OF FAE & FATE

EDITED BY BETH BUCK

Appropriate for Teens, Intriguing to Adults

Immortal Works LLC
1505 Glenrose Drive
Salt Lake City, Utah 84104
Tel: (385) 202-0116

EDITOR'S NOTE

If you were to ask an average person to list all the fairy tales they know, they would most likely between eight and twelve stories, most of which are also titles of animated films. I've always thought this unfortunate, as the corpus of world folkloric literature contains many hundreds of stories.

Andrew Lang collected a number of these in his series of "Color Fairy Books," which were published in the late 19th and early 20th centuries. I received *The Olive Fairy Book* (c. 1907) when I was eleven or twelve years old and found it enchanting. You won't find Cinderella or Sleeping Beauty here, but you will find "Kupti and Imani," "Dorani," "The Jackal or the Tiger?" and "The Snake Prince." The stories depict a fairy tale world much more colorful and diverse than your average fairy tale collection.

Every time we retell "Cinderella," "Sleeping Beauty," or "Beauty and the Beast," we're making a choice not to retell "Why the Sea is Salt" or "To Your Very Good Health" or "Colony of Cats." If you, like many others, have never heard of the latter stories, it is a choice that has already been made for you. You cannot retell a story that you have never heard before.

That is what this volume hopes to accomplish. You are about to read retellings or reimaginings of sixteen lesser-known fairy tales. If, when you think "fairy tale," you imagine blonde princesses requiring rescue from ogres, be prepared to have your paradigms challenged. Protagonists range from poor men and women in their teens to elderly businessmen. The stories retold come from all corners of the globe, from rural Appalachia to South Africa, and in retelling them the authors represent a wide variety of genres: horror, paranormal, science fiction, and of course fantasy.

I hope that as you read though these stories, you'll find some of the magic I experienced as a child in discovering narratives that were both ancient and new.

Beth Buck, Editor

FORWARD

This anthology of lesser-known tales invites the authors and readers to visit wonder stories anew. Most authors attribute their retellings to childhood encounters with the tales they have chosen, cherished, and pondered over time. These stories have been known to them for a while, and now, they get to be shared with us.

Given the countless numbers of stories told across the ages, it is rather a conundrum that only a handful get most of the attention. Charles Perrault's *Histoires ou contes du temps passé, avec des moralités: Contes de ma mère l'Oye* (1697) conveyed some of the most lasting tales to our day thanks to translators, illustrators, and other collectors and storytellers, like the Grimm brothers and Walt Disney. In English, the tales are known as "Sleeping Beauty," "Little Red Riding Hood," and "Cinderella." Other recognizable stories from Perrault's collection include "Puss in Boots" and "Bluebeard," with a new version of that story included here. Clearly, what is unknown to many may be already a favorite to a few. Sharing some of those lesser-known favorites becomes a welcome contribution of this anthology.

The international associations of the stories retold here, from Africa, Ecuador, and Scotland to the United States and Europe, also remind us that tales make themselves at home in specific places and times while also deftly moving across those same spheres. Our authors attribute their retellings to specific people and books and circumstances, admitting the sense of ownership that accompanies many traditional narratives. While fairy tales often are defined as fictional stories of two-dimensional characters, our authors work with elements of mythic beginnings and legendary feats and supernatural encounters as well.

By making an anthology, our editor, Beth Buck, strings stories together like gems forming a prismatic necklace. In a 2019

Convocation speech at Snow College, I referred to the "contemporary-antiquary" quality of fairy tales, suggesting that these stories carry forward troubles from earlier times. Tales remain relevant not only because we remain in suspense about the predicaments these characters get into but also because they require us to take on issues of human wellbeing. These stories confront issues of romance, health, wealth, and close relationships that the characters, and contemporary people we know, grapple with. Even if not every ending is simply happy, these stories take us into compelling worlds where almost anything is possible.

Jill Terry Rudy

THE GIRL WHO MADE THE MILKY WAY

SIERRA WILSON

Author's Note: My story was inspired by a myth from the Khoisan people of southern Africa. In the myth, a girl tosses embers from her fire up into the sky, creating the Milky Way. The beautiful imagery of this myth immediately pulled me in. I grew up going to star parties with my dad and studying astronomy. The magic of the night skies has always made me dream. I was also drawn to this myth because it left me with questions. Every version I've read of the myth is quite brief and I started to wonder what the rest of the story might be. Why would the girl throw embers into the dark night? What was happening before? The story you'll read here is my imagination's answer to these questions.

Amahle hunched her shoulders as she crouched, stirring the fire with a long stick. As always, the night was darker than a rhino's eye. This was long ago, in the day before stars, when only the moon's bright orb lit the night sky.

"Umama and Ubaba should be home by now," Amahle muttered. She narrowed her eyes, straining to catch a glimpse of her parents' forms coming down the red dirt path, but it was no use. The moon's slim crescent nestled in a bed of cloud and Amahle's fire cast a glow no farther than a stone's throw. "Where could they be?"

Though the night was warm, Amahle shivered. She shuffled closer to the fire and took comfort in the gentle popping sounds of the burning wood. Surely her parents would be home soon.

From the bush, a jackal howled, loud and long. Amahle's muscles tightened. She moved so near the fire that her toes were in danger of roasting.

"It's a dark night to be alone, child," the jackal called. His voice sounded cunning and hungry.

Amahle trembled, but willed her voice to sound calm. "I am not alone, Brother Jackal. Even now, my parents are coming."

The jackal laughed. "My eyes are made for night time and I see no one near but you, Little Sister."

Again, Amahle narrowed her eyes, peering into the distant blackness. She could see no parents and no jackal, though she knew the latter was all too near. Still, her parents must be close. All she needed was more time. "My parents are humble and walk softly, Brother Jackal. Someone as great as you would pay them no notice."

Once more, the jackal laughed. "Your words are sweet, but they quiver like grass in a breeze. Perhaps you had better come with me. I will help you seek your parents."

Amahle sent a silent prayer to her ancestors. Surely one among them knew how to outsmart a jackal. The sharp sting of an ember hitting her arm gave her an answer. "Your offer is very kind, Brother Jackal. But my eyes are not made for night as yours are. I am too frightened to go out into the dark. Instead, come and sit with me. We can wait for my parents together."

The jackal gave no reply for a time. Amahle began to hope he had gone off in search of easier prey.

A rustle in the tall grass told her otherwise. Stepping into the clearing on the far edge of the fire's glow was the jackal. His long, pointed nose sniffed at the air and his golden eyes glinted from the firelight. "What a kind offer, Little Sister. I must admit, I have always been curious about the fire your people love so well." The jackal put a foot forward, then hesitated. "Still, I know of how your fire can burn. I think you had better come with me."

Amahle's heart beat swifter than a dancer's drum, but she cheerfully replied, "Oh, no, Brother Jackal. Come and sit by me. The fire is very pleasant. See how it flickers and dances so beautifully?"

The jackal cocked his head and watched the fire. "It is beautiful, but dangerous as well."

Amahle shook her head and smiled. "It is not so dangerous. See how I am safe, sitting here so near?"

The jackal took another step closer. "I will wait here until the fire dies down a bit."

Amahle glanced to her side. She had only a few twigs left to add to the fire and the jackal sat between her and more firewood. Using her sweetest voice, she said, "Do not wait, Brother Jackal. The fire will not be near so warm or so beautiful then."

The jackal gazed at her, then took another two steps. "You are very eager, Little Sister."

"It is lonely here, waiting for my parents," Amahle said. "It will be much better sitting with company."

The jackal narrowed his gaze and slowly crept closer. His stiff fur looked jagged in the firelight. Amahle gripped her stick, keeping her eyes on the jackal.

"You are right, Little Sister," the jackal whispered. "The dancing fire is beautiful." The jackal looked beyond the flames to Amahle's crouching form and licked his lips.

Amahle smiled and nodded, but inside her blood raced faster

than a fleeing antelope. A few more steps would bring the jackal and his knife-like grin beside her. In her heart, she sent up another prayer to the ancestors. Let her will be steady and strong.

The jackal crept closer. One step. Two.

When the jackal stepped up to the far edge of her fire, Amahle thrust her stick into the flames and flung it upward again and again shouting with all her might.

Sparks, embers, ash, and flaming wood flew at the startled jackal's face. He yelped in pain and turned to run back into the darkness. Amahle continued to shout and throw sparks higher and higher. She had to be sure the jackal was gone.

Finally, panting, she crouched again at the edge of her mangled fire. Smoke filled the air and she wiped her eyes. When she opened them she had to rub them again to be sure of what she saw. The sparks and embers from her fire had flown so high they'd become stuck in the sky. Stretching out all above her was a blanket of black dotted with sparkling, glowing lights. Through the center, a river of dusty white made from the ash she'd thrown up from her fire twisted across the sky.

Amahle gazed and gazed, then dropped her head to give thanks to the ancestors. When she raised her head again she saw two dark forms approaching along the path. Umama and Ubaba were back! As they approached, their brown skin glowed from the soft light of the new stars.

From that day on, no child ever sat alone again in darkness. The light of Amahle's fire burns on in the heavens, and Brother Jackal is still hiding in the bush, fearful of the flames.

CAPTAIN
THRUSHBEARD

RACHEL HUFFMIRE

Author's Note: I decided to let fate choose my retelling. Closing my eyes, I picked up a book from one of my favorite fairy tale collections and opened it to a random page near the middle. I had never read "King Thrushbeard" by the Grimm Brothers, but I was instantly charmed by the mysterious minstrel and the princess's biting wit. I couldn't wait to work with these characters. The idea for adding pirates came from my nine-year-old. This excellent mashup, combined with research on French Corsairs and the Anglo-French war of 1778, created the perfect setting for a historical retelling.

Oil lanterns lined The *Promontory's* port side, shimmering brightly against the starlit night. The harbor lights of Weymouth lay far beyond the dusky, red horizon. Adelaide rested her silk-gloved hand against the rail of the freshly swabbed quarterdeck and took a deep breath. The salty ocean spray and vanilla scent of the oakwood deck cast a romantic ambiance around the party below.

Her father approached from behind her, his sword brushing against her skirt. She clicked her tongue as she rescued the delicate fabric from his blade's reach.

The old Naval Lord straightened his own uniform apologetically. "Your dress is lovely, my dear."

Adelaide smirked. "I'll be lucky to keep it so, with all these officer's swords and boots on deck." She turned back to the finely dressed crowd milling about below her. "The *Promontory* may not be your fastest ship, Father, but she definitely knows how to host a party."

"So—you *like* what you see, Adelaide?" Father clasped his hands behind his back and rocked on his heels. His overly casual stance bothered her. Adelaide's shoulders stiffened as her gaze flitted across the crowd. Very few of the naval officers had wives at their sides.

Her mouth pinched into a hard line. "I should have recognized this as one of your courtship traps."

"You're twenty-three, darling. You can't run away from marriage forever." Father pulled out his pocket watch and polished the glass face against his black, woolen sleeve.

"I won't be forced into a diplomatic romance." She crossed her arms.

"I expect you to be civil tonight, Adelaide. I've had enough of you taunting prospective suitors. Such a childish habit will come back to haunt you when you're an old spinster, withering away on your own." Father pulled Adelaide's hand into his own and clenched it like a vice in the crook of his arm. She struggled against him as they made their way toward the stairs. Below, the crowd bowed to the Senior Naval Lord and gawked at Adelaide.

"I don't see why you refuse to enjoy this. See how your beauty astounds them?" Father whispered as they made their way down the steps.

"Only because they've been at sea without sight of a woman for months." She cast a false smile at the crowd.

"And what of that ball in Paris? I remember *Monsieur Barbe de'Mugeut* was quite infatuated with you... Until your pontification about his 'beak-like chin'."

Adelaide patted her father's bicep and put an especially saucy edge to her voice. "It's a good thing I rejected his advances. If you'd had your way and I married him, you would now be at war with your very own son-in-law."

Ahead of them, a rather robust officer shoved his half-eaten plate back onto the serving table and approached them with an eager countenance, resisting the gentle sway of the boat on unsteady feet.

"Ah, Cromwell. Nice to have you aboard. You remember my daughter?"

Adelaide could already see the familiar longing for her father's position glinting in the corner of Cromwell's eye. Father claimed these men sought after her beauty, but Adelaide doubted that very much.

"Good evening, Miss."

She held out her free hand for a kiss. "You look as hearty as a wine barrel tonight, sir. I am glad to see you enjoying appetizers so early in the evening."

Cromwell's hand froze in mid-air, his ruddy cheeks turning an even deeper hue of red. Father pinched her arm even tighter in his vice like grip. At Cromwell's hesitation, a stalky beanpole of a man reached his bony fingers out to claim her gloved hand first.

Adelaide opened her eyes wide with dramatic surprise. "Admiral Langley! Still tall as a mast I see. No wonder you've climbed ranks with such ease."

Father clenched his teeth. "You insufferable child."

She smiled and tilted her head toward her father's ear. "I'll have these men diving into the sea before they subjugate *this* happy bachelorette." She ran her gloved fingers demurely across her collarbone before turning to the next unsuspecting suitor. They were closing in fast.

"Why, sir! You're as pale as death! Quick, someone bring ale. We must ruddy up those cheeks." She turned and covered her mouth with surprise. "Oh, please. Not you, sir. Your nose is already red as a prized rooster."

Father grabbed her arm, forcing her to face him, and growled with an unfamiliar ferocity. "Adelaide, I'm warning you."

She narrowed her eyes. "Father, the man who is willing to marry me shouldn't be so fragile that a simple observation sends him scurrying." She scanned another officer from tricorn to boots. "Though this man couldn't scurry fast enough with such short legs. And this one already seems bent enough without my observations—like a piece of green wood dried behind a stove."

"Enough!" Father's voice echoed across the deck, and the boat fell silent. The sound of lapping waves against the sides of the ship amplified the tension. "These are good men, Adelaide. How dare you reject them for nothing more than their appearance."

"And how dare you only introduce me to men with a lust for promotion in their eyes." She pointed her finger at his nose.

The veins in Father's neck looked ready to burst. "These men have served their country dutifully. You mock them too freely. It's shameful, and I'll have no more of it."

"If you only value them for their titles, I should be allowed to equally esteem their appearance."

Father sputtered, his eyes blinking rapidly in disbelief. "You'd take a handsome pauper, would you? A vagabond—so long as he stood gracefully enough? Well, I've heard the last of it. I swear, I will marry you off to the first attractive beggar I meet!"

A low murmur trickled across the deck. Adelaide narrowed her eyes, bracing her feet on the deck, unwilling to budge. Father always spoke rashly in the midst of a temper. He never meant what he said.

The muttering from the guests grew louder, but she didn't take her eyes off Father. Let them whisper. She refused to back down. As they stood glaring at each other, the officers surrounding them shuffled, putting their hands on their swords. The few women aboard screamed and Father's eyes grew wide.

"Brace yourselves, lads!" someone cried, and Adelaide turned around just in time to see the dark outline of a foreign ship looming so close that it completely blocked out the moonlight on the water. Metal hooks and wooden ladders clanged against the starboard rail. A battle cry sounded as men swung from their rigging over the rails of the *Promontory*.

Pirates.

Adelaide froze in place, unable to run, unable to cry out. One of the men swung through the air toward her and she crumpled with fear to the ground. The man's wild beard curled in the wind while his sword flew from its sheath. Narrowing his dark eyes, he threw himself toward Langley, the only man on board who stood taller than he. Their boots stomped back and forth, and the pirate quickly disarmed the lanky admiral. But before any blood spilt, a cannon went off below deck, rattling Adelaide's bones. She pressed her eyes shut tight and when she opened them again, the pirate and Langley had both disappeared.

Gathering her wits, Adelaide scrambled toward the stairs of the quarter deck, hoping she could make it to the safety of her father's quarters. Pirates darted between the officers, blocking her way. They stepped on her skirt, ripping the hem.

Surrounded by the tumult, Adelaide felt small compared to the confident officers. They were in their element, doing what navy men do. She, however, fell onto the stairs unable to control her shuddering body enough to pull her up to safety.

The Englishmen cheered. Adelaide turned and saw the officers holding fifteen pirates at swordpoint. Cromwell and Langley dragged the tall, dark-eyed captain toward Father. Blood trickled down the captain's face and into his wavy beard that fell to his chest. The toes of his boots scraped along the deck, making a horrid sound that sent chills down Adelaide's spine.

They dropped the pirate at Father's feet, holding a sword to his neck. "Tell me, pirate. What on earth did you hope to achieve by taking on a full ship of naval officers?"

"Ending the war for France with a single raid would be nice, *n'est-ce pas, monsieur?*" The pirate mumbled, as if with a numb jaw.

"Ah, a French Corsair. A pirate with papers," Father said, strolling around the man. Adelaide recognized all too well his intimidating stride.

"Enough legitimacy to keep me from the gallows." The pirate tilted his head, looking from beneath the brim of his crooked hat into Father's eyes.

"Don't I know you?" Father pulled the pirate's hat from his head, revealing thick brown curls tied behind his neck with a blue scrappy ribbon. "Why Durand! It *is* you! What on earth?"

A murmur echoed among the officers. Was Adelaide the only person on deck who didn't know the man?

"War can turn a friend into a pirate, sir." the man, Durand, said.

"It doesn't suit you," Father said, glancing at Durand's captive crew.

"I'm still learning." Durand shrugged. "Though, at the moment, my career seems to be cut short."

"You threw yourself into an unfair fight, Durand. I have no intention of punishing your foolishness. It wouldn't be sporting."

"But sir, this is war, not a gentleman's game," Langley protested.

Father waved off the complaint. "No, in fact Durand, you arrived in time to do me a great service. I offer you a full pardon—" Several cries arose from the officers, but Father held up his hand. "—on one condition."

Durand narrowed his eyes and bit his bottom lip in thought before he spoke. "And that would be, *monsieur?*"

"That you marry my daughter, Adelaide." Father swept his hand across the crowd to Adelaide, who remained sprawled out on the steps. Her breath caught in disbelief.

"Is this some sort of joke?" the pirate asked. Adelaide wondered the same.

"I assure you, I am in complete earnest. I took an oath to give my daughter to the first handsome vagabond I see and I will keep it." Father laughed then cleared his throat. "In fact, being Senior Naval Lord, I have the authority to perform the ceremony myself."

Panic rushed through Adelaide's entire body. Madness. It was the only explanation for her father's actions. Marry his daughter off to a French Corsair? In the middle of a war with France? Ridiculous!

The realization calmed her.

Father intended to inspire humility and submission with this ridiculous spectacle. But she would call his bluff. She took a deep breath, and though her limbs still shook from the terror of the recent attack, she pushed herself from the steps, smoothed her skirts, and wiped a few stray curls from her face. She stepped forward and held out her hand toward the privateer, trying not to take offense at the look of horror in his eyes.

The pirate shook his head at Adelaide's hand. "No, *demoiselle*." The pirate turned and glared at Father. "I am not so selfish as to save my own skin in this way, sir."

Adelaide raised an eyebrow. How interesting. While an entire boat of Englishmen scrambled for her hand, this pirate wouldn't even consider her under pain of death.

"For your crew, then?" Father tipped his head to the side in a playful manner. The pirate's eyes flitted around the crowd, looking for his men. They muttered a few words in French and shrugged.

Father didn't wait for a response. "I'll jump to the quick. Do you, Monsieur Durand, take my daughter, Adelaide, to be your wife?"

Adelaide froze. He was doing this now?

Durand seemed torn between the offer to free his men and the confusion of the moment. Adelaide felt a brief flicker of pity for the man. He was merely a pawn in Father's scheme. Even if the corsair agreed, Father would never let him and his crew go.

"I do," Durand said, his brow wrinkled in anger. Apparently Adelaide wasn't the only one upset with Father's matchmaking schemes.

Father turned to Adelaide. "Do you, Adelaide, take Monsieur Durand to be your husband?"

Adelaide looked into Father's eyes. Though his face wore a smug look of confidence, she recognized a glint of fear that she might not back down. Every person surrounding them leaned forward, waiting to hear her answer. They didn't realize she knew his game. He would never finalize the ceremony to seal their vows. Adelaide raised a single eyebrow and smirked.

"I do," she said, nodding in defiance.

Father's eyes widened in shock, and his tongue clicked as he struggled to find the next words to say.

Adelaide laughed aloud, she was right. He never intended to go through with this farcical marriage at all. She clutched her stomach and leaned forward, gloating that she had forced his hand. Now *he* must be the one to withdraw. Some of the men sniffed and whispered loud enough to be heard.

"Let the heartless wench marry a pirate. This sort of behavior isn't becoming for a Naval Lord's daughter."

Father's eyes widened at this and Adelaide stopped laughing. Nothing set Father on a rampage like a shot to his honor. He worked far too hard for his place in His Majesty's navy to let anyone criticize it.

Father's voice grew low and cold. "Then if there are no objections, I now pronounce you..."

"Father," Adelaide whispered.

"Man..."

"No!" Adelaide shrieked.

"...and wife," he said with finality, a smirk running across his face.

And so, before Adelaide could blink, she was married to a pirate.

"Now, *monsieur*. My pardon?" Durand asked, nodding toward the two gaping officers who still held his arms behind his back. Durand rolled his broad shoulders in an effort to shake off Cromwell and Langley's hold. Father waved off the officers and they reluctantly let go.

"Does his stature suit you, Mrs. Durand?" Father asked, straightening his jacket as the pirate rose to his full height.

"You can't be serious?" she said, clutching her torn skirts in front of her.

Father narrowed his eyes. "Durand, I spared your life because you are my daughter's husband. But, expect no further pardons. Away with you. Go terrorize the Spaniards." He dismissed him with a wave of his hand.

"*Merci, monsieur*. I promise to learn from my mistakes." Durand offered him a sweeping bow then turned to his crew, still held captive by the English navy, calling out commands in French.

The corsairs scurried to the starboard rail where a few ropes and ladders remained. Adelaide crossed her arms, watching them go. Good riddance.

Behind her, Father cleared his throat. "Madam, it is not proper for the wife of a French pirate to be seen in the midst of so many of Her Royal Majesty's officers. I can't account for your safety. It is in your best interest that you depart with your husband at once."

She scoffed. "This sham has gone far enough, Father—"

Father's eyes widened in alarm and he drew his sword. But, before Adelaide could turn around, a strong arm wrapped around her waist and pulled her over the rail of the deck and swung into the dark night.

"No!" Father called after her as the deck disappeared from view. The pirate dropped her aboard the smaller vessel and she rolled to a stop beside a barrel that smelled of week-old fish. Officers leaned over the rail of the *Promontory* and Father stared into the darkness after her with a terrified expression.

"*En avant, les garçons!*" Durand ran along the port side of his mangled ship, cutting the ropes that fastened them to the *Promontory*. The sails whipped taut, catching the wind and bearing them away.

Father looked helpless, gazing over the rails after her.

"Shall we pursue, sir?" Cromwell shouted as the navy men pressed against the rails. Father didn't move. Langley raised a musket and aimed toward the pirates' vessel. Adelaide scrambled for cover behind the fish barrels as his shot blasted a hole in the deck near the helm.

"Hold your fire!" Father raised his arms and Langley lowered his weapon. He gazed down at Adelaide, crouched behind the barrels with a look of genuine remorse. Oh, curse her family for being so proud!

The slow *Promontory* lumbered along after the pirates. Before long, the oil lamps disappeared across the moonlit water. Only the disbelieving laughter of the liberated pirate crew surrounded her.

ADELAIDE SHIVERED as the night grew colder. The mangy crew seemed to forget her existence behind the barrels as time passed. Plugging her nose at the stench of the fish, she poked her head up and searched in vain for the *Promontory* on the horizon.

"Still looking for the old sea dog?" a voice asked from behind her. Startled, Adelaide turned abruptly, and fell against the barrels. Captain Durand stood with his arms crossed, looking down at her.

She threw him a scowl. "A hundred of Her Majesty's naval officers will have your neck when they find me."

"Yes, yes. I'm sure they're all dying to see you safely returned. I saw the looks of adoration those officers fired at you like spears."

She pushed herself up from the ground. "Any one of them would marry me in a heartbeat." The wind blew her fallen hair into her mouth and she sputtered.

He chuckled. "You forget, I already spared them the honor."

She furrowed her brow. "I am not your wife."

"You need not fear me, *demoiselle*," he said, raising his hands. "I don't plan on keeping you. Our marriage afforded us escape. Nothing more. To prove that I am a man of my word, we'll drop you off in Spain. It's the nearest I can afford."

"You expect me to stay here on this piece of flotsam till then?" she asked, glancing across the vessel that rode low in the water. It seemed hardly seaworthy with parts of the deck blown off by the recent cannon battle.

"I do, unless you plan on swimming back. An impossible feat in water-logged petticoats." Durand winked.

Adelaide's face went red with heat, hearing him speak of her petticoats. "My father will finish blasting off your rails with a hailstorm of cannons if..."

"...*If* he can catch us, *demoiselle*. Corsairs don't make a name for themselves by sailing slower than everyone else."

"And you've made a 'name for yourself' with this piece of driftwood?"

"Of course, in France I am known as the honorable Captain Thrushbeard. You'll do well to use my name with respect while onboard." His dark gray eyes glinted like steel.

"Respect is reserved for gentlemen." Adelaide turned away from him. A cold wind picked up, and she shivered again.

"Ah, I see your meaning. Gentlemen don't allow *mademoiselles* to die of cold. If you desire a warm room, follow me." He stood and without waiting for a response, crossed to the captain's quarters and disappeared inside.

Adelaide couldn't believe it. Was this a dream? She wouldn't follow that scoundrel into his quarters, as tantalizing as its warmth seemed. But as the night pressed on, the wind grew colder, turning Adelaide into a frozen pile of irresolute slush. She glared at the men on deck, envying their thick coats.

She could take it no longer. Gathering the skirts of her evening gown around her, Adelaide crept along the deck, trying not to draw attention to herself. The squeaky boards beneath her slippers gave her away and the men smirked as she slunk toward the captain's quarters.

Pushing open the door, Adelaide found a pathetic room piled with refuse and clutter. The captain must have left the room hours ago when she wasn't looking. An assortment of rumpled blankets rested on the empty, red velvet bed built into the cedar wall. She eyed them with frozen jealousy. She closed the door behind her and grimaced at the filth surrounding her. *"The Honorable Captain Thrushbeard's"* personal effects laid strewn across the floor in heaps. Dirty dishes, navigational tools, and crumpled maps lay scattered around the room. An empty chalice rolled back and forth across the floor with the swaying of the ship.

Her stomach rumbled. She hadn't eaten so much as an *hors-d'œuvres* before Thrushbeard took her hostage. A small cupboard on the wall looked like it might hold a promising morsel or two. She pulled open the door and it squealed on rusty hinges.

"You're not a very discreet thief," a voice said. Adelaide startled and turned around, plastering her back against the cabinet. Captain Thrushbeard reclined in a hammock hung in the corner. "If you want to be a real corsair's wife, you have a lot to learn."

"If I wanted to be a *real* corsair's wife, I would have married someone who lasted more than a few minutes onboard the *Promontory*."

Thrushbeard clicked his tongue. "How do you think it feels, to hear you wish for another husband all the time?"

Adelaide pursed her mouth and changed to a less ridiculous subject. "I don't know how you sleep in here. It's filthy."

"Ah, now you're beginning to sound like a wife. If you must know, I inherited the ship and its cargo only a few weeks ago. The untidy habits belong to the previous *capitaine*. And you must agree that it smells better than that fish barrel you chose to inhabit outside." He yawned and slid deeper into his hammock. "But, I am tired, having battled, been arrested, escaped, and sailed away all in one day. So, wherever you decide to rest, please, do so quietly."

Adelaide looked again around the dismal cabin. As much as she hated to admit it, the worn, velvet lined mattress looked tantalizing.

She sidestepped over the refuse, holding her nose as she passed a moldy bowl of pottage.

The narrow bed looked mussed but untouched, likely because Thrushbeard's tall stature couldn't fit into the short bed frame. She pulled on the blankets to arrange them and a mouse fled from its disturbed nest. Adelaide screamed.

"Just give the poor thing a good stomp and he won't reclaim his home while you're sleeping." Thrushbeard mumbled from his hammock.

Adelaide wrinkled her nose in disgust. "Do you honestly expect me to…"

"…I expect *you* to let me sleep."

"In the middle of this wretchedness? How do you bear it? Certainly, your men could clean this up for you!"

"My men aren't servants. And I have better things to do. If this room isn't living up to your standards, then fix it yourself."

"You have absolutely no dignity," Adelaide muttered under her breath. She wrinkled her nose as she scooted the pile of dishes away from the bed with her foot. They toppled with the swelling waves, joining the chalice as they clattered across the floor. Thrushbeard sat upright, making both her and the mouse squeak. The mouse ran over her foot and she screamed again.

"*Quelles bêtises!*" Thrushbeard stood from his hammock. His untucked white shirt hung past the waist of his black trousers, and the cuffs flapped loosely at his wrists. He opened the cabin door and threw the clattering dishes out one by one onto the deck. The pirates keeping watch outside looked up, startled. Then with a mighty swipe of his boot, Thrushbeard shooed the mouse out the door.

"Are you incapable of doing anything for yourself?" he asked, pushing his long brown hair from his iron eyes. "Go. To. Bed. *Couche-toi!*" he demanded, then dropped back into his hammock. Adelaide fled to the mattress and wrapped herself in a threadbare blanket for warmth. She couldn't breathe, and fearing another outburst from Thrushbeard, she was glad her breath made no sound.

~

"Get up! Get up, *demoiselle!*"

Adelaide startled and sat upright. Thrushbeard stood above her, dressed in a captain's jacket with his wild hair smoothed back into a clean tied queue.

"Your dissatisfaction with this cabin resulted in me losing sleep. It won't happen again. So, adjust the cabin to your standards, then you shall have breakfast."

"Pardon me?" Adelaide asked.

"I have work to do and I will be back in an hour. By then, I expect this room to be ready to mop. *Bien compris?*" He stepped out the door, shutting it behind him.

Adelaide blinked in confusion. Last night Captain Thrushbeard said his men weren't servants, yet he didn't have any issues ordering *her* about. She looked around at the clothes, books, and papers rocking back and forth. Not even a few barleycorn's worth of clear space surrounded her. How dare he demand this of her! Too angry to fall back asleep, she crossed to the mirror and spent the next hour dressing her hair and smoothing the wrinkles from her skirt.

When Thrushbeard returned, he looked around in surprise. Adelaide sat with her back straight, her hands resting in her lap, undaunted by his harrowing glare. She sent him a saucy little smile.

"You preened the wrong things, *demoiselle,*" Thrushbeard said, shoving a dirty shirt across the floor with his foot.

She raised her chin. "This room is fit for one thing—burning."

"Then I shall tell the *cuisinier* the same for your breakfast." Thrushbeard planted his feet and crossed his arms.

She turned back to the mirror and resumed smoothing a few stray wisps of hair from her eyes. "Are you the kind of captain who deals orders with threats?"

"I'm the kind of captain who doesn't hesitate to throw *camarades* in the brig for such mutinous behavior."

Adelaide whirled on him. "You wouldn't dare."

"Not on a first warning. No. Withholding breakfast is enough punishment for now. Perhaps if you finish in time, you many have dinner." He turned and slammed the door. She heard scraping noises, and after testing the door latch, found her entry locked. Rather than yell in protest, Adelaide turned her fury on the room.

England and France *were* at war after all.

She pulled every item from its place on the walls, not caring if it broke on its way to the floor. Blankets, compasses, maps, books, tobacco, ribbons—everything came down.

A few hours later, Thrushbeard inspected the mess with fire in his iron eyes. Without a word, he grabbed her by the wrist and pulled her deep into the heart of the boat, dropping her in a cage filled with rats and damp floors. For hours she sat there. Missing dinner. Then supper. The boat rocked back and forth and Adelaide cried. All night she sobbed, yet no one came to visit her.

The next morning, a lantern's light revealed Thrushbeard, descending into the brig. She felt emptiness settle into her stomach when she realized he brought no breakfast with him. A day and a half without food already caused her to suffer from all sorts of shakes and lightheadedness. How dare he neglect her in such a wretched manner.

"Good morning, *demoiselle*. After a quiet, restful night, I feel like offering you a second chance. You shall ready my room for a good floor-scrubbing, and when it is clean you are welcome to a meal on my ship."

"Is this any way to treat your wife?" Adelaide asked, scowling.

Thrushbeard laughed. "You are no more my wife than you are a mermaid; even if you are just as treacherous. You are a siren that kept me from a good night's sleep, and not in the way most men enjoy on their wedding night. So no, my *demoiselle*. When the day comes, I will treasure my wife above English rubies."

She watched the lantern light flickering in his smiling eyes and for a moment, beneath the hardness, Adelaide recognized something. Something familiar. Though, she couldn't be sure what. Men never looked at her that way, with relishing enmity, so how did she recognize his stare?

"Still no answer for me? Well, perhaps dinner will tempt you tonight?" Thrushbeard turned on his heel and disappeared with the lantern.

For the next few hours in the dank, musty cell, Adelaide mulled over his accusations. He had called her a mermaid and a treacherous siren. For the first time, she considered that perhaps her father was right, and that her habit of taunting suitors had come back to haunt her.

Adelaide struggled to sit upright. The stale bucket of water in the cage did nothing to soothe the gnawing hunger in the pit of her stomach. Five whole meals had gone by. The war between England and France could not be won on an empty stomach. The next time Thrushbeard's lantern appeared, Adelaide stood out of mere human preservational instinct. She swayed back and forth on wavering legs.

"Will you come?" he asked.

She struggled to speak. "Yes." Her eyes offered as much smoldering hatred as she could muster. The captain pulled out a set of keys and after opening the door, walked her to the deck. He didn't offer her his hand as she climbed the stairs toward the fresh, humid air. Some of the men whispered as she passed. One even chuckled.

As Captain Thrushbeard opened the door to his cabin, Adelaide looked around the room in dread. How could it possibly be worse than she remembered?

"I'll return in an hour," Thrushbeard said and locked the door behind him again.

With shaking hands, Adelaide scooped papers and laundry from the floor, piling them in the hammock and on the bed. She feared if she didn't finish, the awful captain might lock her away in the galley again. She shoved every last scrap into cupboards, onto the bed and hammock, and then across the desk.

When the captain finally returned, Adelaide stood in the center of the room with her hands pinned to her sides. "The men may now mop."

Thrushbeard walked around the room, his boots clicking on the sticky, crumb-ridden floor as he circled her. Then, he motioned with two fingers for her to follow him. Holding her filthy skirts in her fists, she followed him to the kitchen where she smelled a less-than-savory meal waiting for her. Her knees quivered at the thought of food. At the table, a round bellied cook slid a plate of steaming fish and French onion biscuits in front of her. She devoured the serving, then held the bowl out for more as she finished.

"You ate all you need," Thrushbeard said, looking offended. "If you want more, you must complete another job. Earn your keep, *demoiselle*." Thrushbeard snapped his fingers and the cook held out a bucket and a mop toward Adelaide.

She slapped her hands down against the table top. "You don't expect me to mop too?"

"You will mop your own quarters, be it the cabin *or* the cell below. The choice is yours."

Adelaide stood, tensing every muscle in her body, and snatched the mop from the cook's hands. She envisioned herself slapping the dirty tassels in Thrushbeard's face, but resisted. The captain merely chuckled at her ferocious grip on the handle.

Back in the cabin, Adelaide slid the heavy mop back and forth across the floor. She slipped as the boat tipped on the waves. Her fine hem became heavy with dirty water and stained with the bits of food she mopped up. She pushed everything out the door and finished just before the dinner bell rang.

The men gave her a wide berth at dinner, wrinkling their noses at her ruined clothes.

She couldn't believe they found *her* filthy.

Careful not to aggravate the blisters on her hands, she cut through her burnt potatoes and chicken. She didn't notice Thrushbeard standing beside her until he reached down and took her hand in his. He turned over her palm and inspected the blisters on her skin.

"I see mopping doesn't suit you. Perhaps dusting the shelves in my quarters will serve you better?"

—Late into the evening, Adelaide cleaned the cupboards of his cabin, stirring up feathery dust that settled in her hair and eyelashes. Thrushbeard folded his arms when he came back that night and found his hammock still laden with odds and ends.

"I'm beginning to think I made a bad bargain with you. You have no sense and are hardly suited for any sort of work," he said.

Adelaide was too tired to retort. Thrushbeard studied her for a moment, as if bracing himself for sharp words, but she merely blinked at him. Pursing his lips, he gathered up a blanket and stepped outside to sleep on the deck.

Adelaide crumbled onto the hard but clean floors, pulling a blanket over herself, and promptly fell asleep.

For the next ten days, Adelaide awoke to Thrushbeard standing beside her with new orders. Her hands grew rough from earning her putrid meals. To her dismay, Thrushbeard soon began working beside her. While Adelaide oiled the wooden cabinets, he sorted through papers. While she polished his boots, he re-feathered his tricorn. While she did his laundry on deck, he hovered above her in the rigging and mended the sails with his men. A gloating smile floated down from him and she hurried her pace, determined not to let him work harder than herself.

Before long, the cabin became a comfortable refuge that smelled of soap, oiled wood, and clean linens. And then, one morning, she awoke to the captain holding a frayed length of rope.

"Come. I'll teach you how to splice a rope. I figure you're handy with a needle."

Adelaide sighed. The thought of sitting on deck in the open air and sewing was a welcome task for a change. But instead of dainty stitches and smooth fabric, he offered her thick needles and scratchy twined fibers. She repeatedly pricked her fingers and the ropes cut into her already raw hands, leaving blood stains mingled in the twine.

Thrushbeard spliced his own rope next to her, showing her how to cut and weave the fibers back together. When he noticed her wounds, he pulled out a strip of torn linen and bound her palms.

"So you'll stop bleeding all over," he explained. But the tender way he held her hands in his spoke of other concerns.

Adelaide shoved the rope to the ground. "Why do you care to salvage frayed ropes? You have plenty of others aboard to replace it." She motioned to the rigging above their heads.

"After our siege on the *Promontory*, we are short on supplies. Every rope on deck is spoken for and serves a crucial purpose. Cutting out the damaged threads can make a rope just as strong as it was before. Should one rope go bad, there isn't a replacement. The forestay, the boom, the shroud—a ship can't function without them. It's a bit like my crew, I feel."

"My father never hesitated to throw out old ropes," she said, twisting the strands together and securing them with the needle. She laughed ruefully. "Perhaps that's why he married me off to you. He hated my determination to marry outside the navy." She pricked her finger again and sucked on it.

"What's wrong with marrying a seaman?" Thrushbeard asked.

"My mother, a navy wife, endured lonely stretches without my father while he was off at sea. I saw her worry he might never make it home."

"So, instead you married a pirate and joined his crew?" Thrushbeard smiled

She set the rope in her lap and clenched it tightly in her palms. "At least being part of the crew means I wouldn't get left behind."

Thrushbeard's dark eyes staring back at her made Adelaide feel foolish for saying such a thing. For the last few days, they had continued to throw quick quips at each other, though nothing was so malicious between them as it had been the first few days. But this— this was a far too familiar sort of speech.

Captain Thrushbeard turned back to his work, focused intensely on weaving together the strands. "Tomorrow we'll stop to port in Spain for a few repairs. That is where we will bid each other *adieu*. I am a man of my word."

Adelaide's chest tightened, remembering his promise to drop her in Spain. But to bring it up directly after her *faux pas* was like a slap in the face. "You're going to dump me onshore and hope I find my way back home on my own?"

"You are incapable?" He didn't look at her.

She spread her hands and let them fall to her lap. "I'm penniless, don't speak Spanish, and thousands of miles from home. It's a tall order for anyone."

"Fair enough. Since I do owe you my life, *demoiselle*, I can offer you a few of our spoils to sell. Enough to purchase a passage home, I should think. Or, perhaps with your newfound industry, you could make a living. The port in Cadiz is *magnifique*." He gave her a smirk. Adelaide didn't know what to say. She watched him tie off the end of the string and bite through the thread. He tested the rope by snapping it taut, then stood and walked away.

"Goodbye, *demoiselle*. Send my men back once you are situated in the market," Thrushbeard called. Adelaide didn't look behind her as she walked down the plank. Two of Thrushbeard's men followed her, carrying pillaged china in boxes and sacks. If any of Father's navy men saw her selling stolen dinnerware in the marketplace, she would never find a place in society again. She couldn't endure that kind of rejection. Just because she now possessed thicker skin on her hands didn't mean she bore thicker skin on her back as well.

As she reached the docks, she felt the world spin beneath her, tossing like waves made of wood and dirt. She heard Thrushbeard laugh and cast one final look behind her, feeling frightened at the thought of wandering the streets alone. As she looked back toward the ship, she felt strangely sentimental. She felt a small bit of ownership now that she had worked so hard to improve it. Thrushbeard was nowhere to be seen. Did he even care to see her go?

She shook her head. This was her chance to return home on her own merit. What was wrong with her? She heard a clink of china and hurried to catch up with the pirates, scurrying toward the market. They stopped at a busy corner and helped her spread out her wares.

And then she was alone.

Standing tall, she did her best to appear dignified in the dirty marketplace. A few men stopped to browse, but she found them more interested in her than in dinnerware. Fear burned inside her chest, but she didn't let it show. Thrushbeard gave her this chance and she wouldn't waste it. Unlike Father, the captain hadn't coddled her like she was fragile or planned her life like she had no ambition. Now was her chance to take fate into her own hands.

By evening, she had earned a few coins, but not enough to pay for passage back home. As the sun neared the horizon, she shivered, wondering how on earth she would carry all of the remaining glassware on her own.

Suddenly, shouts from the other vendors rang down the street.

"*Borracho jinete!*"

"*Cuidado!*"

Adelaide turned just in time to see a cavalry horseman galloping through the streets, swaying drunkenly on his steed. The beast reared his head in fright as he tore at breakneck speed around the corner, trampling through the center of her wares, shattering them before her eyes.

Panic rippled through Adelaide at the sight of her dashed

livelihood. The hussar didn't stop, but continued down the street, careening down the alleyway. Her hands trembled as she picked up the broken pieces, trying to shove them back together. She couldn't return home now. Night would come with no place for her to stay. She didn't speak the language and possessed no useful skills. Thrushbeard had been brutally honest about that fact.

At the thought of the captain, she realized he was likely the only person who could help her. *If* his ship still rested in port. She raced to the docks. Deep in her heart she already suspected she was too late. Rounding the corner, she saw his crew casting their lines off from the dock. She ran with desperate speed as the ship pulled in the gangplanks.

"Captain Thrushbeard!" Adelaide cried out, stumbling over the uneven wood planks. The boat drifted too far from the docks. He couldn't hear her. Oh, what had her father called him? "Durand!" she shouted even louder.

The captain peered over the edge of the ship. "*Demoiselle?* What are you doing here?"

Adelaide cupped her hands to her mouth, trying to cast her voice over the splashing water to him. "I have no money!"

The boat drew even further away.

Captain Thrushbeard—Durand—scowled down at her, then disappeared from the side of the boat. Her jaw dropped. He didn't care. He was going to leave her here on the edge of the dock, completely destitute.

And then, he leapt over the rail at a full sprint, rope in hand, gliding through the air toward the docks. She stiffened, watching him swing toward her in a wide arc. He wrapped his arms around her waist, snatching her for a second time and swinging back toward the ship. However, this time instead of dread, Adelaide felt relief at being scooped up.

The men on deck hoisted the rope, sending the two of them flying into the air. Adelaide squeezed her eyes shut and clung to his neck, burying her face in his beard.

His thick, curly hair smelled like soap and warm barley tea. Their bodies swayed back and forth a few times before she felt her feet rest on solid ground. Durand's grip around her waist loosened and she stumbled back. His eyebrows knit together in concentration as his gray eyes studied her.

"Why change your mind and bring me back aboard?" she asked, feeling a flutter in her chest.

The corsair wound the rope into a coil around his arm until he reached a thicker portion. He held it in front of him and tugged, testing its strength. "Your splicing held up. Seems you're not unteachable."

She crossed her arms and eyed him saucily. "And not because you didn't care to see me go? I am your wife, after all."

The look in Durand's eyes told her that she had indeed, gone too far. "You're not my wife and you're not a guest. If you're here, you are part of the crew. If you don't agree, you're free to swim back to shore."

Adelaide pinned her fists to her side and nodded, frightened. The men surrounding them chuckled.

Durand turned to his men, speaking in French. They shuffled. "*Personne?*" he asked. Adelaide didn't have to speak French to know no one wanted to take her on as help.

"*Oh, tant pis, demoiselle,* I'm afraid if they don't want you..."

Adelaide didn't allow him to finish. She stepped toward the men. "I am a willing hand." She held up her calloused palms. "I have the wounds to prove it." She knew they didn't speak English, but hoped they would understand her all the same.

As the silence stretched on, Adelaide sadly realized the only interaction she had afforded these men during the last few weeks was to cast them mistrusting glances. Now they rewarded her with the same.

Then the ship's cook stepped up. He mumbled something she didn't understand and the men surrounding her chuckled. Durand looked at Adelaide. "*Notre cuisiner* said he's seen you grimace plenty at his food. Now perhaps you can do penance by scraping dishes." He stepped back, seeming to wait for Adelaide's snarky retort.

"You may tell him I am grateful for his offer," she said. The entire crew went silent as she curtsied to the cook.

"*Eh bien, commençons,*" the cook said, nodding at Adelaide. He turned and walked into the hull, expecting her to follow. She cast a sideways glance at Durand, who watched her with interest as she followed the cook below deck. She knew they drew close to the galley when she smelled the hint of rotting beef and moldy dishes. Stepping inside, Adelaide gagged, trying not to breathe in the thick smell.

"*Nous voila,*" *Chef* motioned around the room. It seemed two people would hardly be able to work side by side in the kitchen. The cook grabbed a salted fish, slapped it onto the wooden table and cut off its head with one clean swing of a butcher knife. She jumped back against the wall as the head rolled onto the floor and slid into a corner piled high with other unlucky comrades. Her stomach flopped around when she noticed how the partially decomposed fish heads had likely been there for days.

Cook handed her a dustbin and motioned to the filthy floor. She wished once again she had found better success in the marketplace selling her china; then she could be resting in a private bunk, waiting while others worked onboard to take her home. But instead, she sailed farther away from England as a scullery maid in a pirate's galley, sweeping slimy fish heads from the corner to earn her passage.

But then, she would have missed Durand soaring off the side of his boat to sweep her into the air. She smiled despite herself. Though she still wanted to make her way home, she wouldn't ever forget that moment. She considered it a prize for her suffering.

Cook showed her how to discard unwanted scraps out the window and she quickly tossed out the most potent and fermented contents from the counters, adding to the long streak of dried slop painted on the side of the ship's hull.

Once the counters and floors were clear of refuse, Adelaide moved on to the barrel of dishes. She had never smelled so many atrocities in her life. Perhaps her stomach would settle if she took a breath of fresh air above deck. She staggered to the doorway just as the Captain came to see her progress. She didn't want him thinking her weak, so she smiled painfully and returned to the galley.

She felt even more nauseated as she thought of all the meals she consumed from such conditions. No one should ever eat like that again on this ship. Covered in sweat and with shaking legs, she stopped as the cook laid a gentle hand on her shoulder.

"*Les dames d'abord.*" He handed her a tin plate filled with clam stew.

Taking the plate, she found her place atop a barrel in the corner of the dining room, separate from the rowdy men. She didn't notice Durand's boots planted in front of her until he cleared his throat.

With his hair pulled back, she saw the smile lines around his eyes. She remembered the soap and barley smell of his beard and felt furiously self-conscious of how dirty and smelly she must be after a day in the galley. She straightened, hoping her ladylike demeanor proved her to be more than just a pile of grease and stench.

His voice was quiet and respectful. "You worked hard today."

"Is it so apparent?" she asked. "I feel filthy."

He smiled and tucked a stray wisp of her hair behind her ear. "Dirt can wash away." As she stared up at him, he flinched, retracting his familiar gesture. His cheeks grew rosy with embarrassment, and again, the thought that he seemed familiar dug at Adelaide.

"Do you treat all your crew this way?" she asked with a smirk.

"I've never married any of *them*," he said, smirking back at her just as wickedly. Hearing him joke about their sham marriage made her feel immediately less self conscious about her own recent witticisms on the subject.

"Tomorrow we reach a port in Biarritz. While my men refresh themselves I must report to my commanding officer, the *Commandant de' Gabon*. He is holding a grand ball for his son. However, if I were to be recognized there as a corsair, the results could be disastrous. Would you help me, *Ma chérie?*"

"What do you need?" she asked, trying not to get her hopes up that she would be invited to a French grand ball. Perhaps she would meet with someone who would recognize her and help her get home. Although, it could be just as equally risky. Either way, the thought of attending was tempting, if only for an excuse to obtain a decent bath and steal a few scraps of food.

"After the Commandant's son arrives, I need someone on the inside to signal me when the coast is clear. You are the only one onboard who could possibly pass at a party like this."

Adelaide lifted her ripped and stained skirts. "This is no longer a suitable evening dress."

"We shall buy you a new one," he laughed.

The thought of a new dress made Adelaide smile, but it was short lived as a new concern came to mind. "I don't speak French, Durand. I can't attend. If I arrive, people will ask me questions. If I respond in English, they will assume me a spy."

The smile slid from Durand's face and he pinched his bottom lip in thought. "Perhaps if you attended as a maid? People at balls don't typically speak to the servants."

Adelaide scowled. "I'm not the type to serve at parties."

"Would you rather your captain go in alone and uninformed?" he asked, placing his hand on his chest in mock surprise.

She scowled playfully. "I'll accompany you on one condition. I require a proper bath."

"I think I can afford you your day's wages in advance. A few coins should afford you such an indulgence," Durand said.

ADELAIDE STEPPED from the Biarritz bath house in her newly purchased serving girl's dress. Although these clothes were plainer than anything she had ever owned before, she felt grateful and clean. She even had a few coins leftover, which she stashed in her pocket. Perhaps if she continued to serve the captain well, she could earn enough in the coming days to afford her passage back to England.

Following the street that Durand had pointed out to her, she sneaked into the back door of a grand manor. The kitchen was a bustle of noise and trays. Someone yelled indistinct directions at her. Wide eyed, she nodded, picked up a tray, and followed the rest of the serving maids into a room filled with laughter and music.

Stepping into the ballroom felt like stepping into another world. The walls were lined with porcelain, paint, and gold. It was a stark contrast from the filthy ship. Adelaide gawked at the beautiful ladies surrounding her and felt even more plain. Her English beauty could never match their French styles. Instead, she hid in the shadows of the ballroom, pretending to make herself busy while waiting for the guest of honor to arrive.

She feasted her eyes on the plates of food passed around the ballroom. Delicacies loaded atop banquet tables made Cook's food sit like a rock in her stomach. She clenched her hands into fists every time an uneaten dish passed back into the kitchen. She couldn't allow perfectly good food to go to waste.

Sneaking back into the kitchen, she slipped four empty jars from a corner table. Then, finding a secluded corner, she tied them to her pockets beneath her skirts with a length of wool yarn. When she returned to the ballroom, she offered to clear people's uneaten food, and pocketed the best scraps into the jars hidden beneath her skirts.

As she passed among the partygoers, she felt a rush of anxiety. All around the room, Adelaide heard Durand's name cast among the French conversations. It didn't matter where she turned, Durand's name floated among the guests. If he hoped to sneak into a meeting without being noticed, he'd fail. It seemed everyone already knew he would be attending tonight.

Adelaide faltered in gathering more food, the worry and stress made her stomach turn. If Durand were found out, would he be upset with her? She wondered if she should run to the signal point by the door early to warn him. But before she could move, the entire room went silent as a young man, dressed in French velvet and silk and covered in gold chains round his neck stepped into the ballroom. The announcer called out in a loud clear voice *"Je vous présente, l'honorable Monsieur de la Barbe de' Mugeut!"*

Adelaide froze in place at the familiar name. She knew this man. This was the first suitor her father tried to push her toward. The first man who had ever suffered from her critical taunts. The *Barbe de' Mugeut* was where her nasty habit of eviscerating men began.

She remembered how the clean shaven man approached her at a ball in Paris a few years ago. She was spooked by his perfectly flourishing bow, his strange accent, and most vividly the fear of becoming the wife of a navy-man. Her father pushed her too hard to dance with the *Barbe de' Mugeut.*

"I shan't, for fear his beaklike chin shall puncture my cheek should he make the smallest misstep. Honestly, look at it, Father. It is shaped like the beak of a thrush!"

The world whirled around her as she once again stared at the nobleman who once looked embarrassed and wounded by her words. Although looking at him now, she knew she had been far too hasty in her criticism of his appearance.

The guests released a series of surprised laughter and clapping as the host of the party rushed to the man, embracing him. Adelaide felt a rush of relief as half a dozen women likewise rushed to his side. With this important guest so distracted, there would be no chance of him recognizing her.

She easily understood why women paid this young man so much attention. His previously sharp features had been softened beneath a close shaven beard. The women flounced and batted their eyelashes at him, though he seemed politely disinterested. Adelaide smiled, imagining herself in a similar position a few short weeks ago; though this man spoke kinder words of rejection to his suitors than she ever had to her own.

Unfortunately, the *Barbe* caught her eye and smiled with a raised eyebrow. Adelaide blushed and returned to her work, hoping he wouldn't recognize her. It was time to go. Besides, with this man receiving so much attention in the room, it would be the perfect time for Durand to sneak into his meeting with the Commandant.

She found a small pile of dishes that needed to be returned to the kitchen and used them as an excuse to leave. The pile clanked against each other as she hurried into the hall and delivered them onto the trolley bound for the kitchens.

In the hall, she delivered the signal for Durand to seek entrance by extinguishing the lantern in the third window. With her worry for Durand slightly abated, she noticed a delicious-looking tart laid out on the kitchen trolley with a single bite in the corner. She slid the pastry into her pocket just as she heard footsteps behind her.

A butler stomped toward her, shouting and Adelaide made a quick curtsy.

"*Qu'est-ce que tu as dans ta poche?*" he asked, pointing to her skirts. Her eyes widened. A few other servants hesitated in the hall to watch.

"*Monsieur?*" she asked. She knew at least that much French. He scrunched up his mouth, grabbed her wrist and yanked her closer. The jars tied beneath her skirts crashed to the floor and food spilled around her. The other servants in the hall gasped and giggled. A few more heads poked out of the ballroom.

The butler shouted. "*Voleuse!*" Adelaide felt too afraid to be embarrassed of the food pooling fragrantly around her feet.

"*D'où vient tout ce bruit?*" a voice inquired. Adelaide's breath caught as she saw the *Barbe de Mugeut* step into the hall. The butler released her wrist and stood at attention. Adelaide wished she could sink a thousand fathoms beneath the sea. How could this have happened? Caught stealing scraps at a *French* nobleman's party? And even worse, she now faced a nobleman she had rejected harshly. She tried to run past the guest of honor, but he caught her round the waist and pulled her close.

"Adelaide?" he whispered. She stopped struggling and gaped at the man. He laughed in surprise at her wide-eyed expression, but quickly seemed to lose the confidence he held moments before in the ballroom. His grip loosened around her waist and he waved off the servants, excusing them from the scene. They each bowed and scurried into the ballroom or off to the kitchens.

Adelaide's heart sank into her stomach and she refused to look up at him. "*Monsieur Barbe*, I am incredibly sorry."

He straightened his coat jacket nervously. "You—recognize me, then?" he asked.

"Oh, sir. Those words so many years ago... I am so ashamed." She raised her hand to her lips, as if to call back the words. Father was absolutely right. Her cruel words had absolutely come back to haunt her. The man sent her a sympathetic smile.

"Would you dance with me now then?" the *Barbe* asked.

Surprised, Adelaide took a step back.

What would Durand think, if he saw me dancing with this man?

"I'm sorry sir, but I am not dressed for the occasion." She looked down at her serving woman's dress and gave him a brief curtsy.

"Please?" The man tilted her chin to face him with a gentle hand, this time a firm question in his eyes. His gaze lost a bit of it's gentility and filled with steel. She caught the scent of flowered water and barley tea. And then, Adelaide recognized him.

"Durand?" she whispered.

A mischievous smile flickered at the corner of his lips. She no longer saw the wild pirate, or the embarrassed French noble from so many years ago. This man, with his hair combed, his beard trimmed, and confidence brimming, stared at her with so much affection that she felt even more self conscious about her thieving hands and serving gown. But she couldn't back down. She swallowed, burying all her pride and fear beneath her, then nodded.

Holding onto his arm, she allowed him to guide her back into the ballroom. The lights felt brighter than before but she shivered under the cold, judgmental glance of every woman that noticed them.

A song began, and Durand bowed to Adelaide. She curtsied, and together they spun around the room. No one seemed to say a word as they cleared the floor. The servants stood agape. The butler turned red.

But as she danced, Adelaide stopped looking at the others and stared solely at Durand. She felt his firm hand on her waist and relied on his sure step as he guided her across the floor. As they fell deeper into the rhythm of the swelling music, she felt like she was riding away atop the ocean waves with him.

When the song ended, the room offered a polite applause. Adelaide couldn't stop smiling, and Durand refused to take his eyes off her. The host of the party approached the two of them.

"*Qui est-ce, Durand?*" the man asked, motioning toward Adelaide's hand, taking it and kissing it. He paused and sniffed her skin, smiling as he savored the smells of the warm kitchen.

"Father, this is Adelaide," Durand said in English. The room fell silent at the use of the enemy's language.

"*Monsieur!* She is a thief! I caught her stealing food, but your son excused her," the butler said, stepping out of the crowd. Adelaide narrowed her eyes.

"*Père*, she saved my life." Durand said, standing beside her and placing his hand on her waist.

"An English serving girl? What would cause her to do that, my son?" the man asked.

"Because,—" Durand smiled and looked down at Adelaide. "Because she's my wife."

Men shouted in surprise and women whimpered. Adelaide glanced up at him in surprise. His hand wrapped tighter around her waist. Durand's father smiled and raised an eyebrow.

"You married an English scullery maid?" he asked, as if it were a joke.

"No, *Père*. May I present Adelaide Palliser, daughter of Vice Admiral Palliser, Senior Naval Lord of England."

There was another round of gasping in the room. Durand's father stepped forward and scooped her up in an embrace. She blinked in surprise.

"You cannot know how happy I am to hear my son has found such a beautiful and courageous wife! Even among enemies! What better place to announce such a match than at a party!" Durand's father shouted. He motioned for the musicians to play and dancing commenced. While the host's back was turned, Durand pulled Adelaide quietly through the crowd to a balcony, away from the contemptuous glances of the swirling women inside.

Outside, lamps lit the perimeter of the wide balcony, reminding Adelaide of the *Promontory* the night Durand stole her away.

A smile tugged at the side of Adelaide's mouth. "You sir, are a master of disguise. First a French nobleman, then a corsair, and now the son of a Commandant?"

"And don't forget a drunken horseman with an aptitude for trampling pottery." Durand raised his chin into the air proudly.

"You dirty scoundrel!" Adelaide shouted, swiping at him in an unladylike fashion. He caught her hand, laughed, then kissed her fingers. A happy shiver ran up her arms.

"I wasn't ready to sail off without you," he said. Adelaide studied his gray eyes. His smile had remained hidden behind his thick beard for so many weeks, but now she saw the hopeful curve of his mouth, the crooked smile that waited for her response.

"You know I don't like being left behind," she said.

"Then you won't be," Durand said, cupping her cheek in his hand. With his gentle kiss she realized, even though she swore never to love a naval officer, she had indeed married a pirate.

CANTUÑA

IMOGEAN WEBB

Author's Note: From an Ecuadorean folktale. Inspiration for the story comes from my love of Ecuador. Much of traditional Ecuadorean culture was destroyed or converted by Spanish settlers. I've taken this part of their history and applied it to my retelling as the foundation of where their two worlds collided while hopefully bringing attention to an almost forgotten folklore.

Under a full moon, a man named Cantuña lay on his back and stared up at the night sky. Cicadas and toads chirped as he gripped a dusty brick in his hand tightly. Its surface so covered with sharp, jagged edges that every time he ran his thumb across it almost cut his skin. As he waited for morning to break, he closed his eyes and sighed, for he knew that tonight might be his last.

"It's beautiful, isn't it?" A voice from behind him echoed through the cathedral.

Startled, Cantuña rose to his feet. The wind whipped at his loose fitting hemp pants and dark hair. His muscles tensed as Ramos, followed by his *compadres*, stepped closer. They smiled with their long-nosed guns ready in hand.

Cantuña wasn't a special or wealthy man. He was an ordinary builder who happened to be in the wrong place at the wrong time. Sergio Ramos and his loyal guardsmen of the Spanish Conquistadors had stumbled their way into his small shop passed down to him by his father. A few months ago, they demanded that he take their offer to build part of their cathedral in exchange for good money. With a sick sister covered in small red bumps and an unstoppable cough who needed medicine at home, he had reluctantly agreed. Besides, with their freshly polished guns, how could he refuse?

So, in forced agreement, he took the money, bought Sasika her much needed medicine, and got to work.

"Morning hasn't arrived yet." Cantuña said.

"I wanted to hear your excuse. As a proper businessman it's imperative that deals involving transactions are kept in good standing. Although that may be hard for *you* to understand. I want an explanation as to why you haven't finished." Ramos picked a cobble stone from the ground, his pale skin semi-glowed in the dim light. The conquistador walked around the builder's wooden work bench; his loyal men positioned near the entrance.

"If you're going to shoot me, then why wait?" Cantuña argued, shoulders slumped.

Ramos stopped in front of Cantuña, leaned forward until the tips of their noses almost touched, and smirked. "Oh no. Death is an easy escape for a thief. You are of no value to me dead, so since you owe a balance for your unfinished work, I will take your sister as repayment. Yes, she'll make a nice slave back home."

Blood boiled under Cantuña's terra-cotta skin. He rushed the snake of a man and tucked his forearm below Ramos's chin as he shoved him against the wall, ready to crush his throat. Both guardsmen raced forward, barrels of their guns pressed against his back. With his nostrils flared and eyes wild, Cantuña stood his ground.

"You... still have until sun...rise...." Ramos choked. He pulled and tugged, trying to get away, but Cantuña pushed harder before he finally let go. The greedy man dropped to a knee and coughed several times before he scurried behind his men. Unable to waste anymore time, Cantuña marched back over to the pile of bricks, grabbed his trowel, and slathered another brick to an in-progress wall.

As the Conquistadors moved to exit, Ramos turned to face the builder with his hand over

his throat. "You better hurry. The moon almost meets the middle of the sky, Cantuña. If you fail, your sister's life belongs to me. And next time you pull that sort of stunt, they *will* kill you." And with that, they were gone as quickly as they had appeared.

Cantuña payed no attention to his warning. He continued to slather heavy brick after heavy brick with gray, creamy Ecuadorian mortar. What else could he do other than try to finish? Soon, a tower of newly stretched wall grew high. As he moved to start the next section, he stopped to catch his breath. With his skin drenched with sweat and his arms on fire, the stench of grit and clay scratched the back of his throat. He needed a moment to rest.

What would his sister think when the news of his death made its way to her? Who would take care of her after his passing? She had gotten better— the terrible cough and fever had subsided— but what if it returned? Who would be there for her then?

An eldritch breeze rustled the leaves of the walnut tree outside the half-finished atrium window. Cantuña gazed around the incomplete cathedral and stopped upon a shadowed figured that lurked in the dark, hiding on a large branch.

He stepped forward. "Show yourself." Long, nimble fingers with sharp overgrown nails stretched towards him.

"My dear," she whispered, her voice raspy and old. Unable to see more than the obscure outline, he walked to the opening and placed a hand on the window's cobblestone frame.

Moving forward, the woman crouched barely enough under the moonlight so he could see her. With no nose and ghost-pale skin that sagged from her face, she cocked her head to the side. A thin film of grayish-blue covered the pupils of her old eyes. Her waist length hair, thin and balding in spots, hung over bony shoulders. On the sides of her skull sat a pair of ram's horns.

"Cantuña Akichik Kapwãna," she spoke with a smile. "I would like to offer my help."

"How do you know my name?" he demanded with his back straight, muscles frozen in place. A smile crept across her face, piranha-like teeth exposed.

She scurried to the end of the branch, now only a foot or two away from him. "I know *all* my children. It saddens me that you do not know who *I* am, though."

Cold air filled his chest. The chill of fear raced over his heart as he locked eyes with her. He knew her from childhood stories, but the possibility sat stuck in his throat.

"*La... Diabla...*" he spoke, almost out of breath. "Why are you here?"

"I have come to make a deal. I know Ramos and his men have forced you into this contract. I also know of your sick sister for whom you provided medicine. Now it is time to pay, and you will fail in giving them what they seek."

"It's never wise to deal with your kind."

"Many who speak of me are ill mannered. I have come with no tricks or false pretenses. Humans have spit on my name because they do not accept the laws of the world. Even someone like myself cannot break those laws. Humans do not understand."

Cantuña shook his head and rubbed his eyes. "This is a dream—it has to be!"

"No," she reached towards him again as she spoke. "You are awake. I help unfortunate souls who have found themselves in an unfair predicament, but let us be honest, it is one that you have brought upon yourself. My magic will not permit me to help without providing something of equivalent exchange. In this case, your soul for hers."

"My sister?"

"I will send my devoted demons to finish your atrium before sunrise. In return, you will owe me your life." He turned his back to the devil. A sharp ringing echoed through his ears as he tried to slow his heart.

"Cantuña," *La Diabla* called again. He looked over his shoulder. "Nothing in this life or the next is free. Someone must pay. Selling your sister into slavery just means you have sold your soul to the conquistadors who continue to slaughter the Incan empire. If you chose to give *me* your soul instead, you will at least die with honor."

She was right and he knew it. He turned to face her, his head lowered and fists clenched.

"Alright. We have a deal, but I have a term to add. You'll grant protection to Sasika from Ramos and his men. I will meet you back here shortly before sunrise. Let me have my last night alive to remember the world I'll soon leave behind."

She nodded, complying with the builder's request. With a snap of her skeletal fingers, the ground gave a subtle tremor. From the street on which the cathedral sat, human-like creatures with the same eyes as *La Diabla*, entered from the shadows. They traveled from the alleyways and behind buildings towards Cantuña and the cathedral.

She gestured towards the city, inviting him to leave. "Now go! Enjoy yourself. Tonight will be your last." The builder dropped his mud scoop, took a few steps away from her, and turned for the exit.

As he dragged his feet along the dusty half-painted floor, heading for home, he knew that in only a few hours, he would have to return. His soul now belonged to *La Diabla*.

Down the dirt road Cantuña ran, intermixed with the horde of the undead, lifeless and empty. No smell. No sounds. Over two hills and under Chawpi bridge, the young builder raced to his home. It was not long before he reached the door and froze, except for the adrenaline beating in his chest.

After sunrise his sister would have enough grief to fill many nights with restlessness.

As he stepped away from their adobe home, he drew his head back, his gaze set on the night sky, and thought, *Let her sleep.* He turned back for the road and blinked away tears.

Unsure of what to do or where to go, he traveled to the edge of the city. Croaking toads and screeching insects hollered into the night. Even the stars above seem to laugh at him as he passed through the gates of Quito. Unsure of how else to spend his time, he headed towards Hermosa Hill which stood a couple hundred yards away. He had been there many times as a child to escape the world and all its troubles. Only this time there would be no escape. When he reached the top, he sat on the lush grass and thought about all the things he'd leave behind.

He'd definitely miss his Sasika. Even if he could go back in time, he'd still take the money for the medicine, if it only meant that she could live the rest of her life as a free, healthy woman. Or so he'd hope. He'd also miss spicy red lentils, his favorite food, and the way each bite scorched his tongue until he'd lose his sense of taste for three whole days. He'd miss the children in his neighborhood running around, happy and free, even if the conquistadors lurked around almost every corner, ready to cause trouble. Quito was far from perfect, but it was the only home he'd ever known. Come sunrise, he'd never see any of it again.

From behind him, a man called out, "What keeps you troubled, son?"

Cantuña turned to face the stranger. He stood much shorter than him, but taller than his sister, with a much larger, round belly. His tawny hair was pulled into a ponytail hung over one shoulder and a thick mustache rested beneath his nose. He walked closer and plopped down beside Cantuña. With skin similar in shade to his, he knew the man was no threat. Everyone in their city was civil and pleasant, unlike the invaders who had taken their land by force.

"Tonight is my last to live. I'm contemplating my life," Cantuña spoke while he stared off into the distance.

"How so? How do you know this is your last night?"

The builder shook his head, closed his eyes, and pinched his brow. "Because I have made a deal with the *La Diabla*. Tomorrow, she will pay my debts, but in return, I must give her my soul."

A loud chuckle bellowed from the short Incan man. Cantuña jerked his head towards him, lips pressed into a firm line, offended and shamed. He brought his knees to his chest and wrapped his arms around them. Of course the stranger didn't believe him.

"I'll tell you what. I can help."

Cantuña scoffed, "How's that?"

"My name is Viracocha." He smirked. "But mostly I go by Raco. I am a God who walks among humans and—"

"Viracocha? I don't believe my ears. Strike me down because the possibility that I would meet you and *La Diabla* in the same night is doubtful. You must be mocking me!"

"No, no! I came after sensing *La Diabla's* curse on your soul. I sought you out. If you can fulfill a request for me, I'll tell you how to outsmart her." Cantuña stared at the old man, eyes squinted and suspicious. He ran a hand through his dark hair.

"I don't think so." Cantuña sighed. Then he stood and patted down his pants. "I'm done with contracts."

Raco pointed towards the other side of the city. "I have two daughters. Both are demigods. One is tamed, married, and has settled down on the other side of the world in lands not yet discovered by

Pale Skins. The other one, my youngest, lives beyond the ridge, by the river, right outside the oldest part of Quito before the expansion.

"Go to her and ask for her hand in marriage. If she says she will give you a chance to prove yourself worthy, I will aid you in defeating *La Diabla*. But, I have to tell you, if you don't take my offer—if you allow this contract with the devil woman to follow through—not only will she take your soul, but the entire city will be in danger."

Cantuña blinked. "What?"

Raco stood and stepped in front of Cantuña. "The land in which the Cathedral was built has been soiled with Incan blood from the rebellion against the conquerors. It's cursed. The part *La Diabla* didn't tell you was, by winning your soul, she will complete the ritual to posses the church. If she is allowed admittance, she will deceive every weak individual seeking refuge. They will then become her prey."

Cantuña turned and walked over to the other side of the hill. The ember of guilt inside his chest ignited into anger. Every choice he made to try and save his sister led to another undesired consequence. Fed up, he stormed over to the closest tree and slammed his fist into the side repeatedly until his skin broke and his hand bled.

Raco walked over and patted his back. "There is still a chance to fix things. Go to Kilya, my daughter, and convince her that she should be yours. Then I will help you."

Cantuña nodded. He needed to fix this. He thanked the old man for his advice, turned towards the river, and ran faster than he ever had in his life.

The moon had reached the second corner of the sky by the time he found the Napo river. When he was younger, his father had taken him fishing here. They caught slimy toadfish for fun and *bagre* for his mother to cook. Sasika made the same dish almost the same way, but not quite. He missed his parents, and being here only reminded him that he couldn't fail.

Cantuña climbed down from a massive moss-covered boulder and paused. Near the entrance of a dark cave, a woman with long, cacao colored curls and warm beige skin sharpened the end of a spear. She glanced up at Cantuña with beautiful hazel eyes. His face flushed red.

"I'm assuming my father sent you," Kilya called out.

He stepped forward and rubbed the back of his neck. "I'm not sure how you know, but yes."

"Go home."

He shook his head. "I'm not going anywhere until you let me speak."

"Why should I listen to you? Even if your face is appealing, unlike the last two men my father sent, it's still not enough. I will not marry. I will not be tamed by any man, let alone a destructive *human*."

He grinned. "You think that I'm appealing?"

She rolled her eyes and stood, the end of the spear planted firm to the ground. "I can tell you're weak. I will never marry, but if I were to, the man would have to be strong."

"You're right, Kilya." Cantuña spoke softly, "I will never be the strongest. If I learned anything about my mother and father when they were alive it was that love wasn't measured by strength or looks. But, what I would do, is make you the happiest woman in Quito."

She scoffed, "*Doubtful*."

As she turned her back to him and started for her cave, he called out, "Please! Your father told me that if you would consider me, he'd give me the secret to defeat *La Diabla*. If I can't convince you that I'm worthy, then I've failed to save my people."

She rolled her eyes. "You're not the first one to come to me for help and I didn't consider the others. People die all the time. Tell me why I should show you favor?"

His eyebrows furrowed. "Because I'm the most honest human you may ever know. I won't lie to you and promise a life of grandeur. There are no parts of the world that I can show that you probably haven't already seen. Kilya, I can't give you the head of some beast or the most gold in the world, but if you would think of me as someone you could give a chance, then I promise to bring you happiness and truth."

The demigoddess glanced away. She held her breath, cheeks full of air, puffed up like a fish while she contemplated.

She let out an exasperated sigh. "You're honest at least. You can't provide any of those things, yet you stand here, asking for my hand and give me your word that you'll make me happy. For that, I will consider you, but only under one condition."

Cantuña's eyes lit up. "Anything."

She tightened her grip around her spear, pointed towards the city, and nodded. "I'll tell you on the way. The sun will be rising soon, so we should leave."

Without argument, he walked by her side, knowing deep in his heart that it was time to face *La Diabla*. On the way, she whispered into his ear her condition. The longer she spoke, the more uncertain he grew, but he kept his doubts to himself. It didn't matter if he was afraid or tired; he didn't have a choice.

Once they reached the gates of the city, they spotted Raco posted against a nearby wall along the gate. With his arms crossed, he grinned as they approached. Cantuña wiggled his fingers and cleared his throat, wishing he could feel the same.

"I see you took his offer," Raco said to Kilya.

"Conditionally," she scowled.

"I see. Well, nevertheless, I will tell you the secret. Bringing my daughter to the city is proof enough for me. Come closer." The god motioned Cantuña to his side. He whispered the secret of how to outsmart *La Diabla*. When finished, Cantuña blinked and shook his head.

"That's it? But that's so easy!" he said.

Raco laughed. "I never said it wasn't. Now, you two had better leave before the sun rises. Don't want to run out of time."

Kilya scowled at her father's grinning face before she spoke to Cantuña, "And remember, even if you succeed, you still have to keep our bargain."

"Wait a minute... what did you say?" Raco stopped. He glared at his daughter, face scrunched similar to a pig's nose. She moved to Cantuña's side, patted his shoulder, and shrugged.

"It's between us. We'll take our leave." She smiled.

Cantuña nodded and walked away with the demigoddess next to him. Completing Raco's instructions would be easy, but alas, carrying out Kilya's terms would prove much more difficult. She agreed that if he didn't show fear when confronting the devil, then she would consider him. If he cowered, then she would allow *La Diabla* to devour his soul as a way to punish him for wasting her time.

How does one stay calm when facing the Bringer of Death? Only in the moment, when staring her in the eyes, would he know. He straightened his back, determined to find out regardless of the heaviness on his heart. They made their way towards the cathedral.

Cantuña rushed into the finished project with the sun on the horizon, night sky changing from a deep purple to a faded grayish-blue. He stopped in the middle of the atrium and gawked about the space, unable to believe the beauty before his eyes. Maroon paint lined the panes of windows and bordered the walls followed by a deep, gold trim along the intricate paintings which covered the panels. From the windowsill where Cantuña first met *La Diabla*, he noticed Abrus Precar vines in full bloom. Many of the locals were familiar with the vines' poisonous properties. Young children living on the outskirts of the village occasionally devoured it while their parents' attention had slipped.

He marched over to his work bench and picked up his carving knife, examining the ridges on the blade. His father had given it to him as a present years ago to add beautiful designs to wood pieces such as tables and chairs. The builder gripped the handle, moved over to the cobblestone wall near the back of the atrium, and chipped away at the dried clay that held the wall together.

After several minutes, a round, smooth rock dropped to the ground. Cantuña picked it up and wiped the surface off in a hurry.

With the tip of the blade, he etched a message. Kilya turned from the entrance towards him.

"She's coming," she said.

"Almost done," he replied.

The demigoddess stepped away from view and moved into hiding behind a bundle of vines. Right before La Diabla stepped through, he turned his back to the door. Even though he couldn't see her, a cold wind slipped across his sweat and mud covered skin.

"My child. The time has come. What do you think of my work? Beautiful,

is it not? They will remember you for many years." Her voice rang through the atrium.

Cantuña then moved to face her with the rock in one hand and his other hand hidden behind him holding the knife. "But it's not done. I found this one on the ground."

She cocked her head to the side. "Oh? Let me see." Cantuña reached his hand out to her, ready for her to grab it. Right before picking it up, she stopped.

"Whoever picks up this stone... will accept the gods are more powerful?" she whispered. *La Diabla* gasped at the etched words, taken aback by the builder's cleverness. As she repeated the message aloud, her body shook, and her bones cracked.

Cantuña held his stare, though his skin crawled. The devil woman shrieked as she began to change. Her loose, wrinkled skin, stretched as she grew four times taller than him. The ram's horns on the side of her head swirled and grew to match her new beastly form. Her fingers—once frail and brittle—now each the size of Cantuña's torso. Hard spikes made of bone protruded from her spine and ripped her clothes. Now, taking neither the form of man or woman, stood the devil, enraged and murderous.

The builder lifted his chin and squared his shoulders. Tiny bolts of electricity swam through his gut. Hairs on the back of his neck stood—his whole body alert and ready to run or fight. Before him, the true form of *La Diabla* screamed into the last seconds of night. A dark energy swarmed the beast, but he refused to look away. In this moment, he had nothing left except for courage.

"I learned of your plan to devour weak souls searching for refuge through this cathedral. You tricked me. There's nothing you can do because this is the last piece of the atrium you promised to complete and you can't touch it. I've won," he said.

The devil shook its head and leaned down to where Cantuña could feel its breath on his face. Darkness from the monstrous creature crawled closer to him. It blocked out the rest of the world as it swallowed him whole. Now, trapped inside some unknown void, Cantuña stood strong.

"I'm not afraid," he spoke.

La Diabla cackled. "You're hiding how you *really* feel."

"I'm not."

"I can taste it on your words. Every time you speak, the fear seeps through. Give in."

He shook his head and clenched the cobblestone tight. "There's a lot of things that scare me in this world. Losing my sister. My city being destroyed. But you? No. I was prepared to give you my soul. I already accepted that my time was going to end. *La Diabla*, you've lost."

As the beast opened its mouth—massive rows of fangs only inches away from devouring him whole—a small amount of sunlight shined through the blanket of darkness. The beast's body trembled as smoke rose from its searing flesh. *La Diabla* snarled in pain and retreated, freeing Cantuña from its grasp. Unable to stand the break of morning, the devil shrank back into the shriveled form Cantuña had seen the night before. She moved swiftly over to the back entrance of the atrium and escaped into the transient shadows.

Cantuña blinked several times, blinded by the sudden burst of light. He rubbed his eyes, confused by what he had seen. Once adjusted to being out of the darkness, he turned to Kilya, who stepped away from the vines.

She grinned, hand on her hip. "I guess there's something under that pretty face after all. Not many humans could do what you just did."

"Then, does this mean I fulfilled our bargain?"

She snorted in amusement, walked over to Cantuña, and ruffled his dark hair. "This doesn't guarantee my love for you. It only means that you interest me enough to not cut off your head for asking in the first place."

Cantuña rubbed the back of his neck and followed her out of the cathedral. "I could live with that."

Ramos and his guardsmen approached the two from the other end of the street. Cantuña stood proud, with his arms crossed and chin held high. If he could defeat the devil, then he could outsmart three mere humans. With their jaws agape and eyes wide, the conquistadors couldn't believe the cathedral was complete.

"H-how?" Ramos asked.

Cantuña shrugged. "It doesn't matter how. It's finished. My debt to you has been paid."

"Let me examine the work, first," he demanded. The three stepped around them and went inside to see if he was telling the truth. They spent several minutes wandering around before they returned to the front.

"So?" Cantuña asked.

Ramos curled the ends of his thick mustache. "You've done an exquisite job. I don't know how, but I don't particularly care. Build another for me? We've already chosen a spot in San Lorenzo right up the river."

"No. No more deals."

"But I would hate for my men to be upset by your refusal. They were looking forward to the new addition." Ramos sighed. The two behind him gripped their guns tighter.

Kilya stepped forward, spear in her hand. "My father is very close to the leader that rules over that portion of Ecuador. Right now, the Incan residents of that region, he, and *your* people have a treaty that seems to be working. It would be a shame if another war were to break out."

The conquistador rubbed his temples. If this woman was right, it would be his head.

He waved Cantuña and Kilya away. "Fine! In any case, I can find a more skilled builder to handle the job. Our debt is settled."

They nodded to each other then headed down the street. He patted his father's knife as he walked, halfway surprised to still be breathing.

After that, they visited his sister who was happy to see he'd finished the atrium and no harm had come. He returned to working on local projects and repairs, always making sure to never take on any job that he couldn't handle on his own. And for years and years, even after his death, the people of Quito would come to visit the cathedral and remember him as the Incan hero who defeated *La Diabla*.

Dr. Knowall

WJ Hayes

Author's Note: *That Doctor Know-All is not more well-known is a mystery. It is catalogued as Number 98 of the Grimm Fairy Tales (for those keeping score at home) and is, admittedly, a very odd piece of folklore. After all, there is no epic quest or great obstacle to overcome. Heck, it doesn't even have a moral lesson.*

It is a story about a nobleman who summons a doctor to find some missing gold. Why would a doctor be qualified to solve a property theft? And, to paraphrase an old aspirin commercial, he's not a real doctor, he just plays one. Despite this and the fact our eponymous hero does nothing but sit down to a meal, the crime is solved, and he is amply rewarded merely for being at the right place at the right time. It's odd. It's absurd.

Why is this story not more well-known? The "fake it until you make it" ethos of our main character cries out to be more well known. This is a story that should have been included in Jay Ward's 'Fractured Fairy Tales'. The absurdity of the character would have been a perfect fit in some of Bill Willingham's Fables comic series. And yet, the good "doctor" languished in obscurity. Someone, I thought, ought to do something to correct this injustice. Then I realized that someone would have to be me.

Dr. Knowall is the result.

John Scarpariello spoke with his friend, the doctor, when the gilded carriage stopped in front of them. An unamused looking footman stepped off the coach. "Are you Knowall?" he demanded of Sacrpariello.

Scarpariello gestured to his friend who was standing in the doorway of a building. Directly over the entrance was a sign that read:

DOCTOR KNOWALL

Knowall looked at the sign, then the footman, and smiled. "How can I help?" he inquired.

"Lordship wants a word with you," the footman said, staring at the sign.

Knowall gave an exaggerated sigh. "Let me get my book," he said, entering the building.

The footman opened his mouth to object, but shut it when he realized it would do no good. He turned his head and stared at Scarpariello, ready to take his frustration out on the man. "Who are you?" the footman snarled.

Before he could reply for himself, Knowall reappeared. Closing the door behind him, the doctor said, "This is my good friend Scarpariello. He is a mender of soles." Scarpariello rolled his eyes as Knowall paused and looked at the footman's boots before he shrugged and continued, "He might be of some use to you."

The footman had only been told to fetch the doctor. This other man was an unforeseen complication. And the footman didn't like complications. That was one of the benefits to being a footman: you didn't have to worry about what to wear. Just put on the uniform and you were set. Was he supposed to leave the second man here? His Lordship had been running around unshod, greatly vexed, when he had sent for the footman. The footman frowned and came to his decision. "I know where I stand with the Creator," he announced, opening the carriage door for Knowall. "But perhaps the Duke does not."

Scarpariello watched Knowall get into the carriage. There was an uncomfortable moment when he realized the footman was staring at him. "Well, what are you waiting for? An engraved invitation? His Lordship didn't have time for that, seeing as there is a great emergency. He only sent me with incomplete instructions. So stop dawdling and get onboard."

From inside the coach, Knowall cried out, "Come on, John. Let's not keep his Lordship, the Duke, waiting."

Scarpariello wanted to argue, but looking into the stony gaze of the footman, realized the futility of it. He was not completely inside when the door closed, propelling him into the seats. The whip cracked and the carriage barreled down the post road towards the Ducal Palace.

Adjusting himself, Scarpariello looked around. This was clearly the Duke's coach. "Why does he want to see you?" he demanded of his friend.

Knowall smiled. "I always knew this day would come. And he wants to see us, not just me."

"But I haven't done anything," cried Scarpariello. "You're the crook."

"I'm not a crook. I am a doctor."

"You're not a doctor. You're a teamster going around with a children's primer, claiming to be a doctor."

Knowall looked at the book sitting on his lap. It was, as his friend noted, a Children's Reading Primer to which he had affixed a lock that held a metal band in place, preventing anyone from opening the book. The cover showed a rooster. Above the picture were the words:

Mynd First Reade

Only someone who saw the cover of the tome up close and had time to study it would realize the "nd" in the word "Mynd" had been carved into the leather cover sometime after the book had been created. And it would take an even closer examination to realize the final word "Reade" was, in fact, "Reader" with the book's lock obscuring the final letter.

"And," Scarpariello continued, "Your name isn't Knowall, it's Lufttache. Sturgeon Lufttache."

Knowall, nee Luftache shrugged. It was true. He had been a teamster, eking out a living until the day he had been part of the convoy bringing supplies to the Imperial Capital. While there, he had been sent by the head teamster to fetch medicine from a local doctor. As he had waited for the mixture to be compounded, he had marveled at the doctor's beautiful home and the large meal a servant was carrying into the dining room.

The doctor had seen him staring in wonder and when asked, had said it was simple to be like him. "Just sell your oxen and cart. Then use the money to buy a nice storefront, good clothes, and lots of equipment that looks vaguely medical. Have a sign made for over the door advertising you're a doctor who knows all. Then buy a large children's reading primer. I find the one with the cock on the cover to be the most useful."

It was here the doctor had paused and, seeing the quizzical look, amended, "Rooster. Find the one with a rooster on it."

"That will work?" he had asked the doctor.

The response had been a shrug and, "So far it has."

The oxen and cart had been sold, the property bought, the clothing and equipment purchased. He hadn't understood why he had to change his name, but Knowall had no great attachment to the old one. And just as the doctor in the capital had foretold, people flocked to his door, seeking his advice on all sorts of ailments. He had even managed to pick up some actual medical knowledge in the process. Looking at his friend, Knowall made a noncommittal gesture. "It says a lot about the state of medicine in the empire that people believe I am a doctor."

Scarpariello shook his head and frowned. "But what would the Duke want with me? I'm just a shoemaker."

"I think," Knowall said with a smile, "the footman misunderstood what I said. He is under the impression you are a spiritualist who tends to souls, not a shoemaker who tends to soles."

This didn't appease Scarpariello's dread. "But we are talking about the Duke. Surely, he will know the difference between a quack and a real doctor."

Knowall gave Scarpariello a reassuring pat on the knee. "It's faith like yours that allows monarchies to thrive," he said, adding, "It will work out. So, don't lose your head over this."

The coach passed through the gates to the Duke's Palace. Scarpariello watched a burly man chopping firewood. Brutal but quick, the job was done. "That's exactly what I'm afraid will happen," Scarpariello muttered darkly.

As the carriage approached the palace, the Duke watched anxiously at the top of the stairs to the main keep. He kept his hands behind his back and out of sight from most of the staff so as to prevent them from seeing how hard he was wringing them. As for the eye twitch, well, there was nothing he could do about that.

The Duke frowned when he saw two men exit the coach. He had specifically instructed Boris to fetch Dr. Knowall. Could there possibly be two people with that name? Whatever the answer, the Dining Master would have to be told to set another place for dinner.

Boris led the men up the steps and bowed before his Lordship. "May I present Dr. Knowall and..."

There was an embarrassed pause. The Duke winced in mortification as Boris hissed to the other man, "What's your name?"

There was another delay before the answer was given in a theatrical whisper, "Scarpariello."

"...Dr. Scarpariello," Boris said, picking up where he left off, "a Healer of Souls. Both were at Dr. Knowalls. Thought you might want the pair."

The Duke, being so preoccupied with both the protocols of his position and his own concerns, missed the whimper from Scarpariello. Instead, his Lordship gave a brittle smile to Boris. "Thank you. Please let the staff know there will be an additional guest."

Looking directly at Knowall, the Duke extended his hand, hoping the shaking wasn't as bad as he thought it looked. "Thank you for coming on such short notice. I couldn't think of anyone else to summon."

Knowall gave a tremendous smile. "Anything for your Excellency," he said, charm oozing everywhere. "Tell me what ails your Lordship?"

The Duke rocked back on his heels, eyes wide in bewilderment before he realized the error. "Ah," he began, "Yes, that's not why I asked you here."

Ignoring the soft moan emanating from Scarpariello's lips, Knowall nodded. "Someone in your household then?"

The Duke shook his head. "No, nothing like that. Let us go inside and I will explain. You too, Dr. Scarpariello. You should share in this as well. Perhaps your insight will be beneficial."

Knowall and Scarpariello followed the Duke. "We're doomed," moaned Scarpariello.

"Shut up," hissed Knowall. "We'll be fine. See, those are stairs to the dungeon. We're headed towards the Great Hall. Do stop whimpering. It's undignified."

As they reached the Great Hall, the Duke motioned for the servants and guards to leave. Doors closed and the Duke said, "This is a rather delicate issue, doctor. I do not need your expertise in medicine, but rather your knowledge of people."

Knowall relaxed slightly. Knowledge of people was something he'd possessed ever since he had been Luftache. And that experience taught when he had no idea what was happening, the best thing to do was nod and smile encouragingly. He did so. Instantly the Duke visibly relaxed. "You see," he continued, "there has been a theft. A portion of the Duchy's tax revenue has gone missing. More to the point, the portion of the revenue due to the Emperor has been stolen. If we cannot find the money or who stole it, I fear the Emperor will be most displeased."

Unpleasant images of what an unhappy Emperor meant filled Scarpariello's mind, causing him to snuffle quietly. Knowall's smile never wavered as he nodded once again. After a moment to determine the best way to phrase his statement, the doctor said, "I am, of course, honored your Lordship has sought me out. However, I am a doctor, not a watchman."

"But I was told you know all," protested the Duke.

"I think you mean know-it...ow!" cried Scarpariello as Knowall's foot stepped on his.

Ignoring the looks from his friend, the doctor said, "I have been blessed with much knowledge, this is true. But as I have focused on the healing arts, I fear my expertise may be limited."

The Duke, whose images of what an unhappy Emperor meant

were based on observed fact, nodded. "Of course, I understand. But I have complete trust you can assist. Finding money must be like finding the cause of an illness, right?"

"Sometimes," allowed Knowall.

The Duke gestured towards Scarpariello, "Having someone who intercedes to the gods on behalf of us poor mortals can only make the task easier."

Scarpariello bit off his protest. This, he knew, was not the time to be overly honest. The Duke, mistaking the stony look on Scarpariello's face added, "It goes without saying that when you succeed, you will find my gratitude deeply rewarding."

Knowall looked at the Duke and the thin, nervous smile on the man's face. The Duke was probably prepared to believe anything even remotely plausible. Turning and looking at the pale face of Scarpariello, Knowall reflected that even an implausible but divine story might work. He just needed time to think of one. Besides, Knowall thought, if he was able to pull this off, who knows where it could lead.

He clapped his hands, startling both the overwrought Duke and Scarpariello. "Your Lordship, I am at your disposal."

The Duke's smile turned to one of relief. "Of course, follow me," he said walking towards the hall doors. Leaving the great hall, the trio left the keep and walked across the courtyard and out beyond the walls. Standing on the drawbridge, the Duke gestured towards the road and the spire of the town some ten miles away. "So, the money was collected in the towns and lands before being brought to Hal of the Assizes. Then Hal, under heavy guard, stopped here and waited for the drawbridge to be lowered."

As the man spoke, it slowly dawned on Knowall that the Duke was going to walk them through literally every step of the process of how the tax money ended up in the keep. As the Duke retraced the steps of the revenue, Scarpariello hissed to Knowall, "How are we going to get out of this?"

"I'm working on it," came the reply out of the corner of Knowall's mouth.

"That's what you said after you told that general I made Seven League Boots."

"That?" Knowall airily dismissed his friend's protest. "It was a mere misunderstanding. And it all worked out in the end. Everything went back to normal."

Scarpariello slowly turned his head and looked into Knowall's eyes. "Not everything. I'm here," he pointed towards a distant mountain range, "and my homeland is on the other side of those."

"How you fret so," clucked Knowall. "Everything will be good. Trust me."

"I don't see how," Scarpariello harrumphed. "I'm telling you, the servants know something is up."

"You're imaging things. Whatever happened to those boots, by the way?"

"Don't you remember? They were stolen by that witch."

"A witch? Hmm...I would have said she was tough," replied Knowall as they followed the Duke, neither man seeing the five figures standing at the entrance to the kitchens.

"WE MIGHT HAVE TO KILL THEM," one of the quintet, the First Dining Assistant, said. "We can't have anyone discover what we've done."

"Who is he?" demanded the man at the far end of the line. This was the Duke's personal Chef.

The Chief Dining Master answered, "I overheard a valet say the Duke sent for the local doctor."

"What good's a doctor?" the Chef said as he spat on the ground.

A young boy, the Third Dining Assistant, said, "He cured me mum's lumbago."

The man in the middle, the Second Dining Assistant, nodded in agreement. "They say he can cure anything."

"Curing aches and pains does not qualify someone to solve thefts," the Chef reasoned.

"He is said to know all," the Second Assistant protested. "Stands to reason. The Duke wouldn't have brought him in if he didn't think the man could find the gold. We should kill them now."

"You want to kill the men the Duke just brought here to find the missing gold?" the Chef asked.

The First Assistant puzzled over this. "You think it might look suspicious?" he said after finishing his lengthy internal debate.

The Chef ground his teeth so hard, he feared he would need the doctor's services. When he was able to relax his jaw muscles, he replied, "Everyone needs to stay calm."

KNOWALL AND SCARPARIELLO followed the Duke into a structure adjacent to the keep. Made from large stone blocks, it was barely high enough for the men to stand without having to bend down. The Duke was still describing the process by which the tax was brought to the keep and counted, when he pointed to the middle of the room and said, "And this was where the three large chests were deposited."

Scarpariello looked around. There was only one chest in front of them. The only door was behind them. "You would think someone would have noticed chests of gold being moved," he mused.

The doctor walked around the room in a figure eight pattern, stopping occasionally to look at the walls and ceiling. Once, he stared at the floor and grunted. "Yes, this is most interesting. I shall need some time to reflect. And of course, I will need to consult my book," he said, tapping his tome.

The Duke saw Scarpariello wince and again misunderstood. "Where are my manners?" he asked no one in particular. "I have prepared a meal for us. Come, let us eat. Chef is master in preparing all manner of culinary delights"

The Duke turned and almost ran towards the keep. Knowall turned to Scarpariello. "See, we're getting a meal out of it."

"The condemned usually do," his friend muttered.

"You worry too much. As your doctor, I advise you to cheer up. I would hate to have to give you a leeching. Besides, you have never eaten like this. There will be multiple courses. We shall eat until we can eat no more."

Even in his glum state, Scarpariello had to admit the dining hall was impressive. Everything, it seemed, was gilded. As they sat, the Duke rang a bell at his end of the table. Instantly, a door opened near where Knowall and Scarpariello sat, and the Third Dining Assistant appeared carrying soup. As he passed, Knowall nudged his friend. "Look John, that is the first."

It was something of a minor miracle the Third Assistant didn't drop the tureen. When he had heard Knowall speak, the young boy was convinced it was just the beginning of a sentence that would end with, "of the thieves." With more rattling than was customary, the Assistant ladled the soup to the diners.

As he approached, Knowall caught the wonderful aroma of the soup, reminding his stomach how hungry he was. Looking appreciatively at what was being ladled into his bowl, he smiled at the Assistant. "Yes," Knowall said, "it is good to get the first."

The server forced his body to put one leg in front of another and march out of the dining room. Entering the kitchen like a mechanical doll, the boy cried, "He knows."

The Dining Master looked up from his inspection of the second course plates. "Lower your voice," he hissed. "And pull yourself together."

The boy shook his head. "You don't understand, we're doomed. The doctor knows all," he replied, albeit at a lower volume.

The Master and the Chef exchanged a look. "That's impossible," the Chef announced.

The First Dining Assistant nodded in agreement. "It is just your imagination."

"Then how do you explain why, as I walked into the hall, the doctor looked at me and said I was the first."

The First Assistant developed whiplash from turning from the Third Assistant to the Chef. The Second Assistant groaned and reached for the cooking sherry for courage.

"And how did you respond?" demanded the Chef.

The Third Assistant shook his head. "Nothing," he said and then paused. Realizing what he had done, or rather not done, the boy puffed out his chest and repeated, "I told them nothing."

"We should have killed them when we had a chance. Now, we need to run," the Second Assistant announced. "Before we are seized."

The First Assistant nodded. "Or better yet, poison them all now."

The Dining Master shook his head in disgust. "Stop acting foolish," he snapped as he pulled the bottle out of the Second Assistant's hands. Turning to the First, he admonished, "For once in your miserable life, think. Killing them now would only raise suspicions."

The First Assistant, who never enjoyed the chef's cooking, wasn't so sure. But he wasn't sure this was the moment to begin a career as a food critic. The Chef pointed his knife at the servers. "They know nothing. Just act naturally and serve the next course."

The Second Assistant began to protest, but the Dining Master, having placed the final selection of meats onto the vesper board next to the breads and potatoes, made a final presentation adjustment by repositioning an olive which strayed dangerously close to the mustard. Nodding with satisfaction, the Master shoved the second course tray into the Second Assistant's hands as the First Assistant pushed him towards the door.

∼

In the dining room, Knowall and the Duke were discussing, much to Scarpariello's discomfort, whether vesiculation was appropriate for treating gout. He had seen the Second Assistant enter the room. Knowall followed his friend's gaze. Seeing the Second Assistant, the doctor smiled and tapped the table lightly in approval. "This is the second," he said to Scarpariello.

The Duke, preoccupied with conversing with the doctor instead of imagining what would happen to him if the gold was not located, failed to notice the wild-eye look of fear in the Second Assistant. Instead, as he was trying to think of something to say in response to Knowall's view of the treatment, the Duke raised his wine goblet, saluting Knowall. "I applaud your keen insight."

The Second Assistant nearly slammed the vesper board onto the table before fleeing out of the room. When he got to the kitchen, the Second Assistant declared, "The boy's right. The doctor just marked me as the second thief. And the Duke acknowledged it. The guards will be here any minute. I will not go out there again."

"Nor I," squeaked the Third Assistant while the First Assistant reached for what he believed was sherry but was, in fact, red wine vinegar. Whether his failure to notice the difference was a result of his emotional state or Chef's poor quality control is unknown.

The Dining Master rolled his eyes at the assistants. "Idiots. You're both acting like idiots," he announced as he put the cover on the fish course. "If the guards were going to seize us, there would be nowhere to run. Besides there has been no cry of alarm."

"I don't care," the Third Assistant said sullenly. "I'm not facing the doctor again."

With a sigh, the Dining Master turned to the First Assistant. "Since these fools refuse to do their duty, you must take it in."

Scarpariello was looking towards the kitchen door, ignoring the conversation of medical ills. He was confused by the actions of the serving staff. Admittedly, he had very little experience in such things. But they seemed to be acting odd. They were behaving as if they had guilty consciences. His train of thought was derailed as he heard the

Duke ask a nonmedical question. "Tell me doctor, are you familiar with the study of a person's name in divining their fortune?"

"I'm afraid your Lordship has me at a disadvantage," the doctor answered. "Very rarely do I encounter such practices when seeking to cure the ills of my patients."

Dabbing the corners of his mouth, the Duke warmed to his subject. "It is something my wife had told me is all the rage at Court. They have a soothsayer who can foresee a person's future by knowing nothing about the person but their first name."

Knowall and his friend exchanged sideways glances. The doctor smiled at the sheer audacity of a kindred spirit. "It is an interesting theory and I would love to know more," he responded carefully.

The Duke nodded approvingly. "I shall write and have my wife submit your name to the soothsayer to see what your future holds."

Scarpariello put his wine goblet to his mouth. "Now that is something I would like to know myself," he muttered.

The Duke stopped his head in mid-nod. "I'm sorry," he said, a tinge of embarrassment in his voice, "But I don't believe anyone has ever told me your first name."

The First Assistant chose this auspicious moment to enter the dining hall, the covered tray resting on his shoulder. When no cry of accusation was leveled on him as he approached, he relaxed. Lowering the tray towards the table, the First Assistant happened to catch Knowall's eye as the doctor answered the Duke's question. "It's Sturgeon."

The First Assistant had been in Service since he was a child. He had always been a prime example of grace and elegance in the course of his duties. Until this moment. He tried to act nonchalantly as he removed the tray cover to reveal the fish course consisting of vinegar-poached sturgeon with thyme-butter sauce. Still, he soldiered on, his nerves only weakening when he mistook Scarpariello's scratching his neck for a throat cutting gesture, almost dropping the plate into the man's lap.

"I was wrong," the First Assistant wheezed as he staggered into the kitchen. "The doctor is a genius. He knew what was under the tray cover before I made the presentation. We are doomed."

The Chef threw his hands up in the air in despair. The Dining Master crossed his arms and looked at his staff. "What is wrong with you?" he demanded. "Never in all my time have I seen such fools as you three. He is a man. He is a doctor. What does he know of thieving? We are this close to getting away with it and you are going to pieces."

The First Assistant jabbed his finger at the Master. "Then you go out there next time and see for yourself. Dr. Knowall is not a man we can fool."

The Chef shook his head. "Go," he said to the Master. "Just bring them the main course and be done with it."

Muttering oaths under his breath, the Dining Master lifted his first tray in over thirty years and went into the dining room. No one at the table took any notice of him. There was no sense of excitement or alarm. Everything he saw suggested a normal dinner. His heart did skip a beat when the Duke asked Knowall, "Do you know what became of my gold?"

Knowall made a noncommittal gesture. "The symptoms, or should I say evidence, you have provided me has done much to encourage my thinking on the subject. But I have not yet formulated any coherent thoughts on the answer."

Scarpariello rolled his eyes. "That's because there aren't any," he said under his breath and then noticed the odd look of relief on the Master's face.

The Duke was about to ask another question when he saw the Dining Master and the covered tray with the main course. Clapping his hands, he announced, "Ah, Doctor, perhaps you can demonstrate your skill right now."

Knowall raised his eyebrows as Scarpariello choked on his wine. "I'm sorry your Lordship, I don't follow what you mean."

The Duke smiled. "Such is the renown of your skills, undoubtedly you can discern what we are having for dinner."

Knowall felt the coils of panic wrapping around his intestines as he looked at the covered dish. He had no idea and was trying to decide how to get out of this predicament. The sotto voce moaning of his friend was not helping him concentrate. "Be quiet," he hissed.

"We're doomed," moaned his companion.

Knowall knew this wasn't good. He didn't need Scarpariello to point out the obvious. He needed time to think. And his friend's whining wasn't letting him concentrate. "Oh Scarpariello," Knowall groused louder than he realized, "such a chicken."

"Ah ha," cried the Duke as he lifted the tray cover. Even before the dish was revealed, the aroma of chicken, sausages, and peppers wafted into the dining hall, with hints of wine, rosemary, garlic, and roasted onions detected by Knowall and Scarpariello. "You are correct, Doctor. It is Chicken Scarpariello."

Knowall gave quick prayer of thanks to any deity who might have been listening. The Dining Master stumbled backwards, striking the wall. Only Scarpariello saw the reaction as the man lurched out of the room. "Say doctor, can I have a word?" he whispered to Knowall.

Inside the kitchen, the Master appeared. "He knows," he croaked before fainting.

The servants and Chef looked at the form on the floor and then one another. The Chef raised the cleaver menacingly and said in an unnervingly calm tone to the assembled coconspirators, "Any of you scream or panic, and I'll do you in. Now give me a moment to think."

The Chef stared at the unconscious Dining Master. "We have only one chance," he said. Looking to the First Assistant, he instructed, "Have the doctor come in here. Tell him the truth, the Dining Master has collapsed, and we need his services."

The First Assistant wanted to object, but he could not see how he could do that without being cleaved by the large knife in the Chef's hand. Swallowing hard, he did as he was told. A few moments later, he returned with Knowall in tow. The doctor looked at the Dining Master and said, "What happened?"

The chef smiled. "He heard you correctly guess the main course and was overcome by your prowess. We all are."

Knowall smiled and nodded. "It is a gift," he conceded, amazed at Scarpariello's insight. Maybe this crime solving wasn't as hard as he thought it was.

"And," the Chef continued, "that is why we confess to you now, in hopes of striking a deal."

The doctor looked around. The dining assistants were as pale as corpses and seemingly seconds from joining the master on the floor. The Chef was staring at him. It was a familiar look. It was the one used when people sought to make deals that were best if they never became public knowledge. "What is it that you want? You can't take the money."

"We don't want the money," the Chef said, "we want our lives. Let us return the gold to the treasury. Tomorrow, you tell the Duke you had a vision most of the gold has returned to where it belonged."

Knowall scratched his chin thoughtfully. "Most of the gold?"

The Chef reached behind his back and produced a small pouch. "If you do not tell we took the gold, I imagine a small bag of coins will be waiting for you. We will take the other to cover our expenses as we flee. You could say the missing gold was taken by the gods."

Knowall raised an eyebrow. "The Duke knows my friend is a Spiritualist," he said, thinking out loud.

"Fine, you take one, your friend the other. We'll figure something out."

The doctor looked at the men. They all stared at him pathetically. He held their lives, he realized, in his hands. There was the chance they would try to double cross him or set him up. "Where is the gold now?" Knowall asked.

The thieves looked at one another. They were terribly uneasy about revealing the information. From the floor, the Dining Master, having just come around, said weakly, "There is a secret passage behind the fireplace to the treasury. We hid the chests there."

The Chef looked at his confederate. The Master returned the

glare. "The doctor knew the answer. This was a test. If we lied, he would have known. And where would that have left us?"

"That's right," Knowall said, getting into the spirit of it. "I will agree not tell the Duke who stole the money. But I will tell him I am getting close to discovering the location. Leave after the meal is done and never return. By midnight, I will tell him where the gold is."

The deal struck, Knowall returned to the dining hall, a bounce in his step, and the jingling of two bags of gold barely audible. "Is the Dining Master alright?" asked the Duke.

"He will make a full recovery," Knowall said, adding as he glanced at Scarpariello, "And better than that, as I was ministering to him, suddenly my mind assembled all of the pieces of the puzzle and I believe I can now discern where the gold may be. However, I must first consult my tome."

He removed a key from his pocket and inserted it into the book's lock. There was a click, and Knowall pulled the metal band away from it, allowing the tome to be opened. As he hummed to himself, leafing through the pages, Scarpariello once again marveled at it all. Almost no one ever questioned the odd spelling on the book's cover. And those that did always seemed satisfied by Knowall's explanation that it was an instruction to use the mind and first read before diagnosing.

The Chef began pacing in the kitchen. The problem with being a thief, he reflected, was the you always expected other people to treat you the way you treat them. Since the Chef had sold out his own mother, he fully expected the doctor to do the same to him. He left the kitchen by way of a second secret passage, this one connecting to the dining room of his personal quarters. The entrance to this hidden door was concealed behind a large tapestry. The Chef listened intently. At the first sign of betrayal, he would kill the doctor and then make his escape.

Knowall was standing at the table, flipping through the book. He knew there was a picture of a pot of gold in the primer, he had seen it before. "They took it," Scarpariello whispered, barely moving his lips.

"Yes," Knowall said under his breath.

He was getting annoyed. He could not find the picture. Since he had started his practice, he had added other pages to the book, containing actual medical knowledge. Now, it was making it difficult for him to find what he needed. "I know you are there," he growled in frustration, "So you had better show yourself. It is foolish to hide from me."

There were two small holes cut in the tapestry, almost at eye level. Unless you knew where to look, they were completely hidden. That Knowall had uttered those words while looking directly at those holes froze the Chef where he was. How could the man know he was there? Before he could do anything, he saw Knowall's face flush with anger as the man slammed his book closed and smacked it with his hand. It was icy terror that prevented the Chef from moving even as he saw the book fly off the table and come directly at him. Struck full in the face, he fell backwards into the secret passage.

The book ricocheted off the tapestry, striking the mantle of the great fireplace in the exact place necessary to activate the hidden passage. The Duke cried out in joy as he saw the two chests of gold, "We are saved."

Scarpariello slid down the chair in relief. "Yes, we are," he sighed before gulping the remainder of the wine in his goblet.

"But tell me, who took the gold?" asked the Duke.

Knowall shrugged. "Alas, your Lordship, that is something I cannot say."

"Why?"

The doctor paused, trying to think of something. Making random hand gestures, Knowall said, "Sometimes we are permitted to know how something may be corrected, but not what it was. And sometimes it is the other way. It is very complicated and has something to do with felines. Or maybe it is pigeons."

The Duke nodded approvingly. "Yes, that makes sense."

"It does? I mean, it does, doesn't it?" Knowall replied. "I am glad you understand."

"Understand? My dear doctor, I more than understand. You shall be amply rewarded for what you have done."

The Duke trailed off as he clapped for his guards and issued instructions about returning the gold. Knowall took the opportunity to drink some of the wine. "You were very observant, John," he said to Scarpariello. "I think we could do quite well in this line of business."

Scarpariello blinked. "We? What is this we? I solved it."

"But they told me where to find the gold."

"And bribed you, no doubt."

"And you too. They were very keen on getting right with the gods."

"I'm still not doing it anymore," Scarpariello announced as he stuffed some of the chicken into his mouth. "I want to finish this meal and go home."

As the guards, under the watchful eye of other guards, removed the chests from the fireplace to return them to the treasury, another servant entered the room, handing a letter to the Duke. Reading it, he said with a chuckle, "You are certainly in great demand, Doctor."

With a nod and smile, Knowall said, "Oh?"

"Yes. There is a messenger outside from one of the neighboring kingdoms. He was sent to find Doctor Knowall. Seems an entire castle has been put under some sort of spell after a princess suffered a small prick while using a spinning wheel. The King wants your assistance."

Scarpariello shook his head and said with a sneer, "Knowall is an expert in small pr..."

"Good," interrupted the Duke with a clap of his hands. "I shall let the King know Doctors Knowall and Scarpariello will be happy to help."

"What?" asked Scarpariello.

"And I will let the Emperor know of the service you are rendering an ally of the Empire," the Duke cried as he left to tell the messenger the good news.

Knowall and Scarpariello were alone in the room. After a few minutes, the silence was broken when Scarpariello asked in a small voice, "What just happened?"

Doctor Knowall swirled the wine in his goblet. Smiling at his friend's discomfort, he answered, "You just volunteered to help out a friend of the Emperor."

Scarpariello pinched the bridge of his nose. "So much for living happily ever after," he moaned.

KILCONQUHAR LOCH

KAREN EDWARDS PIEROTTI

Author's Note: Scotland and Wales have many obscure folklore or fairy stories so there was a lot to choose from. I chose to write an urban fantasy in which the everyday is touched by the mysterious and fey. The Scottish kelpie story has several variations. The majority of kelpie tales are about kelpies that appear as a beautiful horse that bewitches people to ride it. Once they climb on its back, they cannot dismount so the kelpie plunges into the loch (lake) and drowns and eats its victims. The kelpie can also appear in human form as in my retelling. I incorporated a version where myth says that the McGrigor family owns a bridle that tames kelpies.

Diana could barely read the chiseled inscription on the crumbling tombstone:

Elspeth Mackie, born 3 January 1640 vanished i' the loch, 17 April 1658, aged 18.

Her own age. How sad.

Diana took a photo and texted her grandmother in California along with a picture of the tombstone of Elspeth's older sister, Andrewina Mackie Guthrie. Andrewina was Grandma Elsie's direct ancestor and had led a full life with a husband and seven children. Unlike poor Elspeth.

Tracing her fingers over Elspeth's inscription, Diana wondered why they'd carved "vanished" rather than "drowned." She lifted her head to gaze at the sheen of water sparkling through the trees from Kilconquhar churchyard—the place where Elspeth died.

But she wasn't going to puzzle over that right now—she was starving. The seventeenth-century Kinneuchar Inn across the street from the church called to her.

Diana stepped into the small pub where a lone man sat at the bar. Diana glanced at him a few times as she waited to be seated in the dining room. Tall, devastatingly handsome with a long patrician nose and a lock of black hair falling across his forehead, he studied his beer before lifting the glass to his full lips. As he did so, he met her glance. His eyes were a curious greenish color and Diana felt she was drowning in their depths.

A waiter with hair only a shade darker than her own auburn tresses—she'd never seen so many redheads in one place before—called her name, interrupting her bemused staring match. He almost rushed her through the dining room door.

Diana shook her head; she was getting weirded out. It was unlike her to feel such a pull of attraction. Maybe she was just hungry. Or perhaps traipsing through small village churchyards snapping photos for Grandma Elsie's genealogy for the past two days had tired her. She should have stayed in Edinburgh and waited for Mark to come with her. He'd warned her in particular not to come to Kilconquhar without him.

Why? Big brothers! What did they know? This was her adventure, her chance not to be mollycoddled. That was the problem being the youngest—and only girl—with three older brothers.

"May I join you? All the other tables are full." Diana looked up from studying the photos she'd taken in the past two days. The man with the green eyes stood before her.

Diana gazed around the room with its framed public notices from bygone days. True enough, her table was the only one with extra seats. What else could she say but yes?

"Of course." She smiled at the man whose eyes gleamed emerald with his answering grin.

"Lachlan Douglas." His voice was a deep baritone. He gave a small bow.

"Diana Brown," she said, putting out her hand. She wasn't usually this formal, a wave of the hand was more her style, but she felt compelled to shake his hand.

The waiter appeared and thrust the menu at Lachlan, stopping the handshake. Puzzled at the sudden rudeness of the waiter and the more-than-irritated glance Lachlan threw at him, Diana lowered her eyes to the menu not wanting to get in the middle of an obvious clash. The menu consisted of plain Scottish fare with a few French dishes. She toyed with the idea of eating pigeon pie, but settled for chicken in puff pastry with mussels in white wine as a starter. Lachlan ordered a salad.

"And what brings you to Kilconquhar, Miss Brown?"

"My grandmother's family is from Fife. She asked me to take photos of tombstones in the villages. She's related to the Mackies that come from Kilconquhar."

Lachlan started and he ran his tongue across his lips.

"She's an avid genealogist," continued Diana.

"Genealogist?... I see." Lachlan crumbled bread on his plate, his hands trembling. "And you are here alone?"

"Well, my brother, Mark, was supposed to come with me but he went off to Ireland for a couple of days. He'll be back today though. He's studying history at Napier University in Edinburgh." Diana sipped her lemonade. "So what about you? Are you from here? What do you do?"

"Aye. I have lived here always. Are you studying at Napier University also?"

"No, I'm studying English lit at the University of Washington. I start in the fall."

Their food arrived and they began to eat.

"Would you like some chicken?" said Diana. "I have a lot and that salad won't fill you up."

"No. I do not eat the flesh of fowl."

"A vegan, huh?"

"No. I eat flesh, but not fowl nor beast."

Diana took a bite of her chicken pie and shrugged. She guessed he ate fish, but the way he said *flesh* was creepy, rolling the word around in his mouth as though tasting it. But his eyes were so striking, soulful.

"So you never told me what you do. Are you an actor? Your speech is so interesting, almost early 17th century. Straight out of Shakespeare with a touch of Scots."

"Ah. Shakespeare." He smiled.

That smile was devastating and doing all kinds of things to her pulse. He really ought to be a movie star. But why was he so cagey about himself? Was he famous? Talk about a strong silent type.

"I thought you might be studying the seventeenth century? Getting into a role for a play. Or are you a linguistics professor?"

"Play? Linguistics? Seventeenth century? Nay. Earlier than that." His eyes had a faraway look.

Diana waited for more, but Lachlan toyed with the horseshoe pendant that hung on his chest. The sight of the column of his strong neck rising from the loosely buttoned shirt distracted her so much she couldn't think of any other questions.

The waiter kept hovering, asking if she wanted more lemonade and if everything was alright. She was pleasantly surprised at the quality of the food and told him so then quickly turned her attention back to Lachlan.

"Have you been to the loch, Miss Brown?" Lachlan looked up from his salad and stared at her with his mesmerizing eyes. "I would be delighted to show you. I ken it well."

"Please call me Diana." She blinked as his eyes flamed, sending an answering fire within her. "Yes, thank you." She was a little breathless. "I'd like to learn more about Kilconquhar."

As they made their way to the foyer, Diana was satisfied to see that the waiter was cornered by a belligerent customer.

"You need to take care of your other customers instead of spending so much time mooning over a pretty lassie."

The customer's loud voice could be clearly heard as Diana and Lachlan stepped out of the door. Serve that waiter right! She wanted to concentrate on Lachlan, not be interrupted all the time by that intrustive man.

"Don't go off alone with strange men." Her mother's voice came into her mind. What could be the harm? The village was small with several people walking their dogs or chatting in the street, so she felt safe. It was not yet the gloaming, as the Scots called dusk.

Lachlan intrigued her. His manners and speech seemed so old-fashioned though he wouldn't admit to being an actor or academic. He couldn't be more than thirty. But those eyes! His physique. Wasted in the ivory tower of academe. What *did* he do?

"In the winter time years past, people would use the loch for curling."

"Yes, I've heard of that. It's an Olympic sport now."

"Indeed?" Lachlan wrinkled his brow, then his eyes once more had that distant look. "There used to be a thriving linen weaving industry but so many families moved away. Now there are strangers. But you came back. A Mackie of Kilconquhar."

"What do you mean? I've never been here before." Lachlan was attractive but a little weird. A frisson of alarm ran up her backbone. Diana slowed her steps as they walked past the red-stoned church with its unusually tall square tower.

Lachlan didn't answer but merely gazed at her with longing in his eyes. He tried to take her hand.

She'd already refused to take his arm. This was the twenty-first century for heaven's sake. She was quite capable of walking on her own. Diana was torn between reluctance—he was getting too friendly too early and it irritated her—and yet she had an aching to feel those strong white fingers intertwined with her own.

They came to the end of the path where a dense hedge skirted the churchyard wall.

"It's hard to reach the loch, but I ken a secret way." Lachlan shook back the lock of hair from his forehead and an excited gleam came into his eyes, but several times he looked up where a few pink clouds streaked the pale sky.

It was tempting to follow him to a secret way. She loved hearing the lilt and cadence of his voice and the way his gaze caressed her.

A woman's voice whispered in her ear. *Dinnae go.* Don't go. Diana looked around and tightened her grip on her shoulder bag, her pulse leaping erratically. What the heck? Words tumbled out of her mouth almost without thinking, coming from a deep sense of self-preservation—and *not* from the voice—she told herself.

"I must meet my brother in Dunfermline tonight. I don't think I'll have time."

"Please, I pray thee, Diana."

Was that a flash of temper in his eyes? Spouting old-fashioned jargon wasn't going to change her mind, but his voice was strangely soothing.

"'Tis not far. We have all the time in the world." He reached out to grab her arm.

She stepped back, fumbling in her purse for pepper spray.

"Don't come any closer. I'll use this." She held up the spray, finger on the button.

For a moment, Lachlan's eyes registered shock and bewilderment as he stared at the small canister in her hand; he took a step toward her, opening his arms wide. His eyes softened and his lips curled into a loving smile. It was all Diana could do to keep hold of the canister, her hand shook so hard. His eyes beckoned her to submerge herself in his embrace.

A man stepped between them pushing Diana away. The waiter. Where had he come from? She hadn't heard his footsteps on the churchyard path.

"Don't let him touch you." The waiter barely turned his head to address her but kept his eyes on Lachlan who seemed to have grown taller, sturdier, more powerful, menace in his algae-green eyes. His lock of black hair dripped with perspiration.

The waiter stepped in front of her so she could no longer see Lachlan.

"How dare you! What are you? My self-appointed protector?" Diana shook from anger—and she had to admit—fear. "I can take care of myself. I have pepper spray...police strength."

The waiter gave a small chuckle, but didn't turn around. This was no laughing matter. She gripped the spray, not sure if she wanted to use it on Lachlan or the waiter.

Diana felt an overwhelming desire to be with Lachlan and tried to move around the waiter, but he kept moving so he blocked her way and her view. She wanted to pound him on his back.

The McGrigor must needs help you. McGrigor? Who? What? That woman's voice in her ear again. Creepy...and yet comforting, almost familiar.

"Lachlan. I'm sorry for this jerk's behavior," she said in a raised voice. A gust of wind rushed through a rowan tree whisking away her next words. "I do want to go to the loch with you."

There was no answer but the loud rustle of leaves as though a large animal pushed through the shrubbery near the water. Then splashing, and the wild whinny of a horse in pain.

"What was that?" Diana gripped the waiter's arm. "A horse? It needs help."

"There's no horse," said the waiter, shaking off her grip.

Diana pushed him aside. Lachlan had vanished. How was that possible? Was he too cowardly to face this annoying waiter? He seemed so strong. Though she'd known him for only an hour, she was strangely bereft now he was gone. And yet, a sense of relief too.

But what about that horse? She tried to see over the shrubs, but there was only the silver of water now tinged with flame from the sunset and faint ripples disturbing the surface of the loch. A curlew foraging on the bank cried its high plaintive call before flying away. She must have imagined a horse whinny; it must have been the bird, not a horse. She shook her head as though trying to clear her jangled thoughts.

"What's your name?" Diana turned to the waiter who had a satisfied smile on his face as he stuffed a chain with a pendant shaped like a bridle inside his shirt. "I'm going to report you to your employers." She rubbed her dewy forehead. "No, don't tell me. I don't have time now." The urge to leave at once overcame all else.

She stalked toward her car, the waiter striding beside her.

"Wait, Diana. I know your brother."

"A likely story." She snorted. He must have got her name from her credit card. But he was being too familiar. "Nice pick up line though." What had her mother told her? Don't talk to strangers. And these two men were strange, not just strangers. She marched ahead not looking at him. She opened the car door, realized she'd opened the passenger door—why did they have to drive on the left side of the road in this country?—huffed, and hurried to the other door. She almost fell inside, slamming the door so hard the car shook.

The waiter leaned down, looking into the window gesturing for her to open it. No way was she going to have any more conversations with that jerk. And as for Lachlan... He'd run off somewhere hadn't he? Tears welled in her eyes. Why cry? She rarely cried. She turned the key in the ignition that screeched a protest, and drove away toward the setting sun.

Diana was glad to see Mark that evening in the B&B in

Dunfermline. He teased her about her red hair and how she fit in with the natives.

"And why not? I take after Granny Elsie. Her hair, her short genes." Diana paused. "I do feel like I've come home. Weird." *And that home was in Kilconquhar.* No. Wait. What had Lachlan meant about her coming back?

"You've inherited her impulsive nature too. Why didn't you wait until I got back from Dublin to go to Fife? You were particularly told not to go to Kilconquhar."

"Granny asked me to visit the villages in Fife and take photos. You know that."

"Yes, but not Kilconquhar."

"Why not?"

"Because it has a loch."

"Oh. That explains everything." She pursed her lips. Why was he being so cryptic? She'd told him of her experience in Kilconquhar —she was still fuming about the waiter's behavior—and disturbed by Lachlan's sudden disappearance. Mark had merely nodded with a satisfied grin saying he'd explain later as she was too freaked out right now.

The yearning for Lachlan was still intense. It was so odd. It was as though they'd known each other before. She'd had crushes on boys and movie stars, but nothing like this. She was like the knight in Keats's poem, "La Belle Dame sans Merci" though she was the one palely loitering and in thrall to Lachlan.

"You need a trip to Falkirk," said Mark before he turned into his bedroom. "We'll go tomorrow on the way back to Edinburgh."

"What's in Falkirk? A battlefield? A castle?" Diana was not enthusiastic. As a history major, Mark was inclined to drag her to every historical place in the vicinity and beyond. What she really wanted to do was go back to Kilconquhar.

"You'll see." He took out his cell. "I have to text a friend." He tapped out a short message. "Good night, sis."

Of course, on the way to Falkirk, Mark had to stop off at Culross, a small attractive historic village with many 17th and 18th century buildings. Mark was in his element spouting off facts, figures, and stories about the village. Though fascinating, Diana was curiously lethargic.

"Don't you want to go to Kilconquhar, Mark? It's not that far." Diana had asked that question several times.

"No," he said, taking her firmly by the arm and ushering her into the car. "We're going to the Helix and then home to Edinburgh."

On the outskirts on the road to Stirling, the sculptures of two horse heads rose above the barrier on the motorway. Mark turned into the Helix, a large park with tracks for bicycling, running, and a splash park for children. As she got out of the car, Diana began to feel more grounded. This was more like it. A park with modern-day fun for families.

"Those horses don't look historic," Diana said as she put on her jacket against the chill breeze.

"They're no ordinary horses. They're kelpies."

"And?"

"You really need to pay more attention to Grandma's stories. Kelpies are magical shape-shifting horses that live under lochs and rivers and come on dry land in early evening before the setting of the sun to lure unsuspecting people to ride on them. Once on their back the kelpies take them under the water never to be seen again. And it's said they eat their victims."

Diana's pulse jumped. What had Lachlan said? *I eat flesh, but not of beast.* That horse's neigh. Her mind raced, faltered, and raced again—Don't be ridiculous. Kelpies are not real.

"And sometimes they'll appear in human form and bewitch unsuspecting lassies to take them to a watery grave." Mark kept looking around as he spoke. "Their touch fuses with the lassie's skin so they yearn to go with the kelpie. Cannot love any other."

"Seriously? You can't believe this. Whatever happened to Mr. Historical Facts?" She waved a brochure in his face. "Anyway, this says the sculptures are a tribute to the Clydesdale horses that pulled the barges." Diana laughed, but that twinge of longing for Lachlan broke through her scorn. Lachlan a kelpie? Inconceivable!

She gazed around at the families and children enjoying the splash play area and cyclists riding past the pool and canal. It all looked so ordinary, but the memory of her time in Kilconquhar still haunted her. She peered up at the almost hundred feet tall horse heads, light flashing off their steel structures. One head arched in a stoic classical pose, the other head tossed with open mouth as though whinnying before the start of battle. The memory of that eerie neigh by the loch troubled her thoughts even now.

"Ah, there you are." Mark's voice broke into her musings.

Diana turned to see Mark giving a man-hug to an auburn-haired man. She knew that sturdy back well. Hadn't she wanted to pound on it only yesterday? The waiter from Kinneuchar Inn.

"What are you doing here?" Diana spat out the words. The waiter turned toward her and merely grinned. "You *do* know this guy, Mark!"

"Yes. Angus and I were roommates at uni. I asked him to watch out for you in case you went to Fife." Mark's smile was nervous, his gaze troubled.

Why didn't he look her in the eye? He kept glancing at Angus. Diana narrowed her eyes, too incensed to talk. Thoughts built up ready to spew out words hot as volcanic lava.

"He often goes to Kilconquhar and other villages for research on local myths. Lucky for you he was helping out a chum at the inn."

"Lucky for me?" She could hardly get the words out. "You sent him to spy on me? You didn't trust me to take care of myself?" Diana ground her teeth. When was he going to stop treating her like a child? She had been doing fine until the weirdness at Kilconquhar.

"Diana." Mark took her by the shoulders and gave her a little shake. "I do trust you. It's hard to explain... Grandma Elsie had a dream you'd be in danger if you went to Kilconquhar on your own. There are times when you—we—need *extra* help in out of the ordinary situations. And this was one of them."

"Are you kidding me? Oh right. Grandma Elsie had one of her fey moments." Mark normally ignored their grandmother's Scottish sixth sense. Why did he listen to her now? "And you sent this...this—" She gestured in the waiter's direction.

"Protector? Knight in shining armor?" said Angus, smirking.

Was he mocking her? She wanted to scratch the grin off his face. She clenched and unclenched her fists, glowering at him.

"But I'd like to have seen you use that pepper spray." He raised an eyebrow. "He wouldn't be used to a twenty-first century lassie fighting back...though I doubt it would have helped if you'd seen him in his true form."

"True form?" Diana couldn't quite get her head around this bizarre conversation. "You know Lachlan Douglas?"

"Is that what he called himself? Of the lake and dark water. Hmm. Apt." He raised a hand in a friendly gesture. "Hiya! Angus McGrigor. Now you know my name."

McGrigor must needs help you. Hadn't she imagined that woman's voice? Diana scowled at Angus and folded her arms, drawing herself up to her five-foot-two stature. She'd rather eat haggis than be friendly to this man, though now she looked at him more closely, he was kinda cute. He was not drop-dead gorgeous but had a pleasant face and a build and height that suggested he'd enjoy tossing a caber or two. But she was done with cute men...or any other man for that matter. But Lachlan...

"Angus can tell you all about kelpies. Tradition has it that the McGrigor family owns a bridle that breaks their spell." Mark laughed and clapped Angus on the shoulder. "Even if she had pepper spray, I'm glad you were there."

"I'm glad too," said Angus, blue eyes glinting.

Diana frowned. She wasn't going to be taken in again by a man's fine eyes.

Angus winked. A glimmer of light flashed on the bridle pendant around his neck. And the memory of Lachlan dissipated swift as sun on morning mist.

THE
SWAN MAIDEN'S
DAUGHTER

SHIRLEY MEIER

Author's Note: The fairy tales I grew up with were read to me out of an old book called 'Bechstein's Marchen', most of which were not recorded by the Brother's Grimm. The stories I knew were told in the Rhineland and first translated into English by Dr. Wilhelm Ruland in 1906. Some of these stories inspired Wagner. I have wanted to re-tell these stories because the Palatinate had its own sensibility, its own feel of the world, and I want to recreate the magical feeling I got, first hearing "Tischlien, Deck Dich," or "Little Table Set Yourself," or listening to a story where the dogs had eyes like moons. The Swanmaiden's Daughter is a sequel to one of these old stories because I couldn't bear the thought of the woman/swan's children in the hands of their father. The parental figures in these old stories are often the villains, and greed and ownership are the common sins, along with fear of loss, and to be honest, starvation. The fairy stories that grew out of the years of war and privation, un-bowdlerized, were the ones that held my attention.

I was twelve when mother flew away.

She flew away on strong white wings that buffeted me with wind as she plunged through the open window of her weaving loft. The huge glass windows were wide open to let the spring air into the room that had been shut up close all winter. We had huge windows, to let in the light.

I had been cleaning in Papa's study where he kept a flat trunk under his desk locked by a heavy iron key. I wouldn't have opened it, except that I heard a shrill, peeping cry, like a lost chick, from inside. The ornate iron key was usually either in the desk drawer or on my papa's belt. Today he'd hidden it in the drawer, but I knew where to look. My brothers had told me. The trunk cried, so I unlocked it.

I found a splendid white feather cloak inside and pulled out the beautiful, shining, feathered thing across my lap and it called me to put it on, but I knew it wasn't mine. It was too big. And Papa had kept it so carefully.

I took it to show *Mutti*. She leaped from the loom, where she'd sat every day of my life, making our family wealthy, and seized upon it with shrieks of happiness high and wild as a bird.

"Stand away from the window, Gerta. I love you, daughter, but I must fly. You remember that I love you. I love you all..." She flung the cloak over her shoulders and suddenly there was a swan in the room, the thunder of her wings tangling warp and weft, blowing my hair back. She honked wildly and was gone.

"*Mutti? Mutti? Mutti!*" I wailed after her into the evening air.

It was a spring day, wet and cold, and I had no answer but the rain blowing in. As I went to close the banging window against the rain, a single swan feather fluttered to the floor. I snatched it up and cried. I told Papa how *Mutti* had flown away, and he struck me. When he pulled off his belt, I ran and hid in the attic for a day. My father was and still is a brute.

My oldest brother found me, took me back downstairs, past Father's room, down to the kitchen. I tease him that he's only the oldest by a few minutes but Heiner and Helmut are my defenders and best friends in the world. The two of them help me with Elizabet and Lisel. *Mutti's* little flock of goslings, she used to say. Together. All of us were in the kitchen with Frau Jager, a tiny old woman that father had hired years ago to let *Mutti* work.

Over the next days we all stayed out of his sight as Father raged and drank and yelled and ruined furniture. The only coherent words in the roars all revolved around me, that it was my fault she was gone.

I told everyone what had happened and how *Mutti* had flown away. Showed them the feather.

Elisabet laughed and asked why was I telling *märchen*? But she was old enough to understand the truth. I wanted to spank her, slap her for saying I was lying, but I stopped. That would make me like Father. "I saw what I saw."

Frau Jager shook her head at Elisabet as she swept her old broom across the floor, back and forth, back and forth, sweeping the threshold. "You shouldn't disbelieve your older sister," she said disapprovingly. "She is old enough to put her hair up. You aren't. And she is not one to tell stories." We all had bread and milk for our supper and sneaked up to our rooms quiet like mice.

Next day was worse, but Father fell drunk much faster and kept forgetting that he'd called us, called me, to beat us. Helmut and Heiner saw him into his bed and came down to us in the kitchen.

"What Gerta said is true," Helmut said as he sat down. Heiner nodded and lifted the heavy kettle full of water onto the hob for Frau Jager.

"He told us," Helmut said. "So drunk he was hard to understand." *Mutti* was a swan maiden that Papa... My mind stumbled to a stop. Papa was a baby term, innocent and loving. I couldn't think of him in that familiar baby innocence any longer. Father had forced her to marry him. He'd found her feathered skin on the shore when she'd turned into a human, from a swan, and threatened to burn it. That act made his fortune. *Mutti* could weave anything into cloth so fine it went to royal and noble houses all up and down the Rhine.

That was why Oma and Onkel Rheinhart and Onkel Anton were poor farmers near Gruiten and our family lived in Dusseldorf. It also explained why no one ever talked about *Mutti*'s family. She'd said her parents had died young. The fire crackled in the stove in the quiet after he'd told us all this.

I still had the feather as if it could hold me to *Mutti*, wherever she was. But this feather... I wanted to throw it in the fire, enraged that she could so abandon us, but Heiner stopped me. "Gerta. Save that. We might need it one day."

I blamed that poor, precious feather for my mother's abandonment and locked it into a box under my feather mattress, feathers hidden by feathers. We told people *Mutti* had gone to her people to care for her old Oma out in the country, in the Hartz mountains so far away that no one could know anyone from there and catch us in the lie. Then I started weaving in *Mutti*'s place.

My cloths were not as good as hers and Father threatened to beat me if I lost him customers, so I practiced until late into the night. Once, that horrible summer, I was working at the loom with the window wide open to catch moonlight and air in the stifling loft, and a bird flew over. I heard the *whik whik* of wings, and a feather drifted down to weave into my cloth. I was so sleepy, so tired I thought I dreamed it.

I had fallen asleep on the bench and Papa woke me with a shout and I fell awake. "Wonderful! Wonderful, my girl! This is so fine that the Grafin herself will desire this!" I hadn't remembered the work, at least not so much, but the cloth was finished and glistened gold in the morning light. "You have your mother's touch!"

He chortled as he left me alone to finish and cast off and that was when I discovered the tiny down feathers woven through and through. I took the cloth off the loom and took a feather from the garden—how wealthy we were to have a garden in Dusseldorf—and ran it through my fingers.

How could I have ignored the feeling of feathers? The dove who had lost it was gray and white and I knew in my bones that had I wings... I knew. I knew how to fly, how it felt, how the wind held me in its arms, how the clouds felt. Water on my wings. I came to myself and took the cloth down to my father, who smiled and ran a finger down the cheek he had swollen with his fist when *Mutti* fled. "Run along and play now, my treasure," he said. "You've done your work." I could see the greed glisten in his eyes. I'd never seen it before. My father had the eyes of a wolf, of a fox.

The fox, my father, would always demand more. He would not be satisfied with single pieces of cloth, woven with my little-girl hands and fingers. The loom was heavy and the work was so hard. He wouldn't let me go. He wouldn't let me marry and take my skill to someone else. He held my skin captive in his house, wrapped around my bones, just as he'd held my *Mutti's* skin in a trunk locked in his room. I began to understand her desperation.

That was the day I began taking Elisabet and Lisel for daily walks, sometimes with Frau Jager and sometimes with Heiner or Helmut. We would stroll at my little sisters' speed and none of our escort commented that I was collecting feathers into a flat wallet hung at my waist.

Flight feathers. Down feathers. Breast and neck feathers. Elisabet loved the soft grey, cooing doves so she gathered their feathers for me, and Lisel giggled at the ducks and collected their bright, shining feathers. Hard waterproof pinions. But best of all, for me, were the white, soft feathers of the swans.

Then the rains of fall began and Frau Jager put the big feather coverlets upon all our beds to keep us warm. I worked the loom until every muscle ached, until I wept because my hands hurt. I found I need only weave the tiniest scrap of feather into my work for the magic to work. I found that my tears would become silver threads in the weave.

It was a horrible winter. Father said that instead of buying anyone else's clothes or cloth, which was clearly inferior to ours— Ours. Not mine. Ours—I should start wearing *Mutti's* old clothes. I drew on my mother's clothing that she'd made while she made us. It was like armor, and I could feel how much she loved me in every fingerwidth. It is what saved my spirit.

But it made me look more like *Mutti*, and my father watched me, at dinner, at breakfast. He watched me at work. As I grew, the work got easier, but the regard grew heavier. I wore his eyes like I wore the skin of *Mutti's* captivity. I couldn't hide from this hunter's gaze. He'd always called me his *schatz*, his treasure. Now I felt like the girl whose father had touched her and turned her to gold. Heavy, heavy gold.

I began spinning and weaving ramie that winter... the nettle bundles, stings safely retted and spun into golden thread. The fabric was smooth and shining as feathers and very light. The cloth floated on my hand, and when I wove feathers into it I knew I had to save us all from the hail of greed and the weight of sheep's grease, wool and metal, both gold and silver. I was like a swan whose feet were tied to heavy bags of coins, fighting to not be dragged under. I grew to understand my *Mutti's* wild joy when I had brought her skin to her.

Heiner and Helmut were both training to be warriors, should the High King call up all freemen. The wars loomed, and all young men would go to bleed out in fields far from home. The fighting raged year in, year out, every time a petty Graf declared his "kingdom" and defied anyone to tax them. Hessen was so small that the only real work for a lot of boys was to go mercenary and take their skin to market. They began to grow dour and grim under the iron fists of their masters.

The first shirt I wove and finished was for Lisel, bright waterfowl feathers and soft brown. I gave it to Frau Jager and told her that if Lisel was cold at the river she should put it on. She nodded in understanding and her grief was enormous when my little sister fell into the river in front of half the town. People dove into the water to try and save her, but they never found a body, only a small brown duck that flew away, free from all the commotion.

Father never suspected and he wept for his little girl as we buried an empty coffin in the churchyard, weighted with sand.

Elisabet quivered at my elbow as I wove her shirt, her excuse to father was that she was my apprentice as I had been to *Mutti*. He muttered at both of us but mercifully left us alone, as he was bored with listening to me explain "women's work" to my sister.

There is a white bird with a black cap that flies the world, and I found a single albatross feather from a merchant on the Rhine, brought all the way from the Nordzee. Elisabet kissed me when I gave her the new form and that night vanished out of the bedroom she had shared with her little sister. No one knew how, since her window was not meant to open. I think she walked out as human, into the garden. The dogs howled once and were shouted at by the watchmen.

That's when father began to suspect me. And I dutifully wove ells and ells of cloth for sale, till my fingers ached and my calluses hurt and some had blisters underneath. But I had two shirts for my brothers finished before they marched off to war and no one saw an eagle and an owl fly away from a bloody battlefield where Hessen boys lay tangled together with Frankish dead and the Prussians.

For myself, alone under my father's eye, in secret, I wove a cloak with swans' down and tender breast feathers. A mother swan had pulled them from her breast, a father swan had added his to shelter their eggs.

He found that cloak in my room, dragged me downstairs by my hair, and on the kitchen fire burned it. He held me up by my hair to watch as the white down melted away. I wept and wailed as though the world had ended. He wiped my tears away with soft hands and said that was just how *Mutti* had cried in the early days of their marriage.

He was becoming evil. I knew it. I was her replacement in his eyes and in his withered, greedy heart. He thought he had just locked my cage around me, bound my hands to his loom with the stench of burning feathers.

"Gerta, she did me wrong to fly away from me. I loved her. I gave her everything. She was the love of my life and you, my darling, are just like her. Magical. Magical." He shook me a little to silence my sobs. "No more ramie. No more nettles. Just wool and silk. Linen perhaps. Good, solid, earthly weaves. Do you hear me?"

I nodded, barely moving, hanging from his hands, and he let me go. I rose and brushed the ashes of the feathered cloak from my dress. Gray streaks on my hardened hands. "Go to your room and get some sleep. You are no longer Gerta, but Swanhild."

My eyes were on the floor. I dared not look at him, lest he see. I nodded and turned away quietly. But he must have sensed something. The click of the loft's latch is different from the soft sound of my own door. As I opened the weaving loft door I heard him curse below and come thundering up the stairs. I took my time to open the window because I did not wish to hurt myself with smashing glass going through it and as he burst into the room I smiled at him, flung my real cloak around my shoulders and stepped out of the window just ahead of his straining fingertips.

As I stretched my strong, healthy, young wings in the night sky, soaring high and free, I honked back at his enraged howling, out the same window my mother had escaped from. I honked again, stretched my neck. It was spring and I had the whole earth, the whole sky as my treasure.

Sop Paw

Jay Barnson

Author's Note: The first fantasy stories I ever encountered, at least that I remember, were told to me by my father when I was something like four years old. He told me the traditional "Jack" tales as he'd heard them and remembered them, passed down through the generations. Most of these oral folk tales came from Europe, where Jack's cousin had many adventures of his own. One of the few that are remembered today involves magic beans and a beanstalk. You may have heard of it. Anyway, these stories filled my young brain with wonder, and I imagined the world around me full of adventure and magic. I hoped to capture that feeling in my own retelling of one of these folk tales.

Y'all may have heard that story about how a young boy named Jack slew a giant with a magic knife. The honest truth is that I was nearly eighteen and I tricked the giant into killing himself with his own knife. Personally, I think that's the better story, but folks like to take a story and make it their own. That's fine by me. I did keep that knife, though. Its buck-horn handle ain't too big for my hand, and its blade gleams like silver in the moonlight. It never needs to be sharpened, and it can cut clean through thick hide with a light stroke. I reckon it could stab the heart of the devil himself.

That knife was all I had left of that excursion. It turns out that the reward money for killing a giant doesn't last as long as one might expect. As it ran out and I became reacquainted with the hollow gnawing in my stomach, many of the nearby towns suffered problems of their own. Cows and goats dried up, hens quit laying, and a blight hurt many a farmer's crop. I worked the odd job where I could, but there wasn't much work to be had in the whole county.

The town of Howard prospered where many others struggled. I made my way there hoping to find honest work. Howard is mainly farmlands down in a valley by the same name, along the river. It had just one church, the first building along the only road in or out of town. I found the parson patching up the gate to the church's graveyard.

I introduced myself, and he looked me over with his one good eye. He stroked his steel-gray beard and said, "Jack, huh? You don't happen to be the Jack that took care of that giant business up north last year, are you?"

"Yes, sir. I'm looking for work."

"We have no giants in Howard."

"That's good to know. I wouldn't want to push my luck a second time. Would you know anybody in town hiring labor?"

"I might, but I wouldn't be doing my Christian duty if I didn't warn you. Things in Howard aren't what they seem. We've had our own run of bad luck." He pointed his thumb over his shoulder at the graveyard. "We've never buried as many folk as we have this year."

I chewed on his words for a few seconds before answering. "There ain't sense in warning if there's no way to avoid it. Are you saying it ain't just bad luck?" I wasn't in a hurry to rush towards trouble, but where people have problems, there may be opportunity for a man willing to pitch in and help solve them.

"True enough. Some folks believe it's a witch's curse. Some even say there's a whole gang of witches responsible for the woes around the county, and that the witches are here in Howard."

"What do you believe?"

"I don't rightly know, Jack. I've heard witches are harder to kill than even a giant. About the only things that hurt them are fire, silver, or maybe magic. If I were you, I'd heed the warning and keep on walking to the next town and try your luck there."

"I appreciate that. But I've been looking for work for days with nary a thing to eat except wild berries and a squirrel. I'd just as soon try my luck here and hope that I avoid the attention of a witch."

The parson nodded. "Silas Williams is the wealthiest farmer in these parts. He lives at the end of that road." He pointed towards a cart-road winding up the river. "Everyone who has worked the mill for him this year has died." He turned and pointed to the two newest graves in the graveyard. "Those two brothers came to work for him last month. They worked only one day, and turned up dead the next morning, without a mark on them. Some say it was poison."

"So the job is still open."

"I reckon so, Jack, but I'd hate to dig a new grave for you. You be careful."

I thanked the parson, and followed the river road up to Silas Williams' farm. I'd helped at my uncle's mill one year when he broke his leg. While hard work, milling was simple and a lot less dangerous than giant-killing.

The farmer's fields grew thick as I neared his home. The crops showed no sign of the sickly blight that had infected so many other farms just a few miles away. Fat cows grazed in another field. The paint on the Williams house smelled as fresh as it looked. I knocked on the door, and a man answered. Gray peppered his light-brown beard, and he had the body of a man who was no stranger to good food or hard labor.

"Good morning, sir," I said. "My name's Jack Walker. Are you Silas Williams?"

"I am, Jack. Good to make your acquaintance. What can I do for you?"

"I heard you might be looking to hire help for your mill."

"Oh." The man hesitated, and cleared his throat. "I do need the help, Jack. I'd be happy to hire you for half the profit, including food and board at the mill. Afore you answer, have you heard what happened to the others I hired?"

"I heard they died, sir. Poison?"

He raised his shoulders and bobbed his head in something that looked like neither a nod or a shrug, but something in-between. "That's what it looked like. Same thing happened to the man I hired afore that, except they found him four miles away one morning, all his earthly possessions on his back. Not a mark on him. The fellow afore that hanged himself."

"And afore that?"

"The family that worked the mill last year up and left at the end of the season. Didn't offer any explanation."

"I still want the job."

He grinned. "Then I'll take you on down there and show you around." He called back into the house. "Della, I hired a new hand to work the mill!"

A woman's voice called back. "We don't need no one down there at the mill! You can handle it on Saturdays."

"No I can't, especially as we get close to harvest!"

The woman's voice lowered. "He's gonna get himself kilt, and it will be your fault, Silas. You remember that."

Silas closed the door behind him as he stepped out onto the porch. "Don't mind Della. She gets that way sometimes. Now, I checked below the floors last week for snake nests or some other clue as to what may have happened to those two boys last month. I found nothing at all. But that might not mean everything is safe. You be careful and take no chances out there."

"Yes, sir."

The mill was down a side road a bit from the barn. You couldn't see it well from the farmhouse on account of all the trees down the road. When we got there, Silas unlocked the door and handed me one of the keys. He showed me the equipment, and taught me how to raise the gate to let the water run over the wheel out back. Six broad windows allowed air to vent when they weren't shuttered, and then two smaller ones up above the rafters let sunlight into the mill.

Off to the side of the building a tidy living area included a fireplace and three beds to choose from. Silas said, "There's a stack of firewood out back. I'll pay your wages once a week. I'll also bring you supper each night. I'm not the best cook, but there will be plenty. We have no children, and I always cook too much."

"Your wife doesn't cook?"

"No, Della has other things that occupy her time," he said with a hint of wistfulness. "She cooked for me only twice, once while I courted her, and once on our wedding night. They were the best meals I've ever had in my life, no lie."

"I will be happy for anything. Thank you, Silas."

Silas gave the mill one more quick inspection. Satisfied, he said, "I'll head into town now and get the word out that the mill's open again. I'll see you tonight."

"I will do my best. Thank you kindly for giving me this chance." We shook hands, and he left.

I didn't have long to acquaint myself with my new home before folks from town showed up with grain. By mid-afternoon, a line of people waited on me. I worked as quickly as I could, but the waterwheel and millstone couldn't go faster. Nobody complained.

Some chatted with me and asked how I was feeling. I assured them I felt hale and hearty and expected to be the same tomorrow.

They didn't seem convinced.

Later in the evening, Silas arrived with a quarter-loaf of bread and a pot full of stew. He grinned and slapped me on the back as he saw the line of people. He watched me work for a few minutes. I tried to ignore the savory smell of the food and the growling in my stomach as I worked. Silas went out back and filled a bucket full of drinking water from the flume, and set it down next to the hearth. He filled a tin cup with water and handed it to me as I worked. I thanked him. He said, "I should thank you, Jack. You are working just fine. I'll see you tomorrow."

Silas left, and I kept at it until well after sunset. As the last man left with his sack of meal, I was anxious to start a fire and heat up the stew Silas left me. However, my uncle taught me that you wait until things are cleaned first before you start your fire or mess the place up again. Mills could be dangerous if you weren't careful. I ate a hunk of bread to tide me over, found the broom, and tidied things up. Then I started the fire, and set the pot of stew hanging on the hook above it. Shortly before midnight, I was warm by the fire, and I was ready to enjoy a hard-earned dinner and a good night's sleep.

I pulled the pot down and spooned nearly half of the stew into my bowl. There was plenty left in the pot, and I reckoned it would make a good breakfast in the morning, and maybe a little bit left over for lunch. I sat down on the floor with my bowl in front of me, and took a bite.

It was still a little cold, but I didn't care. I was so hungry that it tasted like a feast at a king's table. I found myself closing my eyes as I savored the spoonful. The beef—real beef!—was tender and perfect. The vegetables were well-stewed but tasted like they'd been plucked from the garden that very morning.

I opened my eyes to take another bite and discovered I had a four-legged visitor. A black cat with a white face and paws, had sat itself in front of my bowl. I smiled at it as I fished out a piece of beef from the stew and tossed it onto the floor. "There you go, cat," I said, mostly to amuse myself. "Eat up! I have food to spare for the first time in weeks."

The cat sniffed at my gift, but didn't give even a lick to the meat. It sat straight up and stared at me. Its eyes glowed in the firelight. I thought they didn't look quite like cat's eyes, nor did they seem human. A tiny ice-cold shiver ran up my spine.

"Sop paw," it said. The sounds weren't quite human, but they weren't just feline noises, either. At first, I reckoned I was more exhausted than I thought.

"What did you just say?" I asked. I hoped not to hear any answer.

Almost at once, cats appeared in the lower windows. Besides the black cat in front of me, six cats sat on the window sills. Their tails twitched as they followed me with their eyes. The orange firelight glinted back at me in twelve tiny reflections.

"I ain't got enough for all of you, sorry," I said to the cats. They didn't move.

The first cat moved forward. "Sop paw," it repeated, and dipped its paw into my bowl of stew.

"Hey, stop that!" I yelled. The creature backed off, but my outburst didn't scare it off. Ordinarily, a bit of dirt or cat hair in my food won't give me any fuss, especially as hungry as I was. I felt inclined to eat the rest of the bowl right in front of that nasty little cat and not leave it another drop. It was a lot of stew, as much food as I'd eaten in days combined. Then I thought of the warnings from Silas and the parson, and while it seemed like a waste, who knew if that cat walked through something deadly on its way to the mill?

I replaced the lid on the pot and hung it back over the fire. I expected to see cats fighting over the bowl of stew when I turned back around, but they all sat stock still but for their twitchy tails. The piece of meat on the floor just sat there next to the black cat, untouched.

I picked up the bowl and opened the door. "Ya'll want some of this stew? Then here, it's yours!" I dumped the stew out onto the weeds near door, and for good measure I washed the bowl out in the cool river water in the mill flume. After letting the water flow just a bit to clean things out, I closed the gate on the flume again, and went back inside.

The cats hadn't moved.

I used a cloth to pull the pot back out of the fire. Lifting the lid with the same cloth, I spooned a little more than half of it into my bowl, leaving plenty for breakfast in the morning. While not as hearty a meal as I'd hoped, I reckoned it would be more than enough to calm the rumbling in my stomach.

I sat down, facing the black cat. Like the others, it stared at me, its tail writhing slowly behind it was the faintest of twitches at the tip. I hadn't even put the bowl down when it opened its mouth and said, "Sop paw."

"No, you ain't. There's still that piece next to you that you ain't eating, and you won't have mine. Now git!" I kicked out with my foot, but the motion didn't startle the cat. It just stared. I took a spoonful of the stew and jammed it in my mouth, just to show it.

The stew was too hot, and burned my mouth. Setting the bowl down, I filled the tin cup with the water Silas had brought in for me and drained the cup to cool my mouth down.

I turned around to see the black cat hovering over my bowl. "Sop paw," it said again, this time its voice a little more human, with what I took to be a mocking tone. It dipped its left forepaw in my bowl of stew again, staring at me as it did it. I could have sworn it was taunting me.

Hollering something that shouldn't be said from Christian lips, I once again dumped the contents of the bowl outside and washed it out at the flume. I returned to find the cats still hadn't moved.

With my mouth still stinging from being burned, I scooped the remaining stew into my bowl and sat in front of that black cat. I set the bowl down to let it cool and unsheathed my special knife that gleams silver and never needs to be sharpened. Wiggling the blade in the air, I said, "You try and sop your paw one more time, and I'm taking it off. And maybe cooking myself up some cat stew for breakfast."

If the cat understood, it didn't respond. It just stared. I kept my knife ready in my right hand and took the spoon in my left. Staring directly into the cat's eyes, I took a spoonful of stew, blew on it to cool it down, and put it in my mouth. It was delicious, but I wasn't about to close my eyes this time.

"Sop paw," the cat said. It darted forward to my bowl, dipping its left forepaw. It was fast, but so was I. I chopped at the cat's leg before it pulled away. The rest of the stew went flying, as did the cat's paw. The cat's horrible scream sounded like a woman's shriek. The other cats howled and hissed as they leaped out of the windows into the night. The black cat limped out to a low window, trailing blood and bits of stew. It leaped onto a window sill with its three legs, and paused. It turned its head to look at me, licking at its stump. With a horrible hissing voice, it said, "Sop paw!" and leaped away.

I cleaned the floor as best I could, and closed all the shutters on the windows. I found the cat's paw laying in the corner. I was fixing to throw it into the embers of the fire, but for some reason I set it at the edge of the hearth instead. I suspected the cat belonged to Silas or his wife, and I might have some explaining to do the next day. I didn't want to lose my job over a cat, but it had been a menace! At least it wouldn't have a paw to sop any more.

There were a few bits of food stuck to the bottom and sides of the pot. I scraped these off with my spoon and ate them straight from the pot, and soaked up the last dregs of liquid with my remaining bread. The pot was all but licked clean at that point. I went to bed, but didn't sleep well. My stomach growled a bit, and the awful cat appeared in all of my dreams, crying, "Sop paw! Sop paw!"

I awoke to knocking. I tumbled out of bed to answer the door. A farmer from town with a sack of corn seemed half-surprised to see me. I greeted him and went around the back to start the water on the wheel.

As I ground his corn, the farmer said, "I wasn't sure you were going to still be here today."

"Why not?"

He hemmed and hawed. "Well, you know, them other boys didn't even last a night. I was afraid I'd come here and find…"

"You were afraid you'd find me stiff and dead this morning?"

The farmer nodded nervously. I laughed. "I'm fine, aside from a pack of cats coming around last night acting strange and getting into my vittles."

"I'm glad you're working the mill, Jack. Silas runs this place for a few hours some Saturdays, but he ain't got the time to..." He trailed off, looking towards the fireplace and beds. I kept running the grain through the wheel. He cleared his throat and mumbled something I couldn't hear over the sound of the grinding. I asked him to speak up.

"Why do you have a hand sitting on your hearth?" he asked.

"What? Oh, that's a paw from one of those cats I told you about."

"That's no cat's paw, Jack! That's a human hand!"

I stopped the millstone and examined the side room. Sure enough, a human hand sat on my hearth, white and dead. One finger even wore a beautiful gold wedding ring. I scratched my head. "That don't make no sense at all. That came off a cat last night."

"It means you done chopped the hand off a witch!" The famer's eyes grew wide, and he began looking around the mill like he expected some one-handed witch to pop out from behind the millstone and grab him.

"Maybe I did. It's a good knife. Ain't that something?" I shrugged. "Let me finish grinding your corn for you."

"No, you keep it. I'd best be leaving. If I were you, Jack, I'd hightail it out of here this morning and get as far from here as you can get."

He left and hastened back up the road towards his house. A few moments later, a woman appeared coming up the road with a poke slung across her back. I thought it might be a sack of grain for the mill, but she walked right past towards the Williams farm. She glared at me as she passed, and I shivered in spite of myself, recalling how the cats stared from the windows the night before.

Nobody else showed up that morning, so I had time to wash up and clean things up. I couldn't decide what to do about that hand on the hearth. Ordinarily, I'd either want to bury it or return it to its rightful owner. But there was nothing ordinary about it. I didn't want to get close to the owner of the hand.

The trouble was that there was no place on Earth I could hide from a witch's curse. By chopping her hand off, I'd angered her for sure. My only chance was to find her and kill her before she cursed me to death. Now, I can be pretty clever when I'm scared, but this time it was no help. I had no idea where to search for the witch.

Silas showed up at lunchtime with a small cloth poke. His face was grim and distracted. He handed the poke to me and said, "You looked pretty hungry last night, so I put some bread and fruit in there to tide you over until suppertime."

"Why thank you, Silas. Say, you don't happen to own a cat, do you?"

"Not anymore. Afore I married Della last year, I had a couple of mousers. But they ran off, and I ain't seen them since last summer. Why?"

"A whole clutter of cats showed up last night, getting into my vittles and acting strange. The leader was a black cat with a white face and paws."

Silas shook his head. "I can't say I've seen it. I'll ask Della when she feels better if she knows who owns it."

"Is your wife sick?"

"Yep, she's a might peaked this morning."

My gut told me I could trust Silas. I didn't know why, but I fessed up. "Silas, I believe I have something to show you, but you won't like it."

"Is there a problem with my mill?"

I took him inside and showed him the hand as I explained what had happened the night before. "This was that cat's paw last night. Then this morning, it became a hand."

His mouth fell open, and he shook his head slowly. "That ring! That looks like Della's wedding ring."

"Are you sure? Did she have it on her hand this morning?"

"I didn't look." He shook his head. "I can't believe she's a witch. I thought we'd just been lucky avoiding the blight this long. If she was responsible…"

"We don't know for sure, Silas."

"It would explain so much! How she always seems to hold court over this group of women, and why her first husband hanged himself. Oh, Jack, what am I going to do? I married a witch!"

"What are *we* going to do?" I corrected him. "If your lady is a witch and I done lopped her hand off, she's going to be madder than a nest of hornets at me. I reckon you could just play dumb and she'd ignore you until she was finished with me."

"No. If she's a witch, she likely deceived me into marrying her because I was one of the wealthiest men in the county. If this misfortune is her fault, she's got plans that probably don't involve me much longer. I may end up like her last husband afore I know it."

"But we must make sure it's really her."

"And then what?" He shook his head slowly, casting his eyes down at the floor. "I hear witches can't be hurt by weapons."

"I've got me a very good knife. It killed a giant once, though it wasn't really me that used it against him."

"A giant?" He looked back at me, his eyes wide. "So you're *that* Jack!"

I shrugged. "I just got lucky is all. Do you mind if I eat that?" I pointed to the food he brought in. "The cats came and kept messing with that stew last night, so I threw it out."

Silas nodded. "Maybe that's how she poisoned all those other folks I had working the mill! Oh, I should have known. I condemned them all to their death."

I looked at the food Silas had brought me, then back at Silas. "Could she have poisoned this?"

He shook his head. "Nope, she ain't been near the kitchen. That's all from me, and if you want I'll take a few bites first to make sure it's all safe."

I grinned back at him. "Naw, but thank you."

I wolfed down the food as we made our way back to his house. As

I ate, Silas recounted misfortune after misfortune that had befallen his neighbors, making the connection as to how they'd earned his wife's ire. "And that one time we got into an argument with Margaret-Ann Church over the property line, and the next month their animals all died from grazing on noxious weeds. And ol' Mitchell Howard... he was a friend of her former husband. He died over the winter. Oh, how could I have been so wrong about her?"

Part of me hoped we were wrong and that Silas could forget his suspicions and go on like nothing had happened. But the part of me that wished to go on breathing hoped we were right, because I didn't have time to find the real witch otherwise. Not that I knew what to do once I proved her identity. Witches, so much as I knew, looked like people and acted like people, but they weren't really people. Their human form was just a skin they wore, like the cat. I hoped that meant my knife would work.

Silas invited me into the house. Four women were already there. Three sat silently in the parlor, including the woman I'd seen earlier carrying the poke. One stood in front of the bedroom door, arms crossed. Silas explained to me that they'd come that morning to help take care of Della.

"Oh?" I asked. "Did she send you to fetch them?"

"No. She just..." He scratched his head. "I reckon she must have sent somebody. Well, never mind." He turned to the woman by the door. "We're here to see Della."

The woman shook her head slowly. "Della is resting and will not be disturbed."

Silas scowled. "I have need to talk to my wife. Step aside, if you please."

The woman and Silas glared at each other. The woman relented, lowering her arms and standing aside. "Fine. Just you." She sneered at me. "Not the smelly boy."

Silas glared at her some more. Della called from behind the door, "It's fine. Let them in."

We entered the bedroom. It smelled faintly of earth and herbs.

Della lay on her left side facing us in the bed, her long black-and-light-gray hair spread over the pillow. I'd never laid eyes on her before, but her sunken eyes and pale complexion didn't look healthy. "Why do you trouble me, Silas?" she asked. "And why do you bring that boy from the mill?"

"I wanted to see your wedding ring, Della."

"Oh, my husband, I ain't worn it much these last few weeks. I've done worked so hard that my fingers have swollen, and that beautiful ring won't fit right. I'll get up and find it for you once I ain't nearing death's door."

Silas straightened his back and said, "I'm sorry I've worked you so hard, Della. I didn't realize. Can you show me your hand so I can see those swollen fingers of yours?"

She raised her quivering hand out from under the blanket, so we could see it. It was her right hand, of course. Then she let her hand drop and pulled it back under the blanket. "Now, let me be, Silas. I need to rest."

"Let me see your other hand," he said.

She rolled over on her other side, facing away from us. She raised her hand, just long enough for us to see it was there. Except I noticed that it was pointed all wrong–she showed us the back of her right hand again.

That almost fooled Silas for a few moments. He stood with his eyebrows drooped in a look of befuddlement. Then his countenance changed, and he frowned. He yanked Della's blanket off the bed. She lay in her bedclothes. A bloodstained bandage capped the stump at the end of her left arm. She leaped up onto the bed, shrieking. Her eyes blazed fire, and her hair writhed about on her head like they were snakes. She pointed at us with her good hand, her fingernails now clawed like a cat's, and screamed at us.

The woman at the door bared her teeth at us, which grew into fangs like a wolf. The three other women stalked fierce-eyed towards us. Two had kitchen knives in their hands. I drew my own knife, and

Della hissed and howled at the sight of it. One of the women grabbed Silas.

"Kill them!" Della howled. I grabbed the wolf-fanged woman, and put my knife to her throat. I ain't never killed a person before, but I've hunted a-plenty, and like I said, a witch ain't a person. Leastways not anymore. "Let him go or I take off her head like I took off your hand," I hollered at Della.

Della's nostrils flared as she breathed hard, hesitating. The other women looked to her, and then back to me. The one holding Silas relaxed her grip a little. Della nodded and said, "Let them go. There ain't nowhere they can run to, anyhow. Tonight we will curse them sore, and they'll die slowly and in agony. Come dawn, I'll be a widow again."

The witch holding Silas let go, and I released the fanged witch. We hightailed it out the door, only to see two more women approaching the house. They glared at me like they wanted to burn me to cinders with their gaze. I wasn't entirely sure they couldn't, but they let us pass. We kept a-running until we got to the barn. We panted and looked behind us, but the witches weren't following us. There was no need.

"Is there anything the pastor can do to help us?" I asked Silas.

He put his hands on his knees and leaned against the barn. "Besides digging holes for us in the graveyard? No. You heard them. We're dead men, Jack. I'm sorry."

"We ain't dead yet. We've just got to figure out how to stop them from casting that curse on us tonight."

"I'm plumb out of ideas. How about you? You've killed a giant. You got anything that'll work against witches?"

"Only my knife, and there are way too many of them." Now, I've learned that my cleverest ideas come when I'm scared. At this point, I was plenty scared, but didn't feel clever. "The pastor said that fire, silver, or magic can kill a witch. I reckon my knife is magic."

"I have no magic, and my silver is back in the house with the witches," Silas said. "Maybe we could set the house on fire?"

"No sense in trying that. They can see us plain as day and either stop us or just get out with plenty of time. No, we need to be tricky and think ahead of them." I kept talking, hoping an idea would hit. Instead, I only thought of questions. "If they could just curse us to death, why did they try to poison me last night? And the others?"

Silas shrugged. "Maybe it's easier? Maybe they all have to gather for a big curse. Folks told me they saw lights in the mill house some nights, and I reckoned it was just vagrants taking shelter for a night. I reckon that's where they meet to cast their curses, and they wanted it vacant. I'm such a fool!"

"Della said tonight. We have a few hours afore nightfall. Maybe we've got time."

"Time for what?"

I didn't answer right away. I thought of the cats sitting in all of the windows of the mill. My uncle's mill had a lot of windows, too.

I had an idea. I turned and looked at the silo beside the barn. "Do you have grain in there?"

"Plenty. Mostly from last season."

"Good. How about ropes and wheelbarrows? And maybe pokes or blankets or the like?"

"Surely. I've got all that here in this barn."

We loaded the wheelbarrows with grain, covering them with ground cloths. We coiled ropes over our shoulders and took our loads down to the mill.

"You know the witches can see us, right?" Silas said.

"If so, I hope they won't know what we're doing," I said.

"I reckon they won't, as I don't even know what we're doing."

"Honestly, I ain't too sure myself. But I have an idea."

We spent the afternoon milling the grain and bringing more supplies from the barn. I made a sail out of the overlapping poke-cloth and blankets up above the rafters, supported by bits of lumber. We tied ropes to the corners, and ran the other ends of the ropes out the two top windows. We tested the assembly, and made some adjustments and greased it up so it moved smoothly. Then we filled the sail with processed meal and flour as quickly as we could mill it.

We hadn't made as much progress as I'd hoped before sundown, but I hoped it would do. We shuttered all the windows except the two above the rafters. We swept up the grain that had landed on the floor, which filled the mill with a slight haze of dust. I started a fire in the fireplace. It was a good roaring fire, with plenty of logs for fuel. By then it was plenty dark, and I wasn't sticking around. Sore and tired from frantic work, Silas and I hid down the road a bit and waited on the witches.

We didn't wait long. Seven lights appeared up the road, candles carried by a procession of seven witches, led by Della. I guess since they didn't need to fool us, they didn't take cat form this time. They entered the mill, and shut the door behind them. The glow from the fire and candles peeked through the slats.

We crept up on the mill. From inside, the witches chanted something in a foreign tongue. It sounded like Dutch or German, but I couldn't really tell. But as we took the ends of the ropes, we heard our names spoken so clearly I half-thought the witches spotted us and called out to us. We didn't have much time. We moved as far back from the mill as the ropes would allow, and pulled.

Nothing happened. We couldn't test my trap once it was fully loaded, and hundreds of pounds of weight from finely-ground flour changed the mechanics of things a bit. Inside, the witches howled and stamped their feet in rhythm, like a dance. I reckoned the end of the dance would mean the end of us. We pulled harder. Inside, the witches chanted and stamped even louder.

Silas looked over at me. I looked back at him and called, "Give it everything you got!" As for me, I ran closer to the mill, wrapped the end of the rope around my chest, and ran like Hades itself was chasing me. I hit resistance that almost yanked me off my feet, but something at the end of the rope shifted. I pulled. Silas kept pulling. Everything moved, and we stumbled back on the ropes.

Inside, the sail pulled back, dumping its contents through the rafters. The witches stopped their chanting as the flour rained down on them, coating everything with powder and filling the air with a thick dust.

That much flour dust is like kerosene in the air when it meets an open flame, like those candles or the fire I'd set in the fireplace. With the sound of a thunderclap, the mill exploded, knocking us flat even outside the building. The whole place ignited like a giant bonfire.

Folks from the town came up with buckets, but the best we could do was keep the fire from spreading. The next morning, there was nothing left but ashes and the millstone. No trace of the witches was ever found, and as far as anybody in town knew, seven women just up and vanished that night.

The blight and misfortune which had so bedeviled the county faded over the course of the month. While much of the damage had been done, folks were in far better shape entering into harvest time than they'd feared.

I worked for Silas until the following summer, helping him rebuild and work the mill. He paid me better than fair wages for my labor. By summer, my feet were itching to wander. I wished him good luck and prepared to take my savings and food and see a bit more of the world.

"I'll miss you Jack," he told me. "You are a good worker. On top of that, I reckon Della would have had me killed by now. You saved my life, and saved a lot of folks from greater misfortune from that witch-gang."

"Thank you. I'll miss you too, but I learned last time that it's best to leave a place afore wearing out a welcome."

"You'll always be welcome in my home, Jack. You are very clever, and I was very lucky to have you come when you did."

"All things considered, I'd rather be lucky than clever any day. Goodbye, Silas!"

"Goodbye. May you always be lucky, Jack!"

OUT
OF THE
FIRE

AMY BEATTY

Author's Note: *I have in my possession a thoroughly disreputable copy of Hilda Boswell's Treasury of Children's Stories. The spine is half torn away on the outside, the corners are dented and peeling, and the scotch tape that once shored up the unraveling webbing by which the front cover is barely hanging on is itself beginning to flake off with age. At the top of the first page a shaky preschool hand has written in fat black marker, "Amy."*

It was in this book that I first met many of my favorite stories in the form of abridgements and extracts from works by such great authors as Charles Dickens, Nathaniel Hawthorne, Hans Christian Andersen, and C. S. Lewis.

Nestled in among the wonderful tales selected by Ms. Boswell, is a fairy tale called Through the Fire, by Mary de Morgan, first published in 1876 in her collection, On a Pincushion and Other Fairy Tales. As a child, I adored this story of the brave boy who helped two star-crossed lovers unite at last. As an adult, I love the story's theme that the way to overcome divisions caused by seemingly irreconcilable differences is to come together with love and a willingness to be changed by each other.

In my retelling, Out of the Fire, I've made adjustments, taken some liberties, and put my own stamp on the tale, but hope I've been true to the original story's heart. Mary de Morgan's wind fairy is a little man in dust-colored clothes, whereas mine is a tall man in a gray woolen cloak who can turn into a dragon. I've kept the original names for Princess Pyra and Prince Fluvius, but I've made little Jack, the main character, slightly older and changed his name to Knut to make it truer to his culture. The setting is the biggest change I've made. The original story was set in Victorian London. My adaptation is set in the same universe as my fantasy novel, Dragon Ascending, though it takes place in the distant past, before the Breaking of the World, in the times when the fae still roamed the lands. (Dragon Ascending is the first book of the Vanir Dragon Series, published by Immortal Works Press.)

Knut set the grinding stone aside and carefully scooped the freshly ground flour into the clay pot beside the quern stone. The other boys in the village would mock him, if they knew, for doing women's work. But they were all at the chieftain's longhouse for the midwinter feast, so there was no reason anyone should know. Besides, they tormented him anyway because of his crooked leg. Giving them one more reason to target him would make no difference.

He sighed and scooped another handful of whole kernels from the basket on the other side of the quern and began milling again, first pounding the kernels to crack them, then scraping the grinding stone back and forth, round and round, wearing the fragments down to powder. If he didn't do it, his mother would have to, and she would be worn down herself from entertaining the crowd at the feast with her music, not to mention wet from traveling in the cold drizzle that was fast melting the scanty snow outside. She might not get home before dawn, and in the morning, she had the washing to do and the goats to feed and milk.

He wished she didn't have to work so hard to keep food in their bellies and clothes on their backs. He wished he could find some way to help her more. He was no longer a child—ten years old was old enough to hire out as a light laborer on a farm or to find work at the docks. But no one would take on a cripple. He also longed to see his mother perform at the feast, but he couldn't hobble that far with his crutch, and she couldn't carry both him and her instruments. So, he told her he preferred staying at home to tend the fire, and she always saved a small sweet from the party or picked up a pretty stone or seashell along the way, and they both smiled and pretended they were content with the arrangement.

His arms and shoulders were beginning to ache from the rhythmic motion of milling the barley, so he stretched and glanced about the one-room roundhouse, checking again that everything was as it should be. Sometimes when he was alone in the house— especially at night with the sighing wind, the faint, tickling patter of rain against the conical thatched roof and the lonely, layered cries of the seabirds—he had the oddest feeling that something was there that ought not to be, or that someone was watching him, unseen, from the shadows. But all was in order. His bed, with its thick wool blanket, stood on one side of the room beneath the peg that held his spare tunic and his winter cloak. His mother's bed was pushed against the opposite wall, spread with the wolf skin his father had given her before he died in the raid all those years ago. Her loom leaned against the wall beside the tidy storage shelves, stone weights hanging from the warp threads in a neat, still row along the bottom, and her spindle and distaff rested on her stool beside the basket of neatly coiled stricks of flax.

The fire in the stone-lined pit in the center of the floor had burned down to a smoldering black heap coated in a layer of white ash like a dusting of snow. A crimson glow peeked out between the crumbling logs, pulsing scarlet when stroked by the evening air that crept in faint eddies through the thatch and stretched long, inquisitive fingers under the door. There was enough life left in the fire to heat the room until he went to bed, but it would survive the night better if he stoked it one more time and let it burn down again before he banked the coals with ashes for the night. And a little more light would make the milling go faster.

He scooped the last batch of flour into the crock and tied its leather cover back in place to keep the dust out, then shifted closer to the fire, grateful that his mother had brought in a generous pile of firewood from the stacks beneath the eaves before she left. His movement stirred the air just enough to send a cheerful rosy ripple flickering across the surface of the coals. The dancing light made him feel less alone, somehow. He bent closer, blowing gently to coax a brighter flicker from the drowsy fire. Back in a crevice between the logs, deep in the heart of the coal bed, two embers flared a bright red-gold, like a pair of eyes peering dreamily back at him.

Knut smiled. Sometimes he amused himself by finding faces in the fire—jolly grinning faces, rosy with wine; sly, gaunt faces full of unspent secrets; solemn, craggy faces that, like the chieftain's, must have seen too many battles. He shifted around to lie belly-down on the packed earth floor so he could see this face better. A long, steady breath directed at just the right angle woke that section of coals to a scarlet radiance, and the eyes flared golden once again, giving him a glimpse of aquiline nose and the delicate curve of brow and cheekbone. A woman's face this time.

Knut's breath ran low, and the coals settled back to a sullen, pulsing crimson. The eyes, too, dimmed from gold to vermilion, as if the woman had lowered her gaze. She looked up when he blew again, and this time, the embers caught fire around her, like a halo of golden hair blowing in the wind. The flames raced along the blackened wood, startling the rest of the fire awake, and for a moment Knut thought he'd blown too hard and destroyed the illusion. But the woman's gaze held his own, steady amid the capering blaze, and her face came into even clearer relief.

It was a lovely face, young and elegant like his mother's must have been before time and sorrow left their marks. And like his mother's, this woman's eyes held a weight of melancholy that made Knut's stomach clench.

He folded his arms on the floor in front of him and propped his chin on one wrist, tilting his head to an angle that mirrored the face in the fire. "Why are you so sad?" he murmured.

A pocket of pitch in some other part of the fire popped, and the logs flinched and slumped. The embers that formed the woman's face slid slowly toward Knut, as if she were leaning forward to see him better. Then that part of the fire flared, reaching quick, bright fingers out to wrap around the remnants of charred wood.

Knut's body reacted faster than his mind to what happened next, sending him scrambling backward in a sprawling tangle of panic as the fingers of flame coalesced and solidified into an actual hand of flesh and bone. The hand pushed the log aside, making room for a whole arm to emerge from the fire up to the elbow. Knut fumbled for his belt knife as he pushed himself upright—or at least to the awkward, seated position that was as upright as he could manage before another arm followed the first. The delicate hands grasped at the stones edging the firepit and heaved, and like a swimmer coming up for breath, a woman's head and shoulders emerged from the fire, sending embers skittering out onto the floor.

The woman propped her elbows on the edging stones and regarded Knut with skeptical curiosity. "Was it you that spoke to me?"

Knut gaped. The woman was even more beautiful in person than she'd seemed in her image among the embers. Her eyes shone like luminescent amber, and her skin glowed in the dimness of the house as if white-hot. Her hair hung in long curls around her shoulders, their molten copper color set off nicely against the pale blue of her gown.

"Who...who are you?" Knut finally managed to stammer. "Where did you come from?"

The woman pursed her lips and studied him as if deciding whether he could be trusted. When she answered, her voice was low and solemn. "My name is Pyra, and I've come from the firelands. You would probably call me a fire fairy, though I was born in your world to mortals, the same as you."

"A *fire fairy!*" Knut breathed. He had heard of such beings, of course, but had never dared hope to meet one. "So...that's how you..." He waved a hand vaguely at the firepit.

"Came in through the fire?" She laughed softly. "Of course. That's what fairies do. It's why people call us fairies. We ferry people through fae gates from one world to the other."

"But...if your parents were mortals, how did you become a fairy?" Knut's hammering heartbeat was beginning to even out, and his panic was fading into a keen curiosity.

Could he become a fairy too? What a fine thing it would be to swim through fire!

"The same way all fairies become fairies," she explained solemnly. "I was caught by a wisp of the wild magic. Most people only touch the magic of the Deep, which is quiet and steady as stone. It's why alfkin can weave glamors and dwarrows can bind metal and stone to their wills. It's what lets nixies breathe underwater. But the wild magic comes from the Between—the place-that's-not-a-place between your world and ours. Wild magic is fickle and temperamental. No one knows how it chooses who to touch or which abilities to give them. Most often, we fae—that's what we call ourselves, mind you, no matter what sort of people we started as—we fae have an affinity for one element or another. Mine is fire, but there are fae who work in spirit and earth and air and...and water." Her eyes went sad again when she said that last one, and her smile slipped. But she shook her head and brightened again. "And most of us only Travel, but some of us can do other things as well. Watch this."

Pyra heaved herself far enough out of the fire to sit on the edge of the firepit, then cupped her hands in front of her chest. Her brows drew together in concentration, and the fire intensified slightly, sending golden threads of light twining up around her fingers to pool between her palms. The threads twisted and wove together, like the patterns Knut's mother wove on her loom, taking on all the colors a flame could be, and a picture began to form in the air. A pale blue ocean stretched out to the horizon beneath a sunset sky. Two bright figures, a man and a woman, walked along a shore of golden sand, gesturing animatedly as if talking and laughing, edging closer and closer to one another but never quite touching before moving apart, then drifting together again as if connected by an invisible string.

After a moment, she sighed and met Knut's wide-eyed gaze. "It's a pretty trick," she said, "but a picture is never as nice as the real thing, even if it's painted in firelight. And I didn't come here to show off." She let her hands fall to her lap, and the image vanished like a snuffed candle flame.

Knut scooted over a bit so he could lean his back against one of the posts that supported the roof. "Why *did* you come?"

"I was lonely. And you looked lonely too." Pyra shrugged sheepishly and her bright cheeks flushed with a rosy glow. "Sometimes I like to spy on people through their hearth fires. It's not nice, and if my father knew, he'd punish me—not my *first* father, obviously. Surt, the king of the firelands. He adopted me when I was little. Apparently, I accidentally made a fae gate in a fire wherever I came from and fell through. I was too young to explain where home was, so they couldn't take me back, and Surt decided to raise me as his own."

She leaned forward, bracing her elbows on her knees, and smiled slyly. "Anyway, he's already confined me to my room until I come to my senses, so I decided a little spying couldn't make matters much worse." She frowned. "Sneaking out like this might, if he finds out, but as long as I keep the fire gate open, I'll be able to hear if anyone comes and pop right back. And I was so utterly *bored*."

"And sad." Knut stated it as a fact. He'd seen that wistful longing in his mother's face often enough to know it for what it was. If he asked, she always said she was just thinking deeply about something, but her face was different when she thought about his father than it was when she was pondering their dwindling turnip supply. Even after all these years, she missed him.

"And sad," Pyra agreed. She tilted her head and regarded him analytically. "You're sad, too. What are you sad about? Maybe I can help."

"I want to go to the midwinter feast, but I can't."

Pyra's eyebrows rose. "Why ever not?"

Knut shrugged and shoved his crooked leg around where the light caught it better. "I can't walk that far, and I'm too big for my mother to carry."

"What about your father?"

"He's dead. The raiders came when I was little. One of them killed my father and my sister, and a horse stepped on my leg. It never healed right."

"That *is* sad," Pyra said solemnly. "I'm not sure I can help with that. Although, I've heard of earth fae who could do things with crooked bones. Perhaps I can ask around after my father lets me out."

"Why did he lock you up?" Knut jumped on the chance to change the subject. He didn't like talking about his leg. "Did you accidentally burn up a forest or something?"

Pyra smiled. "There aren't any forests in the firelands. Just lots of sand and rocks and a few valleys just green enough to grow food. The forests are farther north."

"Is it because of the man in the picture?"

Pyra's cheeks flushed rosy again. "Well," she said, "aren't you the perceptive child."

Knut scowled. "I'm not a child."

The fire fairy studied him again for a moment. "No," she said solemnly, "I suppose in a way you're not." She sighed and poked at the fire, which was fading again. "And neither am I. Yet here we are."

Knut folded his legs under him, tugging the crooked one into place with his hand, and leaned forward. "Will you tell me about him?"

She studied him a moment, and then sighed. "Very well. It seems neither of us has anywhere better to be tonight. If you build up this fire a bit so I can keep my fae gate open, I'll tell you my story."

Knut happily did as she asked, placing the wood where she directed and blowing on the coals. As the fire crackled back to life, Pyra seemed to perk up a bit as well. Her skin and hair took on a brighter glow, and her gown flushed from pale blue to a rich golden orange. When the blaze had settled hungrily in to gnaw the new wood down to its bones, Knut settled himself beside the quern and scooped up another handful of barley to grind.

"I had a happy childhood," Pyra began. "At least, once I got over missing my mother. I was a quick learner when it came to manipulating fire. Everyone said I must have been kissed with an extra measure of the wild magic—which I suppose might be true, and perhaps that's why I fell through the fire in the first place. At any rate, in due time I grew up and the boys began to vie for my attention, as boys do. It was always difficult to tell, though, whether one or another of them liked me for myself or only because of what he thought my power and my position as Surt's adopted daughter could add to his own strength and station.

"A little over a year ago, Surt was approached by one of his lords, who asked if I might be persuaded to marry his son. I knew the young man a little, and I didn't *dislike* him, precisely, but I wasn't ready to marry yet, either, so when my father asked for my consent, I told him I needed time to consider."

"Is that why he locked you up?"

"No." Pyra laughed. "Surt wants me to be happy, and fae live a very long time, so there's no hurry. He told the young man he must wait and ask again."

Knut grinned. "Mother made my father ask three times before she accepted."

Pyra nodded her approval. "A woman should know her mind before she acts, and her man should know she knows it."

She smiled as she continued her tale. "By that time, I had learned all I could at the school in the firelands, and I was growing restless. My father knew of a powerful fire fae who lived in a smoking mountain by the sea in the Western Reaches. She's a dragon's daughter, so she knows things about fire magic that aren't taught at the school. My father arranged for me to study with her, partly to continue my education and partly, I think, to let me see a little more of the world before I marry and settle down."

She glanced at Knut again, making sure he was following her story, and he nodded solemnly before scooping up another handful of barley.

"She was a wonderful teacher," Pyra went on. "It was she who showed me how to make pictures with firelight. But she was accustomed to living alone, and I was not. For her, the mountain was a place of peace, but I was lonely there. Sometimes I walked down to the beach and looked out at the ocean, dreaming of what might lie beyond." She shot Knut another furtive glance, and her cheeks went rosy again. "That's where I met Fluvius."

"The man in your picture?"

"The very one. He heard me singing to myself one evening when I was sitting on a rock a little back from the water. I was hungry for new company, and we talked long into the night. The next evening, he came back again. And the next. Soon I was dashing down to the water's edge before the sun had even begun to dip toward the horizon, hoping he would be there." Her lips curved in a wistful smile. "He was always there. We walked along the beach and explored the forests on the mountain slopes. There was a little cave we went to sometimes, when the tide was low, where black sand as soft as silk covered the floor and little glowing mushrooms grew in crevices along the walls."

Knut scraped his flour into the crock. "Is Fluvius a fire fairy too? Are you going to marry him instead of that other fellow?"

"No," she said softly. "Fluvius is heir to the throne of Murias, the city of the water fae. We can never marry, for if ever we touch, my magic will dry him up, and his will snuff me out. But I know he meant it when he said he loved me, for he has nothing to gain from it but my own love in return."

She shook her head wryly. "My father came for a visit to see how my studies progressed. When he found out about Fluvius, he was furious and insisted I return home immediately." Pyra's gaze went distant, seeming to focus on something beyond the plastered wattle and daub of the roundhouse wall. "What I wouldn't give to see him again," she whispered. "Just once."

The grinding stone stilled in Knut's hand as he thought that over. Without the grating rasp of stone against stone, the crackle of the fire was the only sound that broke the silence. The shore birds had gone to bed for the night, and the wind had hushed. It seemed a fitting backdrop to the tragic tale.

"No wonder you're sad," Knut murmured.

Pyra blinked slowly in the quiet, but she said nothing. Her brows drew together and she cocked her head.

Motionless.

Listening.

Then her gaze snapped back to Knut, sharp and hot, and she shifted in the fire, sending a shower of sparks spinning up toward the thatch.

"Is it *raining* in your world?" she demanded.

Knut blinked in startlement, and his brows shot up. Could Pyra be snuffed out if a stray raindrop found its way in through the thatch? He didn't want to put her in danger. But he didn't want her to leave yet, either.

Cautiously, he ventured, "Maybe. A little. It's been drizzling on and off today. It'll likely turn to snow later, if it hasn't already." At least, he hoped it would. That would give his mother a drier journey home.

Pyra leaned forward, resting her hands on the stones edging the opposite side of the firepit. "If it's raining at midwinter," she said, her voice trembling slightly, "there are sure to be some of *his* people about."

"Water fairies? *Here?*" Knut's eyebrows rose even more.

"Oh, please, Knut, will you let me call out to them? Perhaps they could fetch him here and I could see him after all." She held his gaze for a beseeching moment, then her light dimmed and she added, "But perhaps he won't come. I left without saying goodbye."

Knut wasn't meant to let strangers in the house while his mother was away, but...well...he'd already let in a fire fairy.

Tentatively, he asked, "What would you need me to do?"

"You'd truly help me?" Pyra sprang upright in the middle of the firepit, staring at him, her flame-colored gown flicking sparks out onto the dirt floor, her expression torn between hope and apprehension. "Just open the door." Her voice was a hoarse whisper. "Open the door so they can hear when I call."

Knut hesitated a heartbeat longer—what would his mother say if she knew? But the look on Pyra's face and his own curiosity overruled his doubts. Quickly, before he could change his mind, he took up his crutch and hobbled over to slip the bolt and fling the door wide to the night.

Light from the hearth fire spilled into the heavy darkness, shimmering off rain-dimpled puddles in the pathway. Clouds covered the stars, and the moon had not yet risen. Far off on the horizon, lightning licked at the sea; nothing else moved.

Pyra began to sing, and Knut turned back to look at her. It wasn't one of the songs his mother sang, so he didn't know the words, but it was sad, and sweet, and full of the kind of longing he saw in his mother's eyes when she spoke about his father.

The fire fae stood in the flames, shoulders back, head high and proud, hands half extended in a gesture of pleading. Her gown flared white-hot at the bodice, shading through blue and yellow and gold as it eddied with the currents of the fire like an upside-down candle flame. She was *glorious!*

And then she went utterly, breathlessly still.

"Tell him," she pleaded. "I beg you, just tell him I'm here."

For half a heartbeat, Knut thought she was speaking to him. Then something brushed his elbow, and he whirled, nearly losing his balance as his crutch slipped. Widening rings rippled from the center of one of the puddles. No one was there.

Did water fairies make gates in puddles?

Pyra's soft gasp made him turn back in time to see her sink to her knees in the firepit, eyes wide, molten copper hair spilling in wild ringlets about her pale face. Her light dimmed again, and she pressed the back of one shaking hand to her mouth.

Knut tottered over and knelt beside her, half reaching to lay a comforting hand on her shoulder before the heat stopped him.

"Are you all right?" *Maybe he shouldn't have agreed to this after all.*

She shook her head and looked up at him, her face a plaintive mask of hope and misery. "What if he doesn't come?"

Never had Knut felt so helpless! What could he do? When his mother was upset, he brought her water, but that might snuff Pyra out. Even patting her hand seemed like a bad idea.

A thump from the doorway. A gasped, "It *is* you!"

Knut jumped at the unfamiliar voice, whipping his head around so fast his teeth rattled.

The man leaning in at the doorway was dressed in a soft gray-green trimmed with silver. His sealskin cloak glistened with water droplets and his hair hung to his shoulders in dark, damp waves. At his hip hung a sword with a silver-wrapped grip and what looked like an enormous pearl gleaming from its pommel.

"I thought I'd never see you again," he whispered.

Pyra rose slowly, as if waking from a dream, or as if she half feared the man would bolt like a wild animal at any sudden move.

"You came," she breathed.

A joyous grin spread across Fluvius's face—for who else could this man be?—and he stepped into the room.

Knut scooted out of the way as Pyra carefully lifted her swirling skirts and stepped over the rim of the firepit to meet her prince. Her radiance dimmed to a soft glow as she left the fire, and her gown darkened to a rich black edged with the flickering red and scarlet of fading embers.

The lovers moved like dreaming dancers, slowly closing the gap between them until wisps of steam began to form in the empty air where they almost, but not quite, touched.

Fluvius raised one hand as if to brush a lock of coppery hair back from Pyra's cheek, and she flinched away.

"You mustn't!" she gasped. "I don't want to hurt you."

Fluvius dropped his hand and heaved a sigh. "And I wouldn't harm you for the world. But I think I'd rather die than lose you again."

Pyra shook her head. "What good would you be to anybody dead?"

"I'm not much good alive without you, Pyra—though I don't blame you for leaving me. It's all quite impossible."

"I didn't *want* to leave you. My father came. He... he wants to keep me safe." She drifted closer to him again, pert chin tilted up as if to offer him a kiss, but stopped before she was quite close enough. "But if... if there was a way... you'd still want to be with me?"

"How can you even ask?" The prince's hands came up again as if to cup her face between his palms, and she swayed back two steps. He frowned. "Have you found a way?"

"Maybe. I've... I've had a lot of time to read since I saw you last. Have you heard of the Old Man of the North?"

"The Truth Teller? They say he was a spirit fae who sought to enslave the Deep itself but got caught in his own spell." Fluvius's frown deepened. "But he's only a myth."

"He might be," Pyra agreed sadly. "But again, he might not. I've read eyewitness accounts from three people who claim to have met him up north of the Spine. One of them even left a map with directions to find him."

"But if he's real..." Fluvius's brow furrowed in thought.

"He might know a way," Pyra finished for him. "I can at least follow the directions and see if anything is there." She shrugged. "I'll go as soon as my father lets me out of my room. Will you wait for me to find out?"

Fluvius shook his head. "You can't go north of the Spine, it's always winter there! The snow and ice would quench you."

Pyra shot him a stubborn scowl. "I'll be careful. *You* would freeze solid."

"You're not going. Let me think."

Fluvius began pacing the width of the room, leaving damp

footprints across the floor from one bed to the other. Knut hoped they would dry out before his mother got home; she didn't like mud in the house.

"I have a friend who could go," Fluvius said on his third trip across the room. "A Vanir wind fae. He could pop up there tonight and be back before dawn."

"A *wind* fae?" Pyra was clearly not impressed. "He'd get distracted halfway there and forget what he was about." She shook her head sadly. "And it wouldn't matter anyway. They say the Old Man will only speak with mortals."

The two of them stood there gazing helplessly into each other's eyes. They were so beautiful and heroic and... and *sad!* The look on Pyra's face was just like the one Knut's mother wore when she knelt atop his father's grave and wove her fingers through the grass to touch the brown earth beneath. So *close*, yet, so completely out of reach.

Knut couldn't help his parents. But maybe he could help these two.

"I'll go," he said into the silence.

Fluvius blinked and turned to look at Knut, sizing him up for the first time since he'd arrived. "You're just a child," he said gently.

Knut's jaw tightened. "I'm not," he said. "If your wind fae friend can carry me, I'll go."

The prince shook his head. "It wouldn't be safe. You'd have to Travel to our world, and—"

"Let me be *useful* for a change!" Knut interrupted. "Please. I can't do much with a crooked leg, but I'm good at asking questions. Let me go."

Fluvius studied him again, then nodded his assent.

While he went outside to send a messenger to fetch the wind fae, Pyra flew into motion coaxing Knut into his warmest clothes and insisting that he wrap himself not only in the blanket from his bed, but also in his mother's wolfskin. Then she found an empty pot on the storage shelves and packed it with old rags and tinder moss before she buried a handful of embers in it to keep him warm on his journey.

When he was ready to go, she said solemnly, "Now, you must listen with great care, Knut, and do *exactly* what I tell you." She waited for him to nod before continuing. "The Old Man of the North is said to be very clever and cunning. There are rules to his enchantment, and if you follow them you'll be safe. But if you don't, he'll seize you and keep you under the ice."

Fear coiled in the pit of Knut's stomach. Had he been foolish to offer to go? But how many chances would a cripple get to experience such adventure? Slowly, he nodded. "I understand."

"The Old Man's enchantment shackles him to the Deep," Pyra explained, "so he knows everything, and he is bound to answer your first question truthfully. But you must not, under any circumstances, ask him more than one question. He'll try to trick you, so you must be very careful. Do you understand?"

"Yes," said Knut. "What am I to say?"

"Say, 'I come from the fire fae princess Pyra, and she is in love with Fluvius, the water fae prince, and she wants to know how they can be properly married and live together in happiness.' And then you shut your lips and do not speak again in his presence, no matter what he says. Can you do that?"

Knut nodded mutely.

Lightning flashed outside, and both of them jumped as the crackling roar of thunder rolled through the roundhouse, rattling the warp weights on his mother's loom.

"He's here," Pyra whispered softly, almost to herself.

She reached out as if to grasp Knut's shoulders, but stopped herself before she burned him. Urgently, she said, "Promise me you will not ask a second question."

Knut cleared his throat and looked her resolutely in the eyes. "I promise."

Fluvius came back inside, followed by a tall man with broad shoulders and a gray woolen cloak.

"This is Torvind," Fluvius announced solemnly. "And Torvind, this is—"

"Princess Pyra," Torvind finished for him. "A pleasure your highness. You are as lovely as Fluvius always says."

He had a light, tenor voice and a ready grin, and he shifted from foot to foot as he spoke, as if impatient to get on with things. When he offered Pyra a quick, sweeping bow, a playful breeze danced in at the doorway to ruffle the fire.

Pyra used the firelight to paint Torvind a map and carefully recited the directions to where she thought the Old Man lived.

The wind fae cocked his head to one side, bouncing on the balls of his feet as he studied the mountainous terrain. "I think I've been near there once," he said. "But high up and moving fast, playing tag with Nyordur's daughter." He shot a grin at Fluvius.

Pyrra made him say the directions back to her three times without mistakes before she gave her approval. Then Torvind crouched down to look Knut squarely in the eye.

"And you're to be my passenger, are you, little brother?"

Knut could only nod.

"Then let's away. I've been still too long already."

Knut stopped in the doorway and turned back. "Pyra... if... if I don't come back... will you please tell my mother where I've gone."

Pyra shook her head. "You can tell her yourself," she said firmly. "You'll be back before dawn."

"But if I don't come home, you'll tell her. Promise me."

"I promise."

Stepping out from beneath the eaves, the wind fae turned his face up to the fitful rain. The firelight spilling through the open doorway glinted off his teeth as he grinned and spread his arms wide to the night, embracing a sudden breeze that tasted to Knut of snow and the wild sea water and something... else. The breeze gusted hard, swirling around the tall man in a great gout of mist and shadow, expanding, darkening, and solidifying until the murky shape resolved into something that was no longer a man. The creature stood on four legs now, digging taloned claws into the damp earth. Every inch of it, from the tip of its sleek, reptilian snout to the end of its sinuous tail was covered in glistening scales. And from its thick-muscled shoulders, a pair of leathery wings stretched out into the darkness.

A dragon!

The great beast shifted around so he could direct his slit-eyed gaze at Knut, and said in a rumbling voice, "Mount up, little brother. The storm is calling, I can taste it on the wind."

Knut couldn't move. *Did that thing breathe fire?*

"The s-storm?" Knut stammered numbly.

Beside him, Fluvius murmured, "Torvind uses them to make fae gates." He laid a sympathetic hand on Knut's shoulder. "You don't have to do this, child."

Something twisted hot in Knut's gut. He didn't need this man's pity. He was crippled, not useless.

The dragon bent low to the ground, and Knut found handholds among the ridge of bony spines running down the center of the beast's back. Soon he was settled at the base of the dragon's neck, high on its shoulders between the wings, clutching Pyra's ember pot to his chest with one mittened hand, and clinging to a sturdy spine with the other, with his crutch bound across his back beneath the wolf skin. The dragon let out a laughing roar and launched himself into the night sky. The ground dropped rapidly away and the roundhouse, huddled up with its shadowy goat pen and fenced garden in the corner of the fallow farmstead, shrank behind them to a pinprick of warm light like a tiny candle flame against the darkness. Except for a muffled light near the docks, the rest of the village was shrouded in darkness, but from this high up Knut could see the lights of the chieftan's town glittering in the distance. What would his mother think if she could see him now?

The Traveling caught him completely off guard. One moment he was trying to decide which lights might be from the chieftain's longhouse, then there was a crackling flash of white light that made his skin crawl and his hair stand on end, and the next moment, they were... well... somewhere else.

Knut choked on the cold, dry air and coughed, spilling out a gout of steam as if *he* were the fire-breathing dragon. The glistening water drops that still clung to the wolf skin froze into diamond stillness, and his eyes stung.

The dragon's voice sounded thin and tinny when he called back, "Stay warm, little brother. We're nearly there. The myths say that light comes from the Old Man's lantern."

There was no mistaking which light he meant; there was only one. It was not a pinprick on the ground like the light from his roundhouse receding into the distance, but a clear pink light that flowed up from below to spill in waves and ripples out across the sky, fading to green and gold where it met the horizon.

Knut huddled closer to the dragon's warm scales and hugged the ember pot even tighter as they spiraled downward. The light grew brighter as they neared its source, shimmering across the sky and reflecting from the ground—which in this place was a flat ice sheet that extended out into the distant darkness, dotted here and there with patches of shadow.

In what must have been the center of the ice field, a blobby white shape poked up from the surface, like a geyser frozen mid-eruption, or a giant mushroom carved from ivory. Seated right in the middle of it was the dark figure of the Old Man of the North.

The dragon landed as near the mushroom formation as he could, and Knut sat still for a moment, glancing about to get his bearings. Then he untied the edge of the blanket that held his crutch in place, and slipped off the dragon's back.

The ice beneath his boots was smooth as glass. His crutch left white scratches across the surface as he hitched carefully toward the mushroom. When he passed one of the shadows beneath the ice, he bent closer, straining to see what it was. A bearded man in a fur coat stared lifelessly up at him, eyes wide, mouth open as if in surprise. Knut caught his breath—and coughed again as the frigid air seared into his lungs. The next shadow he passed was a woman. The one after that, two children holding hands. Knut shuddered and didn't look at any more of them.

When he reached the base of the mushroom, which from so close looked like a thick rime of ice crusting some murky thing beneath, Knut looked up. The Old Man of the North huddled in a heap atop the formation, wrapped up in a big brown cloak. His stringy white hair wriggled out from beneath a skull-cap, and his shriveled face was almost flat except for a large, hooked nose and thick, dour lips. He had his arms wrapped round a big brass lantern propped up between his knobby knees, and it was through the holes in the lantern cover that the rays of pink light shot up to paint the night sky. His eyes were shut, and his head hung off to one side. The Old Man of the North was sound asleep.

Knut hesitated. If he waked the man, would he be angry? Was that against the rules? But if he waited for the old man to wake up on his own, he would surely freeze to death.

Behind him, the dragon called, "Hurry along, little brother! The night is cold and our friends are waiting!"

The Old Man started at the sound and blinked blearily a few times before his gaze came to rest on Knut. Then he perked up, shifting his position and jostling the lantern, which made the lights dance across the darkness.

"What have we here?" he rasped. "Come to ask a question, have you?"

He coughed and cleared his throat, then muttered in a clearer voice, "But of course you have. No one ever comes to see me unless they want to ask me for something. Come nearer, boy, so I can see you."

Knut edged closer to the mushroom, and the Old Man eyed him up and down.

"What is it, then?" asked the old man with a dry chuckle. "Do you want me to tell you how to grow straight and tall, or are you going to ask where to find a big sack of gold to take home to your mother? Speak up, now, don't be shy."

Knut tried to remember what Pyra had told him to say, but the Old Man's watery gaze so unnerved him that it drove her words right out of his head. It occurred to him, too, that he could ask a question of his own instead—how he might earn a living as a cripple, for example —and then just make up something to tell Pyra. After all, the answer to her question seemed obvious enough. How *could* she and her prince possibly be together? Still, he had promised. And a man kept his promises.

He drew a deep breath, slowly this time so he wouldn't choke on the cold, and did the best he could. "Uh... my friend is a fire fae, and she is in love with a water fae and wants to marry him, but they're afraid of touching each other because he might be dried up, and she might be put out, so please, can you tell me how they can be married and live together happily?"

A broad, gap-toothed grin split the old man's face, and he began to chuckle. When he ran out of breath, he sucked in a great gulp of icy air and began to guffaw. He laughed so hard Knut was afraid he might topple right off his mushroom.

"Oh, the stupidity of some people!" he cackled. "The thing they're most afraid of is the very thing they ought to do. Go back and tell that drip to stop dithering and give her a kiss." He laughed again, loud and long, until he seemed to run out of laughter.

When he subsided, he scrubbed at his nose with one sleeve and muttered, "A fire fae and a water fae. What foolishness. They ought to know better."

Then he turned his gaze on Knut again. "Well, now that's out of the way, ask me your real question. That nonsense cannot possibly have been your reason for coming so far. What is it you *really* want to know? Something for yourself this time? Or for that pretty mother of yours?"

Knut was tempted. What if the Old Man really did know how to make his leg straight? And a sack of gold would certainly make life easier for his mother; she could hire someone to work the farmstead. For that matter, how did the Old Man know Knut's mother was pretty? But he remembered what Pyra had said and the looks on the faces of those frozen children, and he only shook his head and turned away, pressing his lips tightly together.

As he tapped and scraped his way back across the ice, the Old Man called after him.

"Come now, you're not leaving already! You've only just arrived, and I'm stuck in this weary wasteland all alone. Stay a little longer and keep me company."

Knut said not a word, just kept his eyes focused on the waiting dragon.

"Suppose I give you one free question," the Old Man cajoled, "in exchange for another moment of your time. What harm could one free question do? Don't you want to know how a cripple could become a king?"

Knut shuffled doggedly onward.

"Don't you want to know what happens to people when they die?"

Knut gritted his teeth and kept going.

"Don't you want to know where to find the man who broke your leg and killed your father?"

Knut's crutch slipped on the ice, and he staggered sideways, then stilled. His head filled with visions of what even he, a crippled boy, could do to exact revenge on the man who'd taken everything from him—his father, his mother's happiness, his little sister's laughter, the life he should be living now, and all the happy futures that might have been. Slow poison. A stealthy knife in the night. A good whack in the head with a fist-sized grinding stone.

The Old Man's chuckle was low and lethal. "That's the one, eh? Come back then, child, and let us talk a little longer."

Knut half turned, looking over his shoulder at the lumpy figure crouched atop his toadstool. The Old Man cackled with glee, motioning him to come closer. But Knut was not a child. And a man moved forward into what was, not backward into might-have-beens. A man kept his promises. Maybe Knut was not a man yet. Maybe he was too small, too broken to be a man. But whatever he was, he was not a child.

He pulled his wolf skin more tightly around his shoulders and limped resolutely back to the dragon, who was impatient to be off. He did not look back again.

The transition was less of a shock this time, despite the blinding flash and prickling sensation, and the air when they arrived back home felt almost warm after the arctic bite of the other place, even though the drizzle had turned to a blowing, grainy snow. More surprising was the gray light of dawn that was already creeping over the hilltops in the east. Either he'd been gone longer than he thought or time worked differently in the fae world.

The dragon circled wide around the village, perhaps concerned that someone might see him in the growing light. When he landed on the path in front of the snow-dusted roundhouse, he waited only long enough for Knut to slide off before launching himself back into the air. Five or six sweeping wingbeats later, lightning crackled through the sky and the dragon, somehow, slipped through the crack it made in the air, vanishing as if he'd never been.

Knut stood staring after him until a big hand landed firmly on his shoulder, making him jump half out of his skin and whirl around, heart pounding in his throat.

Fluvian stepped back and held his empty hands out to show he meant no harm.

From the doorway, Pyra called, "Come inside and get warm, Knut, and tell us what you found!"

When Knut was seated by the glowing coals with a cup of warmed goat milk steaming in his hands, he began his tale. Pyra, sitting on the edging stones with her feet in the fire, was delighted to hear that her information had been correct, and that the Old Man of the North wasn't a mere fireside tale at all. But when Knut told them what the Old Man had said, Fluvius gave a small moan of despair and paced over to stare out the door.

"Give her a *kiss*?" He shook his head. "I suppose he means there's no hope, so we might as well be dead and be done with it."

"Maybe not," Pyra said softly, staring into the coals. "Knut asked him how we might *live* together. And the Old Man is bound to tell the truth—at least, if that part of the myth is also real. I think he meant we'll only be changed. If we want to be married and live happily together, we must be willing to be changed by each other."

Fluvius turned around to look at her, and she met his gaze and held it.

"Changed." He frowned thoughtfully. "What kind of change would it be, do you suppose?"

Pyra shrugged. "I suppose there's no way to know without trying," she said. "And then it'll be too late to go back."

"Commit fully or not at all," Fluvius mused, nodding slowly. He took one step back from the door, closer to the fire, and held out a hand, palm up. "I've already been changed by you, Pyra. Nothing I have, nothing I *am* is more important to me than you. My life has been empty without you in it. I'm willing to try if you are, and if I die, I die."

A slow smile dawned across Pyra's face. "I'm ready if you are," she said softly. "And if we die, we die together."

She rose from the firepit and dusted the ashes off her pale blue gown before she went to meet him.

Knut huddled by the coals, sipping his goat milk, watching wide-eyed as the fire fae and the water fae stood in the doorway between the dying fire and the rising sun.

Pyra reached shyly toward Fluvius's outstretched hand, pausing only for the barest heartbeat when wisps of steam rose up from his palm to meet her fingers. Her eyes locked on his, and her breath caught in a little hitch, though whether of fear or excitement, Knut could not have said. Then her hand twined with her prince's with a sizzling hiss. Fluvian pulled her instantly into his embrace, and bent to kiss her—and they were enveloped in a great gout of swirling steam, through which Knut could see nothing.

Time seemed to slow, and the quenching hiss dropped in pitch to a low rumble like elongated thunder that rolled through the room on a billow of vapor. The glow of the hearth fire embers dimmed, and woodsmoke mingled with the heavy dampness of the roiling cloud. Knut huddled deeper under the wolf skin and brought the corner of his blanket up to cover his nose and mouth.

Was this what was supposed to happen? Or had something gone horribly wrong?

Around him, the mist churned and eddied, coalescing into wispy, drifting tendrils that thickened into tentacles and began to wriggle like blind snakes up the roundhouse's internal support posts and across the floor, probing and exploring as if seeking something. Sunlight from the open door filtered through the thin mist between the tentacles, forming slender rays that twisted about themselves, narrowing and twining tight like silvery flax drawn out between invisible fingers into whisper-fine threads that drifted through the fog.

Knut set down his cup and edged back from the fire pit, trying to stay out of reach of the groping tendrils and gossamer threads, tugging his mother's wolf skin closer about his body—but there was no escape. The silver threads found him first, clinging like cobwebs to his crooked leg where it poked out from beneath him at an awkward angle. When he tried to pull away, he succeeded only in drawing more threads in his direction. Reflexively, he reached to brush them off, and a misty tentacle wrapped itself around his wrist, warm and soft and pulsing with... not life, perhaps, but... something. Knut's pulse quickened, throbbing in the same rhythm.

The thunder-rumble changed pitch again, pulsing higher into an urgent tumble of vibrations that sang along the threads and thrummed at the heart of the tentacle around his wrist. More threads drifted against Knut's shoulder and tangled in his hair. A tentacle of fog wrapped in glittering, twisted threads flowed up Knut's leg and wormed its way under his blanket and beneath the hem of his tunic to wind around his middle against his skin. The vibrating sound—the hiss, the rumble, the song—whatever it was, seemed to draw in around Knut, running up that misty tentacle and into him in a warm, tingling rush that washed through his entire body like an ocean wave, clearing away the fear and exhaustion of his sleepless night, softening the age-old ache in his leg and the stiffness left in his hands from clutching at the dragon's spine in the bitter cold wind, leaving behind a pleasant, peaceful drowsiness.

For half an endless breath, time stood completely still.

And then it all came rushing back at him: the smoldering fire, the rolling fog—which somehow was only steamy mist again—the sunlight falling in shifting rays around the two figures silhouetted in the doorway, and a playful midwinter breeze that came in through the open door, cooling the damp air and painting the scene with a welcome sense of peaceful ordinariness.

Fluvius's arms were wrapped around Pyra, his head bent to press one cheek against her hair. Her forehead was pressed into his shoulder, and her slender hands were pale against his sealskin cloak. As the last wisps of mist dissipated, the lovers shifted apart a little to look at each other.

Fluvius's clothes were dry. His feet no longer left damp marks on the dirt floor. His hair had lost its wet gloss and was dry and slightly curly.

The glow in Pyra's skin had gone out, leaving her face a fine, porcelain white with a pretty rosy glow in her cheeks. Her molten copper ringlets had become a wild tangle of ginger curls, and her luminescent amber eyes had faded to the color of good ale.

She blinked hard a few times and raised her hand to her cheek, then stared wide-eyed at her fingertips as another tear rolled down her cheek.

Fluvius caught the next tear with his thumb. "Oh Pyra! Is it too much? I'm so sorry. I never should have—"

Pyra laughed, a broken, musical sound, and smacked him playfully on the arm. "They're happy tears, you goose. It's just I don't think I've cried real tears since I was Knut's age." She rubbed her thumb wonderingly across her fingertips and brushed impatiently at her cheeks before smiling up at Fluvius. "I think maybe we're mortal again."

"Is that all?" Fluvius grinned. "Well, there's no one I'd rather be mortal with than you." He gathered her up in his arms and kissed her again, long and lingering.

Over by the fire, Knut smiled. He might be crippled, but he was not useless.

When his mother came home, he introduced his new friends and asked if they might stay—after all, they could hardly go back to their old lives, now that they were mortal. His mother chided him gently for letting strangers in and said he was too old to be making up fairy stories as excuses for breaking the rules. Still, she was willing enough to believe the two had fled their families' disapproval to be together, and she couldn't help but sympathize with their plight. She couldn't afford to pay them, she said, but if they helped her work the farmstead, they could clear out one of the storage buildings to live in until they found something better.

They never did find a place they liked better, and Pyra and Knut's mother became fast friends. As the years went by, Knut's leg gradually straightened, much to everyone's surprise, and he grew into a strong young man with a quick wit and a merry heart, and became a sort of favorite uncle to Pyra and Fluvius's children. And when anyone asked how his crippled leg was mended, Knut always said he was touched by wild fairy magic—but no one ever believed him.

THE DOVE QUEEN
AND
THE RAVEN QUEEN

BRAXTON YOUNG CHURCH

Author's Note: This story was inspired by the Grimms' fairy tale "The White Bride and the Black Bride." I wanted to do a Grimms' fairy tale because while some of them are the most beloved fairy tales —such as "Snow White," "Rapunzel," and "Hansel and Gretel"— there are a lot more than this handful that we retell again and again. I chose "The White Bride and the Black Bride" because it has the common tropes of fairy tales with wicked stepmothers and stepsisters, royal weddings, good getting rewarded and evil punished; the latter usually through gruesome deaths. But what I found the most interesting about this tale is that the White Bride is not blessed by a fairy godmother or wizard, but by the Lord. This aspect of Christianity drew me into the tale (even though my retelling is missing any element of religion) because it very clearly states what the Grimms believed a good person is and isn't, what they do and avoid. In my retelling, I wanted to explore how our views on what makes a good person good in the twenty first century is different than the time the Brothers Grimm lived. Essentially, I'm exploring the same question the Grimms did; what is a good person?

Duchess Minett screamed as the carriage lurched to a halt. Her daughter Gwen reached out and grasped hands with her stepsister Melanie.

"What was that?" Gwen asked, while Melanie and the duchess asked Gwen, "Are you alright?"

Gwen pulled away from her stepsister and peered out the carriage door. She saw an old woman standing only a foot away from the horses.

"Gwen," Duchess Minett said, "come back in the carriage. The driver will handle this."

"What's going on?" Melanie asked.

Gwen closed the door before she answered. "We almost ran over an old woman."

Melanie jumped over to the other door and peered out like Gwen had done.

"Please," the old woman croaked to the driver, "I need to get to Hasden. I don't know how much longer I can walk, my feet hurt so much." The village was right next to the Minett estate, Melanie's home, but she didn't recognize the woman with her crown of white hair. Gwen hadn't recognized her either, but Melanie doubted Gwen knew most of the people living in Hasden.

"It's ten miles that way," the driver replied, gesturing back the way they had come.

Melanie turned to her stepmother. "She wants a ride to Hasden."

Duchess Minett shook her head. "We can't help her. We would be late to Cassandra's ball, wouldn't we, Gwen?"

Gwen didn't meet her mother's eyes. "It is a fair walk, and she looks frail ..."

The duchess shook her head again. "We cannot afford to waste time. You know how important this ball is."

Melanie glanced at Gwen, hoping to get her support. "I did promise Cassandra I would be there," Gwen said.

"I'm sure she would understand if we couldn't make it," Melanie said. Cassandra was Gwen's oldest friend—they had known each other before Melanie's father married Duchess Minett.

"No," the duchess said, glaring at Melanie, "you cannot break promises simply because something else comes along."

Melanie glared at her stepmother out of the corner of her eye. "You only want us there because the king might show up." Melanie did her best to keep the edge off her voice.

Melanie's stepmother kept her face neutral. "It's true that Cassandra's sister recently married the king's cousin, and the king might be there. But honestly Melanie, Gwen's promise to Cassandra is far more important." Melanie knew the duchess was only partially telling the truth.

Gwen nodded. "Her entire family have been so focused on the marriage and the king, I'm sure she needs someone to be there with her and not doting on her sister."

Melanie looked out the window. The carriage lurched forward, and Melanie watched the old woman pass them.

"Can't we do anything to help her?" Melanie asked.

"We can't turn around, and I doubt that she would want to wait hours until we return home," Duchess Minett said. "It would be rude to miss the ball, especially when the king might be there."

At those words, Melanie reached for the carriage door and flung it open. She jumped from the carriage and nearly fell over. The main motivation not to fall was Melanie not wanting to give her stepmother another thing to lecture her about.

Gwen and the duchess leaned out the door. "Melanie?" Gwen asked.

"Melanie," the duchess said, "get back here right now." The woman glanced around at the woods. "You know what kind of creatures lurk in these woods."

Melanie turned back and glared at her stepmother. Duchess Minett had raised her and Gwen on stories of faeries, elves, and goblins that lived in the wild forests. How the faeries would steal anyone alone at night here and drag them back into their twisted world. How the creatures were divided into two courts, one ruled by the angelic Dove Queen, the other by the dark Raven Queen.

But Melanie was confident she would get home long before nightfall. Her stepmother's stories included ways to protect herself in case the worst happened. "Give the king my regards," Melanie said, then turned away from her family and stomped further down the road as she heard the carriage rolling away.

"Excuse me," Melanie said. The old woman glanced up at Melanie, a small, toothless smile on her face. "I'm sorry we couldn't give you a ride," Melanie said, "but I thought that you might like some company."

"Oh, thank you, dearie," the woman said. Melanie held out an arm to give the woman some support. "What's your name?"

"Melanie."

"What a lovely name, Melanie." The two of them walked a few steps before the woman continued. "I'm so sorry to pull you away from your twin sister."

Melanie laughed. "I'm sorry, but she isn't my twin. She's my stepsister." She was used to people thinking they were related. Both had golden blonde hair and the same fair skin, even nearly identical faces. Their only difference being Melanie's brown eyes and Gwen's blue. "We've always said that our similarities were a sign that we were destined to become sisters."

The old woman returned Melanie's laughter. "I guess I know who's the wicked stepsister then."

Melanie's laughter died, the comment hitting a little closer than she would have liked—with the wicked stepsister always came the stepmother who always favored her own daughter.

"You must miss your mother very much," the woman said.

"For a year, I hated my stepmother and Gwen. I hated my father for trying to replace my mother."

The woman turned to Melanie. "What changed?"

Melanie chuckled. "One summer night, my brother Alexander tricked me into going to the woods because he told me a faerie princess had invited me to a ball. I was out there for hours alone and scared, wondering why no one was coming to get me.

"Gwen noticed I was missing, and then found me, even though the forest scared her more than it scared me. After that, I couldn't hate her or my stepmother."

"And?" the woman asked.

"And, what?"

The woman gave Melanie a knowing smile. "There's more to that story, young woman. No one can have a perfect family."

Melanie shook her head. "Yes, but just because we aren't perfect, doesn't mean we aren't happy."

Melanie told the woman all about her life with Gwen. How every year they celebrated their birthdays together since they were only a week apart, another sign that they were meant to be family. How just a month ago they both turned eighteen. How in a few months, they would be presented at the king's court

Melanie didn't mention that she felt her stepmother sometimes forgot that she would be with Gwen when they met the King.

Melanie was telling the woman about the ball she would be missing, moments away from mentioning Gwen's promise to Cassandra—why she was eager to leave—when the woman cut her off by asking, "Who lives there?" Melanie followed the woman's finger, seeing the Minett estate. Only then did she notice the setting sun and the ache in her feet.

"My family," Melanie said. "Hasden is just half a mile past it."

"Do you think I could rest at your home? Only long enough until I have the strength to continue."

"Of course. I'm sure we could find something for you to eat as well."

The woman smiled. "Thank you so much, dearie."

When they reached the estate, the woman had to sit on the front steps to catch her breath. Melanie told doorman to find a place for the woman to rest as well as some food.

"I'm sorry," the woman called from the bottom of the steps, "but I'd feel rude coming in without being properly invited in."

Melanie smiled at her. "Of course you can come in." Melanie went down the steps and helped the woman over the threshold. A servant led the woman away to where she could rest.

It was only then that Melanie realized she hadn't asked the stranger for her name.

MELANIE WAS seconds away from changing into her sleeping clothes when a maid told her that the duchess and Gwen had returned. Melanie rushed downstairs to the large front room to see her stepmother and stepsister. Gwen hugged Melanie the moment they saw each other.

"How was the ball?" Melanie asked when Gwen ended their hug.

"It was beautiful!" Gwen said, right as Duchess Minett said, "The king didn't come, nor his cousin."

Gwen gave her mother a look that asked her not to say anything else. She turned back to Melanie and said, "Cassandra and I missed you."

Melanie nodded. "I'll have to make it up to her." Melanie went to apologize to her stepmother—for her behavior at the carriage or for the king not showing, Melanie didn't know. But Duchess Minett's rigid posture stopped her from speaking.

"I thought she was heading to Hasden," the duchess said, looking at the old woman. Melanie and Gwen saw the woman standing next to an open window staring into the night sky.

"She needed some time to rest," Melanie said, confused herself as to why she hadn't left. "She was on her feet all day." Melanie walked up to the woman. "Ma'am. It's late. Do you need someone to escort you to Hasden or would you like a place to sleep?"

Melanie rested her hand on the woman's shoulder. The woman spun around so quickly Melanie jerked away.

The old woman was no longer standing there. In her place stood a woman who towered above Melanie. Even though this woman had a braided crown and not one of gold, her posture and gaze declared that she was a queen. Melanie stiffened beneath that gaze for the woman's large eyes had turned pure orange and black.

Melanie felt Gwen's hand slip into her own and her stepmother clutched Melanie's shoulders. The woman laughed, her teeth as white as her long silk dress. But the brightest part of the woman were her wings. A pair of pure angelic wings stretched out, identifying the stranger, moving her out of a faerie story and into reality.

Gloriana: the Dove Queen.

The duchess and Gwen fell to the floor, bowing, but Melanie found that she couldn't move.

"My lady," Duchess Minett said, "it's... it's an honor to have you in my—"

"Quiet," the faerie queen said, her eyes fixed solely on Melanie. Gloriana reached up and took Melanie's chin in one silvery-pale hand, pulling the girl closer to her. Melanie held her breath while the Dove Queen examined her, occasionally glancing down at Gwen.

When Gloriana let go of Melanie and stepped away from her,

Melanie took in a sharp breath. "You do not bow to me," Gloriana said.

"Forgive me, my lady," Melanie said, curtsying deeply. "I was struck by your beauty, I did not know what to do."

The Dove Queen laughed, her voice like a sharp bell. "Flattery will get you nowhere." Gloriana's eyes made Melanie wish her stepsister had not bowed so she could take her hand again.

"Or it could get you everywhere," Gloriana continued, a smile creeping across her face. The Dove Queen glared at the shaking pair on the floor. "Stand."

They did so, but couldn't meet the queen's eyes. "When I asked for help," Gloriana said, "you turned me away."

"Forgive me, my lady," Gwen said, "I was the one who didn't want you with us."

"Gwen!" the Duchess hissed.

The Dove Queen laughed. "Why? I was just a poor woman in desperate need to rest her feet."

Gwen glanced up at Gloriana and stammered.

"Forgive her," Melanie said. Gloriana turned to Melanie. She backed away from the Dove Queen. "My lady, please. She made a promise to an old friend and couldn't break it."

"You mortals break promises all the time. Surely you could have broken this one."

Gwen whimpered, the traces of words dusting her lips.

"What was that?" Gloriana asked. "Speak up."

Gwen took in a sharp breath and met the Dove Queen's eyes. "I didn't know who you were."

Melanie pressed her lips together. She couldn't fault Gwen for choosing her oldest friend over a stranger, but she wished Gwen had said nothing.

"And if you had known I was a queen," Gloriana droned, "would you have helped? Would you have chosen your mortal friend over me?"

Gwen couldn't answer.

"I'm not going to hurt any of you," Gloriana said. The tension visibly drained from Duchess Minett and Gwen.

"No," Gloriana continued, "in fact, I think I'll leave a blessing upon your daughters."

"Thank you, my lady," Duchess Minett sighed.

The Dove Queen turned to Melanie. Melanie stiffened, waiting for whatever twisted joke the faerie had in store for her.

"For Melanie. For the daughter that walked with me when no one else would."

Gloriana rested the tips of her fingers on Melanie's forehead.

"I give you a blessing of the sun," Gloriana said. "Just as everything in our world glories in the sun, so may everyone you meet glory in your presence. May your generosity and love shine to all, and may you be the center of all lives. May people turn to you like a sunflower, devoting their entire existence to bask in your beauty."

While Gloriana's fingers still felt cold against Melanie's forehead, heat ran through her entire body, as if she had swallowed embers and her blood carried their warmth through her.

But it also seemed like many invisible eyes turned to look at her, all at once. The sensation was the heat of a noon sun that not even shade could stop. When the Dove Queen removed her fingers, the chill of the faerie's touch sent a shiver through her.

"Then for you," the Dove Queen said, wheeling around to face Gwen. A wide grin crept across Gloriana's face, causing Gwen to freeze like a deer seeing a wolf. "I also give you the blessing of the sun.

"May your presence force you to remain as alone and as selfish as the sun. May your presence burn away the love anyone has for you like the sun burns dry summer wheat."

Melanie and Duchess Minett kept their eyes fixed on Gloriana; both of them afraid of what they would see when they turned to Gwen.

"What ..." Gwen whispered, "what have you done to me?"

With a faint smirk on her lips, Gloriana stepped away from Gwen. "Only what you deserve." Gloriana spun and turned into a dove. The dove flew to the open window and away from the estate.

When Melanie looked at Gwen, something screamed in her head to turn away. Gwen still looked like herself; yellow hair, fair skin, blue eyes. Melanie's eyes didn't hurt as if she had been staring into the sun. There wasn't a noise like a screaming child in Melanie's head. Nor did Melanie feel as if someone was clawing into her head as she looked at her stepsister.

But Melanie knew that something was wrong.

The duchess had her head turned away. When Gwen reached out to grab her mother's hand, Duchess Minett flinched, moving closer to Melanie.

Melanie couldn't hide the smile that came to her mouth as Duchess Minett favored her above Gwen in that moment.

She didn't even want to hide that smile.

"FLOWERS," the florist called out to Melanie, "for the beautiful lady."

Gwen closed her eyes to keep herself from saying anything sharp to the man. She didn't even open her eyes when she felt Melanie brush past her, the scent of whatever flowers she received wafting through the air.

When Gwen opened her eyes, she saw Melanie hand the flowers to a little girl who had been eyeing the florist's stall for the past ten minutes. "Your sister is an angel," the florist said. She knew the florist didn't look over at her. If he had, why would he say anything remotely kind to her, even if it wasn't about her? She just walked forward and joined Melanie in their carriage.

Neither one said anything until they could no longer hear the noise of the festival. "That was a nice thing you did," Gwen said, "giving the flowers to the girl."

"I didn't need them."

"So, you gave them to a stranger?" Gwen asked. Melanie glared at her stepsister, and Gwen returned the glare. To neither one's surprise, Melanie turned away first.

"I'm sorry," Gwen said, "I shouldn't have said that."

Melanie gripped her stepsister's hand. "I'm sure Stepmother will find some way to break your curse."

Gwen shook her head. "It's been three months. She's read everything that we have in our library. I doubt that anyone else would have more books about faerie magic than she does."

"We'll figure something out."

Gwen looked out the carriage window instead of answering.

After a minute, the carriage lurched to a stop, and Melanie let go of Gwen's hand. "What's going on?" Melanie called out to the driver as she and Gwen peered out the carriage windows.

"Something spooked the horses," he called back. "Nothing to worry about."

The arrow that went through the driver's neck turned him into a liar.

Both Melanie and Gwen shoved open the carriage doors and leapt from it. They ran away from the body, hoping to intercept anyone that might have followed their carriage.

Gwen screamed as she was grabbed, as did the masked man when he saw her face. In his shock he let go of her. She kneed the man, who groaned and doubled over.

Behind Gwen, Melanie screamed. She whipped around and saw a shorter man grab Melanie from behind. The short bandit pulled Melanie close to his body.

Gwen jumped at him and clamped her teeth down on his arm. With a cry of pain, he lost his grip. Melanie broke away and elbowed him in the face. She grabbed Gwen's hand and they dashed away from the two bandits.

The first man struck Melanie's head with a club as they ran.

Gwen fell with her stepsister, and Melanie's unconscious body landed on her legs.

The two masked men had their eyes on Gwen—or as best they could with Gwen's curse. The first one crouched next to her. He stroked Gwen's cheek and said, "Don't worry. If you do what we say, we can all go home safely."

Gwen doubted he would keep his word.

DUCHESS MINETT SLAMMED the book shut after skimming through the first ten pages. She remembered looking through this book just yesterday, but had forgotten to reshelve it, instead piling it among the other books she had on faerie magic. Most of the stories ended with removing curses through true love or the condition the faerie gave to break the curse.

Gloriana hadn't put any conditions on Gwen's curse. And with her curse, the duchess doubted Gwen would ever find true love. The servants never met Gwen's eyes, and they always found excuses to leave her alone. But they seemed to worship the ground Melanie walked on. The gardener brought flowers to her daily. The cook made meals that Melanie liked. The maids spending hours making her room spotless. They only seemed to acknowledge Gwen as they scurried away from her.

Duchess Minett was about to put the book away when there came a tapping on her window. She glanced up to see a small raven outside, looking at the rings on the duchess's fingers like a small child looking at a freshly baked pie.

The duchess laughed and opened the window. The raven tilted its head at Duchess Minett as she said, "I would happily give you every ring I own if you would tell the Raven Queen that I need her help." The raven jumped once, then pecked at a bug on the windowsill.

Duchess Minett turned back to her pile of books, leaving the window open.

"Though I'm tempted by the offer," a honeyed voice spoke, "you don't have to give me every piece of jewelry you own."

Duchess Minett spun around. Underneath the open window lounged a woman. She had long black hair cascading around her shoulders, blending into the slim midnight dress she wore. This woman's eyes were pure blue and black without any white. But the most prominent feature was the two raven wings sprouting from her back.

The duchess fell to the ground, prostrating herself before Maeve, the Raven Queen.

"Get up," the faerie queen said. "I can't stand it when mortals grovel like that." Duchess Minett stood, but didn't look directly at the faerie.

"My lady," the duchess said, "it's an honor. Why have you—?"

"A little bird told me," Maeve said with a smile on her face, "that my sister gave her blessing to your daughters." The duchess nodded. "Before you ask, no, I can't break it."

Duchess Minett opened her mouth to protest, but her voice refused to work. "My sister is as strong as I am," Maeve continued, choosing to ignore the duchess' attempted protests. "As such, it is impossible for me to remove the blessing from Gwen."

Duchess Minett collapsed into a chair behind her. Maeve looked down at her for a few seconds. The Raven Queen walked over to the table with the duchess' books and flipped through one. "However, I can offer a gift to Gwen. A way of balancing the scales."

The duchess looked up at Maeve, her eyes eager. "What do you want in return?"

Maeve laughed as she picked up another book and leafed through it. "You know, if you had actually listened to what Gloriana wanted when she stopped you on that road, you wouldn't be here now."

Duchess Minett held her back straight and ignored the color filling her cheeks.

Maeve slammed the book shut and met the Duchess' eyes. "And while I could ask you for everything you have, I only want those two ruby rings on your left hand."

Duchess Minett tore them from her fingers without a second thought. "What exactly are you going to do for my daughter?" Maeve held out her hand for the rings, and the duchess dropped them. Only for a split second did she worry that she might have made a mistake.

Maeve slipped them onto her fingers. She waved her hand and two necklaces appeared in it, both with chains of gold and a black diamond pendant.

"Give one to Gwen and the other to Melanie. If both wear them, your blood-daughter will marry the king."

"The king?" She couldn't believe her ears. The Raven Queen could make it so Gwen would marry the king? It sounded too good to come from a faerie.

"You dare question the power of a faerie queen?"

"No, my lady." Everything she had wanted ever since her daughter was born, Maeve was offering to her.

"Last chance," the Raven Queen said. "Either take the necklaces or I take back my offer."

She grabbed them without a second thought.

THE BIGGER BANDIT carried Melanie over his shoulder. The short, bald bandit tied Gwen's wrist to a rope and pulled her several feet behind him. Fortunately for Gwen, the man had hastily tied the knot to get away from her. She could get out of it whenever she wanted, but waited until she could get Melanie free as well.

After a few minutes they arrived in the bandit's camp. They put Melanie down on a bedroll and tied Gwen's rope around a tree. A tree that was several feet away from the others.

Gwen already had the rope free from her wrists as Melanie woke up.

"Don't worry," the taller bandit said. "Whoever buys you off our hands is sure to treat a pretty lady like yourself well." He leered at Melanie and brushed a lock of hair out of her face.

The bald one leaned over and rested a hand on Melanie's thigh. The other one slapped his hand away and snapped, "Go check on the other one."

Gwen wrapped the rope around her wrist to make it look like a knot. The short man walked up to Gwen, but didn't even look at the rope. He was back next to Melanie within a few seconds, and Gwen pulled the rope off again.

Melanie saw Gwen get free and nodded at her stepsister.

"Someone will find the horses, the body," Melanie said. "The moment they realize we're missing my parents will send men to hunt you down."

"Yes, they will send men after us," the tall one said, "but don't think for a moment that you'll be getting away."

Melanie glared at him. "Are you sure about that?"

"Why do you say that?"

With a smirk Melanie replied, "No reason."

Gwen struck the bandit on the back of the head with thick branch. He went down before he could even cry out in pain. The second bandit wheeled around to face her.

The bandit's eyes met hers then darted straight to the ground, giving Gwen a clear shot at his head.

She helped Melanie onto her feet and they ran through the forest, trying to put as much distance between themselves and the bandits as possible before they got up.

When they heard the bandits' voices, they were closer than Melanie and Gwen would like.

When Melanie tripped, Gwen turned back to help her stepsister. "I can't keep running," Melanie said.

"Yes, you can," Gwen said as she got Melanie back on her feet. After a few breaths Melanie ran again, but Gwen didn't follow her.

Melanie stopped when she saw that Gwen wasn't running. "Gwen! Come on!"

"I'll be fine," Gwen said, her voice masking her uncertainty. "Go get help."

Melanie looked as if she was about to protest. But when the men's swearing voices reached her, she dashed through the trees and out of sight.

Gwen stood her ground and watched as the two bandits came into sight. The bald one flinched immediately, while the leader managed to keep staring at Gwen.

"Where is she?" the taller bandit spat at her.

"Gone." Gwen stepped towards the bandits. The bald one took two steps away, while the leader took only one and cursed himself for doing so.

"H-how about you tell us where she went," the short one said, still unable to look at Gwen, "and we let you go? Doesn't that sound like a fair deal?"

"Why? Because you don't want me?"

The two bandits glanced at each other. Gwen folded her arms, daring them to say anything.

Gwen walked towards the one that had grabbed her from the carriage. "Look at me," she said to him. After a few seconds, the bandit looked at her. The twitching of his head told Gwen that he wanted to tear his eyes away from her—maybe even tear his eyes out if it meant he wouldn't see her again.

"Leave. Now." Gwen could almost feel the faerie magic emanating from her as the bandits sprinted away.

MELANIE RAN until her hunger for air forced her to stop. She paused for only a moment, then continued. Maybe if she found someone soon enough, they could rescue Gwen from the bandits. What were they doing to her right now? How fast could they move without

Melanie there? Could her curse be enough to give her another chance to escape?

She let herself hope when she heard the sound of galloping horses.

"Help!" Melanie screamed as she ran onto a road. She saw a pair of riders, and the moment their horses stopped, Melanie ran up to the first one. "I need your help!" Melanie called out before she could even look up at the horse's rider.

"Melanie?" the rider asked. She blinked and recognized the speaker—her brother Alexander.

"Alexander! Gwen is out in the woods with bandits. We need to help her!"

"What's going on?" a man on a horse behind Alexander asked. Melanie glanced back at the man and dropped into a bow.

"Your majesty," Melanie said to King Daniel. The king got down from his horse and walked up to Melanie.

"You said someone was taken by bandits?" King Daniel asked Melanie. "Please, rise."

Melanie straightened her body and met the king's eyes. He smiled at Melanie, and she found herself returning the smile.

After a few seconds of them looking into each other's eyes, Melanie said, "My stepsister Gwen. She needs help."

King Daniel nodded at Alexander. Melanie's brother dismounted and pulled out his sword. Melanie gestured back to the direction she had run from, but kept her eyes fixed on the king.

Alexander found the trail Melanie had left through the woods and followed it, but King Daniel didn't move. "Are you alright?" he asked Melanie. When she nodded at him, the king took a step closer to her and took her hands in his own. "Stay here where it's safe." The king drew his sword to follow Alexander.

The king was here. And he was looking at Melanie, really *looking* at her. She didn't want him to leave. She couldn't let him leave. It was what her stepmother had wanted Gwen to have for years.

Melanie didn't know if spite was her only motivation.

A few seconds after King Daniel finally slipped away from Melanie, she called out, "Your majesty, wait!"

The king stopped immediately and turned back to face her. "Yes, my lady?"

Melanie stepped closer to him, and the king sheathed his sword. "Could you stay here with me? I'm sure Alexander can handle the bandits, and I would feel so much safer if you stayed."

She didn't mention Gwen's curse and the possibility that it might help her.

She didn't want the king to think about her stepsister at all.

"Anything for you, my lady." King Daniel bowed deeply to Melanie, which brought a smile to Melanie's face. "You know," the king said as he straightened himself, "Alexander has spoken of you. His younger sister who he simply adored. He never mentioned just how stunning you are."

Melanie laughed, and he laughed with her. "My king, my stepsister is in danger. Do you really think now is the time to start courting me?"

King Daniel appeared as though he thought that it was.

GWEN WAS LOOKING over her shoulder, so she didn't see Alexander run into view. She screamed when he called out her name and sighed out her tension when she saw her stepbrother there—and internally groaned when even he looked away from her. Alexander had learned of Gwen's curse shortly after the faerie gave it to her. Melanie and his mother seemed to be able to meet Gwen's eyes, but Alexander couldn't find the strength to do so.

"Are you alright?" Alexander asked as he ran up to her.

"Yes, yes, I'm fine." Gwen hugged her brother. "Where's Melanie? What are you doing out here?"

"Melanie's safe. I was out with the king, and Melanie ran into us.

If she had been a few seconds later, she would have missed us. What were you doing out here?"

"Going home after the festival," Gwen said, "when those bandits attacked the carriage. Thank heavens I was able to drive them away."

Alexander nodded and led Gwen back to the road. "Hurry. We should get to Melanie and the king soon."

The king. Because if Gwen had to meet anyone before they could break her curse, if there was one reason that her mother wanted to break it, it had to be King Daniel. Gwen looked around the forest for any doves that might be Gloriana watching her.

They found Melanie sitting on a large boulder, King Daniel standing closer than he should without a chaperone.

Melanie stood when she saw Alexander and Gwen. "Are you alright?"

"We're fine," Alexander said. He stepped to the side, and Gwen nodded at her stepsister. "Gwen managed to drive the bandits away on her own."

Gwen smiled weakly and glanced over at the king. He hadn't noticed her, only having eyes for Melanie. She didn't know if she should be grateful or angry.

Melanie turned back to King Daniel. "Your majesty, we thank you for your service." Both Gwen and Alexander rolled their eyes. "Do you think you could escort us back to our estate?"

"It would be my honor," King Daniel said. The king helped Melanie onto his horse and rode off before Alexander and Gwen could mount theirs.

"WHERE ARE THEY?" Duchess Minett asked her husband, the servants, anyone near her. "They were supposed to be back from the festival hours ago."

"Dear," Duke Minett said, "I'm sure they were caught up in all the excitement." The duchess ignored her husband and rushed out to the stables.

She asked the stable boy, "Have my daughters returned?" He shook his head. She turned to look down the estate road as her husband caught up to her.

"We need to send out men," the duchess said, snapping her attention to the duke. Her husband motioned towards the road, but Duchess Minett continued. "Something must have happened to them. Do you have any idea what kind of danger they're in? Who they could be with? What people would do to them because of their curses? I knew I should have gone with them. What?" The duke pointed out to the road once more, and the duchess turned to see Melanie riding with a man the duchess couldn't quite recognize. She realized who that man was when she saw Gwen riding with Alexander just a little way behind them.

The duchess turned to the stable. "The King is here. Tell the cook to have tea sent up to the white parlor in fifteen minutes, and make sure we have the largest guest room ready if he wishes to stay the night." The servant bowed to the duchess then scurried off into the manor.

When the king rode up to the duchess and duke, they bowed low to him. "Your majesty," the duke said. "What an honor and surprise. What brings you here?"

King Daniel dismounted and helped Melanie down. "Her. Your son and I rescued Melanie and Gwen from bandits, and I couldn't stand not seeing her safely home. These bandits killed the driver. Please organize a party to find them and bring them to justice for committing such a horrible crime against your daughters." His eyes didn't leave Melanie as he spoke.

"We thank you for your service, your majesty," the duke said. The duchess ran up to Gwen as she and Alexander dismounted.

"Are you alright?" she asked, hugging Gwen closer. Gwen nodded. The duchess glanced up at Alexander. "Thank you so much for helping them."

Alexander looked behind the duchess. "It seems like someone else is far more grateful than you that the King and I found them."

Duchess Minett turned to see King Daniel walking into the Minett estate, arms linked with Melanie.

The Duchess clutched the small bag at her waist where she carried Maeve's necklaces.

THREE MONTHS LATER, the Minett estate was near chaos preparing for Melanie and King Daniel's wedding. It was only three days before the ceremony and most of Melanie's personal belongings had already gone to the king's palace. Very little remained to suggest that Melanie had spent her life at the Minett estate.

No one, not even Melanie, knew how much of that was intentional on Melanie's part.

That morning, Duchess Minett knocked on Melanie's door, the black diamond necklace gripped in one hand. Beatrice, the King's personal seamstress who he had sent to the Minett estate, opened the door for the duchess.

The duchess froze when she saw Melanie's dress: gold accented with raven feathers.

"What do you think?" Melanie asked. "Beatrice here tells me that feathers are out of fashion in the king's court and that I should have black roses instead. But doesn't this make me look like some beautiful angel of the night?"

Duchess Minett glanced up to the nearby window to check for any grinning ravens.

"Stepmother?" Melanie asked.

Duchess Minett forced herself to smile. "You'll look beautiful no matter what."

"Then I want the feathers." Beatrice shook her head, but continued with the dress. "Can you believe this? I'm marrying the king!"

The duchess ran her thumb over the black diamond.

"Imagine where I would be if I hadn't run into the king that day." Melanie laughed. "Imagine what would have happened if I hadn't walked with the Dove Queen all those months ago. Doesn't it feel like destiny?"

The duchess sucked in a breath but managed to hold her smile. Melanie, however, wasn't paying any attention, so the duchess turned to leave.

But before she reached the door, Duchess Minett returned to Melanie and held out the necklace to her.

"What is this?" Melanie asked.

"A gift," the duchess said. "I want you to wear it for the wedding."

Melanie snatched the necklace. "It matches my dress perfectly. Thank you so much." Her eyes didn't return to the duchess.

Duchess Minett nodded and left Maeve's necklace—and whatever curse the Raven Queen put on it—to Melanie.

On the day of the wedding, Gwen got into the carriage as soon as she could, not wanting to be in the house as everyone prepared for Melanie's wedding. She twisted the black diamond pendant her mother had given her in her hands, wanting this this day to be over.

Gwen heard the servants fussing over Melanie up until she got into the carriage herself. The identical diamond necklace around Melanie's throat made Gwen flinch.

"You gave us identical necklaces?" Gwen spat at her mother as the duchess climbed in.

Duchess Minett looked at Gwen. The duchess looked at the diamond, and if not for her curse, Gwen would have wondered why her mother refused to meet her eyes.

"We're already late," the duchess said.

They rode in silence. Gwen tried not to think about how the court would react to her curse. Though part of her wondered what she was more worried about, the nobles' judgment, or taking away attention from Melanie on her wedding day.

After an hour, Melanie broke the silence and took Gwen's hand. "Thank you."

"For what?"

"Being here." Melanie turned to her stepsister and held eye contact, despite the curse. "I know that I've been caught up in planning for the wedding, been caught up with the idea of marrying King Daniel. But thank you so much for staying with me." Melanie squeezed Gwen's hand. "I'm sure at the king's court we can find some way to break your curse. I won't let you suffer any more."

"Melanie," Gwen said.

"Maybe if I had just gone with you to Cassandra's ball the Dove Queen wouldn't have ever cursed both of us. I'm part of the reason for what happened to you. So, I think I should ..." Melanie tightened her grip. "No, I must find a way to help you. Gwen, I promise you that I will always be there for you from now on."

"Melanie," Gwen put her second hand over Melanie's, "I promise that nothing will break us apart."

"Take off your necklace," Duchess Minett said. Melanie and Gwen turned to her, and she repeated. "Melanie, take off your necklace now."

Melanie broke her grip with Gwen and reached for the black diamond. "What are you—"

"I don't have time to explain. You need to take it off now!"

Melanie stared. However, Gwen reached up to find the clasp. But she pulled away when Melanie's body shook in a coughing fit.

"Melanie?" Gwen cried. Melanie continued to shake and coughed up raven feathers.

"Gwen, get the necklace off her!" the duchess yelled. Gwen reached for her stepsister again, but Melanie shrank, her gold and feathered dress pooling around her. Before either Gwen or Duchess Minett could react, Melanie disappeared, leaving only her golden dress on the carriage floor.

A raven wearing the black diamond necklace hopped out of the dress.

Gwen and her mother tried to catch the raven—Melanie—but she flew up and out of the carriage window.

"What ..." Gwen started, pausing when she saw the tears welling in her mother's eyes. "What did you do?"

The duchess burst into sobs and told her daughter the deal she made with Maeve. The deal she made on the same day the king had proposed to Melanie.

Gwen clutched the necklace at her throat and tore it from neck. She felt a drop of blood where the clasp cut her. "How could you have done this?"

"How was I to know that the king would want to marry Melanie?" the duchess sobbed.

"With the Dove Queen's curse, do you really think he wouldn't want to marry her? The woman that everyone worships for her beauty?" Gwen glanced out the window. "We need to get her back."

"How? And even if we could find Melanie, do you know how to break that curse?"

Gwen fell back into the carriage seat. "What else can we do?"

Duchess Minett glanced down at the fallen dress.

"No. I won't take Melanie's place."

The duchess sighed. "We'll blame the Raven Queen, say she took Melanie away. It isn't completely untrue."

Neither one of them moved to pick up the fallen dress, nor did they say anything the remainder of the ride. When the driver opened the door, his eyes flitted down to the dress and away from Gwen.

"My lady, what are you doing?" he asked. "Discarding your wedding dress on the floor like that? We're late enough as it is."

The driver stepped away from the door. Gwen and Duchess Minett stared at him, wondering how he hadn't noticed Melanie's absence.

"Duchess," the driver said when they didn't step from the carriage. Gwen left first. In front of her was a line of nobles who had come to the palace for the king's wedding. An elderly couple close to Gwen turned back when she stepped out of the carriage then turned away to act as if they hadn't seen her. Despite the chatter and laughter coming from the procession, Gwen heard the couple whispering to each other and saw them glance at her out of the corner of their eyes.

Duchess Minett tried to shield Gwen from the other nobles. They walked towards the palace, their eyes fixed on King Daniel as he greeted his guests—where he waited for his bride that would not arrive.

King Daniel glared down at Gwen. She said, "Forgive me your majesty," right as the king snapped at her, "Is that what you're wearing for the wedding?"

Gwen stammered, trying to answer King Daniel, but unable to form words due to her surprise. Why would he ask about Gwen's dress instead of Melanie's whereabouts?

"Forgive me your majesty," Duchess Minett managed to say. "It's just that I ... I mean, your bride-to-be ..."

"She's right here, and she doesn't look ready."

Both Gwen and the Duchess took a step back from King Daniel, unable to believe that he thought Gwen was Melanie. "I ... I'm sorry, my king," Gwen said, unsure of what else she could say.

"Very well. You have two hours." The king spun on his heel and stalked into the palace.

Gwen and the duchess stood there until Alexander walked up to them. "What were you thinking?" Alexander asked. "Making the king wait like that. He could have you beheaded."

Gwen gaped at him. "Alexander, Melanie isn't here."

Alexander stared at Gwen, then asked the duchess. "Who's Melanie?"

～

An hour later, Gwen had locked herself and the duchess in her room—Melanie's room, Gwen had to remind herself. The room she had taken from her.

"They don't remember her," Gwen said as she laid across a couch twice her size. "How could Maeve have made everyone forget Melanie?"

"We don't have time to wonder about that," the duchess said. "We've already wasted an hour." Duchess Minett sat near Gwen's head. "You're going to have to go through with the wedding."

Gwen opened her mouth, but could she really go against her mother like this? Did she really have any other options? "But he's in love with Melanie, not me."

"She's gone," the duchess said, her voice lacking emotion. "Do you think she would want you to throw away this chance?"

"Like you threw her away?" Gwen regretted saying it the moment it came out. Her mother pressed her lips together, keeping whatever retort she had to herself. Gwen curled in on herself, or at least as much as her dress allowed.

On one hand, she could go through with the wedding. And if she was lucky, King Daniel would ignore her for the rest of their lives and she would live comfortably as a queen.

But then there was the promise she made to Melanie.

"I know what I have to do," Gwen said as she stood.

"What?"

"All this happened because I couldn't break my promise to Cassandra. I can't do the same to Melanie."

After Gwen locked herself in her room, Alexander went to the kitchens to tell the cooks that the luncheon had been postponed as the bride wasn't feeling too well. The servants grumbled, but no one said anything directly to Alexander.

When he walked out of the kitchen, Alexander rubbed his temples. His stepmother had been pushing Gwen to marry the king for so long. So why would all this happen the moment his stepmother's dreams finally came true?

Though, Alexander found this whole thing a little odd. He remembered that King Daniel met his sister the day she was kidnapped. And that the King had proposed to his sister that same day.

But that made no sense. His stepsister had ridden back to their home with Alexander, not King Daniel. And Alexander couldn't remember the king even noticing Gwen that day.

The raven cawing into Alexander's ear cut off his thoughts. When he tried to remember what he was thinking about, nothing was there. So he assumed it couldn't have been important.

The raven's second noise turned Alexander's attention to it. He found it strange that any bird would willingly land on anyone's shoulder. The necklace the raven wore only added to the odd situation; a gold chain with a black diamond. The raven met Alexander's eyes, then pecked at the diamond.

Alexander smiled faintly. "Best not anger the Raven Queen." He picked up the large bird as best he could with one hand, tossed it up, and watched it fly away.

He next checked the stables to make sure the horses and carriage were ready to take the king and his bride away on their honeymoon. Fortunately, the stable hands weren't upset like the cooks, giving Alexander one less thing to worry about.

Which only gave him more time to think about King Daniel's and Gwen's courtship. And it didn't add up. King Daniel had proposed to his sister that day they met. He only did that because of the curse the Dove Queen gave his sister. But everyone found Gwen repulsive. Wait, hadn't Alexander already thought about this?

When the raven landed on his shoulder again, it broke his thoughts once more. When he tried to remember what he was thinking, nothing came to mind. So he turned to look at the raven, and saw it pecking at the diamond. For a brief moment, Alexander thought the raven was begging him to remove the pendant.

"Ask your queen. I dare not risk angering her." Again he tossed the raven into the air and it flew away from him.

He tried to remember what he was thinking about before, but nothing came back to him.

Once Alexander made sure everyone knew about the delay, he headed towards the hall where the ceremony would take place. Guards were posted at all the doors, so Alexander assumed no one could sneak in for any reason. But with all the oddities going on, Alexander thought he should at least check.

He was surprised to find King Daniel in the hall as well, standing at the altar as if the wedding was happening in that moment.

Alexander bowed to the king and said, "My king." The king turned back to Alexander and nodded at him, not speaking for a few seconds.

"I remember," the king finally said, "a few days ago, my bride talked to me about a curse ... someone close to her had a powerful curse given to her by a faerie queen. She had asked me to scour the land to find a way to break this curse. But now, I can't remember this person my bride wanted to help."

Alexander knew his stepsister had been cursed by the Dove Queen herself. But what were the odds that someone else close to Gwen had met a similar fate? And why wouldn't Gwen ask King Daniel to help her break her curse? Their mother had spent months searching for the cure, she would have immediately jumped at the opportunity to break Gwen's curse. So why had they risked angering the king like this?

Before either one of them could answer, a raven screeched. They turned to see the bird flutter down from an open window and land on King Daniel's outstretched arm. Alexander walked closer to the king and saw that it was the same raven with the black diamond.

King Daniel brought the raven close to his face and stared into the bird's eyes. He reached out and gripped the jewel between his thumb and forefinger.

"Your majesty," Alexander said. He had planned on warning

King Daniel about this strange raven, but about what exactly? The raven didn't seem strange or dangerous; it felt desperate.

Neither the raven or the king moved for a few moments, a silent conversation going on between them. Then with a single nod, King Daniel broke the diamond from the necklace.

The raven fell from the King's hand. But before it hit the ground, it had transformed into a young woman wearing a black dress worthy of the Raven Queen herself.

Alexander and King Daniel stared at the woman. When she met the king's gaze, tears formed in her eyes. "Daniel," she whispered.

"Melanie?" King Daniel asked. Alexander gasped, and in that moment everything came back to the two men.

The king pulled Melanie into a tight hug. "Are you alright? What happened to you?"

Melanie took in a breath and held it—almost as if she was unsure if she wanted to tell him. "My stepmother," Melanie said. She stepped away from the king and took the diamond from his hand.

"She gave me this necklace for the wedding. And as we rode here, she told me to take it off. But I transformed before I could. The next thing I remember, I had flown to the Raven Queen. She laughed and gloated over the deal she made and told me everything her curse had done."

Alexander gaped at his sister. "The duchess did this to you?" When Melanie nodded, Alexander continued, "How could she?"

Melanie looked down. She couldn't voice why Duchess Minett had made that deal; how Maeve taunted Melanie about being unloved.

The king cupped Melanie's cheek. "Then let's test the duchess. Please hide while I question her and see if she regrets her actions. Alexander, please bring your stepmother down here." With a nod, Alexander ran off, and Melanie hid behind the veiled altar to wait to spring the trap on her stepmother.

≈

"ARE YOU SURE?" Duchess Minett asked. Gwen didn't answer her, so the duchess took her daughter's hand in her own. Gwen nodded, then reached for their door to leave.

But before she could, there was a knock at the door. "Mother?" Alexander asked. "The king wishes to speak with you in the grand hall immediately."

The duchess let out a nervous laugh. "At least it saves us the trouble of finding him." Gwen didn't say anything, and the duchess gave her hand a gentle squeeze.

When Gwen opened the door, Alexander stared at her. "The king only wishes to speak with the duchess."

"I have something I need to tell the king myself. Am I not allowed to speak with my groom?" She kept her eyes fixed on her brother's. For a moment, Gwen thought Alexander was going to say something, but he only stepped away from the door to allow Gwen and the duchess out.

Gwen and Duchess Minett held hands the entire way.

When they entered the great hall, King Daniel stared at Gwen despite her curse. "My dear," the king said. For a moment, Gwen thought she heard some hesitation in King Daniel's voice but brushed it off as part of her curse.

"Your majesty," Gwen said, curtsying deeply. "My brother said you wished to speak with my mother. But she ... we have something we need to tell you first."

Gwen paused and squeezed her mother's hand tighter. "I have a stepsister named Melanie. She is your intended, not me."

"A sister?" the king asked. "Surely I would remember if my bride-to-be had a sister."

"That would be my fault," the duchess said. King Daniel turned to her, a frown on his face. "The Dove Queen cursed my daughter so that all who looked upon her would find her repulsive and blessed my stepdaughter, Melanie, so everyone would find her beautiful.

"While trying to find a way to break this curse, the Raven Queen came to me. I made a deal with her so Gwen would become your bride."

King Daniel turned his glare towards Duchess Minett.

"I made the deal before you and Melanie met," the duchess sobbed. "I didn't try to stop it before it was too late."

The duchess turned away from the king and silently cried.

"Not only has everyone forgotten about her," Gwen said, "but the curse turned her into a raven. She's gone."

King Daniel walked close to Gwen. "Do you know how to bring her back?"

Gwen shook her head. "My stepsister and I once promised that we would always be there for each other. We promised that no matter what happened, we would love one another. I've never seen her happier than when she's with you." Gwen's voice broke into a sob. "I would give anything to bring her back."

"Even your own life?"

Gwen replied, "Yes."

King Daniel didn't know what to say. Alexander didn't know what to say. Even Melanie didn't know what to say but she walked around the altar and out of hiding. The duchess let out a short scream and jumped away. Gwen, on the other hand, stepped towards her stepsister and whispered her name.

Melanie took her place next to the king and looked at her family.

"You heard your sister," King Daniel said. "As future queen, you should decide your stepmother and stepsister's fate."

"I decree," Melanie said, "that as punishment for their crimes against the future queen ..."

Gwen and Duchess Minett locked hands, ready for whatever Melanie declared.

"... they shall be required to attend my wedding, and Gwen shall be my maid of honor."

Duchess Minett gaped at her daughter. Gwen let go of her mother and rushed to her stepsister, hugging her fiercely. Duchess

Minett walked up to Melanie and locked eyes with her. "I'm so, so sorry."

"It's alright, mother." She took one of the duchess' hands. "We're all together now."

With the excitement from that morning, Gwen was grateful the maid helping her prepare for the wedding had left. And had left quickly due to her curse. It honestly made Gwen laugh; she was grateful for something her curse did.

She looked in the mirror, examining the pearl necklace she wore in place of the black diamond one. She and her sister had left both black diamonds outside where a raven would find them and get those wretched objects out of their lives.

Melanie had told her and their mother how the king broke the curse. The duchess found it a miracle that the king had fixed her mistake. Gwen thought it was proof of how much King Daniel and Melanie loved each other.

Now Melanie would marry King Daniel in a matter of minutes. All was right in the world, and Gwen got a few moments of quiet to herself. So, in the silence, she jumped when there came a tapping at her window.

Outside sat a single white dove.

When Gwen opened the window, the dove flew in and transformed into Gloriana. She *tssked* at Gwen and said, "You really are a foolish girl, you know. You could have had an entire kingdom."

Gwen shook her head. "A kingdom stolen from my sister is not one that I want."

Gloriana sighed. "No matter how long I live, I shall never understand you mortals."

A knock came at the door. "My lady," the maid said, "we're ready." Gwen nodded to Gloriana, and the faerie queen stepped to the side.

Gwen turned to Gloriana and said. "I should thank you. If it wasn't for you, Melanie would not be marrying the king."

The Dove Queen raised an eyebrow. "Even though those who love her despise you?"

"My sister loves me; that's enough." Gwen smiled at the Dove Queen. Gloriana nodded at Gwen, then transformed back into a dove and flew away.

When Gwen opened the door, the maid beamed at her. "My lady. What will your sister think of you, looking more beautiful than her on her wedding day?"

THE BANNIK
AND
THE SOAP

JOHN M. OLSEN

Author's Note: When the call for stories went out for this collection, I wanted to hunt down something out of the ordinary. Rather than pick something everyone already knew or something out of a typical role playing game, I dove into lore of a different sort.

A fair bit of research led me to the Bannik, a Slavic bathhouse spirit. The idea of a creature with both a hot temper and the rumored ability to see into the future intrigued me, so I was off and running. The next challenge was that I didn't want to do a retelling of lore. I wanted to create a story from scratch wrapped around this interesting creature.

That led to more research on banyas (Slavic bath houses), wedding celebrations, and clothing from the appropriate time. Once I had my creature and a setting, I needed a story to match. This is the part you'll find in most stories. Pick a few characters. Give them desires and needs in conflict with each other and let the trouble commence. A twist or unexpected bit at the end is always nice, too.

Olya kicked at a small rock on the path and scowled as she fetched well water for the banya. The steam bath used a lot of water, and leaving empty barrels would be unfair to both the other residents and to the scrawny, ill-tempered Bannik who they say appeared there from time to time. Perhaps a good soak in the steam would distract her and improve her mood.

She said, "She won't be any good for him, you know."

Her friend Masha laughed. "Are you still upset about Nikolai marrying Tatyana today?"

"No," she lied. "She couldn't cook to save herself, and she's too tall for him. I want him to be happy, and I don't see him being happy with her no matter what people say."

"Right. It has nothing to do with Nikolai breaking up with you to spend time with her. I understand." Masha giggled.

Olya said, "We had something special before she butted in and ruined it." Masha didn't understand. Nikolai promised her they would be together forever. They would build a farm, raise healthy children, and be the envy of the town. He went back on his word and chose to wed the girl with the wavy golden hair and perfect chin and eyes so blue the sky was jealous of her. The thought of him touching Tatyana instead of her made Olya smolder inside. She had every right to be upset at the betrayal.

They entered the outer common room of the banya where people gathered to talk and emptied their large buckets into the water barrels. A group of young men came out of the steam room and headed to the side room with a cold-water tub to dip themselves, just finishing the first session of the day. Excellent timing. She and Masha could go right in for the second session and have it to themselves.

Back in the corner of the outer room sat a shriveled old man she didn't recognize wrapped in a blanket. He had a long beard, but it was his eyes that captured Anya's attention. His dark eyes locked with hers as she entered the steam room. She watched him until Masha shut the door so they could change out of their heavy clothes.

Olya asked, "Is that him? Is that the Bannik?"

"Who? I was too busy watching the boys wrapped in nothing but their towels. Didn't you see them ogle at us? I would think you would pay more attention to them since you're unattached now."

Olya glared at the sideways reference to Nikolai. "He is sitting in the corner on a bench, wrapped in a blanket to stay warm."

Masha held up her hands and wiggled her fingers and grinned. "Did he have long claws, perhaps stained with the blood of children? Maybe a spare leg bone to gnash his teeth on?"

"I don't believe those stories of him flaying and eating children any more than you do. Have you ever heard of a child gone missing in the town? I didn't think so."

"What about the baby born here in the banya just last month? They said it was stillborn, but nobody had time to throw rocks to distract the Bannik before the birth because the baby came so quickly. Is it a coincidence? Sometimes he's invisible, hiding in the shadows waiting for a chance to cause trouble." Masha liked to tease and take the opposite side of an argument for fun. Olya figured sometimes Masha did it just to annoy others. Olya was plenty annoyed right now.

"I don't know. My mother tells the same tales the other old women do. It doesn't mean I believe them." Olya thought about the man in the common room. Could it be him? The stories were meant only to scare children, weren't they? What would she do if the stories were true? What would she want from him?

Masha sat on one of the lower benches and picked up a besom, a bundle of fresh oak branches, and dipped it in a boiling pot of water. "Come over here and scrub my back, then I'll do yours."

Olya gave Masha a good scrub with the bundle of leaves then borrowed Masha's soap to rub herself down. Liberal use of the oak besom and its fresh spring leaves was good for the skin. She sat still while Masha rubbed her back until the skin shone red and clean. She had new soap of her own sitting with her things but was happy to leave it unused and borrow from her friend.

They donned felt hats to protect their heads from the heat and climbed onto the upper benches to soak in the steam nearer the ceiling where the temperature was higher.

Olya said, "I think I'll ask him if I will be happy."

"Who?"

"The Bannik out in the other room, of course. I've never seen the man out there before. It must be my destiny to ask him something today."

Masha rolled her eyes. "Old Sasha said she asked him something once when she was young. Have you ever been here when she comes in for a steam bath?"

Olya shook her head.

Mashsa leaned close with a conspiratorial tone. "Her back is covered with deep scars, shoulder to waist. When she was our age and out courting the boys, she asked the Bannik if she would be rich. She married the town drunk the next year. She and her vodka-soaked husband both insist the scars are from the Bannik to punish her for asking a foolish question. Ask him something if you want, but don't expect anything good to come of it if he's the real thing. He might give a boon from time to time, but it's not worth the risk."

After a good sweat, they wrapped up in towels and gathered their things to move to the cold bath. Olya's soap rolled out of her things and onto the floor. After a moment of thought, she picked up the new cake of soap and set it on a far shelf by the stoves as an offering. What harm could it do to leave a gift for the Bannik?

Olya opened the door, only to find the outer room empty. The young men had left long ago since you could only spend so much time in the cold water, even after a long steam. The wrinkled old man from the corner was gone, too. The Bannik had vanished, if there even was such a thing, and if it was him.

If she wanted to be happy, it was up to her. She would work it out for herself. It was foolish to believe in the fortune-telling spirit of the banya. If he lived here, why hadn't she ever seen him before?

Even after the invigorating dip in the cold bath, she wasn't happy. Tatyana and Nikolai were still to be wed that very day. He deserved to be punished, not married off to the most beautiful girl in town. Olya smiled at the thought of his new wife bearing scars on her back like Old Sasha, but the girl was too dense to ask for anything amiss even if the Bannik offered.

If Olya couldn't have Nikolai, then Tatyana shouldn't have him either. She stewed over how to disrupt their marriage. Something secret. Start a fire during the ceremony? Too dangerous. Put cinders in their bed? There was no way she would be allowed into their new log home. There must be something she could do. Rumors around the town would be a good start. Perhaps Tatyana was barren, or maybe he would sneak out at night to visit an old girlfriend like Olya. She would find a way to destroy them for what they had done to her.

The wedding was awful. Everything went perfectly, and Olya had no chance to ruin anything. If she were seen causing problems, it would produce more stories than those about the town drunk. The people would hate her for taking her just vengeance on the newlyweds. They didn't understand. They never would.

She followed along as a group left to prepare the banya for the new couple. The banya, where she had seen the Bannik. It must be him. It had to be. She hurried to catch up.

One of the older women set out a sack of rocks and cracked pottery. Olya smiled. "I can take care of throwing the pottery if you like."

The old woman laughed. "I bet you'd like to throw pottery at them." It was no secret Olya was sweet on Nikolai for years and planned to wed him before Tatyana came along. "But I see no harm. Make sure you fling it at the walls at the back of the banya where the steam room is. We don't want the Bannik ruining things for the new couple. It's the fourth session for the steam room now, and we can't have him causing trouble for the newlyweds. The fourth is his favorite, you know, but he hates the noise and won't stay."

"Of course. I'm not on the best of terms with Nikolai, but I'd like them both to have everything they deserve." Olya smiled in a way that was more like baring fangs and picked up the sack to carry it to the back of the building. All along the base of the old log wall sat shards of broken pottery and stones used from past celebrations.

She pulled the pottery out and flung it at a nearby tree with all the force she could muster, breaking the projectiles into small pieces. They would easily hear the noise of the destruction from out front and consider her job well done. The rocks made a neat pile behind a tree as well, out of sight where nobody would find them.

Olya carried the empty sack back out front to await the couple's arrival, smug in her growing faith in the Bannik to behave as the stories all said he would. Soon she would know.

The couple arrived and entered the banya with much fanfare, but a short moment later Nikolai poked his head out the door with a sheepish expression. "We forgot soap."

Olya couldn't stand any more delays. She was ready to test the wraith of the Bannik, and their forgetfulness threatened to ruin her plans. "I have a new cake of soap I left it inside this morning. I'll go get it for them."

She stomped past them pausing only to glare at Tatyana as she opened the door to the steam room. Water boiled on the hot ovens and belched out steam that made it difficult to see. She made her way to the back of the steam room where she had left her soap and felt along the shelf until her hand came across the cake of soap. The wet soap, freshly used, was warm in her hand.

The door slammed shut.

Olya saw his gnarled form at the door through the steam as he flexed and relaxed his long, clawed fingers. "You seek vengeance against the boy who took back the gift of his love, yet here you are, taking back the only gift you ever gave me."

He stepped forward to stand between her and the door. "They say I can be kind or cruel. They say I can tell a man's or woman's fate and future. They're right, but I think of myself more as a giver of justice. Some people deserve peace, or joy, or a life of rewards. Then there are others. Others like you."

Olya screamed, but nobody came to save her despite her pleas. She huddled in a corner and howled with every breath as he scraped his claw-like nails down her back, ruining her clothing and cutting into her skin deep enough to leave scars to last a lifetime.

He stopped with a harrumph. "Now go, show them how I've marked you for the fool you are. And leave my soap."

NIGHTINGALE

STEVEN HEUMANN

Author's Note: *The balance between authenticity and artificiality is something we deal with on a daily basis in our modern world. Through computer technology we can create perfection, or at least the illusion of perfection, in our movies, magazines, and social media. I thought a lot about that when reading the original Hans Christian Anderson tale.*

Published in 1843, The Nightingale featured a Chinese emperor being overwhelmed by the song of a lovely nightingale from a nearby forest. Not long afterward he is given the gift of a mechanical nightingale, which instantly enamors him and replaces the real bird in his heart. All is not well however, as the Chinese Emperor becomes more and more despondent through his connection with the artificial, until finally the real bird returns and heals him with her beautiful song.

We see our own struggles with technology thrown back at us in this tale. At times we allow ourselves to waste away in front of a computer screen or tablet while the real world progresses unabated outside our windows. That parallel holds a great deal of power. Eventually the emperor is brought back by the very real singing voice of his paramour, and thus reminds all of us that reality, no matter how flawed, is preferable to the prison of perfection.

"You know," Dutch said, fiddling with the gold clip on his tie. "Everybody loves how she sings, I mean it's a thing of beauty. Truly. But you're going to make more money if you replace her with a Bio-Mech and sell the units as singing companions."

Shang rubbed his beard, scratching at his cheek as he contemplated Dutch's council. A cold current blew across his face, descending from the air conditioning vent fifteen feet overhead. Shang liked the cold and could work comfortably with frost on the Greek statues lining his office windows but understood sixty-five degrees was more than chilly enough for his colleagues. Dutch sat across the glass desk, unfazed by the temperature.

Tapping the crystalline surface of his workspace, Shang pondered Dutch's proposal. His Marketing Director had never steered him wrong, even when focus group data had contradicted his conclusions. Dutch had instincts no other Board member possessed, and they had paid off handsomely, evidenced by a ten-thousand-dollar three-piece Armani suit. Regardless, in this case Shang couldn't help but disagree.

"I'm not sure that's a good idea," he said, touching the tiny leaves of his Bonsai tree growing in a red pot to his left. Dutch's face reflected off the glass desktop next to the plant, smiling as if anticipating his boss' reticence.

"I've had the tech boys draw up some designs," he said, handing a rectangular digital file-pad across to his boss. "It's all early stages, but trust me, she'll be the most advanced Bio-Mech we've ever produced. The Tokagashi Firm won't know what hit them! Our annual projections will go through the roof on this one."

Pale blue holograms appeared on the screen in Shang's hand, complete with measurements, cost analysis, and artistic elements. A perfectly designed woman stared up at him, proportioned like the svelte fashion models he had dated in his youth. Lavender wafted from the device's olfactory fabricator, filling Shang's nostrils with the smell of beauty and serenity. The hologram winked and smiled.

"I had them add the lavender, so you could get a better feel for what we're going for," Dutch continued. "The female secretary Bio-Mech unit with the sandalwood scent receptors sold the best because the smell reminded people of comfortable offices and libraries; crap like that. I figured this one we'd try some type of flower. It certainly beats the weird plastic smell they have after production."

Shang put the pad down and pushed his chair back. He stood slowly, bracing his hands against the desk's cold glass. Lavender lingered in the air, conflicting with Dutch's over-abundance of cologne. Turning toward the large windows behind him, Shang approached the statue of Perseus he'd bought from a collector in Athens. Centuries-old cracks rippled along the arms, evidence of past upheaval and ancient intrigue. The work of art contrasted against the illuminated skyline behind it. Colored lights blinked against the darkness, silhouetting chrome skyscrapers and flying automobiles along the Gravity-Lite Expressway. An animated billboard for the Tokagashi Firm mocked him from across the city; their slogan, "Building a Better You," flashing in bright purple text.

"Over the past two decades," Shang began like a professor about to lecture his class, "art has been marginalized. A machine couldn't create a statue like this if it wasn't programmed to do so. I want people to see beyond the artificial perfection we've fed them. I've never heard anyone sing like her before," he said without looking back at Dutch.

"I agree, but she's not attractive enough to market to the K-Pop and rocker crowds. You can sponsor her and put out a few albums if you want, but that's it. If you digitize her voice and use it in the Bio-Mech, well then you've got something. We've got recordings of her singing. It'll be easy to replicate." Dutch reached across the desk and picked up the electronic pad. "People aren't interested in real singers anymore. It's been done to death. They want perfection, and we can give it to them; the perfect singer everyone can own and serenade them in their homes whenever they want. We need something big if we want to keep Tokagashi at bay. I'm telling you, this is it."

Cold air filled Shang's lungs like the first gasp of a newborn. He made his decision.

"Let's do it," he said, turning to face a grinning Dutch. "I'll talk to Caroline and break the news. She'll be disappointed of course, but we'll compensate her for the use of her voice." He sat back down into his ten-thousand-dollar chair, the cushions electronically folding to conform to his body. A little too perfectly, Shang admitted to himself. "Contact the design crew to begin production immediately. I want these units to hit retailers by this Christmas, so we can crush Tokagashi."

Dutch stood, buttoning his suit coat. "Yes, sir."

"Do you have a name for this thing yet?"

A broad smile spread Dutch's cheeks like the Cheshire Cat. "I do. The Nightingale."

"Wait, so you just want my voice?" Caroline asked, putting her fork down next to her salad, eyebrows arching up in confusion. Long curly hair framed a round face, lovely but less than perfect with its freckles and large nose. Nothing about Caroline would merit a second glance except for her voice, which Shang could listen to every day for the rest of his life. He wanted her to sing even now, interrupting the diners and treating them to something truly special.

"We feel using your voice in our newest domestic Bio-Mech would be something worthy of your talent," Shang said, reaching across the table and patting her hand like a father comforting his daughter after the family dog's death. "Imagine all the people who will wake up to your singing every morning."

"But it won't be my voice," Caroline contested, pushing her salad away and taking a sip of fizzy soda. "It'll be a digital version that some sex-bot will use to sing old men to sleep."

Shang smiled, appreciating her perspective. He took a bite of his grilled salmon before continuing. "The Nightingale will be marketed as a family service unit– "

"They're all marketed as 'Family Service' units," Carline interrupted. "Oh, they're serving all right."

"–And your voice will make them the most unique and sought-after Bio-Mech in the world."

"Do I have a choice?" she asked, sitting back in her chair, eyes cast down in defeat.

Shang opened his mouth to speak but couldn't find the words. Clanging silverware and faint laughter filled the space between them. "Of course you have a choice," he finally spoke. He reached down and pulled out a digital file pad, placing it on the table between them. "I brought contracts for you to sign, and you'll be compensated."

"All I wanted was to sing," Caroline said, standing abruptly. "I thought you wanted to share art and beauty."

"I do," Shang conceded, reaching toward her as if to grab hold and keep her from leaving.

"Do what you have to." Caroline pushed in her chair and turned to leave.

"Caroline, please wait," Shang said, a pleading need in his voice. "You can still sing. You can sing for me."

She looked at the digital pad on the table, contracts flashing on the screen. "I don't want your money or to give up the rights to my own voice. I'm sure your lawyers won't have a problem getting around my not signing anything, but I'm not doing it willingly. Goodbye, Mr. Shang."

"Please Caroline, I still want to hear you sing whenever I can."

"Then buy a Nightingale."

She turned and walked out. He wanted to call after her, beg her to stay and sing one more time for him, but such action would not befit a man of his stature. He took another bite of the salmon, allowing himself to be sucked into the din of noise echoing through the restaurant.

∾

"I THINK YOU'LL AGREE, she's perfect," Dutch said, motioning for Shang to stand and get a closer look at the prototype Nightingale. Eyeing the dozen board members ringing the donut-shaped table, Shang nodded and stood. Each of the executives looked to their leader for permission to either praise or criticize the mechanical marvel standing in front of the windows and the city skyline beyond. Shang tentatively approached the unit.

From a distance he would never think the unmoving woman anything other than a real person. Dark hair cascaded over her shoulders in beautiful curls, accented by the sunlight streaming in through the glass. Flawless skin stretched over every inch of her, with womanly curves that were neither too big nor too small. Her clothing, a simple light blue short-sleeved dress extending to the mid-thigh, complimented the android's beauty without drawing undue attention. Everything about the Bio-Mech seemed perfect. From a distance.

Shang drew close, paying particular attention to the eyes. The eyes always gave it away. No life or imagination, no spark of brilliance ever emanated from the eyes of a Bio-Mech. The Nightingale, while easily the most lifelike unit ever produced, still would never think for itself, laugh spontaneously, or paint a portrait, no matter how advanced the software.

"It looks very good," Shang admitted, touching the warm flesh of the unit's arm. A faint smell of lavender tickled his nostrils.

Dutch skipped over, looking the Nightingale up and down like a man about to buy a painting. "The tech-boys outdid themselves this time. She's fully conversational, performs all household duties with even more efficiency than our Alice-Mech 2.0. Cooks, cleans, everything. She's a work of art."

Whispers of agreement rippled along the boardroom table as executives chorused their approval.

"How does she sound?" Shang asked.

"That's the best part," Dutch gushed. He snapped his fingers in front of the Nightingale's nose. The bio-Mech came to life, blinking and smiling a sheepish grin, like someone who had gotten distracted in the middle of a conversation. "Nightingale?"

"Yes, Mr. Anders?" the unit replied, a sweet innocence to her voice very similar to Caroline's.

"You can call me Dutch, sweetie."

"Yes, Dutch?"

"Would you sing Peter Gabriel's *Book of Love* for us please?"

The Bio-Mech opened its mouth, forming an "Oh" shape. The note that followed flowed through the room like a butterfly riding sunlight. The first stanza began, words dancing between the men and women in the room, filling every ear with a melody so perfect, so otherworldly, several in the audience were moved to tears. Shang was not one of them.

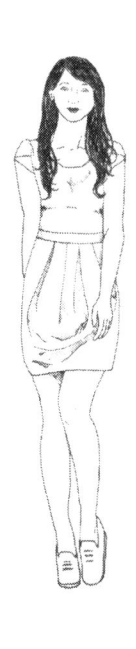

Between the precision of the notes, the purity of the tone, and flawless syllables, Shang could find no fault in the performance. Yet somehow it left him wanting. He longed to hear Caroline sing the song. Maybe then he could decide what the Bio-Mech lacked.

The ballad ended, board members applauding enthusiastically as if at a concert.

"I told you," Dutch said, a slight gloat to his words. "She's perfect."

"What do our pre-orders look like?" Shang asked, returning to his seat.

Dutch handed him a digital pad, flashing with graphs and financial projections. "That's the really beautiful part: we've only been advertising for six weeks, and even then, only in short bursts. We already have over a hundred thousand pre-orders. A hundred thousand, and that's before we really make our holiday push."

Shang nodded at the impressive numbers spinning in a holographic ballet before his eyes. He should be overjoyed, but something kept him from moving past reserved content. "Keep me informed on production timelines. Thank you very much for the presentation, Dutch. You can take the unit back now."

"Well, sir," Dutch smiled. "This one is actually for you."

"What do you mean?" Shang asked, forehead creasing in confusion.

"The board got together, and we all know how you love art and how this project is so close to your heart, so we had the techs make a special unit just for you. This first Nightingale is yours."

The cold air around him suddenly heated up as discomfort moistened Shang's armpits. Not one to expect gifts or special treatment despite his powerful business status, Shang had no idea what to say or how to respond.

Dutch grinned at his boss' speechless stupor. "We thought this might catch you off-guard, but what do you get for the man who has everything? This makes up for your last ten birthdays."

Friendly laughter bounced off the windows, filling the room with good-natured frivolity. Shang smiled despite his embarrassment, accepting the gift graciously.

"Thank you, everyone," he said, standing back up out of respect for his peers. "Thank you. Your thoughtfulness will not go unappreciated." He waved his hand toward the Nightingale. "Dutch, have it delivered to my study upstairs. Starting tonight she will serenade me to sleep with the city at my feet."

≈

"What would you like me to sing, Mr. Shang?" the Nightingale asked. Shang handed her the book he had been reading and sat back into his armchair, snuggling against the cushiony fabric in preparation for his artful entertainment.

"Sing me the second aria from the *Clandestine Colindale* opera, please."

Nightingale placed the leather-bound novel in its place on the bookshelf amongst hundreds of other works of fiction. A soft fire crackled in the hearth across the room, bathing the study in warm shades of tangoing orange and yellow. The perfect environment for beautiful opera.

"Would you prefer the original 2087 version, or the updated 25th anniversary aria from last year?"

"The original, please." Shang closed his eyes, smelling the burning cherry wood and musk of old books.

Deep from within Nightingale's chest a rumbling note resonated, peaking and dropping with each change in pitch and tone. *"The love of fields and flowers wane along the paths of childhood's glance; while billowed smoke consumes the grain amid my passioned stance..."*

Shang listened to every word, again finding no fault in the performance. The Nightingale's voice never faltered, not a single note wavering, and yet somehow the song failed to reach the emotional heights Shang had felt the first time he heard it performed live. Each new stanza brought with it an uncomfortable longing for something indescribable. Words proved inadequate in formulating the emotion of dissatisfaction he felt. The voice, so similar to Caroline's, even better in some ways, never reached the same level. He didn't know why, or whether the fault was his own expectations or not, but either way the music gave no comfort.

"Would you like me to continue to the fourth aria, or sing the male role in aria number three?"

Lost in his confusion, Shang hadn't realized the song had ended. He opened his eyes, the Nightingale smiling warmly down on him like a dutiful daughter happy to perform. "No... sing *Carmen Habanera.*"

Again, the Nightingale began, dulcet tones filling the study like the light from the fire. Crescendos built, reaching their apex and dropping back down; a rollercoaster of sound that promised to never end. But no matter how well performed, no matter how beautiful, no matter how perfect, Shang found no pleasure in the song.

The Bio-Mech's eyes opened and closed in concert with the

notes, no soul emanating from its life-like corneas. The unit swayed along to the music, strutting like a real woman. From a distance no one would guess otherwise, but Shang, trapped now in emotional solitude, knew all too well that the performer in front of him understood no happiness or pain, and in truth, enjoyed nothing.

"Sing Bobby Darin's *Beyond the Sea*."

The Nightingale performed magnificently.

"*Battle Hymn of the Republic*."

Another perfect rendition. Maybe if he tried something a bit more boisterous the Bio-Mech would give him a presentation with greater depth.

"For crying out loud... *Baby Got Back*."

Without a hitch, the Nightingale created a female version of the Sir Mix-a-lot classic that retained the uproarious fun while adding a bit of sadness. It still didn't feel quite right, however. None of the songs carried the weight Caroline would have brought to the refrains.

He asked the Nightingale to perform a dozen different pieces of music, operatic, hip-hop, classical, jazz; nothing satisfied. Like a starving man forced to watch through glass as others feasted, Shang went to bed disturbed by his inability to enjoy his precious art.

The following morning Shang awoke to the Nightingale standing over his bed, artificial smile beaming, hair silhouetted red in the light from his alarm clock.

"This is your wake-up alert, sir. What would you like me to sing, Mr. Shang?" the Nightingale asked.

Blinking sleep from his eyes, Shang had little desire to pick a song. "Sing whatever you wish," he answered.

"I wish to sing a song you will enjoy," the Nightingale said.

Sheng rolled over, checking the clock. 5:30 AM, his normal wake-up time. "Just pick something you think I'd like."

"Should I go through the songs you've already requested of me and pick one at random?"

"Sure," he said, throwing the blankets off and stretching his back.

"Then I shall sing *Baby Got Back* by Sir Mix-a-lot."

Shang cringed, wondering how the most advanced robotic servant on the planet could be so obtuse.

Every night for weeks he had the Nightingale perform and every night her perfection became more apparent. Each note made him long for something he couldn't comprehend, a connection that wouldn't materialize. Finally, his entire existence seemed to crumble around him.

The more time he spent with the Nightingale the more detached he felt. Depression had never been a problem for him, but now the emotion's dank heaviness seemed to claw at his every thought. How could one Bio-Mech make him feel this way?

Nothing felt real anymore. Food lost its flavor, colors bled from the sky, walks in his rooftop garden overlooking the city did nothing to comfort him. No painting or musical performance brought the slightest joy.

Each night the Nightingale sang and each night he fell deeper into despair.

"Sir, the board asked me to check in on you," Dutch said, seated in the recliner across from Shang in the cold study. "You haven't been down to a meeting in over a month, sir. The Tokagashi Firm has been spreading rumors that your health is failing."

"I'm fine," Shang coughed, pulling his blanket tighter around his shoulders. His beard, longer now than it had been in several years, rubbed against the comforter reminding him he needed a trim... and a shower. "I've just been unmotivated, is all."

"Well your lack of motivation could have a negative impact on the company," Dutch said, handing a digital pad across to Shang. "It looks like you haven't left that chair in a week. Good thing no paparazzi can get in the building. For now, the Tokagashi are floundering. Projections from Christmas are still unofficial, but we crushed them. You can see there that we had our best quarter ever. The Nightingale is a massive success."

Shang never looked down at the screen, staring instead at the cold fireplace across the room. Wind blew outside, tree limbs tapping against the window. The random scraping soothed him somehow, as if the branches massaged his brain with their chaffing.

"Where's your Nightingale?" Dutch asked, craning his neck to look out the opened door toward the living room beyond. "I figured she'd be in here with you singing some song to make you happy."

"Did you find what I asked for?" Shang questioned, a terse bite to his voice.

Dutch looked at his hands, lips frowning slightly. "I searched through all the registries, employment services, hell, even the ad-cams throughout the city that log faces against online purchasing patterns. Nothing. There was a rumor she was singing at a bar in the Davies section of Old Town, but nothing concrete; only talk about a girl with a pretty voice that sounded like the Nightingale."

"Find her," Shang said, standing up and walking toward the door, blanket still wrapped around him.

"Sir, I don't know if we can. I had the entire security division scrubbing the net looking for her last week. I don't even know if she's in the city anymore. It's like Caroline just disappeared. She could be anywhere."

"Find her," Shang repeated, looking over his shoulder at Dutch. "Find her or I will fade away amidst the perfect music of her copy."

Dutch shook his head. "I don't know what that means..."

"I need to hear her sing!" he shouted. "I need something real!"

Dutch clawed at the chair armrests like an animal wanting to escape a predator. "Yes sir, I'll keep looking."

"Just find her." Shang walked out.

"WHAT WOULD you like me to sing, Mr. Shang?" the Nightingale asked. Shang rolled over in bed, clinging to the warmth of the blankets. Where he had once loved the cold like a wide-eyed toddler seeing snow for the first time, now even the slightest chill brought him to his knees. The comforting folds of the sheets held him close. He wanted nothing more than to stay here forever, smelling fabric softener and filtered air. Afternoon light shone through the window, casting a shadowy cross over his prone form.

"What would you like me to sing, Mr. Shang?" the Nightingale repeated. How many times had she asked that question in the preceding months? A thousand? Ten thousand? Time had ceased to exist. A hundred years could have passed, and Shang wouldn't have known the difference. The Bio-Mech never changed, never aged, always smiling in fake comfort. He had it sing a litany of songs, every melody he'd ever heard, and yet in the beauty of its perfection he found only ashes.

"I wish for you to be silent," Shang answered. The Nightingale immediately ceased any motion, eyes not blinking to avoid even the slightest whir of servos. It became like the statues in Shang's office, pale, elegant, deceptively delicate.

How had he gotten to this place? Not long ago he commanded an entire army of workers from one end of the globe to the other, dictated terms to foreign companies, and shaped the future of industry. Now he lay in bed searching for something real among the artificiality of his existence. Alone in his home on top of a skyscraper he felt farther from heaven than he imagined possible.

His phone rang, a hologram of Dutch's face appearing above the screen. No force on earth could persuade him to answer the call. The ringing eventually stopped, replaced by a flashing message signal where Dutch's head had been.

"Play message," he commanded.

"Sir, I'm coming up," Dutch's voice said through the digital device. "I found her. She's here." The message ended.

Found who? Shang thought. *What "she" did Dutch mean?* The answers seemed to have been important at one time, but now their meaning escaped him. Nothing, no one outside of his bedroom existed anymore except for the Nightingale. He could never escape it.

His eyes closed, mind wafting toward oblivion content in the reality of nothingness.

Someone spoke his name. Dutch? Maybe. A woman's voice followed as if calling from far away. He didn't want to wake up. The darkness seemed so inviting.

A melody filled his ears, familiar but not quite recognizable. The sound roused him, warming his limbs like a soothing balm. Eyes opening, he made out a blurry shape standing next to his bed singing a lullaby. The Nightingale? No. Similar voices perhaps, but this one held life and imperfection, an energy Shang hadn't felt in months.

Caroline. Her song filled his ears and revived his mind. That's who Dutch had been searching for. Caroline, whose voice had inspired him to promote art and beauty. Caroline, who he'd replaced with perfection and reaped nothing but emptiness.

Her voice soared, radiant in its blemishes; rich in its failings. The passion behind the words gripped his heart and lifted him from his inertia. Dutch stood behind her just outside the room as if not wanting to intrude.

Her lullaby ended. Caroline smiled at him with her full cheeks and large nose, freckles dancing against her skin. "I hear you've been looking for me," she said, kneeling next to the bed.

"Can you ever forgive me?" Shang asked, tears rolling unashamed down his cheeks. "Please, forgive me."

"It's okay," she soothed.

"No, it's not." He took her hand, holding it tightly. "Look what I've created," Shang said, waving his hand at the Nightingale. "What have I done?"

"It's okay," Caroline repeated. "You'll figure it out."

"I wanted to share art and creation with people. Instead I gave them an illusion." He sat up, breathing deeply as if the weight of the ocean had washed off his chest. "Thank you for coming back. It's more than I deserve."

Caroline smiled. "Hey, we can still make music if you want."

"I'd give up everything I have for that," Shang admitted, wiping the tears from his face. "Dutch," he said, motioning to his colleague still standing by the door. "Please remove the Nightingale and return it to the technicians. I have no desire to hear it ever again."

"Yes, sir," Dutch nodded, stepping over to lead the Bio-Mech from the room.

"I would give up my company just to hear you sing," Shang said, squeezing Caroline's hand.

"I don't think that will be necessary." She smiled. "But I would never deny you a request so beautifully spoken. What should I sing for you?" she asked.

"Anything you'd like," Shang answered.

He closed his eyes, face frozen in bliss as the first notes resonated against his ear drums. He had rediscovered real beauty and would never accept its counterfeit again.

ENDA

AMANDA HAKES

Author's Note: I wrote Enda after reading The House on The Lake, the original Irish Folktale about a young man who rescues a fish that turns into a swan, who used to be a princess. I was mesmerized by how much the folktale felt like the dream of a boy to me, with the fairy tale logic, and the feats of heroism, and the wooing of the girl at the end. As I read and reread it I so badly wanted to muddle those lines between reality and dream, I wanted to know the boy who wished he could fight the dragons. I wanted to be in the brain of someone so pure hearted. So I created the boy whose beloved grandma had died, and helped him dream the dream.

While writing Enda, I enjoyed balancing the whimsical fairytale feel where anything could happen, and the weight of a boy moving through grief. It was important to me that, despite his age, Enda did not miss the opportunity to feel the loss and experience the growth that comes from it.

Enda ran his finger over the crack in his grandma's clay cup. She had pressed the knotted design herself along the narrowed neck before he had been born, but when he turned three years old he added the crack. He felt guilty for stealing the cup from her possessions beneath the table where they laid out her body, but surely she wouldn't miss one cup in the Otherworld. He would miss her, though.

The cold wood dock underneath him chilled his skin through his shirt. His legs propped up against the stone wall of their house. Enda tilted his head back. This way the lake that reached their dock looked like the sky—and the sky looked like the lake. He held up the cup against the sun that hung just above the mountain peak to pretend the cup was bigger. When he turned the world upside down, it didn't seem strange to be confused anymore. Not by the noisy relatives gathered in his home who shouted above each other. Not by the druid who whispered directions to the Otherworld into Grandma's ear. And not by how his Grandma's spirit might make it out of the house when herds of people kept blocking the doors and the windows so they could say goodbye to her body.

The thought of his Grandma not making it to the Otherworld in time made Enda want to kick against the stones and scream, but his mamma had asked him to be good. She had to focus on their family right now.

"Enda boy. Please come inside, I can't keep checking on ya out here." His mamma leaned around the corner. He tried to hide the cup on the other side of his leg, but his mamma cocked her head, her dark curls all falling to one side.

"Do ya want Grandma to miss her chance to go to the

Otherworld because she's wanderin' around looking for her favorite cup?" She stuck out one demanding hand and the other fisted on her hip. Enda sighed, let his legs fall to the side, and rolled so he could stand. Finding the crack with his finger one last time he put it in her hand.

"I just thought I could keep one." Enda scraped the bottom of his shoe against the wood so the leather made a soft scuff-scuff-scuff. The crashes of talking from the house mostly drowned the soft sound of it out. Enda wanted to scurry up on the table inside, waving his arms big like wings, and tell everyone they needed to go home.

"I'll tell ya what," his mom said, bending down so her eyes were the same height as his eyes, "I'll give this to ya to keep safe, but please take this back to Grandma. She loved this set very much."

"Will you stay outside with me?" Enda wrapped both hands around the cup, trying to be very careful.

A strange look crossed his mamma's face—like she wanted to cry. But he didn't know why staying outside would make her cry. She stroked his dark, curly hair and kissed his cheek. Usually, he liked that, but now it made him feel sad, too.

"I'm sorry Enda boy. I have to be inside."

Enda held the cup close to him as he watched his mom guide another guest into the house. He did want to keep it forever. But what if Grandma got stuck here in this world looking for this cup because of him, just like his momma said? Enda scrunched his face. It wasn't fair he couldn't keep even one thing of hers, but he would put the cup back.

In the distance, quick bursts of a swan's squawks interrupted Enda's thoughts. At first, it only added to the other sounds Enda wished he could get rid of, but the honk punched Enda's ears again and again. It didn't seem right. He looked out over the lake, trying to find the swan. In a patch of reed at the far shore its white head reached just high enough for Enda to see it. The swan's wings spread, flapping, but it didn't move from that spot.

Strange swan, Enda thought and wiped his running nose on the back of his sleeve. He walked to the opened door and stepped right into the noisy front room. The swan's cries still carried over on the wind.

Enda rocked back and forth, one foot inside his home, and the other on the dock. He needed to return his Grandma's cup, but what if the swan was hurt? He looked back—the swan hadn't moved from the spot in the reeds. He would be quick, he decided, and dove inside to put the cup back. There a sea of hips and legs knocked into Enda as he waded through them, drinks sloshing over the rim of their cups and landing on Enda's shoes, seeping through the seams and making the bottoms sticky. From the middle of the room, he still couldn't see his grandma. Enda huffed and fiddled with the cup. He didn't want to spend too much time trying to get to the wake room. They wouldn't make space for him. The swan still needed help. The cup would have to wait.

Enda pushed his way back out. A small hole at the base of his home where the stones had crumbled away made a space just big enough for the cup. Enda set it inside and covered it with leaves. He would be right back, then he would bring the cup to Grandma.

With one cold, deep breath he ran down the dock to the shore. Enda dipped his foot into the lake as it lapped up onto the dirt. Winter water filled the holes of his leather shoe. He shook the water away. It would be faster to swim straight across, but it was too cold.

He would never be able to walk to the swan and be back home in time. Once his Grandma had walked with him as far as they could before the sun went down. They didn't even make it to the other side of the lake.

Momma kept their currach upside down on the edge of their wooden dock, the oar stored inside. He could push the boat out, free the swan, and be back before his mamma even checked on him. He was strong now, and big enough to handle it. He could free the swan from the patch of reeds. It would at least take him away from the house and his worry over Grandma.

When Enda stepped into the currach it rocked to one side then the other, almost knocking him off balance, but he bent his knees and waited for the currach to be still. He knelt at the front and pushed through the water with the paddle. His arms shook from it. He knew that if his hands got too tired, the oar would slip out of his grip and be lost to the dragon of the lake. They would never be able to get it back, and his mamma would be really angry then.

By the time he made it to the swan, his arms, shoulders, and back ached. From this side of the lake, his little home seemed much farther away than it should, and the distance made a nervous sort of monster grow in his belly. But the bleating of the swan became more frantic, and he couldn't bring himself to turn back now, so he pushed that monster down.

Enda pushed the boat through the water until it scraped the shore. He got out, shoes sloshing in the water, and pulled the boat up safely on to the soggy earth. Then he waded through the water, pushing reeds out of his way to make a path to the swan.

The swan spread its wings and honked so loud that Enda brought his hands to his ears. Its wings reached longer than any grown-up's arms and flapped so hard that Enda stumbled backward.

"I want to help you," Enda yelled over the sounds of the swan. He put out his hands, blocking his face from the beating wings. "I want to help!"

The swan, with its neck stretched up towards the sky, looked at him with one dark eye. Enda thought he saw a tear running down its face. Pushing his way closer, Enda touched the swan's chest, "Poor thing," he said, just the way he had heard his grandma care for others, "I'm here now."

The swan went still.

Looking at the swan looking back at him, Enda thought of his grandma.

"Swans look beautiful," she had said to him one night on the dock, "but be careful around them." She tapped his nose and winked at him, then they watched the lake and the family of swans swimming there. "They need their own space, understand? They can get grumpy when things aren't just the way they like them."

"Like mom?" Enda had asked her. She just laughed and patted his head.

This swan was certainly beautiful, but it seemed kind enough. Just scared. Its neck arched, trying to watch as Enda looked around for what could be trapping it, bleating softly as Enda's hands moved closer to its foot. Exposed roots of some lake plants tangled around the swan's foot. Enda knelt down, knees soaking in the cold lake water. He bit through the roots, grinding his teeth and tearing them apart. The roots fell away, and, feeling the freedom, the swan lifted itself into the air, landing gracefully by Enda's beached currach. Bobbing its head and trumpeting, it sidestepped on the pebbled ground in a way that made Enda think of dancing.

Pride swelled in Enda's chest. He didn't even care that his knees went numb. He laughed on the way to the boat, but when he began to pull it into the water a soft, trumpeting voice called to him.

"Thank you for saving me, boy." A lovely woman's voice came from the beak of the swan. Enda's eyes locked onto the swan's beady black ones.

"Could you help me again?" The swan stepped closer to Enda. This time Enda checked the swan from tail feathers to beak. It looked like a swan, but it certainly didn't sound like one.

"Yes, I'd like to." He nodded his head slowly. Mostly he wanted to hear the swan speak again, to see for sure if he had heard what he thought he heard. The swan waddled quickly to him.

"My name is Maeve. I used to be a princess," the swan said. She came so close her beak almost touched his nose.

Enda let go of the rope to his currach. "A real princess?"

The swan bobbed her head up and down. She had a hard time standing still. She moved in a small circle and then rustled back towards Enda. It made him feel jumpy, too.

"When I grew too wise to listen to my stepmother's lies, she called me insolent and she cursed me. She swore that in this body no one would ever listen to my cries as a swan. Until now, she spoke the truth. You must be a smart and thoughtful boy. You didn't have to save me, but you did anyway. Will you help me again? If you can't help me, I don't know if I will find anyone else."

Enda looked back to the house on the far shore of the lake. Family members still spilled in and out of the house. Surely his Grandma was still laid out on the table. If his Grandma stood next to him now she would do all she could for this swan. Now he would in her place.

He puffed out his chest and put his fists on his hips. "How can I help?"

The princess rustled her feathers, taking two wobbly, webbed steps closer to him. "There's a tale of magic water kept in a golden bowl that can change me back into a princess. The queen of the fairies keeps it in her castle ballroom, but the dragon of the lake guards her castle gates. I can't fight him. I can't pass him."

He turned and broke a long piece of reed and with the pointy end, he showed the princess swan how well he handled a sword, and what he would do to any dragon who tried to stop him. "Nothing is too dangerous for me," Enda crowed.

She honked a laugh. It made him laugh, too.

"You'll need a better sword than that, brave knight. A warrior's helmet too." The swan cooed at him. Enda had never seen a monster in real life, he thought suddenly.

"How will I find the castle gates?"

The swan stretched her neck to the far west part of the lake. "You need to dive to the bottom and walk across the lake floor, following the red light of the setting sun. Then you will find the gates."

Enda thought about his cold knees and shoes. His family told him never to go swimming in cold water. But the cold could not feel as bad for him as not ever seeing home again would for the swan. He would bear the cold.

"I don't know how to walk on the bottom of the lake," he said.

"I have the power to give you a blessing, just for tonight."

In one swift motion, the swan stretched her neck to the reed in his hand, tilted her fine head, and dripped one tear on the broken reed in Enda's hand. Then she did the same to the cloth of his shirt. Before he even felt it seep through the fabric on to his skin, a brightness buzzed all around him. The reed in his hand burned and grew in size and weight, each particle of it glowing like tiny fireflies. Enda wanted to see the glowing orbs more closely, but his vision blurred momentarily as something formed over his eyes. The visor of a helmet glittered in the sun. The weight of it pressed down on his head where nothing had been just moments before. In his hand, the broken reed turned to a spear—thick and sharp. He jabbed the spear forward while the other hand steadied the back of his helmet. Cold fabric tickled his ankles as he stepped into the jab. Surprised, he looked down and saw a shimmering blue knight's tunic. The spear, the helmet, and the knight's tunic were all real. They were heavy. They belonged to him. Enda's cry of excitement echoed off the waters and the mountain.

The swan tucked its feathers in close to its body, looking Enda over. "This is the water-tunic of Brian, one of the three sons of Turenn, and his helmet of transparent crystal. Legend claims he used these to walk under the green salt sea. Together these magic-infused relics will help you face any challenges that wait for you at the bottom of the lake. Now you must hurry. If I do not have the bowl by the time the full moon sits in it's lowest place in the sky, we will not be able to break the curse."

Enda gave the swan a big bow, the way he always imagined a hero would, and said in his most grown-up voice, "I will get thee the bowl of water, and you will be a princess again. I swear it."

As he pulled his currach into the water and paddled west, he thought of his mamma. He ought to tell her about his quest, but what if she kept him there, called him a child and ordered him to be good? What would he do in their home where his momma kept to the guests and the guests kept to his grandma, and no one let him help with a single thing?

No. Here he could do something. He could make his grandma

proud. Here he wasn't a child who needed to be good, he would be a warrior, with a real warrior's armor. He could help this swan, and when he came back, Grandma's spirit would be ready to depart safely. He would be there for that.

Enda didn't feel his body ache from paddling like before, and he'd already made it to the middle of the lake. As he looked over the edge of the currach, though, the monster in his stomach turned over itself with sharp claws. Momma and Grandma didn't let him swim alone.

Enda couldn't see the swan now, but he imagined he could hear her panicked honkings again. He had to be brave.

Enda filled his cheeks with air and swung one leg over the currach. When he tried to get the other leg off, his grip slipped and he fell back-first into the lake. Ice-cold slaps of water rose over his head. The spear in his hand and the helmet weighed him down. He tried to kick himself above the water, but the harder he kicked the further the surface seemed. The waning evening light stretched its short fingertips to him but didn't reach.

In the same instant he watched bubbles of air float above his head he also thought of his grandma's cup tucked away under a damp pile of leaves. Why did he jump off the edge of his currach? He was just his momma's little Enda boy, he wasn't a warrior. His chest hurt, his head spun, and even though he knew he shouldn't open his mouth under water, his body did it anyway. He took in one big gulp of water-

-and it turned into air in his mouth. He took in another, a fresh breath of air, and then another as his heart slowed its pounding.

The knight's tunic really did let him walk under water.

Enda punched his free hand through the water, then laughed at all the little bubbles that exploded there. He gave in to the weight of his armor and let it drag him to the bottom. There, only shadowy outlines of the plants and stones could be seen. Enda squinted, and he couldn't even make out where his currach waited above him. To the left and right, rocky mounds seemed to move and reform.

He needed to find a starting point, a direction to head. "Get to a higher point," his Grandma had taught him. The memory made him feel close to her, more than he had in all the days of her wake. He smiled while scrambling up one of the mossy boulders, trying several different holds before his fingers found secure places to launch himself further up. When he found a perch, the shadowy floor of the lake spun out before him. Fish moved like one in and out of tendrils of plants. The farther away they got the more they seemed like ghosts. A gate with white rungs that were set deeply into a stone ledge gave off a white glow that stood apart from the dreariness of the rest of the lake. *Surely no person made a gate at the bottom of a lake,* Enda thought and turned so his belly slid down the other side of the boulder. His feet landed in the silt, sending a cloud all around him, and he trudged across the lake towards it.

Moss and slimy plants covered the white rungs completely. Enda scrunched his nose but reached out to rub some moss away. It made his insides creep just as much as it excited him. Enda searched the gates up and down, but there was no handle. When he pulled on the rungs they would not budge. He kicked off the lake floor and swam to the top, hoping he could squeeze through somewhere, but the gate was swallowed up in rock. There was no way in.

Frustration burned in his chest. If he were big, he could open the door. He tore a plant out of the ground and squished it hard in his hand. If a grown-up were here, they would be able to do it. But grandma was gone. The only grown up he had left was too busy. Enda clenched his teeth together. The back of his neck hurt. With a furrowed brow he turned in place looking for something. A key maybe?

He huffed and glared at the stream of bubbles floating up, up, up until he saw the shadow of a creature floating in the distance. Enda froze. That was a big creature. Its shadow stretched out too long, and spikes seemed to come off every side. The way it wiggled towards him made Enda's insides itch to run away. The gated rock wall against his back trapped him. Every moment he stared at the creature, the bigger it grew. Enda looked at the sprawling lake floor—nowhere to hide. He felt like food.

Enda whimpered. He wanted his grandma, right now. With the spear clutched in his hand, he side stepped along the ledge. He closed his eyes, though he knew he shouldn't, and reached out his free hand, hoping to feel a spot big enough to hide him. It was all pointless.

Enda willed himself to look again, and his heart skipped. It wasn't a shadow anymore. Bright red eyes and a maw of bared teeth as long as his whole hand were perfectly clear now. Talloned claws propelled the beast through the water, and webbed spines burst through green scales all over its body. The dragon of the lake was staring right at him, and the closer it got the wider its mouth grew.

Enda's screams were swallowed up in water, but his fear was not. He raked his fingers over the stone ledge. He needed to crawl up, he needed to escape the lake. His warm bed, his momma—she would never find him down here. She wouldn't be able to protect him. Enda's grip slipped and it slipped again. Long claws crushed into the rock around him. The rock crumbled under the force, and Enda felt immensely small. He curled in a ball and sank to the floor.

No. No. No. Why isn't grandma here to help me? Why isn't anyone here! Why am I not big enough?

The dragon lowered its massive head and roared right over Enda. The sound and fear shot through him like sharp electricity. Its cold tail slithered around his belly and squeezed the breath out of him, pulling him up off the ground.

Slam. It thrust him head first into the rock wall. Clanging filled Enda's ears, inescapable. He clenched his eyes shut. There was too much noise; he couldn't make it stop. His hands pushed against each side of his helmet, trying to make it stop.

The dragon gurgled a frustrated growl and smacked Enda against the wall again with enough force Enda knew his head should have shattered, but it didn't. He rubbed the cold surface of his helmet again. It protected him. As more ringing cleared, and Enda felt himself being pulled away for another thrashing, he realized that the helmet matched every blow the dragon inflicted perfectly, never denting, never moving. Perfect.

The swan, she protected him. The thought filled Enda with hot air. He might not be big enough, but this magic was. Enda thrashed his body as wildly as he could, pushing against the tough scale of the dragon's tail, gripping his spear. He popped out, suspended for a moment in the water. Quickly, he looked for the white gate. Perhaps the dragon was the key, he thought. Could he move faster than the dragon? Fast enough to get to the gate first? Enda kicked through the water, but each movement was too slow. A rough growl rumbled from Enda's chest and he kicked harder, pushed faster.

The dragon turned to face Enda head on. He could reach out and touch the gate now, but he could do nothing to stop the dragon from swallowing him. Not alone. If the helmet had protected him against its strength, the Swan's spear must be able to do the rest. The thought gave him courage as he readied himself. Hand latched onto one rung of the gate, knees bent, Enda launched himself at the dragon. With an anger so much bigger than him, he roared and thrust his spear forward. The water resisted his every movement, but the spear's tip found its mark, piercing the dragon's gleaming, red eye. The light behind it dimmed as blood floated upwards like a cloud in the water. Its pained cry rattled every inch of the lake, sending ripples through the water.

Enda thought the sound rattled the gate so fiercely that the white rungs started to hum. But as the cry settled, the humming only grew more intense. Enda wanted to watch the gate begin to shine even brighter, vibrating against the rock, but two thuds of the dragon's feet landed solidly on the ground in front of him, its mouth pulled back in a snarl. Before it could clamp its teeth around him, a current of water sucked Enda away from the beast. The sight of the dragon blurred in the rush of water.

Enda landed rump first on sun warmed sand, sputtering. He grabbed his spear and scrambled to his feet. The surprise would give the dragon the seconds it needed to finish him off. Yet, where he expected to see it charging after him, instead he saw the gate squealing shut against the water and back into the stone of its own accord, blocking Enda from the lake and the dragon.

His clothes dripped as his fingers pressed down on coarse sand and small white rocks. A gentle breeze dried the baby hairs on the back of his neck. Enda looked around at this strange place he'd been pulled into. The shore he sat on met no waves, only the edge of a rocky wall. The same wall, Enda realized, that had once been under the lake. Behind him, a forest of trees full of green leaves and flowering fruit sat a short distance from a grassy, green meadow. This didn't feel like a place for a little boy. Why hadn't he told his mamma that he had left?

From the darkness of those trees Enda heard a voice, or at least he thought he did. He took a step closer, tilting his head so he could catch the sound better.

"Enda boy!" called his Grandma's voice.

"Grandma?" he mouthed, the word caught in his throat. It had been days since he last heard her voice. How did she get here, though? He couldn't see her, or anything else, past the large trunks and thick branches.

"Grandma, come out. I'm right here." His voice squeaked. A shudder shook him from his head to his toes. If Grandma was here she would give him a warm hug; he would ask her not to ever let him go. Holding on to the thought like a string, he scurried to the tree line.

"Enda boy." His Grandma's voice sounded like a soft whisper now, something he felt in his heart more than heard. In the darkness of the forest, a pulsing orb of light appeared farther ahead, tree trunks almost obscuring it. His heart raced and he took a couple steps into the forest, squinting to see it better. From behind one tree trunk to the next, Enda crept toward the light and the feeling that he wasn't going to be alone anymore. The closer he got, the more a shadowed form flickered within the light. Grandma! He sucked in a breath and jumped out from behind the tree.

The orb burst. Heart sinking, Enda scurried to the spot. There wasn't even a singed blade of grass to prove it had been there.

"Enda, have you been good?"

Enda turned, and the light glowed for him again further in the forest, waiting. He must be faster this time. Dashing through the trees, he leaped over roots and scrambled through bushes. Yet the light burst again just as his fingers could reach it. Enda put his hands on his knees to catch his breath. Very slowly he scanned the forest in one wide circle. Where had the sand gone? Or the gate? In chasing the light he hadn't thought to keep track of where he came from. He couldn't even see the sun through the cover of leaves. And for all of this he still couldn't see the orb of light.

Enda kicked the base of the thick tree next to him. The leaves didn't even quiver. He kicked it harder, then he kicked it with the other foot. He yelled and kicked it until it hurt his knees. His Grandma had been here, he was sure of it, but now she was gone. She didn't even say goodbye.

He hadn't either. Enda ran off to play that night, his Grandma wrapped in her blanket, his mom warming up soup for the three of them. He didn't want to wait; he had treasures to find. His grandma had called out for him to be safe, but he let her words carry off on the wind without even looking back.

Just like now, she had been there, and then she hadn't.

"Why won't you come back?" Enda called out to his grandma, wherever she was. What would a real warrior do?

"I'm sorry I wasn't good," he whispered. "I'll be good now, just please, Grandma, help me one last time." He turned in a circle again.

"You are my little warrior. My little Enda boy."

Enda whipped around. The light, a hand swipe away from him, lit up the forest. He expected the light to be warm, like a fire, but it didn't feel like anything. He expected to see Grandma, and though a shadowy form bobbed somewhere in the middle of the orb, he could never seem to catch a good look at who or what it was.

Enda rubbed his hands, not trusting he could keep himself from touching the light and knowing he couldn't stand to lose it again. "I just want to help the swan princess. I can't do it by myself. Stay with me?"

In the distance, a tinkling floated to his ears. Was the sound laughter? Was it music?

"Is this it, will this take me to the fairy castle?"

The orb didn't change. He reached out and put his hand just on the outside of the brightness, holding his breath. This time it didn't burst. He wanted to ask it to follow him, to stay just a while longer. Would he be able to say goodbye?

"Thank you," Enda said. For the last time, the light burst.

Enda ran towards the sound, stopping now and then to concentrate on where it must be coming from. The trees thinned around him. The air smelled like flower petals. When the sound and the smell overpowered everything else, Enda finally saw a meadow full of fairies dancing to their own laughter and the sound of tiny harps. They wore bright fabrics in yellows and purples and reds that flowed when they moved, their hair twirled around them. They held blades of grass in their hands like streamers that twisted and flowed around them in loops, and as the grass unfurled, they tumbled laughing.

Enda was entranced. It seemed to him they turned into flowers and then back into fairies as they danced. He wanted to touch one, to see if they disappeared like the ball of light had. He wanted them to dance on his fingertips to see if their feet tickled. The wonder was so strong he couldn't help but step out from the cover of the foliage and into the meadow. The light cracking of leaves under his leather shoes made the fairies freeze. Every tiny head turned in his direction, eyes wide with fear. Before he could reach out to stop them, they darted under leaves, behind pebbles, and into rotted logs. Just like that, the meadow emptied and stilled without a lick of evidence there had ever been a fairy there at all.

Except for one. In splendid glory, she stood tall on a branch that stuck out from a tree into the meadow. This fairy wore a dress with a skirt full of the burnt red leaves of fall and a crown of gold wire on her head.

"I know why you're here, Enda," she called in a chirping voice, then stomped her foot on the branch, making the leaves quiver. In response, the rest of the fairies stepped timidly from their hiding places, heads down or turned away from Enda. The fairy on the branch, the queen, leaped from the branch and fluttered to face him.

"Your helmet and spear scare my subjects, knight. There's no need for them here. Leave them in the meadow."

Now that she hovered closer, Enda could see the beautiful features of her face, her fierce eyes and opal skin. Enda dropped the spear on the soft, carpeting grass. He lifted the helmet off his head and let it roll from his fingers. The Fairy Queen smiled at him then flew once around his head. He tried to keep her in his sight, but to turn so fast made him dizzy.

"Shall we welcome our new guest?" The queen crowed. All at once, the rest of the fairies joined her in the sky, their laughter and singing filling the air once more.

"You come for a bowl of golden water, young Enda." The queen laughed from overhead. "You can have it, but only after you dine with us first."

The fairies cheered and made a colorful line that threaded through the trees deeper into the forest. Enda felt a giggle bubbling in his chest. The queen beckoned Enda to follow, before joining her subjects. He felt strange not taking his helmet and his spear with him. What if he needed them? He hesitated for a second. The sound of the fairies started to fade. He ran after them into the depths of the forest until the line of fairies sang over his head once again.

No STONE or gem had ever shone as brightly as the queen's castle. Built into the trunk of a grand tree that grew out of a split in a rock, the walls only reached his knees. Enda's hand would never fit through the front door, let alone the rest of him.

The queen landed gently on his shoulder. She whispered in his ear, "We'll have to make you the right size first." Her whisper tickled, but he didn't wiggle for fear of squishing her. That tickle spread down his neck and his arms and all the way to his toes. It made him laugh and he couldn't stop. When he finally caught his breath, the castle had grown so much he had to tilt his head all the way back to see the tallest spires. The doors alone now looked taller than his house.

"Call the bard! Call the jesters!" The queen twirled like a leaf on the breeze. "Tonight Sir Enda dines with the fairies!"

Magnificent cheers erupted all around Enda. Lulling harp music pulled them into the castle where fairies in red dresses laid out fresh petals for the queen. Fairies flooded into the ballroom. Long golden tables set with jeweled dishes held glorious piles of food. In the middle of the display, where Enda expected to see the grandest dish of all, the court presented the cracked, clay, hand-pressed cup his Grandma made instead. It was plain in comparison to the fairies' dishes, but Enda couldn't take his eyes off it. With sap-slow steps Enda let the music of the festivities fade into the background and moved to the cup. He tipped the edge towards him and a golden liquid came right to the brim. When fairies passed by, they bowed their heads and whispered reverently before dancing on.

The fairy queen, who stood at eye level with Enda now, pulled his hand, suggesting he step away from the table, but this time he couldn't move. He needed to know how the cup moved from the safe spot in the wall of his house to the queen's table.

The queen's thin fingers cupped his chin and turned his head towards her. When his eyes could no longer see the cup, she spread the edges of her beautiful dress and curtsied.

"May we dance?" She smiled, and Enda nodded slowly. He would ask her about the cup, about when he could have it back. As she led him in a lilting dance, spinning them around the room, the colored windows, bright court clothes, the gleaming table all blurred at the edges of his vision.

"You must be brave to help someone you don't know, Enda." The fairy queen smiled at him. Enda's cheeks felt warm; he had never been complimented by a queen before.

"Can I have my cup now, please, so the swan can be safe?" Enda's voice came out a whisper. If the queen heard it over the music she didn't show it, so Enda cleared his throat and tried again. "I wondered—if you don't mind me asking—if you had the golden water and knew the swan needed it, why didn't you give it to her?"

"Silly boy, just because something seems it could be easily solved, doesn't mean that it is so." The queen's tinkling laugh made Enda smile, but something nibbled at his heart that made the smile feel like it didn't belong on his face.

"Could you not give it to her because of the dragon? Does it trap you here, too?" Whatever trapped the queen so she couldn't even free herself despite all her magic, would certainly keep him here forever as well. Was anything he had done to this point enough?

"Maybe." She shrugged. "Maybe I'm trapped just as you trapped the cup in the hidey-hole. Just as you were trapped on the dock. Just as your momma is trapped with her family. Just as the swan is trapped. If things are where they must be, does that mean they are trapped? Or are they free?" As they spun around and around, her dress flowed in ripples around them both. The music played faster and faster as they moved. All the colors of the fairy's clothing flashed too quickly. He riddled through her question, trying to focus, but he couldn't understand one bit of what she asked.

"I heard my grandma calling me. Is she stuck here, too?" His heart squeezed, remembering the sound of her in the forest. Was she here because she was looking for the cup? Perhaps he was too late, and she'd missed her chance to the Otherworld. Enda chewed his cheek, and his throat tightened.

"Oh, little one, you worry too much for someone so young. But you fight like a true warrior. I could use someone like you on my guard. You could go on adventures every day. Doesn't that sound like fun? Not a single of my guards has ever defeated a dragon."

Not a single one? Enda's eyes grew wide as pride washed over the worry.

"I could order armor to be made just for you, a sword just for you. Can you imagine it? Your grandma would be so proud."

"She always told me stories of adventures," Enda said, wondering what it might be like if one of those stories had been about him. How wonderful would that be?

"So you'll stay here with me then?" The queen smiled. She tightened her hand on his shoulder. Perhaps she didn't mean to, but it hurt him. Enda looked down at her hand just as they spun past the table. They moved too fast for him to see his grandma's cup. He wanted to slow down. He wanted to think. He wanted to be a warrior. Except... the cup.

"I want to go home," he said. It sounded like a whimper. He didn't mean for it to, but he had never wished his grandma stood next to him more than he did right now. She could tell him what he needed to do.

The queen's head pulled back, her brows pinched in the middle. "You don't want to go back home, Enda. To feel ignored? To live without your grandma? That sounds so lonely. You aren't needed there. But look what you've already accomplished here. Look who you could become! Don't go home, stay with me."

Enda tried to pull away, but the queen's grip tightened on his shoulders. Before a thought could stop him, he stomped his heels hard on her toes.

She cried out, a tearing sound that broke through the merriments.

The music, the dancers, the jester—they all came to a screeching halt. All eyes narrowed at Enda. The guards who posted at the doors of the ballroom drew their spears, ready to defend their queen.

Tears welled in Enda's eyes. He had not come this far to not make it home. He took a step back, but even a step away from the queen meant a step closer to her subjects or the guards. Enda felt the loss of his spear and helmet now. If only he had kept them.

"I'm sorry," he said, hands balling up in front of his eyes. "I'm sorry, but that's my grandma's cup. There's a swan waiting for me. I want to stay, I do. But I wouldn't be a hero if I did. I only came here to be a hero."

Moments longer than any Enda had experienced ticked on while he waited for the queen to send her guards to take him away.

Instead, she smiled as if she had won a game. "If we could get the cup to the swan? If I promised her safety, would you stay?"

The swan would become a princess. He would be her hero, a true warrior, just like in grandma's stories. This beautiful castle and all the queen's promises could not replace his home. And maybe he could live as a warrior here, but he wanted to be Enda boy there. With or without his grandma.

Enda bowed his head and shook it. "I'm sorry." He thought that getting away from his home, that becoming a strong warrior, would make him feel better. But now the world seemed so much bigger than he had thought.

The fairy queen sighed and stroked his head in a way that reminded him of his mamma.

"One last dance then," she said and waved her hand above her head. The music struck up in slowed drawn-out notes, and he couldn't spin away from the sadness it brought to him. The queen pulled him along in a slow waltz. She smelled like roses and wet dirt, and the smell made him think of their lake. The bursting colors of the hall became fuzzy. The sounds came to him through a tunnel. Enda stretched his face, trying to stay alert, but as the fairy queen spun him around one last time, his eyes finally closed.

～

WHEN ENDA WOKE UP, he wore his own clothes again. They were drenched through with lake water. The sun had almost disappeared, and the evening air smelled like something familiar, but Enda felt too tired to remember what. He lifted his head just slightly from the floor of the currach. Every muscle in his body ached, and even that much movement seemed beyond him. From what he could see, no spear, helmet, or knight's tunic were with him in the currach.

The boat tipped suddenly to one side, and his mamma's face, the skin around her eyes red and puffy, appeared.

"Enda MacGearailt thank your lucky stars I found ya," She pulled herself into the boat, her own dress soaked from the waist down, and she scooped Enda onto her lap and squeezed him so hard he would have complained, but this time he didn't. A shiver ran through them, and only upon her lap could he see over the edge of the boat. The rope that tied the currach off trailed loosely in the water, and they drifted just a couple lengths from their home. Not as far as the reeds that caught the swan, and not as far as where he found the Lake Dragon. How had he ended up here? Where had the swan gone?

Enda's mamma kissed him on his wet hair, the tip of his nose, and every bit of skin on his cheek.

"The currach isn't yours to take out! What in your right mind were ya thinking?" His momma bent her face so that their noses touched and he could see the fury in her eyes up close, but a tear, or maybe a drop of lake water, dripped from her cheek to his. She pulled him close again. "Oh my Enda boy," she muttered.

"I had to save a swan, Momma. She was a princess. No one could help her but me." Enda tried to explain in between his momma's kisses and squeezing.

"A princess swan?" His momma pulled away just long enough to look at him and shake her head.

Enda thought he should explain more, but the cold of the water set in, and his body began to shake. Curling up into her embrace warmed him to his core. His body ached more than ever. Maybe now they could go home. Maybe Momma would ask everyone to leave so he could sleep. Then his grandma could have plenty of space to find her way to the Otherworld.

He wiggled on his momma's lap until his legs wrapped around her waist, his arms wrapped around her neck and his chin rested on her shoulder. Her arms secured his place there, her cheek pressed against the top of his head. Enda wondered about the fairy queen and the orb of light in the forest near her home. He wondered about dragons lurking in the water on the other side. Had it all been a dream? If only he had held onto the spear and the helmet. Then he might be sure.

Like a low moan, keening started from the house. The mourning cries of women turned into wailings. Now Grandma's spirit would find its place in the Otherworld.

Enda's momma let go of him for the first time so she could row them back home. "It's time to go." Enda's eyes went wide and he pointed behind her where a bend in the shore hid a part of the lake from them. She turned to see a great white swan, whiter than any others on their lake, drifting towards their currach until it was close enough to put its head over the side and press it against Enda's arm.

Enda's momma leaned sharply away to keep them from the swan, but Enda reached out to stroke it's beak anyways.

"Don't worry, momma." Enda looked her right in the eyes, so his momma knew she could trust him. To his surprise she allowed him to guide her hand straight to the swan's long neck, and when she felt the softness for herself he heard her catch her breath. Enda wondered if she ever touched a swan before, or if his momma ever danced with the fairy queen as a little girl? If not, he, his momma's little boy, got to show his momma something new. His mom would see him as a big boy now, just like grandma always had.

His Grandma. Her cup. The swan only swam to their curragh because she expected him to have the cup.

The keening behind them grew louder. It echoed off the mountain walls. Enda thought at any moment it might shake the lake.

"Enda, if we want to say goodbye we need to go now. Ready?" his momma asked. He couldn't say yes. He had sworn to help this swan. He had conquered the lake to do so, but he had come back with nothing more than memories for himself. Could he leave her here to say his goodbyes? Enda couldn't quite answer yes to that either. He never took his Grandma's cup back from the Queen. He had been too distracted. Could he go back and say goodbye, knowing that he lost his grandma's cup? Knowing she'd certainly go looking for it, if she wasn't already?

As his momma turned to situate the oars, Enda curled up tighter in her lap. Tears stung his eyes. His adventure had been for nothing. The curragh shifted far to one side, and then the other in the water as it turned. Before it came back to an even place, a solid *thunk* against the canvas side made Enda's head popped up, and his mom turned to look. Turned upright, having slid under the wooden seat of the curragh, his Grandma's cup hid perfectly intact and full of a shimmering golden liquid. Enda's heart pounded. He scrambled off his mother's lap. He tried to move carefully so the curragh wouldn't rock and spill all the precious liquid, but Enda could only go so slow in his excitement and some slipped over the rim of the cup anyways. With two gentle hands, Enda picked up the cup and dripped its contents on the head of the swan. The swan ruffled her feathers, specks of water beading and shooting off in all directions. She stretched out her wings, neck pulling towards the sky. Enda turned to his mother. He could feel his smile, so big it made his cheeks hurt.

"I did it, momma," the whisper buzzed out of him.

"A princess?" He mother gaped. Enda turned back to the swan. She pressed the side of her head against Enda's cheek. Enda wondered if she would miss her feathers at all. Without any more of a goodbye, the swan turned and swam towards the far shores where, Enda hoped, she would make her way safely back home. He leaned on the side of the curragh, waving frantically. The boat tipped sharply.

"Oh!" His mother gasped, and then laughed as she steadied herself. Enda liked the way it sounded. Happy. Lighter than she had for the last few days. She kneeled and reached for Enda again, setting him in her lap and nuzzling the hair on her head.

"I'm ready to go home now." Enda laughed. He had his Grandma's cup tightly in the crook of his arm. He would always miss it, but he knew now that he could give it back to his Grandma and still have her close by.

Together, Enda and his momma brought the boat to shore. When Enda's momma lifted him out, she didn't let go of him again. Not when they went into their home to join the keening, and not as she said goodbye to all their family. Then, as they nestled into bed, Enda caught a glow from the shore out of their window. A woman dressed in all white illuminated in the moonlight stood waving just to him.

THE HOUSE ON
BLAUBART STREET

SARAH LYNN EATON

Author's Note: When I was a child I was obsessed with the French fairy tale, Bluebeard. It originally appeared in the 1697 compilation Histoires ou contes du temps passé by Charles Perrault. What a horrible story for young children. Do as your husband says or you'll find out he's a serial killer? Should she not have looked? Would they have lived happily ever after if she had never looked? Was that the lesson in the story?

Of all the fairy tales, I understood the message of that one the least. I read it as a cautionary tale about the world. Where, in Beauty and the Beast the monster is revealed to have become a good man, in Bluebeard the good, wealthy, land-owning man is revealed to be the monster. It could have been a modern story. We're still discovering monsters hiding in the open as community men in good standing.

I didn't want to retell the horror. I didn't want to sit in his head. How would you react to learning that you lived with a monster? What if you discovered you were connected to someone capable of such atrocities? Where would that sit in you? Would it be possible to move past it? What might that take?

What if Bluebeard's horrible act was the beginning of someone else's story? Soon after that thought, a scene unfolded in my head. I met Laurel and Anne, in their apartment kitchen, a week before this story takes place. That moment resulted in the birth of this story.

A warm summer breeze floated down Blaubart Street as a yellow four-door Volvo stopped at the curb halfway down. The woman inside glanced curiously at the unoccupied red-brick manor house nestled generously between two modern family homes. Laurel Jefferies leaned her elbow out of the open car window, drumming her fingers across the outer door. A thick envelope sat in her lap. She tied her dark hair back in a ponytail and sipped water while contemplating the abandoned house.

It hid partially behind an iron gate and a thick yew hedge, and Laurel was grateful that the house was unable to stare back at her. She supposed the decorative iron grates over the windows kept out trespassers, and the trimmed hedge was meant to discourage ne'er-do-wells, but there was no life to the place. Two young boys walking home from school hesitated at the edge of the property before they raced each other to the other end.

This house is not a home, she thought. *Children always know.*

This one had an ugly history. Five women had been murdered in the Blaubart House by a madman who had been a pillar of the community. Laurel's parents had been the last to die inside it. Her hands shook.

Yay, she thought, staring at the deed in her lap. *I own the murder house now.*

Beneath the deed was a last letter from her aunt. Its content was mundane enough that Laurel searched it for a cryptic cipher. It was the first one she had ever learned, containing a message spelled out by every seventh word.

Cleanse the house on Blaubart Street.

She'd been studying to do just that her whole life, but staring at the house, Laurel was terrified. Her world had been upended. The two women had meant to do it together.

We waited too long.

The leaves on the trees whispered outside the car. They lifted upside-down, gently stirring, and the daylight shimmered leaving an almost invisible trail towards the car. Laurel's heart quickened at the familiar sign. She rooted through her bag for one of her jars and placed a small sprig of lavender under her tongue. Laurel softened her gaze on the empty passenger seat.

"Reveal," she whispered.

A subtle human shape swirled like smoke and dust trapped in a sunbeam in the corner of the vehicle where shadow met light. A woman with curly hair and the transparency of fog flickered in and out of focus. In life her hair had been strawberry-blonde and she held the softened look of someone who had been beautiful in her youth.

"Hello, pumpkin."

"I wasn't sure I'd see you again." Laurel took measured breaths. Her heart was trapped between joy and sorrow, just as her aunt was trapped between death and life.

"You've always been able to see beings in the spirit world. Why should I be any different?"

"I wanted it too much."

Anne reached across the seat to grasp her niece's hand and chuckled as her hand passed through the living flesh. Laurel felt it as a whisper against her skin of what-almost-was and it caught in her throat.

"I guess we knew it might be like this," Anne joked.

"I'm not laughing," Laurel said sharply.

"I know." The ghost turned to stare at the house. "It doesn't look nearly as impressive as it thinks it is. I didn't mean to leave you with my unfinished business."

"I know," Laurel replied. After Anne's cancer surfaced they thought her treatments would buy them a few more years. Laurel's young body suddenly shivered involuntarily at the thought of being in a house that had sat empty and lifeless. "I'd like to be done before dark."

"You've never done a job this big on your own before."

"I've never had to." Laurel bit back the bitterness, focusing on having gratitude for the mere sound of Anne's voice. She braced her shaking hands against the steering wheel. "I'm a Jefferies, Aunt. I can do anything."

"Magic's in the blood. Which I no longer possess." Anne laughed weakly. "Sorry."

"I found something else in your safety deposit box." Laurel fished a small velvet pouch out of her bag, pouring out a necklace made of small black faceted beads. A two inch-long, rectangular three-sided iron pendant hung heavily off a silver fob. Laurel cocked her head questioningly.

The ghost struggled for the thread of memory attached to the object. "You were wearing that when I found you. It belonged to Mary. I forgot about it." She glanced at the house. "The stone is black tourmaline." Anne brightened in sudden recognition and then quieted down.

"What?" Laurel looked expectantly at the necklace in her hand. *My mother's necklace.*

"I left the oven on when I collapsed," she said, heavy with regret. "Would you believe I was going to tell you everything over some birthday cake?"

"What's left to tell?" The seconds sitting between them seemed to lengthen and twist and eat away at the oxygen in the car. The ghost blinked away.

Laurel's ribcage ached. She took deep breaths. She pulled on the door handle and got out of the car, grabbing her messenger bag. There was nothing unusual about her cargo pants and embroidered peasant blouse. She was an average woman of average height coming to do an average, run-of-the-mill spirit cleansing on a murder house.

Aunt Anne won't be able to rest until this business is done. That was true. Then Laurel would lose her all over again. But everything dead deserved peace. She had to see it through. She pushed the key into the lock.

Anne flickered onto the porch. Laurel turned to her. "I shut the oven off when I found you."

"Oh. Good. It was quick, when it happened," Anne offered.

"That's something then," Laurel said.

"I'll see you inside," said Anne, disappearing again. Laurel turned the key and her stomach went with it as she opened the front door. It was solid and heavy and swung inward easily.

The house was modest inside. Light-colored walls were framed with dark wood. There were no signs of break-ins or squatters. It looked as if the inhabitants of the house had disappeared where they stood, and the house had simply fallen asleep. Waiting. There were no strange voices. No flickering lights. No floating furniture. No creepy sensation. It was wood and drywall and paint and memories that didn't belong to her.

But something was there. Waiting.

"It's like a horrible time capsule," Anne said, unsettled.

"It's just a house." Laurel didn't feel anything more than that. She moved into the living room where the dust was riotous. She folded all of the sheets up into wads to keep the offending grit at bay while she worked sorting her supplies.

She had herbs in jars, bottles of oils, ancient salts, sage bundles, candles, and a handful of small but mighty lanterns. She had a box full of crystals, including the ones meant to imitate the bones of those victims found in the house.

Laurel shivered at that thought now that she was on the inside. *This is where my parents died.* Their bodies had never been recovered. But their blood had. There had been too much blood for them to have survived. She looked at the floors around her.

"We cleaned up that much," Anne said from the hallway. "I had it cleaned and then I locked the door."

With three deep breaths, Laurel brought her focus to the center of her body. She moved to the first window and drew a symbol of protection and containment taught to her by her aunt, using a small vial of angelica in safflower oil. She was careful not to break the line. She drew the symbol on every window and laid a bundle of sage and holy basil in the outside corner of the house. She felt the edges of her body blur as she moved throughout the rooms with half-sight, marking the openings and laying herbs at edges, building a wall between the house and the world outside.

The floor plan was simple enough. Five rooms on the first floor. Six rooms on the second floor. Open floor in the basement.

Laurel found Anne in the kitchen, staring at the cabinets. "It feels strange. I'm here but not here. Like a dream that flickers in and out of focus and time keeps jumping and it's hard to catch hold. But then it doesn't matter. None of this matters. But it does. I want it to and then it does and I remember and it hurts and there's you and then"—she phased out and back in with a crackle of ozone—"when I come back, there's you again and I remember why I'm here. Unfinished business."

Laurel nodded. It wasn't anything she hadn't heard from other spirits. She couldn't take it personally.

"Down to the center now," Anne pointed to a wood panel next to the silent fridge.

Only then did the gnawing thought in Laurel's brain burst into form. She snapped her head around the hallway. The entrances to the living room, dining room, and study were all sleekly framed in dark wood unmarred by hinges.

"There are no doors on any of the rooms," she remarked.

"Not a one," Anne replied. "When Mary remodeled, she could not stand the thought of ghosts hiding behind doors. So she took them out." Anne faded, barely visible against the wallpaper.

Laurel slid the panel open but looked back at her aunt, worried. Spirits were made of emotional energy. They could be easily trapped by sorrow and regret. She wasn't sure how hard it was going to get for Anne. Turning on a lantern, she descended into the dark.

The cellar was stacked with labeled boxes and pieces of furniture, too grand and ostentatious for the items upstairs. She reached out to touch a hideously carved cherub bedpost and a wilting label fluttered on a nearby box. Laurel snatched her hand back.

Is it possible? Did they belong to him? The man who killed my parents?

All of the boxes around her had eyes. She had never felt it so keenly. Of all the houses she and Anne had cleansed together, the worst had been three deaths to a house fire.

This one would be harder.

"Laurel?"

She looked up the stairs for her aunt.

"Laurel?"

The voice echoed behind her, from the far corner. The hair on her arms slowly rippled to attention. Laurel cleared her throat and spoke to the ether without turning. "Don't be alarmed. I'm here to help."

Laurel cleared a space in the middle of the floor and laid down a generous bed of nettles with two large double-terminated crystals crossed over each other so each point faced an outside corner. If she did it right, the adopted ley lines would connect with the sage bundles in the outside corners of both floors upstairs.

Nothing in, nothing out, she thought. *Not until we're ready.*

She cracked open the jar of asafoetida, wrinkling her nose at the offending odor. It was a smell foul enough to chase away ghosts for good, and she hoped it would do just that as its energy moved through the house. She sprinkled it liberally in a spiral around the nettles, fanning it into all corners of the storage space, leaving the sage bundles to the last.

A soft sigh filled the room. Laurel smiled, placing the lantern at the bottom of the stairs. It was a good start. *So far so good.*

The kitchen was empty when she returned. Laurel went back down the hallway to the front stairwell, paying more attention to the lack of doors. It was the oddest sensation. The house felt completely open, only instead of pockets of air it was as if the house took one giant steadying breath.

There was no room for secrets.

"I'm sorry, Mary," Laurel spoke to the emptiness around her. She replenished her supplies in the living room and then climbed the stairs.

Laurel continued her work through the rooms upstairs, starting in the library, an office, and what must have been a guest room. Each had the bare minimum of necessary furniture. But it felt empty. There were no personal touches. No photos. No art. No embroidered pillows.

The walls of the house responded to the magic, closing in like a blanket. The container was almost ready. The sliding pocket door to the bathroom stood open.

"Close the door," a genderless voice whispered. Laurel's hand was on it, pulling it shut. She stopped and stepped backwards. She hadn't meant to do that.

"Anne?" she called out. *Shit.* Her heart raced. Everything her caretaker had ever taught her flashed through her. "They will try to confuse you, to throw you off track. They have become what happened to them. They are not who they were. Five women were killed in this house. The murderer fled. He came back a year later and killed two more."

Almost three.

She finished the bathroom quickly, giving the voice no attention, before moving on. While the other rooms presented like a forgotten, sad spread of *Neglected Housekeeping*, the child's room, painted in a thick disco-yellow, made her blood turn cold. A crib stood in one corner beside a rocking chair. Their mismatched look read as an afterthought. Her hand left a deep imprint in the dust.

"She would have loved you," Anne said calmly beside her. "She was a little broken, but she would have loved you." Laurel swung away to hide her tears. Anne frowned as she shimmered into sharper focus. "It's garish now, but yellow was a popular color. At the time."

Laurel swallowed hard and finished marking the windows.

"The house feels better already," Anne remarked. "It's not as hard as I thought it would be."

Being a ghost or being in the house? Laurel wondered but did not ask. "I don't think a house can be evil. You know that."

"How much blood can mortar and timber absorb before it gets a taste for it?" Anne replied. "I mean, how can people be evil? No one thought Vincent was."

"Did you know him?" Laurel asked. There was a note in Anne's voice that softened in the way she said his name. The ghost turned her head.

"Everyone did." Her translucent form flickered.

There were two rooms left. The first was a master bedroom. Male toiletries sat on the dresser and the closet was full of men's clothing. Nothing else. Laurel set her bag down and stepped into the second one.

A pang in her gut told her it was her mother's room. The lilac walls must have been bright when fresh but were the same gray as everything else under the dust. A bathrobe hung on the back of the door. Laurel rubbed the silk between her fingers.

Hello, Mary. She balled a fist into the dusty silk. Her heart unexpectedly tripped over the thought that something of her mother remained.

"Why did my parents have separate rooms?" Laurel asked,

returning to the male room. The light through the windows was growing dim. She rifled through the nightstand and found two frames tucked away. The first showed a young woman with strawberry-blonde curls on a picnic blanket, smiling at the camera coquettishly. "Aunt Anne," she said, teasing. The ghost peered over her shoulder.

"I gave that to him as a birthday present when we were sixteen."

Laurel raised her eyebrow. She saw her aunt's heart clearly for the first time.

"You were sweet on him."

"I never told him. Or Mary. I wanted her to have him. That's how much I loved her. She was my baby sister, with the kindest heart, and after what happened... I would have given my life for you to have a normal one."

"I did have a normal one, Anne," Laurel assured her softly, but the ghosts did not seem to hear her. After discovering the separate living spaces, she wasn't sure she would have had a happier life with her parents.

The second photo was of the three friends—Anne, Mary, and Eric. Laurel's insides ran cold. Anne and Mary were both strawberry-blonde and fair. Eric's hair was more platinum. Laurel tugged on the ends of her raven-dark locks.

"Eric was a brother to us. Of course when Mary discovered she was pregnant, he offered to be your father. He would have loved you."

"What are you saying?"

"It was a marriage of convenience," Anne said.

"What do you mean?" Laurel asked, spinning to face her.

"I was going to tell you everything."

"Eric isn't my father?" Laurel lost her focus. "We don't keep secrets, Anne. That is the fundamental foundation of our relationship. Why did my mother live here?"

"You don't know what I saw in this house." The ghost flashed like lightning in the darkening room. "I was going to tell you everything over birthday cake."

A cracking sound split the air in half and Anne disappeared. Laurel's hands shook. Her brain needed words, needed to hear her aunt say the words that her bones were already accepting. The magic was in her blood. In the blood soaked into the house. They were bound together.

The floor groaned beneath her. What payment would be required to bring it peace? Laurel finished the rooms. There were bundles left at every corner of the house on every floor. She had to find the approximate center of the second floor, like she did in the basement. Her aunt stood in the hallway, flickering.

"Leave now," Anne pleaded. "This was a mistake."

Laurel's heart quickened at the sudden fear in Anne's voice. "Let's finish up so we can get you and me out of here—"

"Just go!" Anne yelled. Her face contorted and twisted.

She was upended again. Her heart sank beneath her gut and her gut leapt into her throat. The walls around her weakened. She was too distracted. "Why did you keep such a truth from me?"

"We all found it hard to believe that the charming, charitable Vincent Blaubart was capable of such horror and violence." Anne paused. "I wouldn't have believed it possible till your mother found the bodies. Vincent disappeared. Mary discovered she was pregnant."

"With me." The skin Laurel had worn all her days felt foreign and familiar all at once.

"Can you blame me for not wanting to tell you?" The specter's voice was a whisper. "The night you were born Mary called me. 'I just gave birth to a murderer's baby,' she said. 'He's here,' she said. And the phone died."

Laurel felt the walls slide away around her. She spun her fingers in the air, holding the threads of the magic in place as she listened to her aunt's story.

"I broke laws speeding to get here. The house was empty, except for you, wrapped in a blanket at the bottom of the stairs, your head covered in downy blue-black hair. The cord was dangling out of your belly and you were crying... Next to a pool of blood. A second one trailed down the stairs. Mary was gone. Eric was gone. Vincent was gone."

My father. On the lam. She shuddered.

"Why did she stay?" Laurel asked. "It would be like living in the Amityville house after sitting through the movie."

"Mary blamed herself for not seeing the monster in Vincent. She couldn't leave the murdered women in limbo. And she felt the magic stronger than I did. Eric stayed with her, did what he could to help her heal, but in the end, they both died in this place—" Anne's words broke off as a sudden rumbling shook the house.

Laurel braced herself in the door frame. The wood warmed beneath her hands. It moved against her skin. Lights that could not have been lit flickered on and off as a banshee wail hit her sternum, throwing her backwards across the room. She gripped the photograph of her aunt tightly and clipped her shoulder on the corner of a side table. Pain shot through her.

Just as quickly the quaking ceased. Laurel righted herself. "Was that you?"

"No," Anne said, shaking her head. "Maybe one of the spirits. Maybe the house."

"Which one should I be hoping for?" Laurel asked, rubbing her shoulder gingerly. She put the photograph in her bag.

"You have to leave. This was a mistake."

"We have to stop being sentimental and speed up our timetable."

"Laurel?" Anne hadn't moved. "This is going to be a bigger job."

"I'm prepared for that." Laurel moved to the landing near the stairwell. She set five crystals in a circle and placed a bay leaf beneath her tongue.

"Recall," she said. The bay leaf vibrated, and with deep intention she associated the quartz points with the bones of each victim, offering them a safe berth through which they could escape the confines of the house.

Which she could still feel moving beneath her palms. It was inviting her a berth from her body. But she was stronger than that.

The house moaned lowly, another good sign. They were ready. Laurel steadied herself as the air shifted and grew hazy. Silhouettes formed over each crystal, like flickering flames.

They're coming! It's working.

The shapeless forms began to waver and stretch out, bloating and folding into each other. Laurel frowned. The crystals snapped into shards, spraying everywhere. Laurel ducked her face and covered her head. She felt blood dripping down her arms.

No room at the inn, she realized. There weren't enough crystals for the lives at unrest in the house.

Anne's voice was cold. "I was there. On their wedding night, Vincent gave Mary an unusual antique key. He said it was a sign of his trust. That there was a door it opened. That she was never to use it. That he'd know if she had. She didn't even think about it. She made a necklace of it."

Laurel pulled it from her bag. Anne nodded.

"'He changed,' she said. It's all she said. He changed and she found his secret. Eric and I came over. Vincent had Mary by the throat. She had called the police. His hands were bloody. She was bloody. Her throat was black. He fled at the sound of the sirens. We saved both of you that night."

Laurel shuddered.

"There were five mutilated corpses behind the locked door," Anne said.

"What locked door?"

Anne pulled herself into focus for a moment. Her face was somber.

"Did I never tell you?" The words hung in the air, creating a void like vapor neither of them could fill. Anne's specter spun slowly, facing a wall behind them. "There's a hidden door to a storage space. It was his space."

Laurel moved closer, running her hands along the carved wooden panel. It was hot to the touch, definitely the source of spirit activity. She found a tiny opening hidden in the overlap of sculpted leaves. She peered closer at the keyhole. "We need a small triangular key."

"Leave it," Anne said fearfully. Sadness and failure radiated from her aunt. "Magic held the horror inside before."

"You know we need to cleanse the whole house." Laurel's chest was tight. Anne flickered out of view and reappeared behind her. The house groaned around her. Laurel hefted the necklace. *What kind of man gifts his new bride the key to his murder room?*

She didn't mind speaking the truth about the man who was her father. He was just a blip in her genetics, one bad seed in generations of philanthropists. His choices didn't mean anything to her.

Anne was my mother and my father.

The windows rattled, and an impossible wind lifted Laurel to her feet, the necklace gripped tightly in her hand. Anne flickered in and out of focus, walking towards her. Laurel's feet slid of their own volition. She leaned back against the magnetic pull of the key to the lock. Behind the hidden door came a pulsing drone that made her want to run for the front porch.

The floorboards beneath her feet pitched and pulled, rushing her along. Laurel gasped. Her toes scraped across the wood. Anne rushed through her, disappearing through the wall first.

The wind died.

Laurel clattered to the ground, disoriented in the absence of the screaming wood grain. She steadied her hand against the small door with the key still in her grasp. Something on the other side of the wall ran towards her. She heard it. Laurel clambered to her feet. Every nerve in her body was on fire.

Vincent could still be alive.

She bolted. Blood pounded in her ears. She couldn't hear anything but she didn't look back. The door was unlocked and Laurel threw it open.

A flock of mad sparrows swarmed in. One after the other they pecked at her. A thousand wings forced her backwards across the threshold. The door slammed shut. Laurel tripped and fell to the floor. The house had been waiting, waiting for her. Her last thought was of darkness as the birds filled the room and turned to smoke and ether, filling her breath.

~

THE OUTSIDE WORLD began its twilight song. The house sat quiet. The walls stood still. Laurel eased her eyes open. Anne wavered at the bottom of the stairs, a horrid look on her face.

"You look pale," Laurel croaked, laughing. She tried to shake the cobwebs out of her eyes but winced when the back of her head began to throb. Her arms were covered in tiny, bloody cuts.

"I thought you were dead," Anne whispered.

"What did I just run from?" Laurel asked. Anne looked away. "What was in the room?"

"Bodies. Like before," Anne said, ghost eyes glazed and wild. "Just like before."

"It's okay, Anne," Laurel said. "I got this. I'll finish the cleansing and then we'll call the police." Her aunt blinked away and Laurel's pulse trilled.

Can spirits be in shock? She stood shakily, said a silent prayer for safety, and made her way up the stairs of the dark house with a lantern. She was still gripping the key in her hand. The metal was cold on her skin. She could taste it at the back of her throat. With every step she pulled the walls of the container she magicked up around her like armor.

She slipped the key into the sculpted wood, where it became a handle she used to push the door inward. She bent low and stepped inside. The smell was dank and fetid, but years past overpowering. It was mostly empty, save for a wooden trunk and some boxes just inside the door. The lantern could not penetrate the dense darkness. A low, rushing wind tugged at her clothes like a million wings, pulling at her corners and hems.

The door behind her slammed shut with a sharp snap, and Laurel jumped, stumbling into the trunk. The lantern tumbled across the floor. It stopped, illuminating a horrid tableau.

There were three bodies. There were more than three ghosts.

An unintelligible voice crawled across time to reach her. Something grabbed her by the wrist. Laurel's skin aged old to new and then unborn. She was unmade. A light began to glow in the room, and she could see that the darkness was made up of solid black highlighted against inky black. Shapes slid, moving and writhing against each other until one was more visible than the others.

Laurel couldn't see the light of her lantern anymore. She couldn't catch a breath.

The shape moved again, carrying indigo fire in one hand. The hair color was different but the face and the eyes were the same as hers. *Mary.* Laurel's mother walked towards her.

And then through her. An electric jolt shot through her limbs and ran through her heart. Breath caught in her throat as Laurel stood with a foot in the past. Every cell in her body felt dimensionally wrong. She couldn't turn her face away.

Mary, bleeding, dragged herself in through the small door and sat against the wall, collapsing there. Eric was prone on the ground, his head bashed open. A third man with dark hair and Laurel's jaw leaned against another wall. His throat was cut open. His eyes were still full of fire.

The look of horror on her mother's face wrenched at Laurel's heart. The sound of an infant's bleat shattered the silence of the room and a cold shiver flooded Laurel's arms and legs, spiraling up through her torso and into her chest.

All this death to protect me. Laurel knelt before her mother, who had blood on her mouth, whose eyes were a slow burn.

"It's time to go now," Laurel said, and her words swam like bubbles, rippling out to reach the other. "Let me help you." She closed her eyes and drew the symbol of fire on her forehead.

"Laurel," a deep voice said.

He said.

She looked up as her father's ghost grinned at her. He drove his fingers into the wooden floor. It splintered beneath him and the cuts the sparrows delivered on her arms widened and began to bleed.

The man on the floor who might have been her father yelled her name. Her mother screamed it. The ghosts began to repeat themselves, quicker and quicker in succession until Laurel was deafened by the storming of her name moving about the room, spoken by the people who might have loved her, in the house they died in. In the house she was born in.

She couldn't think about it. She couldn't think about them. A murmur of moth wings flapping from her world filled the enclosed space. She was doing this for Anne.

Vincent pushed his energy into the brick and timber. Blood dripped down her arms, and she let the house absorb it. And then she connected her thoughts to the sage bundles in the corners and the crystals in the basement like dots on a grid and she connected the dots with lines in every possible dimensional intersection until the sigil was complete. Every window in the house blazed with light, a dozen eyes open to other worlds.

Vincent's ghost roared. His dark cloud swarmed in the corner, growing larger. Laurel stared into the emptiness of his eyes, so unlike her own. A grin broke across his face. She shook her head and snapped her fingers.

"The way is open."

The light burned so brightly it became phosphorous white. The spirits of the murdered women flared into view. Everywhere they touched the darkness it burned away. They broke him piece by piece. His voice drowned beneath their song.

The darkness brightened as Laurel cried. Her breath came easier. The bleeding on her arms slowed. The women lifted up, passing through the ceiling like smoke.

Mary and Eric were pillars of blue fire, standing aside the murderer's black husk.

Laurel limped to the door and opened it. Anne stood on the other side, her face drawn and pained.

"When I lifted you up off the floor, she was in here the whole time. I never looked. It was locked, after the bodies. It was always locked. I never came back." Anne hung her head. "The house terrified me. I never came back. She was in there the whole time."

The hallway darkened around the ghost. Black threads began to spool themselves beneath her, tethering her down into the house. The walls rippled, shrinking in on them. Laurel watched the birth of a new haunting.

"Stop it," she said.

Anne's lips moved softly. "I was afraid of this room."

"Mom—" Laurel said. At the sound of the word, Anne lifted her head. "I was born in this room."

The tethers fell away.

Laurel smiled bravely. She couldn't always grasp the idea of grieving that the dead were gone from the physical world, because her daily one was filled with non-corporeal spirits. But a new sorrow spread heavy in her limbs. This was an ending.

"It's okay," Laurel pasted a grin on her face. "They're waiting for you. You've waited long enough."

"You are the best thing that ever happened to me." And the ghost smiled.

The light of Anne Jefferies grew luminous and swam around the room like a spring storm turning over the earth. Laurel felt a gentle breeze kiss her cheek and closed her eyes as Anne walked through her. She opened her heart to the blending.

Delight crept into her body and a seedling thickened, climbing up towards the sun, turning her heart and her head towards the light. Love created a deliberate melding of life to earth to air to heart. A fullness like heavy water passed hope back and forth like licks of fire, and there was no darkness in the shadow anymore, for the tinkling of a child's giggle became her talisman against it.

The three spirits turned to white fire and became one flame.

They advanced on Vincent's ghost, passing through what was left and absorbing him. The light expanded and broke into a thousand glittering pieces and burned away to stardust.

Laurel was alone. Truly alone with dried blood on her arms. The lantern on the floor illuminated the room, empty now except for bones that would need to be laid to rest.

She collected her bag in the upper hallway. She left the iron key in the small secret door. She made her way down the stairs and exited the empty house.

Laurel locked the front door. It was just a door. It was just a house now.

She breathed in the heady summer scents and the cooling air cleared her head. The past settled back into the earth as crickets sang a song welcoming the darkness. Fireflies danced along the edge of night while spirits became new stars overhead. The remains of the dead could wait until morning.

CASH FOR GOLD

JD SPERO

Author's Note: Cash for Gold is inspired by Rumplestiltskin. The original story was compiled into a collection of children's tales by Brother's Grimm in 1815, though sources claim its origin dates back 4,000 years. I was inspired to use this as a basis for my retelling after a friend of mine, after having 4 children of her own, became a surrogate mother three separate times for three different couples. Intrigued, I asked about the process and even considered doing it myself. Along the way, she told me about a doctor who had arranged illegal surrogacies and sold babies black-market style. That, and the shady essence of those ubiquitous Cash for Gold shops in strip malls, brought my story to life.

Candice McGreer steps lightly on the cracked sidewalk along Main Street, the unstable surface testing her poise. Her long cloak interrupts her stride with its awkward, weighted bottom. What a lame attempt at a disguise. She's more conspicuous than ever in this silly cloak, in this town where she's lived nearly all her adult life. But turning back isn't an option. Not without the money.

Shame seems to have changed her very essence. She fights a disembodied feeling, as if she could dissolve into the backdrop of old downtown or fade into the concrete like ash. She pinches her lips, intent on moving forward in bits.

The dry wind chills her. The mild North Texas winter she'd expected has turned as bitter as the barren, browning cornfields behind her home. She pulls on her hood as she passes Charley's Drug Shop, where the usual suspects linger on the stoop. There are more than normal, although it is not yet ten am.

"They're harmless." Her whisper manifests as a wisp of steam curling from her hood.

The next jumble of thoughts is loud in her mind: they're just trying to earn a dollar. No matter that their tongues are foreign and as dark as the dirt beneath their fingernails. The creature her mother warned her about—Lord rest her soul—is not among these men.

The tune reaches her as if from a dream. It takes her a moment to connect her own shaky voice to her mother's favorite lullaby. "All I have to do is dream," she sings the old Everly Brothers tune to herself, feigning courage... or apathy. Anything to ward off danger.

"Ma'am," says one, a greeting.

The song halts as if someone powered her off. She barely nods, too startled to speak.

"Nice coat you got there, Red," says another, prompting chuckles from the rest of them.

Candice hugs her purse tighter and starts to cross Main Street. A dead bird is splattered there, right in her path. Candice swallows bile and retreats. She creeps along the painted curb, a child's balance beam, to the crosswalk.

A gust of wind throws back her hood, and she feels exposed. She sprints across the street, her heart thundering in her chest, to the exterior wall of National Bank. Pressed against the cool stone, she fumbles to replace her hood. It takes ages for her breathing to settle. A couple passes by holding to-go coffees. The man takes the woman's hand, and she laughs breezily at something he said. They don't notice Candice hiding, thank goodness.

It's only a few storefronts away. She can see the sign from here. Black block letters on a yellow background, the most distinct combination of colors. There's also a sign tented on the sidewalk, forcing people to side step around it. Such extremes weren't necessary. If the sign were in pastels, she would've found it just the same. Yet, here it is screaming at her: *You desperate louse!* in the name of *Cash for Gold*.

The wind follows her inside, rustling the blue curtain behind the counter. She stares at the fabric, sure someone will appear from the other side. Its dance is brief, though, and she's surprised to find herself alone.

No one is here? Candice checks the storefront window. Reflected there in square neon letters: OPEN. She taps a bell on the dusty counter. The sound feels enormous. Too soon, it is quiet again. No one appears.

The small tiled room smells of mildew and rotten fruit. Triangles of dirt are caked in the corners. Candice can hear music playing faintly, probably from the restaurant next door. Something tinny, perhaps Middle-Eastern. Sweat collects beneath her cloak, and she shrugs it off her shoulders.

Candice turns to gaze out the front window. Main Street looks unfamiliar from this viewpoint... and lonely. The salon across the way has closed. Bookstore too. She hadn't noticed. The traffic is sporadic, and there isn't a soul on the sidewalk. It may as well be black and white, like a deserted street in an old Western.

A dark hopelessness presses down.

She never thought she'd be in this position. How did her life come to this? She and Earl married on wings of wealth. With his lucrative job as a construction engineer and hers as an executive assistant, they wanted for nothing. With their move to the suburb, they were comfortable enough for Candice to stop working completely. She spent her days decorating their large home, assuming children would soon fill the bedrooms. They even drafted plans to put a pool in their sprawling backyard. But then, construction jobs dried up. Layoffs happened, and the picture of their lives went out of focus.

Now, they could barely afford to pay their bills. How could they ever support a child? Candice held onto hope as long as she could. But Earl has been out of work for two years now, his severance long gone. And their savings is dwindling fast. They've recently had to plan for foreclosure.

She had to do something. What good is gold if you're homeless?

After a weepy morning, she emptied her jewelry box. "I'll sell it all."

Earl looked pained. "What will that do, really, in the scheme of things?"

"It will pay the mortgage." She squeezed his hand. "It will buy us some time, so to speak."

Tears swam in his pale eyes. "For just one month's mortgage, all your treasures gone?"

"It will give us that month. It will give us another month."

Earl wagged his head. "No, I won't have it. It's not worth it. There are some things money can't buy."

Candice smiled at her husband, pity tugging her heart. She loved his innocent spirit, but she would prove him wrong. Of course it would be worth it. Besides, how could Earl possibly think he'd have a say after being out of work for two years? He's not being practical.

Still, she would complete the mission secretly so as not to upset him.

But now, alone in this room of sinful exchange, her anxious stomach begs her to go back, to abandon the mission. Return to the safety of her home and find a new plan.

Nerves fill her legs with lead. She can't run out now. Her bag is full of gold to trade. She's come all this way.

She turns to prayer. "Please, Lord—"

The curtain clicks open behind her. The air in the shop shifts, and the scent of fresh mulch fills the room. No longer alone in the small shop that buys gold, she spins around, pressing a hand to her chest.

Then she sees the clerk, and nearly chokes with fright. The stooped man before her barely seems human. His bumpy, weathered skin looks active, like tiny bugs crawl beneath its surface. His body is slight and contorted, as if used to hiding in cramped spaces. He studies her, his bulging yellow eyes cautious.

"How can I help you?" His voice is equal parts screechy and hoarse.

Candice is too stunned to speak. She swallows the words that come to mind: troll, urchin, hobgoblin...

She nods, choosing no words at all. Rifling through her purse, she doesn't take her eyes off the troll. Under his unblinking gaze, heat crawls up her spine. She tries a smile as her hand wanders blindly inside the bag. His wide grin in response is full of grimy, crooked teeth. Finally, she takes out the satchel, squeezing it like a stress-ball.

The troll raises his bushy eyebrows, his forehead creasing around a raised mole. She sees now something in his aura she hadn't seen before. His eyes are not only jaundiced, but bloodshot. He doesn't look well. That smell is so strong: soil and manure. A nurturing instinct kicks in, surprising her.

"Sir, if you don't mind my saying—"

"Would you like to show me what's in the little bag, or do you want me to guess?" His eyes twinkle despite the sickness. "I've been known to have some of that."

Candice stammers, "Some of what?"

"Oh, a splash of vision, so to speak. Let's see." He dips his head, showing the hump on his back. He ticks off the contents of her satchel on his misshapen fingers. "Two gold chains, one thicker than the other. An antique broach you never wore but hope is worth something. Four pairs of gold earrings: one dangly. Quite fancy! Two bracelets, one with diamonds. Oh, and an empty locket. That's something that will be hard to part with, but you're willing to do it, considering your"—his eyebrows lift—"situation. Your wedding band is off-limits, of course. And you plan on keeping the gold cross that's currently around your neck, although you'd be willing to negotiate. The Lord will understand, you figure."

Candice's mouth would be hanging open if the cloak fastener wasn't choking her. Her satchel of treasures has dampened in her grip.

"Of course," he continues, chewing on a toothpick that materialized like a magic trick. "What you have in your satchel may or may not give you another month. But then, what will you do?"

Her lips tremble. "How... ?"

His eyes narrow as he leans toward her. He's so close the pores on his nose are visible, as well as the cone of fur on his chin. She holds her breath against the stench, working to keep her gaze steady while her insides sting alert.

What he says next rattles her to the core. "The ring your mother gave you—the one that's hidden away—the one your husband doesn't know about—is reserved for a different kind of emergency."

Candice swallows, shakes her head slowly. "But - but I don't..."

While she falters, he waits patiently, digging a thick-knuckled pinky into his oversized ear. His voice is oddly calm. "I need to collect a debt that's owed me. For you, it is a great price to pay. At another time, perhaps unthinkable. But considering your obligation."

His eyes are sharp on her abdomen. She steps back, covering her midsection, shock and confusion swirling.

"Wait. What did you say?"

The few beats of silence hang heavily in the air. His piercing stare cuts through her. "Do you know you are with child, Candice?"

The room seems to spin. She breaks eye contact with the troll, her ears ringing. Tears spontaneously fill. She blinks them away, feeling a hint of a smile for the first time in days.

Oh, my goodness. She's had a hunch for a couple weeks now, but was too scared to confirm it. She and Earl have always hoped for a baby. A few years back, this news would've been cause for celebration. But, oh, now is not the best time.

It must be very early, but of course, she feels it now: the tender breasts, the constant fatigue, the stubborn bile this morning. How could she have missed it? She blinks at the troll, who at once seems less frightening. Her heart lifts despite the fear. A baby!

But wait—he called her *Candice*. How does he know her name? And the ring. How does he know things he couldn't possibly know?

And then, like a flash from a vivid dream, it hits her.

Hiding her shock, she summons all the strength she can muster. Her entire life she'd been preparing for this moment. Of all places, it happens here at the shop that buys gold, right in her hometown. She must proceed appropriately. Her mind spins, trying to catch the right move. She knows it's hers to make.

She mustn't let on. He can't see a crack in her carefully polished veneer. Working to keep her features smooth, she straightens herself so as to look down on the creature her mother warned her about decades ago.

She tosses the satchel on the counter. "How much then?"

THE RING. *The ring.* The thought consumes her entirely. In a blink, she's home, but has little memory of how she got there. She flies through the door, blood roaring in her ears.

"Earl, are you home?"

No answer. Thank you, Lord!

Relief gives her fresh energy. Must move quickly. Earl could return any moment. No time to take off her boots or cloak. She rushes directly to the master bedroom closet and uses the step stool to reach the top shelf. There, beneath a stack of wool sweaters, is the small box her mother gave her so many years ago. For the first time since seeing the creature, Candice takes a full breath. She sits at the foot of her bed, holding the box like an offering. It feels empty. It should weigh a ton, considering how heavy its lay on her conscience. But no, it sits in her hand like a dainty bird.

The ring—it must be inside. Flinching into her cloak, she imagines something evil there instead. A ball of fire or toxic charm. She's tempted to stuff it back beneath her sweaters and never think of it again. Her fingers clench around the box, the sharp corners pinching her flesh. A ping of irritation. Why is this her burden?

She swallows down the question. *Reserved for emergency*, the troll had said. How right he was. Her entire life, she knew this time would come. And here it is.

She sets the box on the duvet, her hands trembling. Memories of her mother rush to the surface. Little things, like snapshots in time. The way she pulled her long hair into a low bun whenever she cooked. How she would hide her laugh behind her hand, almost embarrassed. The surprisingly gentle touch of her strong hands. Her soft singing voice, the soundtrack to Candice's childhood. The old tune she still sings to soothe herself, just this morning, in fact.

And of course, Mother's words. She filled their days together with stories and poetry, reading from the greats around the globe. A natural orator, Candice would recognize the elevated tone, the flourish of her hand, as Mother recited something significant. It was in this manner she delivered the caution around the ring. So many important things she'd heard from Mother's melodious voice. It's no wonder she forgets some. The bit with the ring would get confused with Keats and Rumi and Browning and the others. Even though Mother recited it every few weeks, with the cycle of the moon, compelled by a kind of cosmic energy. Her usual tenderness hardened, it was as if the words caused her pain. What was the exact warning? Part of Candice doesn't want to remember, because the words cause her pain as well.

The ring. The thing that's protected me—and us—from my past. It belongs to the creature. If he comes for you, just give him the ring and leave. You do not owe him any more than that, no matter what he says. Do not entertain the thought of making a deal with this man. The risk is too great.

The rest of the story eludes her, the details patched together with inadequate glue. Her mother had been in trouble—pregnant out of wedlock. The creature offered her the most impossible kind of out... and Mother took it.

What did she agree to, exactly? Candice can't remember.

The ring was the contract. Mother wore it without fail until Candice turned eighteen. That was the magic number. That's when they could stop running. Finally, they were safe.

Though Mother insisted their safety was a fragile, ephemeral thing. *You should never assume the danger is gone. Dangers are lurking all around you.*

Dangers—not as in tigers or muggers or rapists or snakes. Dangers —as in the creature and his avarice.

How she wishes she could call her mother now. If only she could hear her voice once more. There are too many questions. Too many unknowns. Should she just go back and hand it over and be done?

There's got to be more to it.

She runs a hand absently over the stitching of the duvet, and forces a breath before opening the box. Inside is only a red silk pouch. Confusion muddles her thoughts. No letter, no instructions?

A wave of regret washes over her. How could Mother expect a girl to remember everything? She should have listened more closely, locked it in her memory, repeated it like prayer. Perhaps in the pouch?

Candice opens it. Inside is just the ring. A simple gold ring.

She turns the ring to the light, studies the inside for an inscription. Aha! There it is: *ab incunabulis*

Why Latin? She wants to cry out in frustration. Frowning, Candice stomps to her trusty Webster's. Her fingers tab the pages with the same proficiency she'd used as an executive assistant.

Ab incunabulis: Latin. Translation: From the cradle. Thus, "From the beginning" or "From infancy"

Candice shudders, and then scolds herself. It's just a piece of gold, after all. Still, it seems to radiate heat in her palm. She clamps her fingers around it, as bile once again rises in her throat. She barely makes it to the bathroom before her stomach turns inside out. She washes the colorless liquid down the drain. In the medicine cabinet, she finds Earl's mouthwash and gargles until her gums sting.

She catches her reflection after, which makes her pause. *I'm pregnant*, she wonders with awe. A burst of laughter comes out. Equal parts delighted and dazed, she cries into her closed fist. A baby! Candice swoons inside, thinking of the hope this child has already brought her. How she would love to run into Earl's arms right now and tell him he will be a father.

But first, she must go to the creature and give him the ring. Fulfill her promise to Mother and be done with the whole ordeal once and for all.

She shoves the ring onto her finger so it won't be lost on the way.

Oh, the wad of bills in her purse! How could she forget?

Perhaps superfluous now that she has the ring. Still, she wouldn't want to pass the usual suspects outside Charley's Drug Shop with all this money on hand. In haste, she empties the cash from her gold into the coffee can in the cabinet. Earl's hiding spot. Though he hasn't used it in months.

Huh. The bill roll seemed larger in her purse. Was Earl right? It isn't much. Barely makes a single mortgage payment. A wave of guilt makes her knees give way, having defied Earl like this—for nothing. Just a few dollars. She presses the plastic cover back on, which smudges out the guilt a bit.

Once Earl hears about the baby, he won't be angry. She would find a way to make this right too. She always has.

∽

OUTSIDE, she tucks her hair into her cloak's hood and makes her way back to the shop, *Cash for Gold*. Her swift footfalls soften into a comfortable rhythm. The Everly Brothers' tune keeps her company. She sings to the sky. Thoughts of Mother warm her from the inside out. The winter sun is high, illuminating the few muted leaves that still cling rigidly to their trees. She basks in the light, tilting her face to it, grateful for the ubiquitous Texas sun. She twirls the ring with her thumb as the clouds in her mind dissipate.

There are notably fewer usual suspects outside Charley's Drug Shop. The one with the mustache is still there—*Nice coat you got there, Red*—a wad of tobacco tucked in his cheek. He spits, and brown sludge splats at her feet, missing her boot by inches. The nerve of this man! Candice steps over the filth, averting her eyes.

Onward. She weaves through Main Street, which is busier with the rush of midday foot traffic. The journey takes minutes—a runner's high pushing her like a tailwind.

Candice enters the shop with purpose. Empty, again. Impatient, she taps the bell. The troll appears from behind the blue curtain at once—the bell's song still hanging in the air. Was he waiting for her? His eyes are moist, and his wide grin seems lewd.

Candice hides the ring in the drape of her cloak, unsure suddenly. "I've come back to—"

"I know why you've come back. Let me see it." He clasps his gaunt hands—an old-lady gesture.

Why does she hesitate? She is in control now. Just hand over the ring and have it over with. But she is paralyzed by uncertainty. There must be something else. It can't be that simple.

The troll's skin crawls with anticipation and he leans over the counter. His base, earthy odor wafts as he reaches for her.

"It's been so long," he whispers, ecstasy swimming in his eyes.

The ring's heat radiates through her fingers. Yet dread weighs her hands.

If only she could reverse time and think this through. Perhaps she would remember exactly. *Oh, Mother!* Candice trembles. Something is wrong.

The troll is greedily fingering her clenched hands. Candice must see it through. Neither can wait any longer. When she finally uncovers the gold, she is weeping.

With a gasp, the troll leaps onto the counter. His wicked laughter echoes in the small shop as he towers over her. He points and laughs like an impish tyrant, breathless with triumph.

Oh, no. Oh, please, no. Candice's tears come steadily. *What's happened? What have I done?* She awaits her punishment, sure now that she's made a mistake. A terrible, irreparable mistake.

The shop begins to fall away like an efficient set-change on Broadway. Flats are lifted, shifting the backdrop, changing the scene. The tiles beneath her boots sink into damp earth.

In a blink, Candice stands in a mossy jungle. The shop's fluorescent lighting cracks and dims. The thin sunlight battles through draping, lush greens. The jungle stretches out before her, endless. The air is thick with moisture. That smell. That raw, intestinal smell... is everywhere.

What's happening? A hollow panic strikes. *Where am I?*

The ring offers a brilliant glow, and she holds it out like a lantern. The troll has galloped away from her—out of sight but not out of range. She follows his malicious cackling, too terrified to cry out. Her steps along the soggy, uneven terrain are clumsy and slow.

Behind her, the dark is cold and daunting. The only way is toward the sound, the light...

About twenty yards before her is the troll's silhouette. He dances before a fire that's tucked within a shallow cave.

"Please," she calls to him. "Help me, please!"

His laughter pauses as he skips to her. He leads her by the elbow to the clearing before the fire. Its orange flames seem alive, tormenting her. The troll circles around like a court jester, humming a giddy, maniacal tune. Vertigo strikes, and as Candice catches her fall, she recognizes the tune he's humming is the same her mother sang at her bedside.

Candice shivers, a damp chill blanketing her. The heat of the fire is swallowed into the rock. The feral jungle smell smudges out her modest stamp of perfume. She hugs the cloak tightly, but it is no use.

"Please, take the ring and let me go. It's what you want, isn't it?"

He hops to face her, taking her hand to his lips. He settles a humid kiss on her knuckles, tapping his yellow teeth on the gold band.

"Ab incunabulis," he sings.

Candice tries to wrestle out of his grip, but his hold has superhuman strength. He leads her beyond the circle. At once, she is blinded by darkness, shaking from the chill. It is eerily quiet but for her boots sucking swamp with each unsure step.

The troll pauses. She waits, disoriented, hoping her eyes will adjust. Out of nowhere, a small wooden bowl is placed in her hands. It's warm. Her stomach lurches as she realizes she hasn't eaten all day. Guilt pings—has she neglected her unborn child? She drinks, and is relieved to taste coconut milk. It settles her stomach and leaves a sour tang on her tongue.

The troll is busy nearby. She hears the swish of fresh banana leaves, the subtle squeak of braided vines, the squish of wet moss. She blinks, trying to focus. It's no use.

Suddenly, she's struck by debilitating fatigue. Bone tired. She closes her eyes. If she must be in darkness, better to be in her own.

Perhaps this starts a dream, for there is warmth now, beckoning her. She steps into it, and has an urge to

"Go ahead. Lie down."

She hears his voice. She knows it is the troll, yet she's no longer afraid. Just exhausted. She rolls onto the bed, easily and naturally, as if she were home. It's a cradle of moss. She melts into it. Her cloak is a hindrance. The boots needless. She shucks them off, unwraps the cloak and discards it. A heavy warmth surrounds her like a sauna. She sheds all her outer layers, yearning for the silky moss to caress her naked skin.

Now enveloped in its warmth, like Earl's strong arms. Peaceful. Sleep is creeping close. She revels in its addictive pull, longing for it. But then, the troll's voice nudges her consciousness a bit longer.

"Rest. You have lots of work to do."

Work? She doesn't say the word aloud, but it seems he's heard her.

"Your *body* has lots of work to do."

What's that? She must not have heard him right.

"Nothing but a healthy baby is acceptable."

It's like a wind catches at the base of her skull, the draft pulling her alert. She fights sleep now. There are too many questions.

The creature will not outsmart her!

Her mother's warning roars in her mind. How could she have missed such a crucial piece of information? It now throbs in her memory like an alarm siren:

You must remember, Candi, do not wear the ring. That gold should not find your finger. Ab incunabulis cannot touch your skin!

She tries to speak but her tongue is thick and the pull is too strong. The moss hugs her snugly, a false sense of safety.

Wake up, Candice!

She tries, but it is no use. His words are faraway, perhaps underwater. She hears it like a dream.

"Nine months seems like a long time. But here time doesn't exist."

Time doesn't exist...

"For your husband and the rest of the outside world, it will be as if no time has passed. After the child is born and transferred, you will return to this day and go home to Earl as if you'd just finished your afternoon errands. And all your real-life problems will be gone. Vanished!"

All problems gone... but also the baby. My baby?

No! No, no, no. Surely, he wouldn't. He couldn't mean—

She lashes out, kicking with all her might, trying to wrestle herself free. But it doesn't work. Her body misses the brain's signal, and she can't move. She sinks deeper into the thick putty of warmth.

His voice is a mere echo now. "It's a small price to pay for a lifetime of comfort, really. My dear Candice, you'll never have to worry about money again."

Money? Who cares about money?

My baby, my baby...

Everything goes soft. An energy swirls inside her. Her body is working on something. She can feel it. Candice's breathing deepens, her mind empties. She is slipping...

"And to think," he says dreamily. "I didn't even have to come find you. You came right through my door."

As if from the end of a long tunnel, she can barely hear him. He's laughing softly, and singing her mother's favorite lullaby as she succumbs.

THE FOUNTAIN,
THE BIRD,
AND THE TREE

JM UTRERA

Author's Note: "The Fountain" is based on the popular Spanish/Catalan fairy tale more commonly known as "The Water of Life." This story is an old one, retold again and again throughout Catalan and into Spain, mostly by oral tradition until it was collected by D. Francisco de S. Maspons y Labros in his folklore anthology Cuentos Populars Catalans in 1885. Since then there have been a few, but not many, retellings.

I chose to write my own adaptation of the story because it has always been one that has fascinated my imagination. My grandparents and great-grandparents came to Brazil from Spain, and that Spanish legacy has always held a spell over a corner of my heart. This story came with them, so for a long time I've tried to imagine what the sister protagonist was like and what kind of love or ambition drove the motives of the story. There is such a quintessential fairy tale quality to the whole thing that convinces me it deserves a space next to Cinderella and Snow White as one of the world's most beloved fables. It was a joy to explore that story further and write the kind of character I hope my daughters can find in themselves one day.

ADRÍAN: THREE DAYS BEFORE

Laughter spilled out into the balmy night air, conversation flowing and ebbing with the same rhythm of the tide against the nearby shore. People moved between taverns, eating at tables outside or standing in clusters inside. Sunset painted the town in warm touches of gold. Adrían couldn't feel it. For him, the night had chilled.

He stood at a table by himself, nursing a drink ordered more for the pride of its expense than the taste. It wasn't too long ago that he wouldn't have been able to afford a drink like that, or tapas like these — finer and more exotic offerings than those found at the places lower in town where he used to dine. Where they didn't know how to treat him anymore.

All around him, heads swiveled over fine fancy collars to steal glances at him. They weren't as subtle about it as they pretended to be. Their mouths would turn down, their attention would return to their companions, and scandalized murmuring would spill among them in tones too low for Adrían to properly hear.

Except one man, who snorted as he moved past Adrían's table and said loudly, "This place isn't what it used to be. They'll let in any riff raff with a shiny penny, won't they?"

Adrían's spine remained stiff and straight and he signaled for more wine and another plate of olives with cheese. The serving man — no waifish daughters of tavern owners here — acknowledged him.

"You don't belong here," someone said smoothly, sidling up to the table and placing his own drink next to Adrían's. "Do you?"

Adrían gave this stranger a critical look. He was older, with pale skin, reddish blond hair and blue eyes. He had the look and accent of someone from the North. From that witchy region of devil-language and devil-workings they called Vasco. Yet no one here seemed to give *him* suspicious glares or muttered grievances.

"I have every right to be here," Adrían replied.

And he did. He could afford it. His house was finer than theirs. His income was greater than theirs, in most instances. He'd become polite and well-spoken and had learned the nuances of their manners well enough. He was just as good as any of them — never mind that he had been born with dirt in his mouth, and they had come into the world on imported linens and golden camel's milk.

"You certainly look the part, yes," the man acknowledged. "The right beard style, the right clothing, even the right air of superiority. But you're a fake."

Adrían bristled. He couldn't help it. "Have you come over to harass me, then? A man who comes from where you do?"

"I inherited my wealth, same as they did. They can sense it." He motioned airily to the people around them. "I haven't come to harass you, though. Unlike them, I don't mind mingling with interlopers."

"Who are you?" Adrían's eyes narrowed.

"An envoy, here to propose a marriage between my liege lord's daughter and your own eligible duke, Don Augustín."

A stab of jealousy flashed through Adrían. The don interested in *his* sister, not some far-flung duchess from heathen Vasco. "Then you have come to the wrong city. Don Augustín is dear to the king, sir, and the king himself will need to be the one to approve such an advantageous match."

It was one of the obstacles Adrían did not know how to overcome to help his sister take advantage of the don's fascination with her. Not that she knew much about it. He'd kept those conversations with their duke secret from her, lest she get her hopes up — or worse, reject the whole idea.

"Oh, I don't care what these men above my head can and can't do without their king's permission. I was told to come here to speak to the don, so here I am."

"Mingling with interlopers."

"Precisely," the man grinned. "Your kind are so much more interesting than my own. Grown too big and important for your own people, but not good enough for your new peers, is that about right?"

Adrían thanked the serving man for his refill of food and wine and picked at his olives instead of answering.

The man plucked one off the plate for himself. "I feel pity for you."

"Don't." The olives were suddenly bitter in his mouth. He pushed the plate towards his companion. "I can't use pity. It doesn't make me richer."

"In this case, it could."

"What is that supposed to mean?"

"What do you know of the Sacred Fountain?"

Adrían laughed — a little too loudly for this crowd. They gave him sharp, offended glances. He lowered his voice. "Like the children's story?"

"Well, if you don't believe in it, I don't need to waste my time with you," the man sniffed, turning his face away to browse the other tables.

"I didn't mean to offend you," Adrían said quickly. "What of the Sacred Fountain?"

"Consider, *amigo mío*, that all stories begin with some grain of truth."

"Are you trying to say that the three treasures of the Sacred

Fountain are real?" Adrían had to work very hard to keep the bemusement out of his voice. Whatever nonsense this was, he didn't want the man to go away again and leave him washed in the icy stares of isolation again.

"Yes, and that many have tried to claim them. Remember the stories, boy. They told us about these heroes."

"Heroes who chased after phantom riches and never returned," Adrían pointed out.

"No, quest-seekers who knew the reward awaiting them if they succeeded!" The man's eyes gleamed. "Fame. Honor. Wealth. Consider, would the owner of the Tree of Beauty, the Water of Life, the Bird of Prophecy ever be turned away by this crowd?"

Adrían looked around, frowning. An old hunger stirred inside him, roused by restlessness. If any of this were real, it would be desperately satisfying to become the owner of these mythical treasures and flaunt, not only his equality but indeed his superiority, over these highbrow denizens.

But what a wild fantasy.

"I can see you want to protest. But they are *real*, my friend," the man said emphatically, leaning forward. "I have learned that they are in the mountains to the east, and I intend to go get them. Straightaway in the morning."

"What?" Adrían stiffened.

"Why should I care about returning with an agreement for my liege when I am so close — barely three days' walk away from the very heart of the mountains where the treasures are? I'll never be this close to them again! I'll find the treasures, I'll return richer than my liege can ever imagine and he'll put away his dreams of your Don Augustín. I will become a more powerful ally for him."

"I thought you were already wealthy," Adrían said, but only because the rest of it was too ludicrous to address. "Why are you not already an eligible option for marrying his daughter?"

"The king's cousin is a much more powerful match than a

provincial landowner," the man chuckled, as if Adrían were silly and boyish for even wondering.

"So you're just going to go marching after some fairytale treasures?"

"They are *real*, for the last time! A friend of my brother-in-law has been to the base of the mountain. He has spoken with the guardian who keeps the way. His courage faltered and he turned back, but he told what he saw."

This gave Adrían some pause. A friend-of-a-brother-in-law seemed thin as far as a reliable source went, but even still. He'd never heard of anyone who had gone to the place in person and returned. A real man who could confirm its mystical existence...

Suddenly Adrían's imagination was galloping away from him. Not even the king himself would be able to deny that Mercedes was not a worthy bride for Don Augustín if her brother were the keeper of the sacred treasures. The entire family would be elevated by it. No one in any region in all of Catalonia would be able to deny entrance to or turn up their noses at the presence of the Martín siblings. Their wealth would expand, their ranks would soar, and everything they'd been carefully building their whole lives would finally, finally come to fruition.

Despite all logic, his heart began to thud faster and harder. Mercedes was the cool-headed one who held him back when his flights of ambition soared too high, but this was different. He could feel it pricking along his bones like sparks of fire. If this stranger didn't succeed and the three treasures remained unmolested — and if Adrían himself found them...

"Where is it, then?" he asked.

∽

MERCEDES

"Congratulations, Mercedes," said Rosa genially as she handed over her payment. She leaned on the doorway to her house. "I hear Don Augustín has been paying visits to Adrían these days. You know what that means..."

Mercedes finished wrapping the fish in paper, glancing up from her work to see the woman's eyebrows waggling suggestively. She laughed. "It means our business is doing well and has caught his attention, that's all."

"That's not it, *mija*. They say the don's interest isn't in your business so much as it is in you."

"Rosa," Mercedes handed over the parcel. "We aren't the sort of people who catch the attention of royalty."

"Maybe not before," conceded the baker's wife. "But now? As you said, you four are doing very well for yourselves. Too well, I think, for any of our sons to be eligible matches for you now, or our daughters for your brothers. I heard Adrían won't even go for tapas at our own taverns anymore. He goes up there."

She motioned to the streets higher up the hills.

"Oh go on, Rosa. Go, and take your *chisme* with you," Mercedes said, laughing and affectionate even as she summarily dismissed the old woman and her gossip.

Rosa grinned and gave Mercedes a quick kiss on the cheek before heading back inside her house.

The final delivery. Mercedes could go home.

Years ago, when she was negotiating with some of the town's most prominent businessmen about investment in their growing fishing business, she'd promised the early investors personal deliveries from the day's catch. This had proved a profitable enticement, and her list of such deliveries had grown quickly. She'd managed to arrange them strategically, so this last stop at Rosa's meant she could quickly check on the hired hands working the market booth before heading back to the villa she shared with her three brothers. It was a pleasant day, with salty ocean breezes sweeping through the streets and a mellow sun hanging low on the horizon. Business was good, which meant life was good.

So she was in a cheerful mood when she arrived home. As soon as she walked in, however, she froze. They had a visitor.

Don Augustín himself.

The lord of the duchy stood in an archway leading out to the little courtyard in the center of their villa, deep in conversation with her brother Adrían. Her other brothers, Luis and Santiago, sat at a table near them, mending torn nets.

Mercedes set down her empty basket and dipped her hands in the fresh rosewater she kept by the door to remove the smell of the day's labors. She quickly wiped them dry.

"Mechi," Santiago called, waving when he saw her.

Everyone turned to look. Mercedes steeled herself against the sudden attention.

Don Augustín strode towards her quickly, smiling. Adrían followed suit with a sharp, appraising glance.

She resisted the urge to glare at her brother. He didn't complain about her appearance at any other time, knowing how her negotiations and personal deliveries directly affected the growth of their once-tiny fishing operation. He knew why she looked like she'd just spent all day walking around in the sun and dust, while he'd had enough time to put on his fine fancy clothes to receive their guest.

But the duke politely pretended not to notice. Or maybe he genuinely didn't mind, because he extended his hand to her as if she were some grand lady anyway and smiled as he bent to kiss the back of her fingers.

"*Buenas tardes*, Señorita Martín," he said warmly.

Mercedes tried not to blush at his attention, though warmth flooded through her just the same. "*Buenas tardes*, Don. I apologize for my state. I did not anticipate receiving such a distinguished guest today."

"Of course not, don't trouble yourself. You are lovely as ever." His eyes never left her face, didn't drop to see what dirty clothes she might be referencing. They sparkled in a way that made her feel like the only one in the room. "I have been discussing business with your brother."

Adrían gave a nod. He had a conspiratorial look on his face, and Mercedes recognized it. He was scheming again, probably about money.

"Will I have the pleasure of seeing the Martín family at my ball next month?" Don Augustín asked.

Mercedes didn't think they would be welcome among all those nobles — but all three of her brothers were eager to accept. "We were honored by the invitation, my lord. We will be there."

"I'm very glad to hear it." The duke beamed. Mercedes expelled a soft breath and looked at her feet as he turned back to her brother. "Well, Adrían, I take my leave. Good luck with your endeavors."

"Thank you, Don," said Adrían, bowing.

He gave Mercedes' hand one last kiss by way of parting. Adrían escorted him to the door.

Mercedes went over to her other brothers and sank into an empty seat at their table, feeling that her cheeks were too warm.

"He wants to marry you," Luis said knowingly.

"Don't be ridiculous. Of course he doesn't."

Don Augustín was young, eligible, and the aim of every noble family with a daughter of age in the kingdom. His kinship and particular friendship to the king made him even more desirable. Mercedes knew these were supposed to be his most recommending qualities, but she enjoyed his warmth and kindness more than his fortune or royal favor. His world of highborn denizens terrified her.

Adrían returned, silencing them all with a swift report. "I have an announcement."

He'd said the same thing six years ago, when he declared it was time for them to get out of poverty. He'd decided that they would all work together to become rich enough to build a beautiful villa and never go hungry again. He didn't know how to begin, but Mercedes quickly put together a plan. And they'd done it. All four of them together had clawed out a fortune for themselves and built this magnificent home. Adrián was satisfied with their success for a while, but lately he'd been getting that look about him again.

"I'm going to find the Sacred Fountain."

All three of them gasped, laughed, saw that he wasn't laughing, and then spoke out at once.

"But that's not—" Luis began, rising out of his seat.

"You're joking—" cried Santiago.

"What do you mean?" demanded Mercedes.

Adrián waved them off. "We've done well, but we need to improve our fortunes further. Only the treasures of the Sacred Fountain can do that for us now."

"We have more money than we need, Adrián. That cannot be the reason." Mercedes didn't even bother to point out that the whole pronouncement was nonsensical anyway. He knew that already — didn't he?

The Sacred Fountain was a legendary place from where all beauty and life flowed. At least, that's how the children's story went. Adventurers from all walks of life had struck out in search of its three treasures — the Water of Life, the Tree of Beauty, and the Bird of Prophecy. None had succeeded, or even returned. Fewer and fewer attempted it in each generation. It was probably all just a story anyway. So why this mad plan, and that mad look on his face?

"Well, for one, Don Augustín wants to marry you, Mercedes," Adrián said.

This was a bigger shock than the earlier revelation. Luis and Santiago guffawed in triumph and elbowed one another while Mercedes gaped at him.

"But why?" she asked breathlessly. "I'm nobody!"

"Not anymore. We have become the most important business family in his stewardship. He knows you are the architect behind our success, and he admires that. He thinks the two of you, together, could orchestrate a better administration. He wants you as his partner as well as his wife."

Mercedes drew in an unsteady breath, her mind and heart spinning into eddies of emotion.

"What are you waiting for?" Luis demanded at once. "Strike the match, Adrían. Agree to it, already!"

"I haven't agreed yet for two reasons," Adrían explained, looking at Mercedes. "Firstly, he wishes to talk to you about this himself. Secondly, I needed your answer. You will tell me what reply I should give him. I won't sell you to the highest bidder. This is your decision, little sister."

"But what does this have to do with going to the Sacred Fountain?" Santiago interjected.

Adrian turned to the others. "Though the duke doesn't care about how poor we once were, the rest of the grandees and nobility certainly will. They still look down on us. They see us as up-jumped urchins. Besides, the don is not free to choose anyone he wishes. If Mercedes agrees, and if I agree, he will have to take his proposal to the king. And I don't believe the king will agree to let him marry a fishmonger's sister."

So he explained his plan, first by explaining that someone he met confirmed its real existence, not far away from them in the eastern mountains. He would go, bring back the three treasures, and secure their place in the upper climes of society through fame and fortune. People of every strata would know their names, and the great lords, princes, and kings of every nation would come to their villa to see the rare prizes. Then no king or noble could object to Don Augustín marrying Mercedes, the most famous woman in the land.

"And it will improve our own marriage opportunities, too," he concluded, motioning to Luis and Santiago. "The highborn of our city will practically be throwing their daughters at us, begging us to become their sons in marriage. Think of it — great names and fine old lineages eager to join their heritage to the *familia* Martín. That's why I'm going. I leave tomorrow."

"Tomorrow!" Mercedes cried. "This plan is lunacy, Adrián! We are happy here. We have more than enough. Your marriage prospects are already good enough. Why should we seek to reach for more when we've accomplished so much?"

"It will allow you to marry the don," he said again.

"I don't care about that." Augustín was handsome and agreeable and kind, but Mercedes had never aspired to such a lofty marriage.

"Anyway, it isn't just for you," he persisted. "We can all still climb higher."

"I think it's brilliant," said Luis. "Mad, but brilliant. Nobody will ever again be able to look down on us if we have those treasures. And you're *sure* they're real?"

"Adrián," ventured Santiago, even as Adrián was reassuring Luis. He was the youngest, still caught between boy and man at sixteen. Right now he sounded like a frightened child. "Nobody who has gone looking for the Sacred Fountain has ever returned. How will we know if you are alright, or if you are... dead?"

Adrian produced a knife. "I knew that would be a problem. My friend gave me something he acquired, said he didn't need it. It will keep you all from worrying too much."

The knife, he explained, would stay with them. He would prick his finger on it and let it taste his blood. Then, while he was away, if they should wish to check on him, they need only check the knife. If the blade was clean, he was alright. If it should run red with his blood, it meant he was wounded or dead.

"Where did your friend get this?" Mercedes demanded. "Items like this aren't just found in shops. This is *brujería*, Adrián, witchcraft."

"Where he comes from, it isn't so taboo. Anyway, it's efficient."

"No, you're not doing this!" she cried. "It's lunacy. You can't."

"I can. You'll keep things running smoothly while I'm away, as you always do." He kissed her forehead. "Trust me. It will work out."

"No one has ever succeeded. Why do you have the arrogance to think you will?"

"Because we were born with nothing, with the fates against us, yet have seized our own destiny and bent it to our will, little sister."

~

ADRÍAN

On a normal morning, the Martín siblings would rise before dawn to begin their preparations for the day, and then Adrían would lead his two brothers out to the docks where Luis and Santiago would fish while Adrían negotiated with their contracted fishermen. Mercedes would keep the books and the personal deliveries. They worked well together, and they were good at making money.

But this morning, things did not proceed normally. They all rose at the same hour, but Luis and Santiago went to the docks alone. They hugged Adrían farewell and divided his responsibilities among themselves. None of them knew how long Adrían would be away, but they all pretended this new arrangement would only be needed for a couple days.

After they'd gone, Mercedes gave him a bag of bread and other items she had spent the night baking. He thanked her and pricked his finger on the knife. Together they watched the droplet of his blood soak into the metal.

"There," he said. "Now you will know if I'm alright."

"But not where you are or when you'll return," she said unhappily.

He gave her a warm hug. "It will all be alright."

She didn't believe him — he could see that in her frown and the tension in her brows when he waved goodbye from the road. It didn't matter. He believed it himself.

Within him thrummed a steady cadence, excitement pulsing in every beat of his heart. His parents used to talk about the brave adventurers who went in search of the Sacred Fountain and the three treasures it held. The Tree of Beauty, rumored to grant the keeper of any of its twigs or branches matchless esteem in the eyes of their peers, or turn any home into a sanctuary for the soul. The Water of Life, which was said to cure any ailment of the body or mind. And the Bird of Prophecy, a creature who could answer any question about the future, even if the truth was terrible to hear.

Adrian's parents told these stories to help their children dream of better things than their empty bellies as they fell asleep, as well as to caution them against striving for something unattainable. But the promise of a better life with those treasures had burrowed deep into his psyche. They'd made him hunger for more, and he forgot the part about caution.

The stranger from the tavern had never returned. He'd given Adrian the dagger with his own blood staining it, telling him that he needed someone to know if he had succeeded or not. If it never turned red, it meant he had obtained the treasures and gone home, and word would soon come of the fabulously wealthy man with the sacred items. But it had turned red yesterday morning, setting Adrian's plan into motion.

He walked for a long time, eventually departing from the manicured roads and striking out into the untouched wild. He slept beneath the stars and ate the food Mercedes gave him. He thought of her, and was grateful. His little sister. The third born. He loved her best of all his siblings. Yes, he was doing this for her.

Or so he told himself.

He traveled far and further, until the mountains drew near and he passed into their shadow. A path departed from the valley and climbed the nearest slope. At the base of this path grazed a modest flock of sheep. Keeping watch over them sat an enormous man.

Was this a giant? The stories always said there were giants in the world, but Adrian had never seen one. He approached half in awe, half in fear.

"Who trespasses on my pasture?" the giant said. "A flea?"

"A man," said Adrían as loudly as he could.

"A man? A flea? One word, both the same."

Adrían motioned up the path. "Is this the way to the Sacred Fountain, where the Water of Life flows and the Tree of Beauty gives home to the Prophetic Birds?"

The giant had a tremendous beard tangled with twigs and branches. He scratched at it, and a few leaves fluttered to the ground. "Aye. And I, the keeper of the way."

Adrían's heart skipped a beat. Would he have to fight the giant to be allowed to go up? "What must I do?"

"Turn back. You ought to know, little flea, that no one who goes this way ever returns."

"I understand the dangers," said Adrían confidently.

"Of course you don't. But you men never listen. You can't be dissuaded from your foolish dreams. Symptom of greed, probably. It's a common affliction of your kind."

Adrían frowned. He didn't need a lecture, he needed to be moving on. "Can you just tell me what I need to know about finding it?"

The giant sighed. "Very well then. This is what you must know: Do not stop. Do not look back. Keep going until the end."

Adrian blinked at him. "That's it?"

"The only *it* there is," the giant confirmed.

It was almost laughable. Adrían pictured great beasts and specters of evil, shadows protecting the Sacred Fountain and bringing battle to any who sought it. He'd imagined fighting for his very soul against these agents of hell. But just...keep going?

He'd be the wealthiest man in the kingdom by this time tomorrow!

He thanked the giant and set out, setting his feet on the path to begin his ascent.

At first he hiked through dense trees and warm woody scents. The occasional animal crossed his way and fled from him. It was cool, even pleasant on this wide dirt trail. But soon the trees began to thin, and the grass didn't grow, and before long, an enormous field of rocks stretched over the whole face of the mountain leading up to the peak. Adrían didn't stray from the path, but he did notice how beautiful some of the stones were. Dazzling colors dotted the rocky slope. He pondered them, but did not stop. The sun rode high on his back now without trees to shelter him. It drew out his sweat and sapped his strength. He was tired — so very tired.

Whispers began to swirl around him in human voice, at first faint but growing louder.

"Presumptuous fool!" someone hissed nearby, making him jump. "You think you can claim the treasure at the top?"

"Who does he think he is?" someone else agreed. "Look at him. He's obviously a street urchin someone dressed in nice clothes. You can't disguise a pig as a gentleman."

"It's the stink that gives it away," another voice chimed in. "No matter how high they try to rise, they never get the sewer stench off of them. They're born with it when they come into this world in the gutter."

"Were you birthed in a gutter, boy? Did your mother whelp you while she was begging for money?"

"Of course she did. Look at him."

Adrian's face felt hot, and it wasn't just from the exertion. He thought of his mother and grew angry. She and his father had died of illness a few days apart, leaving Adrían the head of the family at too young an age.

Don't stop, the memory of the giant's words echoed.

But this wasn't right. These voices, which seemed to be coming from the very stones themselves, had no business invoking her memory. His blood heated to a living magma in his veins.

The sounds grew louder. The host clamoring out, hurling cruel insults at him, swelled in size. They protested, objecting not to his dreams for finding the treasure, but to his origin of poverty. They drew out every insecurity he possessed and flung them at him in sharpened points.

Adrian's nerves were slipping. He wanted to hit something. Or someone.

Mid-step, he decided to hurl a stone into the midst of the noise to shut them up. He just needed a moment's peace!

So he reached.

~

LUIS

Mercedes had been checking their dagger five times a day for three days now.

Luis was every day more confident that Adrían would come back — and he was very much looking forward to it. Not just because he would come with treasures, but also because Luis was tired of doing his brother's work. The fishermen didn't listen to Luis the way they did with Adrían. He hated it when people thought he was the lesser brother — and too many of them thought exactly that. He was barely two years younger, but they all acted like he was some kid, as if Santiago were trying to give them orders. And what if he were? All three of them were the employers of these men. All three of them had become some of the most important employers in the whole duchy. They should have had as much respect for any one of them as they had for Adrían.

He trudged home from work with a belly full of simmering anger. Santiago tried to cajole him out of it.

"It's just a change, Luis," he said. "Most people don't like change."

"They don't even give me a chance to show them that things haven't changed that much," he growled.

"Hey Luis!" someone called, waving to them from the doorway of his own house. "I hear Don Augustín has paid a visit again. What keeps bringing him back, eh? What's she doing without Adrían around to supervise?"

Luis waved him and the insinuation off. The gossip about Mercedes and the duke was much worse now. No one had thought twice about Adrían's trip — they all assumed he was off to expand their business interest in another town. But Don Augustín had come directly to find out what was really going on, and Mercedes told him of Adrían's mad plan. She did *not* tell him that one of the reasons for it was to boost their marriage prospects. Since then, Don Augustín had come every single day to learn if they had heard any news. He was concerned for Adrían, but the rest of the town thought he came in pursuit of Mercedes.

Though maybe that was part of it too.

They were nearly to their house when they saw Mercedes running out of the door of their villa and into the streets. Something was flashing in her hands and as soon as she got near enough, they saw that her eyes were filled with enormous tears.

"Luis!" she cried, stumbling almost blindly. "Santi!"

"What is it?" said Luis, alarmed.

She shook her head, covering her mouth with one hand and producing the object in the other.

It was the dagger. And its blade was red with blood.

"Adrían," gasped Santiago.

Mercedes's shoulders heaved as she tried to suppress a sob. Luis took the dagger from her. He wiped the blade clean on the bottom of his shirt and pressed his fingertip against the point until a spark of pain zipped through him and a droplet of his own blood slid down the side.

"What are you doing?" Santiago cried.

"I'll go find him," said Luis, chin lifting a little with the certainty of his choice. "I'll find out what happened, and I'll bring him home."

"But he's probably dead!"

"Then I'll bring his body home, at least."

Mercedes shook her head and forgot her tears in favor of anger. "You can't, Luis. Whatever happened to him could happen to you, too."

"It won't. You know how Adrían is. He probably rushed into some situation without thinking it through first. Or got distracted by a shiny coin. That's his way. I'm not like that."

That last bit came out proud and harsh. The anger from the day's difficult labor fueled his need to prove that he was equal to their elder brother.

"Luis," Santiago began, but Luis overrode him.

"You can't dissuade me. Let's go to the house. I'll change, gather supplies, and leave now."

And he did. With his two younger siblings hovering around him, nervous and reluctant, he gathered a few things and filled his bag with food. He kissed them each goodbye, then headed out into the evening gloom.

He didn't know exactly where or how far Adrían had gone, only that he'd said he thought the treasures were somewhere in the mountains. So Luis went in that direction for as long as he could before a moonless night forced him to stop and sleep. He slept well, too, with fiery self-satisfaction burning his belly. It felt good to be going to rescue Adrían. Everyone would know and see that the brothers were equal. And if he found the treasures as well, so much the better.

In the morning, he traveled swiftly and with increasing cheerfulness. Being out here in the wild reminded him of being on the sea. Like he was at the mercy of the elements. Like anything could happen.

And something did happen, after a couple more days walking.

He found a giant at the base of a mountain. The huge creature was dozing against an enormous boulder while sheep grazed around him. Luis squared himself up for a fight and went to him, tapping on his hand.

With a deep baritone sigh that shook the foundations of the earth, the giant opened his eyes and squinted at Luis.

"What is this? Another talking stone?"

"I'm not a stone. I'm a man."

"I have seen so many of you, you all look the same."

"You've seen another one like me? A few days ago, maybe?" Luis suggested.

"Hmm," he grumbled. "Could be."

"He was looking for the Sacred Fountain. He's my brother. I know that something has happened to him and I want to get him back."

The giant sighed again, and Luis felt the rumbling through his whole spine.

"Your brother went the way of the stone. If you want to save him, you have to find the treasures. That is the only way."

"Why do you keep talking about stones? Tell me what to do," Luis demanded, his heart quickening with excitement. "I'll save him."

"So foolish." The giant shook his head. "Very well then. This is what you must know: Do not stop. Do not look back. Keep going until the end."

Luis lifted a brow. "That's all? Didn't you tell that to Adrían?"

"I tell that to everyone," the giant sniffed. "None of you listen. You won't either."

The instructions were absurdly simple. Luis wanted to laugh — he'd never let Adrían live this down. "I'll be back with my brother and the treasures in no time."

The giant yawned, shrugged, and leaned back against his boulder. "*Hasta luego*, then, if you're so confident."

"I am."

Luis left him and headed for the mountain. He reveled in the idea of his heroic elder brother failing at something that Luis himself would accomplish. It stroked his pride in a very pleasant way.

The climb was easy enough at first, but soon the voices began to sweep all around him.

"Look," they whispered. "Another pretender, come to claim the prize."

"He won't make it," they said.

"He doesn't deserve to make it."

"He's not even as interesting as the last one. He's weaker. And obviously less intelligent."

Luis became incensed. Who were these uppity voices questioning his ability? He let his anger drive his pace, and he climbed faster. The peak was hidden in cloud cover, but he thought it was probably near.

His ears were ringing and his head pounding with the cacophony of voices when a single one cried out to him.

"Luis!"

He stumbled in his step, turning reflexively. "Adrían?"

SANTIAGO

The dagger turned bloody again three days after Luis had gone.

Santiago was home when he heard Mercedes' choked cry of dismay. He went into the den where she balanced the accounts, hoping to discover that she was only upset because of some discrepancy in the ledger. Hoping, but not expecting.

She held it in her trembling hands, the blade stained crimson. When she looked up at him, her black eyes were swimming in unspilled tears.

"Santi," she choked.

He went to her and took the dagger, setting it aside and pulling her into a frightened hug.

For most of his life, Mercedes was the only mother he really knew. She had held him and comforted him through his darkest hours. But he'd grown nearly into a man by now, and she felt so small and fragile. It disconcerted him. His sister was never fragile.

"Don't you dare think about going after them," Mercedes whimpered.

Too late. Luis had already committed him to that promise before he left, even though the prospect terrified him. Santiago wasn't sure he could do it. The task was huge, and filled with unknown dangers. But icy fear gripped him at the thought of living in a world without his brothers, too. The business probably wouldn't succeed, they'd sink back into poverty, and the emotional wound of their loss would be too great to overcome. Mercedes might get married and go away, and then he'd be alone. He couldn't be alone.

"I have to," he said, his voice faltering and giving him away.

"Am I to have no brothers, then?" Mercedes snarled. "Will you throw your life away too?"

Santiago picked up the dagger again. He did what he'd seen Luis do, though he did it with trembling, nervous hands. When he returned it to Mercedes, it now bore his blood.

"I don't want to be here without them," he said simply.

"And I want to be here without all three of you? Forget it, Santi. If you're going, then I'm coming with you."

"No, Mechi. Let me do this. I...*can* do it. Stay here and be safe. None of us would want you out there."

She pressed her lips tight together and said nothing for a long time. He didn't know if that look she gave him meant she was angry or wounded. And he didn't believe his own words — so she probably didn't either. He'd never been brave like his brothers. He loved comfort and safety and assurance more than risk. Building their fortune hadn't felt like a risk. They were already at the bottom. And he was young enough when they began that he didn't understand it all. Now he had a comfortable life he loved, and it didn't have anything to do with fighting monsters for mythical treasures. But he loved his brothers too...so what other choice did he have?

Eventually, she spoke again — this time to persuade him to sleep at least one more night at home, and then leave directly in the morning.

Santiago couldn't rest easily. The long night passed with frightful dreams of what could happen to him out there — of what had happened to his brothers. He didn't share Luis' hot temper, or

Adrían's ambition. He was good at following orders. He preferred to follow orders. Did that make him more suited to the task, or less?

Don Augustín appeared at dawn. Mercedes must have sent him word in the night. He'd come to persuade Santiago to abandon his task — but Mercedes had miscalculated, for once. Santiago looked into the face of this intimidating, honorable duke and felt the sinking certainty that he was more bound to his task than ever.

"Your sister needs you here," Don Augustín insisted.

But she didn't. And Santiago knew that if he backed down now, he'd feel like a coward for the rest of his life. Augustín was the kind of man who would ride into *El Infierno* to save someone. So Santiago shook his head and pretended to be that kind of man.

He thought he saw a glint of respect when the duke, realizing his attempt was futile, offered to give him a ride to the edge of town. Santiago was grateful for this, and thanked him when he climbed out of the carriage.

"I know you want to marry my sister," he told the duke, holding on to the last moments before he had to begin. "It's one of the reasons Adrían went in search of these mad treasures. Will you still marry her if we don't find them?"

The duke gaped at him, horror descending over his features. "Santiago, I never needed your family to possess treasures to find your sister worthy. You must believe me."

"Good. Because I'm bringing my brothers home, not going after the Fountain. You understand?"

"That is the only thing I want for all of you. Are you certain you won't let me help?"

Santiago wanted to accept that help. He wanted the duke's own army at his disposal. But again, he flinched away from being thought of as a coward, and shook his head.

"It isn't necessary." Santiago extended a hand, even though he had no business shaking hands with any grandees. "Thank you. *Hasta luego*, then."

With that, he turned and began his journey. He traveled most of the way in a nervous sweat, wishing he were back on his boat scouring for fish instead of launching himself into the unknown. He liked the water. He liked his work. He did not like marching through endless fields, sleeping in the cold under the open sky where any nocturnal predator might snatch him.

By the time he found the giant, he was homesick and tired.

"Have you seen my brothers?" he asked, wondering if this strange ancient-looking shepherd was the cause of that twice-bloody dagger.

"It is probable," said the giant, not bothering to look up from his whittling. "They were searching for a fountain?"

"Yes." Santiago watched that big knife dance over the wood. He swallowed. Did giants eat grown men?

"Then I change my answer to *definitely*. Will you follow them?"

"I don't care about the Fountain. I don't need to go that far. I just want to get my brothers home again, so things can go back to how they were."

"You will get them back when you get to the Fountain," said the giant. "To get to the Fountain, you must climb."

"Climb?" Santiago looked at the path winding its way into the ascending trees.

The giant recited in a baritone sing-song. "This is what you must know: Do not stop. Do not look back. Keep going until the end."

Santiago grit his teeth against those ominous words. He closed his fists, mustering what courage remained. For Adrían, for Luis, for Mercedes. He could do it.

...Couldn't he?

~

MERCEDES

Mercedes stood on the docks and recorded the catches of the various fishermen with a blazing fire of anger inside her that kept any of them from objecting twice to being ordered about by a female. She was barely holding things together by herself, but she *was* holding them. If her brothers were fool enough to go traipsing off into the wild after some fairytale, she would be the logical one who held their fortune together so they had something to come back to.

And if they didn't come back at all...

No, she wouldn't let herself think that way. Not yet. It had been three days and the dagger now sheathed at her side was still clear and clean. Of course, it was about this time that it had turned red for the others, but she was pretending otherwise. It made it easier to cope with the now very hectic days consuming her time while she waited for the others to return.

During a break in the work, she went to sit down on some barrels, wiping the sweat from her eyes. If Don Augustín could see her now, he might think twice about wanting to marry her. She knew she looked a sight. But she hadn't been sleeping — she'd never been alone overnight in her whole life, and the villa felt much too big and grand without her brothers there. Only a few servants stayed overnight, and Mercedes sometimes forgot they were there altogether. During the day, she'd been working herself to sufficient distraction, but nothing could ease the nights.

She reached for the dagger to check it, reflex more than anything. But even as she grasped the handle, her heart skipped a beat and she found it suddenly very hard to breathe.

If it was bloody...

What? What would she do? No, she told herself she didn't need a plan because the blade would be clean. Precariously teetering on this confidence, she pulled it from its sheath.

Instead of glinting metal, rusted scarlet smeared the blade.

Mercedes cursed and dropped the dagger as if it was made of molten steel, standing to hastily get away from it. Santiago was lost! Right on schedule. Her whole body began to tremble as the implication of this descended upon her.

"Mercedes?" someone asked nearby. "Are you alright?"

The words yanked her back into blinding, painfully sharp

awareness and she whirled, looking around to meet the concerned eyes of a fisherman's wife staring at her. She grabbed hold of the woman.

"Carla, I need you to go to the palace of Don Augustín. Tell him I had to go after them. Do you understand?"

Carla blushed violently. "Me? Speak to the don?"

"You can do it. I need you to do it. And then tell your husband that I need him to run things here for a few days. Keep an accounting of everything he does, and when I get back we will see what we can do to promote him to dock foreman."

Carla nodded, but Mercedes didn't stick around to see the surprise fully unfold. She was already moving. She picked up the dagger, slipped it into her belt again, and set off. She stopped by the villa long enough to lock everything up and grab some food and a jug for water, and then she was gone.

A feverish madness had taken hold of her, laughing in the face of logic. Three had gone, and three had fallen. She was certain to meet the same fate. But Mercedes and the madness embraced this possibility. She would not lose her brothers. They were the only ones in this world who truly loved her, and the only ones who she truly loved. If they had crossed into that distant country from whence no traveler returned, she would follow. And no prince, duke, friend, or employee could convince her otherwise.

She carved a trail eastward, towards the mountains.

Night fell more quickly than she expected. After she'd stumbled yet again and fallen on her face, she decided to stay in the cool grasses and doze until morning. As soon as the sun began to paint the horizon in gradient red smoking up into darkest indigo, she rose once again. The urgency driving her febrile steps had not diminished in her deep, oblivious sleep. It drove her like the doe before the wolf.

After two more nights, she came upon a path leading up a steep, towering mountain. Mercedes might have passed it off as unimportant, except for the giant sitting at the trailhead while sheep grazed around him. What road required a giant to guard the way, except one of great importance?

"A little moth to a big flame," the giant hummed when she approached.

"*Buen dia, señor.* I'm sorry to disturb you," said Mercedes.

"You're all coming quite regularly now." His booming tone was conversational, but disinterested. He didn't even glance at her. "It used to be every few years. Now it's every few days."

Despite herself, her hopes flashed bright and hot for one glorious moment. "Does that mean you've seen my brothers?"

"If you mean three foolish young humans all racing up the same mountain, one right after the other, then yes."

"They haven't come back this way?"

"Of course not." Now he did turn to look at her. His enormous green eyes sharpened when he saw her, and he leaned towards her. "Oh. You're different. I don't see many of your kind attempting the slope. Not for a long time, anyway. Are you also after the Sacred Fountain?"

"I want to get my brothers back, if they can be brought back. Are they dead?"

"Not in so many words, no." He cocked his head and peered at her. "To get them back, you have to climb the mountain and get to the Fountain."

"Tell me everything I must do, if you please," she asked, making her voice more gentle than desperate. "I will do whatever it takes."

"If you can." Here, the giant sounded amused. "I told these brothers of yours the same that I am about to tell you, and all of them failed. Tell me, who will come for you when you have failed as well? Am I to expect your whole village? I might as well make a signpost and save myself the trouble of repeat conversations."

"I'm the last one," she said. "There's no one else."

"Well, then, Señorita Moth, listen well, or you will all of you be gone forever. This is what you must know: Do not stop. Do not look back. Keep going until the end."

"Just...don't stop?" Was that it? The only instruction?

He went back to his fire. "It's harder than it sounds, isn't it? Or your brothers would not have been lost."

That was true. "What is it that will try to make me turn around?" she asked.

He blinked at her, surprised. "No one has ever asked me that before."

"I will trade you my dagger for any information you have." She produced it. "It can let you know when something has befallen someone you love."

The giant picked it up between his thumb and forefinger. "This is a special little trinket indeed. But it's nonsense to me. You keep it, little Moth, I'll tell you what you want to know. This mountain is littered with dashed dreams turned to stones. Those who have tried it and failed now believe it cannot be done. There will be many on your way who will rail against you, who will be angry, or who will laugh at you, who will say it is impossible because they could not do it. Despair will creep in. Doubt will hunt you. But do not listen. Keep going, and keep going. Until you have done what you came to do."

It was cryptic enough that Mercedes still didn't know what to expect on the path, but it settled in her like the comfort of weapons against unknown enemies. The giant's gaze held her, gentle and sincere.

"Thank you, sir," she said. "I won't forget your patience, or your kindness."

He gave her a nod. "I very much hope you do not become a stone, little Moth."

Mercedes left him and walked until night fully fell and forced her to stop. As soon as light began to leak over the horizon, she began again and soon found herself on the eastern path, climbing up a thickly wooded slope and waiting for the voices meant to dissuade her. Her jaw was set, her mind focused to a razor sharp edge. Her body wasn't quite as prepared for this steep climb as it perhaps should have been. Before she'd even left the trees, she was panting heavily and forcing herself onward, step after step.

But when the trees finally did vanish, she forgot her weariness for a moment and her breath caught for an entirely different reason.

The rest of the way up was marked by a vast and endless field of rocks. Large and small, dull and brilliant, they littered the slope in a numberless expanse. Stones. The giant said he hoped she wouldn't become a stone. Were these rocks around her those who had failed?

"And are three of these my brothers?" she murmured breathlessly to herself as she kept walking, a shudder working its way down her spine. Would they suddenly spring back into the shapes of men when she reached the summit? Would they be alright? Would they remember anything?

"A girl?" Somewhere nearby, a sharp voice rang out, making her jump. She scrambled forward before instincts could make her pause to look for the speaker.

"A woman thinks she can make this climb? How insulting."

"How dare she leave her home unattended to come here?"

"She must not have a husband. He would never allow this."

"Her? A husband? Absolutely not. Look at her. What man would ever want someone so poor and filthy?"

"Don't stop," Mercedes whispered to herself, pushing aside these disembodied voices crying out all around her. She stared at the peak above and kept climbing. These jeers were no worse than she imagined the nobles and grandees said of her and her brothers when they presumed to appear at high society functions. Certainly it's what they would have whispered to each other when they went to Don Augustín's ball in a few weeks. And it would be what they said more loudly if he really did proceed in his plan to marry her.

"You're so cruel!" another voice cried out. "To shunt us aside with your feet, to step on us. Why won't you help us?"

"Help us!" several more joined in.

"Don't look back," said Mercedes more loudly. Somewhere in this cacophony, her brothers had succumbed to temptation, one by one.

She couldn't afford to do that. She hadn't pricked her finger, and nobody was watching the dagger to see if she would return. If she gave heed to the outraged host of voices, they would spend eternity among the stones. Forgotten.

"Wild, savage thing. She must disappoint her mother terribly."

"Of course her mother is disappointed! Heartless child. Don't you care about your mother at all?"

"Keep going until the end," Mercedes growled, shutting her ears to them. Shut her heart against the hurt and anger that flared at their mention of tender memories. The peak was nearer now. Just a few more minutes...

"Mercedes," a strong, clear voice called out above the throng.

She nearly stumbled. "Adrían," she gasped, hurrying forward and away from her impulse to stop.

"Mercedes," cried Santiago. "Help us!"

"I will," she sang in reply, keeping her eyes fixed on the peak even as they filled with tears. "I promise, I will."

"Why do you keep going?" said Luis. "Why are you leaving? Help us!"

They didn't know what had happened to them. Or they didn't realize what would happen to her if she stopped. Or they were trapped under the same sort of spell that compelled all the trapped souls here to disparage the climber.

"Mercedes!" said Adrían again, urgently.

She couldn't stand it. She wanted to turn around. To look for them. To scour through the stones until she found the three belonging to her brothers. She could carry them home and take them to some bruja or magician and beg for them to be changed back. Instead, she began to run. The last stretch was so steep, she had to use her hands to help her scrabble up the mountain side, fleeing the voices growing in volume and desperation, assailing her senses until she knew nothing but the roar of an anguished crowd.

But eventually she pulled herself up onto a ledge — and there, all sound ceased.

Even though it wasn't the least bit cold, a pristine field of snow blanketed the peak. In fact, she felt warmer now than when she'd been climbing the rocky slope, with wind nipping against her chapped skin.

An enormous tree stood in the very center of this snowy plateau. The branches twisted and tangled into a complex web, adorned with leaves so brightly green it almost hurt to behold. Interspersed among the green were patches of autumn, bright red and yellow and orange. And here and there were the cheerful pink blossoms of springtime, flecked with frost, as though this tree existed simultaneously in all seasons.

At its trunk flowed a little spring, seemingly fed by the snow. It bubbled merrily towards the edge of the cliff and then tumbled away down another side. In the tree conversed a host of birds. Mercedes couldn't see them, but she could hear their murmured, muted conversation in sounds that closely resembled human spccch.

She'd made it.

Quickly, without really taking time to truly experience her awe, she ran towards the stream and withdrew the jug she'd brought with her. She dipped the spout into the flow to let it fill. Where the water touched her skin, it healed what cuts and chafes she'd gathered on her way. After the jug had been filled, she thrust both hands into the spring and drew it up to her face, splashing it over every inch of exposed skin she had. After, she felt much refreshed.

Next she went to the tree. Standing beneath it, she felt deep vibrations in the air, like some primeval song humming on currents too deep for her to hear. She touched the trunk and felt its warmth. Looking up into its tangled branches, she saw the birds. They were white at first glance, but as they hopped and flitted about, she saw that the light cast rainbow hues shimmering along the edges of their feathers.

One of them spotted her and flitted down to the nearest branch, cocking its head and peering at her with one violet eye.

"Hello," Mercedes whispered.

The bird fidgeted and hopped from one foot to the other, but it didn't say anything.

"I need to know how to save my brothers," she said. "I was told I would find the answer up here. Can you help me?"

It turned and seized hold of a slender twig in its beak. It shook the twig so violently, it snapped off. Hopping down onto her shoulder, the bird seemed to whisper around the twig. "Let's go."

"Go where?" Mercedes had the Water of Life, this Bird of Prophecy had in its beak a branch of the Tree of Beauty. All three things that Adrian had set out to find, but surely the little bird didn't mean to come with her all the way—

"Home," it said.

She didn't move right away, wondering if she should take this little thing away from its beautiful home.

The bird peeped a normal bird sound and flapped its wings, reassuring her.

Mercedes went to the edge where she'd climbed up. Looking down, the rocky slope plunged away from her, down towards the tree line. She wasn't eager to face the cries and shouts of the lost again. But Adrían, Luis, and Santiago were down there too. So down she went.

The bird fluttered where it needed to when her climbing disrupted its balance, but otherwise it kept hold on her and kept hold of the twig. She crouched and slid on her heels down to where the path was no longer so steep. No voices cried out to her. No one said a word.

"What do I do?" she whispered to the bird, unnerved by the unearthly silence.

"The water," said the bird.

She opened the jug and sprinkled some of the water onto the ground.

All at once, people began to appear around her. Man after man, and sometimes a woman. They were all dressed in various outfits of adventure or climbing. They all scratched their heads and looked around in confusion, or looked at Mercedes and began to weep.

"I've been trapped here for so long, I forgot I was ever a man," one knight in very old armor sobbed. "Thank you. Thank you."

Apparently none of them remembered the cruel things they'd said to her. She didn't remind them.

A little further on, she sprinkled more water, and more people joined the host now growing behind her.

"Mechi!" cried Santiago, running to her from somewhere in the crowd.

Mercedes whirled around and caught him just in time. He threw himself into her arms and hugged her so tight, she thought her ribs might crush. The bird fluttered onto her head to avoid the squeeze.

"Mercedes, you did it!" Luis came next, beaming from ear to ear.

And Adrían. This time, Mercedes was the one to run to him.

"Well done, little sister," he murmured against her head as he folded her into his embrace.

"Come on," Santiago urged. "Let's get off this mountain."

The whole congregation of lost adventurers produced a great rumble of agreement. Mercedes laughed.

The host of them together descended the path that each had ascended alone, and when they emerged at the bottom, the giant woke up from his nap with a grunt of surprise. Mercedes grinned and waved to him as they passed. She would have to learn what giants valued, and return to thank him one day.

They marched out across the fields until the sun sank low. Just when they were wondering whether or not they should camp for the night, Santiago spotted something in the distance, gleaming in the sun.

The something moved towards them quickly, and as it drew nearer, materialized into a large, armor-clad company of soldiers. The soldiers were led by Don Augustín himself, bedecked as if for war, proud and handsome on his charger.

When he saw them, he gave a shout and spurred into a mad gallop over the rest of the distance.

"He didn't ride out with the cavalry when you went missing," Luis chuckled, elbowing Adrián.

"It's an expensive gesture," Adrián agreed with amusement.

Mercedes was tired, and emotionally drained from her journey. The glow of triumph had carried her this far, but she'd planned to sleep more deeply than ever tonight. Yet somehow, in the midst of her exhaustion, her heart began to race all over again and her stomach flopped with pleasant surprise at the sight of the duke racing towards — her.

He dismounted immediately and pulled off his helmet. His cheeks were flushed from the heat of his ride, his hair disheveled, and his eyes shone with wonder. Mercedes blushed at the mere sight of him.

"My lady," he choked, shaking his head. His hand reached out as if he wanted to touch her face, but he faltered and pulled it back. "You're alive!"

"And you're all the way out here," she laughed, looking around at the vast open fields around them.

"I got your message. I made preparations as quickly as I could." He didn't tear his eyes away from her. "I was afraid I'd be too late."

"You *are* too late," said Adrián. "Mercedes has done it all herself."

That finally persuaded Augustín to take in the whole scene — the bird on her shoulder, the missing brothers, the assorted host — and his astonishment grew in spades. He embraced Adrián and from there things began to move very quickly. Mercedes seemed to slip out of immediate reality as everyone went into motion around her. Explanations were made, greetings spread, the soldiers began to make camp and distribute rations to the all wayward adventurers. Adrián fell into lively conversation with one of the rescued adventurers, an older blond man with blue eyes. Luis and Santiago jumped in to help the soldiers.

But Mercedes didn't feel quite part of it, as if the sight of Augustín out here in these circumstances had transported her back onto the mountain peak. Mercedes watched him work with her brothers to organize everyone. She wondered at the little bloom of warmth flickering to life in her chest. The bird brushed its soft feathered head against her cheek.

"I thought I was alone," she whispered to the bird, running her fingers along its silky breast. "If I became a stone, no one would come looking for me."

But she'd been wrong. Someone had risked a great deal. For her.

In the last of the evening glow, the duke sat down beside her and gave her a plate of freshly prepared food.

"You deserve a queen's feast, but this is the best I can do out here," he said, flashing her a bashful smile.

She glanced at him, pleasure scattering goosebumps across her skin. "I'm grateful you came after me."

"I didn't do it because I doubted your ability," he said, his voice low. "I knew that of all of the Martíns, you were the most capable.

But I wanted to be your safety net, should you need us. I — I couldn't stand..."

His words trailed off, and she thought she knew how he might finish that sentence. She knew he was interested in her — and she knew he'd become close to her family, his daily visits since Adrián's departure had proven it. But she hadn't known, hadn't guessed, how deeply these feelings ran. And she hadn't guessed anything like it could glow to life inside her too.

He didn't say anything further, but turned his attention to the setting sun. Mercedes let the full weight of the day escape her in a long, slow breath. Here, at the end of it, she discovered something new within her that seemed just as rare and lovely as the Fountain treasures. For the first time since the death of her parents, Mercedes felt that she could relax and the world wouldn't fall apart. Someone else was keeping watch. Her family was safe.

~

DON AUGUSTÍN

"Come, *primo*," said the king, striding out of the palace doors, towards the carriage awaiting them. "You may have already seen these legendary treasures, but I have not. You'll indulge my impatience."

Augustín sighed good-naturedly and adjusted his coat once before following his cousin into the carriage. It was silly to be nervous about his appearance, but he was going to see Mercedes and that always made his stomach turn funny, childish flips.

"I knew you would do great things," the king was saying. "Finding these treasures — you're a credit to the kingdom, cousin."

"I didn't find them. Mercedes Martín did," he reminded the king.

"But you and your knights played a part."

"Not really. I went to help her, but we found her with her

brothers returning home already, with an enormous following of people."

"I heard about that. People who we thought were gone forever. Well done, Augustín, well done."

Augustín sighed again, this time with a touch more exasperation. Many of the town thought the same thing as the king, at first. When they saw their duke and his knights returning with the missing Martín family and their extraordinary treasures, they gave him all the credit. He was quick to deny their praise and declare publicly that it was Mercedes who deserved their love. Adrían backed him up and told the story of how all three brothers were lost until Mercedes came.

The word spread quickly, and Mercedes soon became the talk of the kingdom. Not that she enjoyed that very much.

La Villa de Martín had become a crowded place these days, as people from all walks of life and all corners of the kingdom came to see the artifacts from the Sacred Fountain. Now, though, the villa was empty. Nobody else was allowed to visit today — it was the king's very own day to come and see for himself.

When they emerged from the carriage, all four of the Martíns were there to greet them. The man Mercedes had made foreman turned out to be exceptionally well-suited to the task, and he could manage affairs for them when they had other duties — which was often, now. Wealthy daughters from all over the kingdom were suddenly being presented to the three very handsome brothers as eligible matches, and new business partners were springing up out of the woodwork. Their fame had opened many, many doors.

Men had come calling on Mercedes, too. Augustín kept a respectful distance so she could explore these options without feeling any obligation to him. According to Adrían, however, these would-be-suitors did not interest her. That gave him some hope.

She glanced at him with a half-suppressed smile now, and his hopes soared into the stratosphere.

"Your majesty," Adrían said when the king approached him. He bowed low. "Welcome to our humble home."

"Yes, it is very small, isn't it?" said the king cheerfully. "You must be Adrían. Augustín has told me much about you and your remarkable family."

"It is an honor to be spoken of so highly."

Augustín watched the king make all the introductions, and then followed him into the house. He went directly to the courtyard — where all the visitors were going these days.

A beautiful tree stood in the middle; summer mixed with autumn mixed with springtime. Augustín had been there when Mercedes placed the twig in the ground, and watched as a full, glorious tree sprang up in an instant. The marvelous Bird of Prophecy on her shoulder had hopped up into the branches and began to sing happily.

It still sang now, flitting from branch to branch, sometimes dipping down to bathe itself in the pedestal basin wherein she'd poured the Water of Life.

"I think it likes having the tree all to itself," Mercedes said quietly, coming to stand beside him.

Augustín glanced at her. "It knew what it was doing, then, when it volunteered to come with you."

She nodded.

The king perused the treasures for a while, and then returned. "This is the most remarkable thing I have ever seen. And this is the most remarkable woman, for having brought them here. Tell me, my dear, how can I get some treasures of my own? I will send my best men to do it."

"Some have already begun trying," Mercedes admitted. "But stones are gathering on the slope again. They do not listen. It's best if you enjoy what you see before you here, your majesty."

Augustín nodded in agreement. "Love of money, or pride, or comfort won't be motivation enough, sire. Your motives must be purer than that, or they will not carry you to the top of the mountain."

The king barely heard them. He grinned and clapped his hand on Augustín's shoulder. "Yes, indeed, a very remarkable woman. If I didn't have an excellent wife of my own, I'd marry her directly. You're a fool if you don't take the opportunity before you, cousin."

Augustín chuckled and glanced at Mercedes, whose warm olive face had gone as red as the autumn leaves. "That's up to my lady. I think you'll agree that she has earned the right to decide for herself, sire."

The king gave Augustín an absurd look. He turned to Mercedes. "Did you know, this daft cousin of mine originally had his sights set on a peasant? Some fisherman's daughter?"

"Sister," Augustín corrected.

"When he consulted with me, I told him *out of the question*! He deserved someone much better than that. Aren't you glad now, Augustín, that I didn't let you make such a rash decision?"

Augustín watched as Mercedes frowned a little when she thought the king wasn't looking. He cleared his throat. "I am pleased this new prospect delights you more, your majesty, but for myself I would have been happy either way."

The king made a noise of incredulity, but Mercedes looked at the ground and smiled a private little smile.

"Perhaps, sire, might I suggest that you get the whole story yourself from Adrían," Augustín said, addressing the king but never taking his eyes off Mercedes.

Freed from their royal inquisitor, the two of them together walked over to the tree and looked up into its colorful branches. The beautiful white bird peered down at them.

"Well, Señorita Martín," Augustín said softly. "I would be honored to have a fisherman's sister for a wife. Could you bear to stoop so low as to marry a duke?"

Her dark eyes met his, and in those fathomless depths he saw all the treasures of the Fountain, and more. "Not for your money, or your reputation, or your comforts. But for your kindness. For — for love. I have learned to keep moving forward...towards what I want. And what I want now..." her gaze dropped shyly and a smile crept over her face. "Is you."

Augustín could have kissed her with the sudden rush of joy that flooded through him. Instead he took her hand and brushed his lips against her knuckles. She laughed. He grinned and looked up into the tree. "Bird of Prophecy, how long shall we live this happily?"

The bird with dazzling colors hopped down to the lowest branch. It regarded them, and said with certainty, "For ever after."

THE
BIRDBATH

DAVID CARTER

Author's Note: Inspiration for 'The Birdbath' came from various directions but perhaps from the same basic source, not unlike the birds in the story. At first the idea was vague, and prompted by the racket I heard one day being made by what seemed to be a convention of starlings in the boughs of a shrub on the lawn of the Harvard Divinity School Chapel. Not long after that I came across a simple but remarkable pencil sketch of a birdbath on the cover of a book about Sacramental Theology in the library; that's when the title suggested itself to me and I knew that I would write a story called 'The Birdbath' one day. Somewhere along the way I read a passage in a collection of letters by the author Virginia Woolf describing one of the episodes of what she called her 'madness;' she could hear the birds outside her sickroom window singing in ancient Greek. But it wasn't until I encountered the Sufi pir Idries Shah's discussion of the Persian poem that recounts the ancient legend of 'The Conference of the Birds' that the voices all came together. It's an extravagant, delightful poem that demands close attention, as it is packed with allusions that can be obscure especially for those of us who haven't been brought up in the traditions that nurture it. But at heart it is just a sweet story about the creative tension that leads us on. I can only hope that my retelling is faithful to its spirit.

I really thought it was the end of the world, and I was surprised by that, believe it or not, and surprised by the fact that I kept thinking about killing myself. At the same time a part of me, the rational part, I guess, kept insisting that I was taking it all too hard, that I was making a big deal over what, in the long run, would be nothing. *So she dumped you*, said that part of me – I could practically hear its disdain for the terrible agony I was in—*So what? There's plenty of fish in the sea.*

Even as miserable as I was, I considered such clichés beneath me. I wanted to punch that part of myself in the mouth, to feel its lips split against my teeth, and to taste blood. *You don't get it*, I said mentally through mentally gritted teeth. *She was my soul mate.*

Not anymore—I could hear my own self sneering. *To hell with you*, I told myself, and I threw my empty cellophane sandwich wrapper into the birdbath. In my right mind, I wouldn't ever casually litter like that. My mind's eye was only seeing my ex, her pretty, contemptuous face as she said the last words she ever said to me:

"You live in a fairy tale," she said. "You believe what you want to believe. You need to get a life."

Another stupid cliché. As if I didn't have a life. She had *been* my life. I did everything I could to keep her happy, but nothing really made any difference. She was one of those people who can go from hot to cold in a snap, and I probably did spend too much time trying to figure out her moods, but isn't that what love is? To tell me to get a life... she might as well tell me to breathe while she's choking me. Looking back, that very dynamic could sum up our entire relationship. I didn't realize it, you know, until it was ended.

Freshly miserable, I watched the sandwich wrapper expand and sink into the dirty water of the birdbath. I'd forgotten to bring something to read like I usually did when I had my lunch in the park across the street from my office building, so I didn't have anything but my own troubles to keep me occupied that day. My troubles, and apple, and tomato and mayonnaise sandwich.

I hated the conspicuousness sitting there on the park bench doing nothing like some kind of freak; I thought about going back to my cubicle early—but after hours spent within the unnatural, sanitized and self-consciously busy atmosphere of my office building I couldn't stand the thought of going back inside so soon. I had grown up in a suburb a long way away and had spent most of the summers of my childhood in a cottage at the beach, and I have found throughout my life that when I do not spend at least a part of my day out of doors I can't sleep at night.

That day was well into December. A spiteful chill was in the air and I hugged myself in my inadequate blazer after bolting down my sandwich. I told myself that I might as well return to the office before I caught a cold; I could compensate for the short lunch hour by leaving work early. But having only my own company to look forward to after work, the prospect of a longer evening than normal wasn't attractive. Even though I was young and well educated and gainfully, if not meaningfully, employed, I had no idea where to go from there.

To keep myself alive I huddled on the park bench, restless and shivering. I had almost had enough when I noticed two birds perched upon the rim of the birdbath that stood under the canopy of a spreading oak just a few yards in front of me. They were perfectly ordinary birds, but something about them held my attention. I don't know how long I sat there staring at them before I realized their conversation was intelligible to me.

Never having been much of a birdwatcher, I had no idea what sort of birds these were. They were small birds, colored brown with pale freckled feathers on their breasts, and they had small, thorn-like beaks that stayed closed as they vocalized. Yet they stood in front of me speaking what seemed to be plain American English with sharp and small yet clearly audible voices. Because their conversation snuck up on my awareness, it was a while before it dawned on me that what I was hearing I could not possibly be hearing. The sharp breeze rattled the few dry leaves left on the trees; passers-by of my own species chatted and laughed; cars honked and growled on the avenues that bordered the park, and the birdsong in the distance sounded as incomprehensible as ever. But the two little birds perched on the rim of the birdbath were most definitely speaking English. I shook my head to clear it, but the birds chattered on.

"So," said the slightly larger bird, with an unmistakable air of indignation, "it would seem that our summons to convene has been roundly ignored. I suppose our good comrades have all got better things to do than attend a council meeting. We might as well go home, son."

The smaller bird cocked his little head. "But Father, *we're* here. And we just got here. Shouldn't we wait a while? Everyone else was late last time, too."

The larger bird poked his tiny beak at a speck of something in the birdbath water then tossed whatever it was onto the ground. "The indifference of everybird else accomplishes nothing but to waste our valuable time. It is hardly worthwhile for the two of us to meet here merely for form; we share a nesthold, for pity's sake! I am highly perturbed, concerned, and indignant. If council meeting attendance does not improve in short order, it could spell disaster for our community. Regular gatherings to share information and concerns are essential for public safety. Of late, far too few of our city-dwelling comrades seem to comprehend that fact."

"Maybe they'll come along," the smaller bird chirped. "Maybe they're just busy."

"*I'm* busy myself!" said the larger bird. "Don't *I* have mouths to feed? Including *yours*? Don't make excuses for the apathetic, my son. You will find that the excuses sure to be offered by them will far exceed anything you can imagine in sheer preposterousness. But mark my words, they will rue their heedless ways. As anybird with a grain of sense can see, lean times are ahead, and there are preparations to be made. Change is in the air. Let's go back to the nest, son; I must cogitate upon this development. Such a dismaying lack of community engagement calls for fresh strategy. Outreach and engagement! Meeting adjourned."

"Until tomorrow," the smaller bird added.

"Until tomorrow," the larger bird agreed. "Tomorrow is another day."

Off they flew, in parallel arcs, into the canopy of the spreading firs and pines that fringed the park. Tossing my apple core into a wastebasket, I got up from the bench and made my way back to my office, feeling both cheered and alarmed.

∼

BACK AT THE OFFICE, I continued to feel weird. I would have liked to have shared with someone, anyone, the impossible, delightful conversation I overheard— but of course I knew better. I was new there, and I did not really know the people I spent the week with. All literary types. Vaguely friendly, but hardly inviting. Like me, they all seemed to prefer the companionship of the books and manuscripts that surrounded and occupied us as catalogers. And catalogers have a bad enough reputation for kookiness and social awkwardness without my adding to it by claiming to understand the language of birds.

But of course the conversation of the birds was on my mind for the rest of the day as I processed updates in my cubicle. And that night, as I lay in bed in my tiny studio apartment, as the sirens and screams and traffic of the city raised a racket that kept sleep just in the wings, I kept debating whether or not I was losing my mind. And yet when I woke up the next morning, I felt refreshed even as I staggered to the coffeepot. I hummed in the shower for the first time since I was a kid. I was looking forward to my lunch hour, if not to work.

I stayed in a relatively good mood all morning. I worked at somewhat faster than my usual pace and told several of my co-workers that I was leaving early for lunch and might return a bit late. One of these, a young woman who might have noticed that I was out the door without the usual book under my arm, watched me go with a knowing smile on her face, as if she thought I was meeting someone special.

But when I arrived at the park bench, the two brown birds of the day before were nowhere to be seen. The birdbath was deserted except for a couple of small withered brown leaves and sodden pine needles floating on the surface of the murky water. A number of squirrels scampered around the birdbath's base. I threw those squirrels, whose chittering didn't communicate anything to me, the corners of my sandwich, and they stuffed their cheeks hurriedly and furtively like urchins in a Dickens novel.

I glanced at my watch every few moments while I munched on the remains of my sandwich without really tasting it. Half an hour passed, but no birds arrived, and still the birdsong in the distance was as meaningless to me as the undifferentiated murmurings of a human crowd. I sighed. Maybe I *had* been psychotic the day before. Maybe the strain of the break up and a new job in a city where I had no friends and no knack for making any had simply pushed me unknowingly over some unseen psychological edge. Once again I felt so much hopelessness that I considered not going back to work, returning to my third story apartment, and jumping off the roof. I set my jaw and stood. The cold late autumn wind slipped through the cuffs and collar of my blazer and I shuddered like someone being shaken from within.

Then I heard, above all the city sounds, a single snatch of birdsong issuing from the vast spreading canopy of the maple above the birdbath. "Shall we meet? Shall we meet at the bath? All clear. Shall we meet?" Was it chance? Or was it destiny? At any rate, it was then that the squirrels I'd fed, having had their fill, dashed away.

Within a few seconds dozens of birds of various sizes, shapes, colors, and voices descended, some perched upon the rim of the concrete birdbath, some on the branches of nearby trees, some stood pecking at the ground. I sat back down on the bench.

I LOST TRACK OF TIME. I don't know how long I sat listening, but by the time I came to myself and returned in a rush to the office I was shockingly late, and my peculiar new elation was conspicuous to not a few of my co-workers. I explained myself by saying that I had gotten sick and I promised my immediate supervisor, who was, on the whole, a lot more puzzled and surprised at my behavior than she was angry, that it would never happen again.

And yet by the end of the day, in spite of my extended lunch hour, I accomplished much more than usual and left the office at 5:30 with the pleasant sense that I had redeemed myself somehow, that I had managed to lift myself above any petty reproach. When the street level doors of my office building hissed closed behind me and I entered the stream of pedestrians on the sidewalk, I decided that the prospect of returning right away to my third story studio apartment was more unappealing than ever. I checked my wallet for cash and decided that I could afford to treat myself to a decent supper at a nice downtown restaurant and at least one drink.

I ordered a steak, rare, and a vermouth cassis, and as I sat in that warm, dim restaurant, with the murmur of human conversation all around me punctuated by the tinkle of silverware against china, I recalled with a simple happiness all that I had seen and heard over lunch that day.

The larger small brown bird, the "Father," called the meeting and was the first to land on the rim of the birdbath. His son, the smaller brown bird, perched right beside him and gazed at me, I felt at the time, with an air of curiosity and suspicion. After that a cardinal arrived, one of the few birds I could recognize. Then, in very quick succession, a bunch of other birds arrived. There was a large crow, who didn't perch on the birdbath but rather paced like a hunched old British butler on the ground right below. There was a blue jay that settled on the ground, too, along with others I couldn't classify. After the arrivals tapered off, the larger little brown bird raised his voice above the twittering of greetings and general commentary. "If I could call this meeting to order! Everybird's attention, please. I'm afraid I must begin by reiterating the importance of regular, daily attendance at these gatherings by each and every one of us in this habitat. I was alarmed and disappointed by everybird's absence yesterday."

The answer from the gathering was a general musical grumbling that, like the babble of a human crowd, made it impossible for me understand much. Out of this came the voice of a small, rust colored little fellow with a roundish body and a thornlike yellow beak. "I've got seven beaks to feed. Things come up when you have a big family. I can't come to every meeting."

The larger brown bird, whom I was coming to think of as the Patriarch, swerved his head from the left to the right in a quick glance at the entire gathering. "Would anyone care to respond to the chickadee?"

So, I said to myself. That's a chickadee. It did look a bit like a baby chicken, the fuzzy little creatures you see on Easter cards. I decided I would buy myself an Audubon Guide in order to be able to identify all these birds for myself.

In the meantime, the Patriarch called for order.

"Order!" he squawked. "Well, then, I'll explain, for the hundredth time, the purpose of these gatherings. My friends and fellow inhabitants, it is in everyone's best interest that we meet! This park, these trees, this very birdbath upon which many of us are presently perching, is our habitat for the time being, and while is has been carefully selected after rigorous scouting, it is by no means without its dangers. All of us must assume the responsibility of vigilance, which means communication is key. Even in a relatively peaceful setting such as this urban park, our homes and families are in considerable peril due to the constant proximity of beasts who care nothing for us as individuals. Like all civilized creatures, like our fathers and mothers before us, we must come together frequently as one body in order to share perceptions and strategies."

He pause, and scanned the little gathering like a preacher searching out a backslider within his congregation. He fixed his glance on the round fellow. "My little chickadee, how safe is your nest and your hatchlings if I see a vile opossum creeping up your trunk and I don't let you know that he's found you out? Yesterday a flock of filthy human adolescents were terrorizing even their own species in this park with slingshots, and I was nearly killed by one of their projectiles while perching on this very basin. I would never have suffered such a fright, which may well have taken days from my already all too brief life-span, had somebird, perhaps even yourself, chickadee, been paying attention and had the common courtesy to warn me!" The brown bird's tailfeathers twitched indignantly.

The chickadee had his beak in the water and seemed to be paying little, if any, attention to being singled out.

The brown bird continued. "I hope that answers your question. If nothing else, it provides for me a fitting introduction for the first item on the agenda for this meeting. As you know, this is my thirteenth winter as the leader of this particular community, and as I am undeniably becoming ancient in days, it is more than likely to be my last winter among the living. Now that autumn is well underway, and most of us have arrived who are going to arrive, and most of us who are going to stay have remained, it is high time that I presented my firstborn son to the gathering as my successor. For, as you all know, we sparrows..."

(So that's a sparrow! I noted.)

"... As sparrows my son and I are temperamentally and traditionally suited to city life, and so gravitate or ascend, if you prefer, towards positions of responsibility in urban and suburban settings. As sparrows we have connections spanning the globe. My beloved son, whom I have trained assiduously and at length in the skills of community organization and information management, as well as in the retention and transmission of ancient memory, is fully prepared to take over the responsibility of facilitating these meetings,"

There was a brief silence, then a sudden twittering chorus. I felt my teeth chattering and I clenched my jaw, and only then realized that I was smiling broadly and leaning forward so as to better hear.

"Aww, that's nic,." I heard one bird say.

"Don't make no difference to m,." observed a roundis,h dun-colored creature.

"Isn't he awfully young?" a female voice trilled.

The blue jay who had been hopping on the ground, ascended to the rim of the birdbath, forcing a couple of starlings out of place and onto the ground below. "How rude!" I thought.

The older sparrow shot a warning glance at the jay, then turned to his son. "So,." he said. "Why don't you say a few words?"

The younger sparrow nodded, or so it seemed to me, and his feathers ruffled for a second, then settled. He stretched his wings as if trying them for the first time. "Well," he began. "I guess I don't really have much to add to what Father just said. I do think it's very important that all of us who can continue to meet here at the bath for regular information sessions if not everyday..." He glanced warily at his father. "At least three to four times a week. Like Father said, sparrows like to be on top of things and to know what's going on around us, and that's what's made us thrive in these sorts of places and has taught us that we can't just look out for number one, we have to be good neighbors as well. Like Father said, I've been learning the ropes from him for a while now, and I think you all would agree that he's the best there is when it comes to getting the word out and getting and keeping birds involved and organized. I only hope that I can come close to being as good a leader as he has been. No bird could have had a better teacher, and when the time comes to take over for good, which I hope won't be for a good long while, I'll be ready. I guess that's all I have to say." He nodded and edged a bit closer to his father, whose tiny black eyes seemed to glisten.

"Thank you, son." His words were low and melodious and very different in tone from his usual brash chirp, with which he addressed the gathering after he collected himself sufficiently. "Any other business to discuss?"

"Aren't there any other options?" Piped the bright young cardinal. "I mean, what are you all, the royal family?"

The gathering at the birdbath broke into what sounded like mirth to me. "You think you could take over, Red?" Cawed the crow on the ground. "Aw! Give me a break, pretty bird. All you ever think about is tail."

"You're just jealous, you loud mouth creep!" chirped the cardinal sharply and flew several yards away.

The elder sparrow spoke. "I will not tolerate any more bickering. Are there any serious objections to my son's investiture?"

"To his what?" said a pigeon.

"To his eventual assumption of the mantle of leadership," said the old sparrow with a note of impatience.

"He's just a hatchling!" sang the female who had noted the younger sparrow's youth at the beginning. "But he's just as cute as he can be, and with such nice manners...."

A chorus of mostly masculine twitters drowned her out. I turned to look at the younger sparrow, whose expressionless face somehow managed to convey to me an intense, uneasy self-consciousness. After a few minutes of what seemed to be disorganized debate, the father sparrow emitted a long, loud, shrill whistle. "Enough!" he said. "Enough. You all know what to do. Those in favor, sing!"

There was a brief burst of variegated birdsong, including a sustained high note from the old sparrow himself.

"Those opposed?" the old starling called.

The cardinal gave one short, sharp chirp, then, taking off from the branch he was perched on, said, "Oh, whatever. I've got a date." Then he disappeared.

"Good riddance," grumbled the old sparrow. "Malcontents, my son, can only be suffered up to a point." He sidled with his twiglike legs to the side of his progeny. "Now," he sang, "the main order of business has been settled. Let me take this moment to say that rarely have I felt such happiness. It is no small thing for a bird to see his legacy honored so concretely. I..." The old bird's song drifted into silence and he gazed into the distance, clearly at a loss for words. His son, after a quick, questioning glance at his father, raised his beak.

"Well," he said. "I guess I don't need to say that I'm really happy. I *know I can never be as good a leader as Dad here, but I'll sure try. I guess..."* He flexed his wings, a nervous gesture, I perceived. *"I guess, unless someone has something else they want to talk about, I guess we can say that this meeting is over. Does anyone have any other business?"*

Bemused, respectful silence followed.

"Okay then," the young sparrow said. *"Meeting adjourned."*

"Until tomorrow," the older sparrow sang pointedly.

"Oh, yeah... until tomorrow," the young sparrow said. And with a rush of wings and feathers all the birds dispersed. I sat there on the bench for I don't know how long. Only when a group of boys on skateboards dashed between myself and the birdbath did I realize I was going to be late getting back to work.

∽

I'M USUALLY TOO self-conscious to enjoy a meal in a restaurant alone, but that evening was an exception. With the memory of the meeting at the birdbath so alive in my mind's eye and ear I was as completely absorbed as someone reading an exciting story. In fact, the act of eating enhanced the quality of my recollection, because when I finished the steak and the cocktail the odd intensity of my recollection faded, and I became more aware of my surroundings. All around me fellow diners, clustered around tables in cozy groups of two or three, murmured their private conversations and tinkled silverware against their plates. A lady harpist in a white dress on a red carpeted platform stroked and tickled out vaguely familiar tunes. Outside, the twilight had deepened to darkness and through the large street side window I could see lit streetlights and storefront windows. Inside the restaurant the lighting was soft and warm. It was a pleasant atmosphere, and I was in no hurry to leave. I caught the eye of the waitress on her next pass by me and ordered another vermouth cassis.

When she brought it, I thanked her, and was disconcerted when she placed her fingertips lightly, briefly, on my shoulder and asked me if I needed anything else. Like a dumb teenager I fumbled for words, and she laughed and winked. "I'll check back in a few minutes," she said, and then she was gone. For a moment I sat just staring at the place where she had been, feeling her light touch on my shoulder as if it had remained there. Had she been flirting with me? I had no experience or comprehension of the complex, indirect language of flirtation, so I had no way of knowing.

I lifted my glass and downed it. Once again I asked myself if I might be losing my mind. And yet as I considered that possibility, I felt only as mildly concerned as if I were considering whether or not I might be coming down with a cold. Maybe it was the cozy, convivial, insulating atmosphere of the restaurant that made it all seem relatively benign. At any rate, I contemplated my own sanity at that moment with a detached, almost clinical eye. If I were a psychologist, or some other qualified mental health professional, how might I experience a seemingly sane individual who presented to me with nothing more than the conviction that he could hear birds speaking in English? Would I diagnose it as a harmless delusion, or the harbinger of a complete mental collapse? I had no doubt that the whole thing was all in my mind. I was imagining things; the question was, why? My shallow understanding of abnormal psychology, gleaned from an undergraduate elective that I'd gotten a B in, suggested that if I were a psychotic hallucinating the conversation of birds, their remarks would more likely than not contain some reference to me. But the birds weren't talking *to* me or *about* me; they were minding their own business. What would a psychologist make of that?

He would say, I reasoned, that I am an atypically humble psychotic. I lifted my empty glass to my lips to hide my smile. Whatever was going wrong with my mind wasn't having a very bad effect on my mood. I set down the glass. The waitress appeared at my side and I ordered another drink. When that was gone, I ordered *another* one. I'm not sure how many vermouth cassises I drank before the lights of the dining room dimmed and the place was empty except for the restaurant staff and myself. All I know is that I did not feel drunk, only unsteady. So unsteady that I abandoned my bold plan to smile at the waitress as I handed her an impressive tip and invite her to join me for a drink somewhere else. Instead, I left my money on the table and staggered out into the night to catch a bus to my apartment.

~

THE MORNING after was like an injury: sudden, unexpected, and extremely painful. The air in my tiny room, despite the attempt of the ancient and gurgling steam radiator to warm it, was cold, and when I looked out my one grimy window, which faced east over the jagged skyline of the city, the morning sun seemed pale and remote and as half dead as I felt.

With my head pounding and my stomach churning, I forced myself to consume a banana and a mug of instant coffee and rushed to meet the train that would take me to the office. It was pointless to hurry; I was already late. As the subway roared and lurched underneath the city my own intestines squirmed like live bait in a bag. Gritting my teeth, I gazed at the blackness that held my own reflection in the compartment window and berated myself for not having the sense to call in sick, since I certainly felt sick. And yet, I couldn't bear to miss a day. Work no longer meant just work and drudgery, and the dry, halfhearted companionship of my co-workers. It meant lunch and the birdbath. I couldn't have one without the other.

~

CHRISTMAS, like death, can't be avoided. I tried to ignore the excrescence of garlands and ornaments throughout the office building and across the surrounding downtown shopping district as the days passed, but it was no use. Insipid carols seeped from speakers everywhere, and shoppers streamed in and out of stores with the single-mindedness of ants. The first email I opened when I got to my cubicle reminded me in red and green font of the "December Holiday Party" scheduled in the employee lounge during the lunch hour.

I don't know how long I sat staring at my screen. Of course I had to attend. My presence, while not desired, was expected, and my absence, if not regretted, *would* be noted. We weren't a large department. And yet the meetings at the birdbath, as far as I knew, only happened around noon. I couldn't be in two places at once. I'd have to make a decision.

I agonized all morning and accomplished very little. My hangover, in spite of dose after dose of ibuprofen and repeated trips to the men's room, seemed determined not to fade. On top of that, I had the paranoid feeling that my physical and mental discomfort *was not* going unnoticed by the powers that be. As noon, and the moment of truth approached, I could think of nothing other to do but to put my fate in the hands of the gods. I reached into my pocket and pulled out a quarter. *Heads*, I told myself, *I go to the party. Tails, I go to the birdbath.* I flipped the coin and it landed heads up. I knew then, as my heart sank, that I would go to the birdbath instead.

To GET to the birdbath in the park I had to go through the shopping district. I felt so foolish on my delusional mission in the face of all that Yuletide cheer, those streetlamps wrapped to simulate candy canes, the cheerfully secular storefront wreaths. Even the overcast skies that seemed to threaten a snowfall contributed to my sense that I was out of touch with what should be the giving spirit of the season, the fellowship of friends and family. I'd done absolutely no Christmas shopping. My brother expected me to spend Christmas Eve and Christmas Day along with my parents at his new house, to admire it and to marvel over his month old firstborn, a girl. I loved my brother and I didn't dislike his wife, and normally I didn't really think too much about how his situation in life could not have been any more favorably compared to my own.

I settled myself onto the park bench. The slats of the seat felt harder and colder against my backside than I remembered from the days before. I stared at the birdbath. As always, the scattered strains of birdsong in the distance was audible but not understandable, and it occurred to me then, that as a matter of fact, there were birds everywhere—all over the park, all over the city, all over the world—but it was only here, before this ordinary birdbath, that I could understand their speech. The hair on the back of my neck rose, and I sat up straight. The pigeons all over the city warbled and cooed throughout the day, but all morning I'd not heard them as anything but background noise. A formation of geese passing over as I emerged from the subway that morning honked as they always honked, signifying nothing, and I'd thought nothing of it. Only here did I even expect to hear birdsong as human language. Why?

I leaned forward, resting my elbow on my knee and my chin on my hand, and furrowed my brow as I stared at the birdbath. The realization that the phenomenon was localized lent it a kind of symmetry that pleased me. I had some control. Some choice in the matter. If I didn't, where would it end? I contemplated with real terror the possibilities. The chatter and scolding of squirrels, the buzzing of insects, the barking of dogs tethered to owners, would I really want to know what was on the mind of every sentient creature? I would not. It would be too overwhelming, too chaotic. But limited to a time and place, the impossible felt manageable. It was like picking up a book and reading. The analogy was a stretch, but close enough. It served to reassure me that I wasn't mad. Psychotics could not escape their psychosis. I could, simply by staying away from the birdbath. It was up to me.

But where were the birds? The young sparrow had scheduled a meeting. And I wanted to see how he would handle his new role. He was such a meek little fellow.

I settled myself as comfortably as I could on the bench,

unwrapped my sandwich, ate it without tasting it, and waited. When the sandwich was gone I crumpled up the bag and tossed it into the wastebasket. I looked at my watch. If I left now I could probably slip into the office party without drawing too much notice. I could always say that I was in the bathroom or something. But would I break then the spell of the birdbath? Could I bear to? And what about Christmas! My chest tightened. If I went home for Christmas like I was supposed to, what then? A fragment of memory emerged from my early childhood; I'd come across a cheap pamphlet tract marking the place in my Southern Baptist Grandmother's TV Guide. I opened the tract and saw The Good Shepherd to the right, the Grim Reaper to the left. "The Wages of SIN is DEATH" proclaimed the words superimposed upon the juxtaposed images. "And the GIFT of GOD is ETERNAL LIFE! (Romans 6:23) WHICH will YOU CHOOSE?"

But which was which? What was right and what was left?

(*You live in a fairy tale*, said the voice of my ex so-called lover).

My brother had the wife, the kid, the promising career, my parents had each other. I had this, and I didn't want to lose it.

Just like the day before, I shivered and huddled within my inadequate blazer. *If I don't leave, I'll freeze*, I told myself. And yet I didn't move until a sharp, familiar voice caught my attention, "Time to meet! Report to the birdbath, it's time to meet!"

"Rather an informal summons," remarked another familiar, slightly less reedy voice. "But maybe that's best."

And there they were, on the rim of the birdbath, father sparrow and son. "Now Father," the young bird said, "you said you wouldn't make any suggestions until after."

"My apologies," said the older bird. "Reflex."

The younger bird hopped in place, clockwise, looking about. "No one yet," he said. "I suppose we should give them a few minutes to get the message."

"They've 'got the message,' as you put it," said the elder sparrow with not a little acid.

"You can't know that for sure..." The younger sparrow sighed.

The feathers of the elder sparrow's breast rose and fell. "I apologize," he said, rather primly. "Old habits die hard. You, my son, possess a quality I lack, that will serve you well as a leader: forbearance. It may well be that my own tendency to take a hard line has alienated our constituency. At any rate, I will do well to remember that I am no longer in charge of these gatherings. *You* are. One element of authority is the willingness to abdicate when indicated; to allow for change when change is due. But there are limits to patience as well, son. Don't underestimate the entropic lure of indifference."

"I won't, Father," said the younger bird.

Then the two were silent for a while. I found myself, like the younger bird, scanning the skies and the boughs of the surrounding trees, looking for signs of life. Where was everybody? It seemed to me that the absence of the other birds from this, the first meeting officially chaired by the younger sparrow, spoke volumes. He was taken even less seriously than his father. My heart filled my throat.

"I guess everyone's busy," said the younger sparrow eventually.

"Perhaps," his father replied. "Perhaps they simply don't care. You must be prepared to be dismissed sometimes, son, and you must be prepared to respond."

The younger sparrow seemed to shiver. He gazed into the murky water of the birdbath. "Maybe it's too soon. We did just have a meeting yesterday..."

"Perhaps." His father sounded tired. "Daily meetings have always been the rule. But, son, you're in charge now. It's up to you to decide how to proceed. I'll own that we have enjoyed an extended period of extraordinary peace and stability. Whether or not that is the result of, or in spite of, my tendency towards heightened vigilance is for you to consider. I will be off. I'll leave you, son, to your own counsel. I will await and abide by your decision, but it is yours alone to make according to your own lights."

"All right, Father," the younger sparrow said. The elder sparrow flew off, in the same broad arc as the day before, to disappear into the canopy of the surrounding trees, leaving his beloved son alone on the birdbath rim, right in front of me. It occurred to me to wonder; did he know he was not alone? Was he aware that there was someone nearby who knew his struggle? I wondered what would happen if I told him.

My internal response to this internal question was immediate and firm. Absolutely not, I would not say a word. It was one thing to understand, another to participate. Then I really would be crazy, crazy for all the world to see. I didn't think I could bear that.

I had every intention at that point of getting to my feet... but one last glance at the birdbath made me pause. It seemed to me as if the young sparrow had lowered his little head to regard his own reflection in the still, murky water of the birdbath... The very picture of a solitary creature searching his soul for an answer. I leaned back on the bench and abandoned all hope of keeping my job.

I don't know how long I sat there before I realized my eyes had closed. I opened them in a kind of panic to find, to my relief, that the young bird was still there, still deep in what seemed to be thought. It occurred to me that if he had flown away while I wasn't paying attention, I would have wept. *This is insane*, I told myself. *This is complete craziness. Here I am, a grown man, with a decent job, risking it all just to keep a bird company.* But he looked so sad. I couldn't help myself.

I took a breath and let out a sigh that must have been heavy, because the little sparrow looked up from his reflection and cocked his head to the side a little, as birds do. It was hard to believe he wasn't looking at me. I had the strange sensation then, that I was looking at myself, too, from somewhere beyond. "Listen," I, or at least what I recognized as myself said. "I'm here. For what it's worth. You can tell your father that at least I showed up. And I'll keep showing up, too. All you have to do is ask..."

The sparrow didn't move, but just stayed there, perched on the rim of the birdbath, his head still cocked a little bit to the side, looking in my direction. I could see him as clear as day, even to the bright spots of reflected sunlight it his tiny black eyes, but I couldn't, of course, read his expression. I could, though, read my own. I was leaning forward, my own head cocked a little bit to the side and my eyes blinking rapidly, like a child about to cry.

The young sparrow stretched out its wings. A sob rose up in my throat and my Adam's apple plunged. "That's all you have to do. Just ask me."

The little sparrow's wings closed in against his little round brown body. I stood and approached the birdbath. I saw myself approaching and took off into the trees.

"I'll be back..." one of us said. I'm not sure who. So I'll stay right here.

Author Biographies

Jay Barnson is an award-winning video game developer, author, and software engineer. By day, he creates Virtual Reality training simulations for industrial and military heavy lifting equipment. By night, he creates adventures. His stories and non-fiction articles have appeared in several anthologies and magazines, including The Escapist and the Hugo-nominated Cirsova magazine. His Blood Creek series is about monsters, magic, and mayhem set in the Appalachian Mountains, and is also available from Immortal Works.

～

Amy Beatty is a science fiction and fantasy author whose work has been compared to that of Robert Jordan. Her debut novel, *Dragon Ascending* (2018) was pronounced "an extraordinarily entertaining and innovative treatment of dragons" by Orson Scott Card, author of *Ender's Game*.

Amy was raised in the wilds of Yellowstone Park as part of an experiment in combining the genes of a respected biologist with those of a grammar aficionado. She now lives in the mountains of Utah with her husband and two delightfully unconventional children under the benevolent dictatorship of a toy fox terrier.

～

David L. Carter is a writer and illustrator who holds degrees in Theology, English Literature, and Library Science. He lives in North Carolina, and is the author of four novels: 'Familiar,' 'Lustration

Rites,' 'The Dead Man' and 'From the Edge of the World.' He has also published fiction and scholarship in the periodicals *Cities and Roads* and *The Journal of Pastoral Care and Counseling*.

∾

Braxton Young Church knew he wanted to be a writer ever since he was fourteen and took his first creative writing class. He took it because he couldn't be in his junior high's advanced acting class, but has never regretted it. Braxton wants to write young adult fantasy novels, so he is beyond ecstatic to have this story be his first published piece of creative writing. When he isn't writing, Braxton enjoys reading—having once reading eighty-five novels in a single semester—acting, drawing, and doing all of the above with friends. His dream is to be a famous rich novelist living in London where he can go to plays every day.

∾

Sarah Lyn Eaton is a queer pagan writer who is surviving near-death by fire. She lives quietly with her wife and cat where two rivers meet and spends her happiest times immersed in nature. Her published stories can be found in *Pantheon Magazine* as well as the anthologies *On Fire*, *Dystopia Utopia*, *Fracture: Essays Poems and Stories on Fracking in America*, *The Northlore Series Volume One: Folklore*, and *What Follows*.

∾

Before Amanda Hakes started writing stories about mothers and their children, she spent 5 years doing infield research. She lives in Utah where she is teacher, tender, and taskmaster to her three young kids. Amanda is also an in-house writer for Writing Through Brambles, a blog dedicated to supporting other parent writers. When she is not writing or being a homemaker, Amanda likes to play delightfully nerdy games with her husband. Enda is her debut short story, and she hopes it's the first of many stories she is able to share.

~

By day, WJ Hayes is an attorney who specialized in legal research and analysis. By night, he is a writer and his works have appeared in several anthologies. He lives outside New York City with his wife and daughter.

~

Rachel Huffmire lives in Southern California where she enjoys sand at its finest: the beach and the desert. Her debut novel, SHATTERED SNOW, is a historical time travel retelling of Snow White set in 16th century Germany. The upcoming sequel, SPINNING BRIAR, is a retelling of Sleeping Beauty, set in medieval France. She loves playing board games with her two little boys, writes about fairy tales, and reads bedtime stories to her husband every night.

~

Steven Heumann spent his childhood recording stories into his sister's tape deck until she took it away in a huff. Even so, he wouldn't be stopped. After 15 years working as a writer and director in the television industry, he left it all behind to become a full-time novelist...with a wife and six kids. It may sound crazy, but that's who you're dealing with here. He's since written and published five full-length contemporary science fiction books and five short stories, including *Nightingale*, featured in *Of Fae and Fate*.

∽

Shirley Meier is launching her latest book, 'Blood Marble', a Fifth Millenium fantasy, later this year and is working on a YA novel to come out early next year. As well as being an award-winning author, she is an artist with several book covers to her credit. Her archery, horse riding, and other hobbies have to take distant third place.

∽

John M. Olsen is an award-winning author and editor who inhabits multiple genres and loves stories about ordinary people stepping up to do extraordinary things. He hopes to entertain and inspire others as he passes his passion on to the next generation of avid readers. As a long-time engineer, he loves to create and fix things, whether editing or writing novels or short stories or working in his secret lair equipped with dangerous power tools. He lives in Utah with his lovely wife and a variable number of mostly grown children and a constantly changing subset of extended family.

∽

Karen Edwards Pierotti was born in Edinburgh, Scotland, but because her father was in the Royal Air Force (RAF), she lived many places in the UK and a two-and-half year posting to Gibraltar, Spain. She worked for a year in Lugano, Switzerland where she joined the LDS church. She met her husband at a BYU ward and has been in Utah ever since. She has four children and six grandchildren. She usually writes historical fiction and this was a first attempt at urban fantasy. It was so fun to write, she may write more!

∽

Johannah Davies (JD) Spero's writing career took off when her first release, Catcher's Keeper, was a finalist in the Amazon Breakthrough Novel Award in 2013. Since then, she's found similar success with her young adult fantasy Forte series, which won Best Book of YA Literature in the 2015 Adirondack Literary Awards. Having lived in various cities from St. Petersburg (Russia) to Boston, she's now settled with her husband and three sons in the Adirondack Mountains, where she was born and raised.

～

JM Utrera is a Brazilian-American author, mother, and advertising manager. She loves writing fantasy with influences from her own mixed heritage, as well as reading and boosting fantasy by diverse authors from all over the world. A big fan of Star Wars, Star Trek, Harry Potter, Narnia, Stranger Things, and so much more, Jen is an unashamed pop-culture consumer and nerd. Other hobbies and interests include scuba diving, zoology, crochet, swimming, camping, and exploring the magic places of the world with her family. She speaks English, Spanish, and Portuguese.

～

Imogean Webb: She lives out on the outskirts of Memphis, TN with her four-year-old daughter and soon to be newborn. Books and storytelling have always been a *must* in her life. She intends to finish college soon with a dual degree in cyber-defense and programming.

～

Sierra Wilson: Sierra Wilson is a former high school teacher and a forever dreamer. She's had several poems and short stories published and is the author of the picture book *The Atonement of Jesus Christ Is for Me.* Sierra loves studying folklore and is so pleased to be part of this anthology. When she's not reading or writing, she's caring for her three little ones, taking a nature walk, painting, or trying a new flavor of chocolate. Learn more about her and get in touch at sierrawilsonauthor.com.

ABOUT THE ILLUSTRATOR

About the Illustrator: Megan Stern is a mother-artist. To her, nourishing her creative passions and nurturing her family are inextricably intertwined. Megan has a wonderfully supportive husband, a child who thinks making art all the time is a normal thing, and a baby who naps in the studio. She lives and creates in Provo, Utah. See more of her work at www.meganrstern.com.

About the Editor

Beth Buck is the Director of Acquisitions for Immortal Works, but sometimes she writes her own stories, too. When she's not hard at work in publishing, she homeschools her small army of children. She also knits, gardens, and has a real, live spinning wheel. Beth has always wanted to edit an anthology like this one, so all her dreams have come true – just like Cinderella! Except Cinderella was not invited to participate in this project.

All love and appreciation to this volume's production babies, William, Alex, and James.

This has been an
Immortal Production